THE
PHARMACIST'S
WIFE

Vanessa Tait grew up in Gloucestershire. She went to the University of Manchester and completed a Master's degree in Creative and Life Writing at Goldsmiths College. Her debut novel, *The Looking Glass House*, was published in 2015. *The Pharmacist's Wife* is her second novel.

THE
PHARMACIST'S
WIFE

VANESSA TAIT

CORVUS

First published in Great Britain in 2018 by Corvus,
an imprint of Atlantic Books Ltd.

10 9 8 7 6 5 4 3 2 1

A CIP catalogue record for this book is available from the British Library.

Hardback ISBN: 978 178 649 2708
Trade paperback ISBN: 978 178 649 2715
E-book ISBN: 978 178 649 2722

Printed in Great Britain by
TJ International Ltd, Padstow, Cornwall

Corvus
An imprint of Atlantic Books Ltd
Ormond House
26–27 Boswell Street
London
WC1N 3JZ

www.corvus-books.co.uk

For Tristan

CHAPTER 1

Edinburgh, 1869

Perhaps it was her shoes that were making a dent in the afternoon. Because, look there, a little monkey on a gold chain, pulling up its knees in time to the brass band that Alexander had hired; and there, the cymbals crashing away and the trombone glinting in the uneven sunlight. And see, a little further off, stalls selling saloop and whelks and whatnot, and people gathered round them, drawn from either end of Edinburgh; it was all very gay. And the pharmacy itself was looking swish, its broad window polished to a glint and – and this was the proudest part – the name above it, written very bold, in gilt lettering on the wooden board, *Palmer*, which was Rebecca's name, too, these last six months, though she still could not get used to it.

The pharmacy, everyone said, would be the making of North Bridge – the road that ran between the Old Town and the New, connecting the rich part of Edinburgh with the poor. It would draw its customers from the slums and from the toffs, and take advantage of both. As Mr Badcock said, they ought not to care who'd owned the shillings before, just so long as they all flowed in their direction.

But still, and Rebecca was sad to notice it, the *pump-a-rum* of the trombone beat almost the same rhythm as the pulse in her big toe. She flexed her feet upwards to take the pressure off them that way, but if she leaned back a little on her heels t'would be even better … but that was too far! She had almost tipped over, she must clutch at her husband's arm to right herself.

'What on earth are you doing?' said Alexander, pulling his arm away.

Rebecca snatched back her hand and clasped her fingers together. 'Just …'

But Alexander was looking at her feet and frowning. 'You have got your shoes stained, after all the trouble.'

'Stained?' Rebecca had only walked the short distance from their brougham to their place here at the front of the crowd. But she had got the heel hooked on the step – had she marked it then? She could not see without craning down to look, which would not look elegant, standing up here, as she was, as *they* were, she and her husband, on show. Or the shoe had got marked by the water that gathered in the indents of the pavement, hard to avoid, impossible to see. Their leather was so soft and pale and would stain as easy as a blush.

''Tis a pity, after all the trouble that was gone to in the measuring of your feet. All you have had to do was stand, after all,' said Alexander, rubbing at his chin.

'I can clean them for you, madam,' said Jenny. 'If you like.'

'I don't know how, when she is wearing them,' her husband said.

'Thank you, Jenny. P'raps it can wait until we get home.' The shoes *were* stained, Rebecca saw it now: an uneven mark thrown carelessly over the knuckle of her smallest toe. She blinked. She was not made to wear such shoes, she had known it even as she pulled off her old black boots to make way for them, back at the house. Such pale and slender shoes should not go on her great feet, and now she had proven it, for she could not even get out of a carriage without ruining them.

'I have brought a handkerchief,' said Jenny, turning her face so that Alexander would not hear.

Rebecca swallowed. She did not know if her maid meant for her shoes or for her eyes. She must not cry – she was not crying! Not today. She shook her head at Jenny, tried to smile and spread out her gaze.

They stood in front of a crowd of about sixty, and now that she looked she saw that Mr Badcock had been right. A group of women from the New Town, their parasols trimmed with lace, were at the front, nodding in time to the band, but to the side of them an old lady whose skirt was held up by string – from the Old Town, of course – was staring hungrily at the food stalls. As well as those there were a number of actors, swells, tramps and other types of a more middling sort, and a dog who could have been from anywhere. It must have been attracted by the smell of burning sugar, for the first batch of lozenges Lionel had made had been ruined and thrown away behind the shop.

Try again, Rebe, 'tis a proud day, you said it yourself! Rebecca turned to her husband. 'It is going very well, isn't it, Alexander, just as you planned?'

'Mr Badcock is not here yet,' he said, picking a hair from his trousers between finger and thumb and pursing his lips.

'But, still, it's a proud day, Al, that's for sure!' Rebecca smiled hard.

Where other men sprouted beards and moustaches Alexander had nothing but skin. Even the place where his whiskers should have been was bare. Beards trapped disease inside them, he said, and made men ill. (Mr Badcock maintained that on the contrary, beards trapped bacteria on the *outside* and prevented them getting in.) Rebecca did not hold either opinion, she only knew that when Alexander was angry all that bareness made his face terrible.

'I beg your pardon?' he said now, his lips tighter than ever.

Rebecca had made another mistake even as she'd tried to rectify the last. She knew what it was, and how stupid she had been to risk his displeasure! She palpated her toes against the soles of her shoes, as if she could drain away the heat from her face. Other wives had affectionate names for their husbands! She knew of a woman who called her husband Flossie, though he was not light and airy but short and fat.

Rebecca had planned to try out a more familiar name for her husband today, but she saw now what she ought to have seen all along: it did not suit him, did not suit him at all.

After waiting so long … Rebecca shut her eyes and shook her head to banish the word *waiting*, but it was no good: it was there already, plump and falsely bright, with its *ting* on the end. She set her teeth and stared over at the whelk stall and forced the word to dissipate … After *waiting* for more than two years she had been saved from spinsterhood and all the humiliations that went with it by Alexander Palmer, proprietor of a fine pharmacy on North Bridge.

Yes, that was right. That was the story that she would tell and she would feel better for it. And now her father had died she could wait no longer, for her house was sold and everything in it was gone. But she had Mr Palmer, a husband many women would envy, and how lucky she had been to be chosen by him, just by chance, on the street!

But in the anxiety of preparing for today, she had forgot to eat. Eating, that may be counted upon as the opposite of thinking. And now a good smell was coming across from the food stalls; some of the people of Old Town had no kitchens, and this was as good a place as any to set up trade, catering for the stomach as the pharmacy would cater for the rest of their needs.

'I only meant, Alexander, you must be very proud. It is exactly what you hoped for – all this – is it not? And I wondered … I thought, perhaps I may get a cone of whelks. I forgot to breakfast, in the rush of the morning.'

'Whelks?'

'It is unconventional, I know, but I have a fondness for them.'

'It would not look right to eat. Not street food, not here.'

'Well, I would not—'

But Alexander twitched impatiently. 'There he is at last,' he said. And in front of them Mr Badcock was indeed stepping out of his brougham on his tiny feet and shouldering his way between the backs of the crowd with surprising agility.

'Ah, John, you are late.'

'Mrs Palmer.' Mr Badcock caught up her hand and brought it up towards his great beard, pushing his lips down on the back of her glove. 'A great day, a great day. I am late, I was in a desperate hurry, I was almost afraid I had missed it all!'

Alexander consulted his pocket watch. 'No, you have not missed it. I would not start without you, as it is your money that has gone into it.' He nodded in the direction of the large glass doors of the pharmacy with their polished brass handles, still shut.

Mr Badcock raised his eyes to heaven. 'The good Lord would not let me miss such a day; He would not allow that to happen. And may it be the start of many great days.' He brought the tips of his fingers to his chin and moved his lips silently. Then he wrinkled his nose and his eyes snapped open. 'I suppose they,' he motioned towards the food stalls, 'are a good thing, to draw people in. But I wonder if the smell is healthy?'

'Mrs Palmer is asking for whelks,' said Alexander.

'Oh no,' said Mr Badcock, 'you cannot eat whelks! Not at all, not *you*, Mrs Palmer, I am afraid. They operate on women in unfortunate ways. They contain certain minerals – zinc, say – which have properties of an aphrodisiacal nature. Spermatozoa, of course, contain zinc. So if a man eats whelks, he becomes more of a man. But a woman ingesting such a compound, hmmm, may also become more of a man! It would not be the natural order of things. An army of marauding women ... Ah – and who is this?' Mr Badcock asked, turning to the maid.

'This is Jenny, my new maid.'

Jenny made a curtsy. Mr Badcock took up her hand, as if it were a great extravagance. 'Charming,' he said, though he stopped short of kissing it.

Jenny blushed and tried to smile. Rebecca pressed her hand to her stomach. Other women were eating at the stalls: those two there, slurping down their saloop from tin cups; that old lady in the faded hat at the eel stall, spooning jelly into her mouth from a filthy bowl. And at the whelk stall, a woman in a green dress. Her coat and hat were trimmed with matching brown feathers from a rarely seen bird, an owl perhaps. She was as thin as the most excoriating fashion demanded and yet her chin worked up and down as she spooned the rubbery whelks into her mouth.

The woman must have felt Rebecca's eyes on her because she turned. She had the kind of face that was a resting place for the eyes, the kind of face that threw all other faces into unevenness. But her skin was too pale, almost colourless; she had not pinched her cheeks to redden them. Her teeth were uneven. And as she leaned over to get a napkin, Rebecca saw a stain spreading down from the armpit of her dress like a high water mark.

She had a mole on her cheekbone that was smooth, like a flattened piece of chocolate, and it struck Rebecca that she had seen it before.

'*She* is here,' hissed Mr Badcock. 'I told her not to come.'

The front of the woman's hair was frizzed up into a fringe that sat high up on her forehead. The back was plaited into loose coils and wound round and round and twined through with ribbon. She blinked.

'Who is she?' asked Rebecca.

The woman took a few steps towards them; Rebecca caught a glimpse of her leather boot poised beneath her high hem.

But Alexander gripped hold of Rebecca's arm and turned her towards the pharmacy. 'Stop the band, Mr Badcock, now!'

Mr Badcock pivoted away and gesticulated at the bandleader. 'Stop playing this instant! Yes?'

The crash of the cymbals died in the air, the trumpet was put out, the monkey stopped dancing. Rebecca and Alexander came to the pharmacy's window with just enough time for her to see the cut of Alexander's cheekbones and the blunt outline of his jaw. Her own face was less resolute, a badly made image on a glass negative. The hurry had made Mr Badcock pant, the edge of his breath had something milky in it.

Now Alexander spoke: 'Thank you to everybody for making the journey to North Bridge. We hope you enjoy our modest entertainments.' He nodded to the brass band. 'And we further hope that you will all use the occasion to visit our new pharmacy, which we have equipped with the very latest medicine.'

'As well as medicine loved for generations,' put in Mr Badcock. 'All the traditional cures to which you are used. You will find something for everybody here!'

'Thank you, Mr Badcock. And now, without further ado, let us declare the pharmacy open!'

They turned and watched Lionel as he made a swagger of opening the door with his great black key. Then five of them went inside, followed by a small crowd of every type.

'Is he the apprentice?' asked Jenny, as Lionel went up and down the ladder fetching things for them all.

'Lionel? Yes. I think he will do well here.'

'He is very smart,' said Jenny.

'I shall tell him so.'

'Oh no, madam, please don't,' said Jenny.

'Lionel, you are smart today!' Rebecca called out to him.

'For the Grand Opening, I should say so, Mrs Palmer. This came all the way from London.' He pulled the edges of his waistcoat together, pushed out his bony chest and grinned.

'London! Just for today?'

'Oh, I've a cousin who is down there, in the clothes trade.' He looked at Jenny. 'Have you been to London, miss?'

'No. I have only just got to Edinburgh a few weeks ago, and that is noisy enough.'

'Aren't there many carriages and people where you are from?'

'None at all, for I live at the end of a track in the middle of a field. Lived, I mean.' Jenny stood as stoutly as always, her hands clasped easily in front of her, but the tips of her ears were pink.

'A sea sponge, Lionel, please, for the lady here!' called Alexander. 'I told you to fill the jar this morning.'

'I don't suppose there are boys like Lionel, either, in Argyll,' Rebecca said.

'Not many. A waistcoat like his does not do around sheep.'

Across the room Alexander said: 'I did tell him, this morning, to fill the jars. I hope the boy will improve as time goes on.'

'He is just a boy, yes?' said Mr Badcock. 'You can mould him to suit your needs.'

'His mother relies upon him,' Rebecca cut in, for she had been responsible for Alexander taking him on. 'She swears he is a good boy.'

'Mothers ought to think their sons good,' said Alexander.

'Except yours, hmmm?'

Alexander's pale skin flushed, very slightly, along his cheekbone. 'Let us not mention my mother today, John.'

'She was not invited?' said Mr Badcock.

'She was not invited, no.' Alexander blinked once and passed his hand over his eyes. 'She does not often leave her house. As for my apprentice – I do not have need of a dandy in the shop. I have need of a worker.'

Lionel ran his hand through his hair and wiped his palms on the back of his trousers so that Alexander could not see. 'Of course, Mr Palmer. I only thought—'

'Stop toying with the boy, Alexander,' said Mr Badcock. 'You will not get the best from him if he is afraid of you. Will he, boy, eh?'

Lionel shook his head, and then nodded it, and took a step back towards the counter, for the door had opened and the pharmacy was all at once filled with noise. A woman had come in with her baby, who was arched away from her hip and screaming. Dark circles hung under the woman's eyes.

'I cannot put him down and I cannot pick him up!' she shouted over him. The baby started to sob harder, as if he understood. His face was all over red and twisted with fury or desperation. His cries came in a rhythm, as if he was praying to a foreign God: *Allah, Allah, Allah!*

'What can I do for you?' said Alexander.

'My friend told me you could give me something to help the baby. The Quietness, she called it, though I don't know its proper name.'

'Good afternoon,' said a voice quietly at Rebecca's shoulder. It was the woman in the arsenic-green dress. When she spoke the tip of her nose waggled alongside her lips a little, as if her skin was pulled too tight. Rebecca glanced at her husband, to see if he had noticed. But the baby had taken all of his attention. She saw Mr Badcock smile, and almost wink at Alexander, and Alexander in his turn, reach over and tap Lionel on the shoulder.

'Oh,' said Rebecca. Close to, the woman was more beautiful, and more ragged. Her face was glossy but without health. Her skin was translucent, the bones very near the surface. There was a hole in the top of the first finger of her glove and Rebecca could see the end of a nail, and the dirt trapped under it.

'My name is Evangeline – or Eva, as I have come to be known.'

'Oh,' said Rebecca again. 'And I—'

'I know who you are. You are Rebecca. I dare say I know a lot more about you than you do about me!' Sweat broke out over Eva's face. 'Or at least, I know your husband. In a professional,' she swallowed on the word, 'sense.'

'Oh?' said Rebecca. 'How's that?' She felt the first flutter of fear in her chest.

'And Mr Badcock! Both men! I'm afraid I am not making myself clear.' Eva was smiling in her stretched way and shaking her head, but even in this moment of awkwardness her cheeks remained a blanched white.

The noise still went on. 'Ah the poor wee bairn,' said Jenny. But she was looking at Lionel, who was reaching up for a slender bottle full of dark liquid, with *Godfrey's Cordial* written on the side. His shirt had escaped his trousers and a bony hip poked out from beneath.

'Now now, there we are,' Alexander was saying. 'No need to cry. It will soon be better. There is treacle in it to make it sweet for the children. No more than twelve drops a day.'

'I am so glad to make your acquaintance, I have oft wondered about who would be Mr Palmer's wife, and here you are, of all people!'

'Of all people?' Rebecca said. A pulse had set up in her toe once more; it was like a heartbeat.

'I wondered if you would like to call on me one day? I have so few friends and – I know this is very irregular, but if you do, call on me, I mean, I had something in particular I wished to ask.'

'How do you know my husband?'

The mother was trying to rock the baby and twist the stopper from the medicine at the same time. She leaned and tried to sit the baby on the opposite hip. 'Allah, allah, allah!' he cried.

'I was a regular visitor to the other place, and we struck up an acquaintance.' She shivered and Rebecca could see her skin pimple where it met the air, between her glove and her sleeve.

Eva meant Alexander's previous pharmacy, which had been owned by someone else. The flutter in Rebecca's chest became something worse. She looked again at her husband. But Alexander was twisting the bottle open for the mother, instructing her, tapping the top of the bottle with his index finger.

Rebecca thought that Evangeline would move away towards Alexander, but she did not. Rebecca could feel her trembling as they stood, hip to hip.

'Have we met somewhere before?' Perhaps she had seen Evangeline at the last pharmacy, or perhaps, and this was worse, she had seen her hurrying away from her house at night, running out of the back door as she came in the front.

Eva sneezed into her handkerchief and her large blue eyes filled with water. 'Perhaps we have! We could think on it, if you came to see me.'

Rebecca stared. What boldness! She felt her colour rise.

But Eva's manner was not gloating. 'I was often at the other place. We may have caught sight of each other. I have an ailment, you see. I expect it will be the same in here. Though

I am not allowed to get—' Eva stopped herself by pushing down on her mouth with her filthy glove. She looked afraid, her eyes darting over to Alexander again.

Alexander was poised with the dropper just above the baby's mouth. The baby twisted away, fearing mistreatment. But Alexander managed to get a taste of the medicine on his lips, and when the baby tasted how sweet it was he turned his face back towards the dropper.

Suddenly the noise fell away. The baby sucked on the dropper as if it were a nipple. Rebecca heard Mr Badcock say quietly: 'I told you it would work, this situation on the bridge.'

Eva said: 'I live on Blackfriars Street, number nine.' She opened her reticule and riffled through it. Rebecca caught a glimpse of a mirror and something torn out of a newspaper, and a small blue bottle, with no stopper. 'Here, this has my address.' She held out a handwritten card, jabbing the corner of it, in her hurry, into Rebecca's wrist.

Evangeline seemed so urgent, so ardent, and Alexander, who had turned at last, so angry, that Rebecca snatched the card and hid it up her sleeve.

'Remember to call ahead to let me know you are coming. Otherwise I shan't know—'

'Evangeline?' Alexander's voice, in the quiet, was terrible. 'What a surprise to see you here. Are you ill again, that you could not wait?'

'A little,' she stammered out. 'I had not expected to be—'

'Neither had I expected it.' He turned his eyes on Rebecca. 'There is no need for you to be here now, wife. You may go home.'

Mr Badcock took hold of Eva's wrist. 'Now, now; have you been a naughty girl?'

'I am sorry, truly I am!' Out of the corner of her eye Rebecca saw Eva blush at last, suddenly and effectively, as far up as her forehead.

'Go home, wife,' said Alexander, taking hold of Rebecca's shoulder and turning her towards the door. 'Do not wait up for me, I shall be back late.'

Rebecca turned against his hand. 'Alexander!'

'You are tired,' said Alexander. 'Your maid will take care of you.'

'Yes, sir,' said Jenny, hurrying to be by her side.

'Oh please, husband!' cried Rebecca. 'She told me!'

'Who told you?'

'Eva – Evangeline told me!' Alexander stopped walking and grew very still. 'She told you *what*?'

'That – that – she knew you!'

'And what else?'

'That is all – but why would she, and you—'

'Then she told you nothing. She is sick, as you can see.' Inside the pharmacy Eva had been overcome by sneezing and trembling. 'She has a cold, she has come for medicine. As everyone does. She was a regular visitor to me in my last place of work. I hope to get much new custom that way. But,' he tightened his grip on her arm, 'I do not want you talking to her, if you should see her again, here or anywhere. Do you understand?'

'Why? Why not?'

'Because she is the wrong sort of woman for you to know. Go home now, and do not expect me. There is a great deal for me to do here and that boy will not be much help.'

But after Alexander had turned away, Rebecca still stood outside the pharmacy, staring in. Alexander had not gone in to his chores, but was braced into a corner of the shop with Evangeline, taking no notice of the other customers at all. He stood so close to her that the brim of Eva's bonnet pressed against Alexander's forehead.

'Should we get home, then?' said Jenny, the black clouds pressing down on them both.

Alexander's cheeks were flushed and he was talking to Eva urgently. With each word Evangeline blushed and flinched, but she did not take her eyes from his face.

'Perhaps we ought to go. If Mr Palmer sees us still here ...' Jenny went on.

'Mr Palmer,' said Rebecca, her heart cold, 'has forgotten all about us.'

She stood for a moment more, as if she would gorge on the sight, though with every second that passed she felt more sick, until at last Jenny took hold of her arm and pulled her away.

CHAPTER 2

Rebecca sat at her dressing table, put her fingers to her forehead, stretched out the thin skin between them, and started to cry. She could not bear to look at her reflection, so instead she sobbed towards the silver-backed hairbrush, with its long black hairs still caught between the bristles.

'Should you like me to take off your shoes?' said Jenny. 'You've been half hobbling since we left the pharmacy.'

'I had dreamed ...' She sniffed. 'I had dreamed of today! And how proud I would be to see Alexander standing behind his own counter at last. And now everything is ruined.'

Jenny began to ease off Rebecca's shoes. 'You did see that, though, didn't you, madam: Mr Palmer standing behind his own counter? Times will be good now, surely they will.'

'But how can they be good, when he has betrayed me? You saw them together! He and that woman in the green dress, that Evangeline.' She pressed her forehead into her hands and squeezed her eyes shut.

'I saw them,' started Jenny, 'but I did not hear what they were saying.'

'You did not need to hear! I have never seen Mr Palmer talking that way, to anyone. Not to me. And she is so beautiful.'

'She may be a customer, as she said, who is always ill, and he knows her that way.' Jenny looked up and put her hand on Rebecca's knee. 'Don't fret so.'

'Jenny, you are trying to comfort me, thank you for it. But my husband would never talk to a customer that way. He hardly talks to anyone – except Mr Badcock. No, she is his mistress, I am sure of it!'

Jenny took up a pillow and shook it out. 'Even if you were to be right,' she said carefully, 'it would not be so uncommon, so as I've heard.'

'Aye, not uncommon, you are right. But I have not been married above six months!'

'But even that is not so rare,' said Jenny, settling the pillow against the headboard and smoothing it.

'I don't think, at fifteen, and coming from the middle of nowhere, you ought to know what is common, should you?'

Jenny said stoutly: 'The middle of nowhere is as filled with vice as a city brothel. More perhaps.'

'Oh!' said Rebecca. 'I dare say you are right.'

'I think you should rest, madam,' said Jenny, passing her a handkerchief.

'Rest? I do not think I can, not yet.' Rebecca stood up and gazed through the window. A skivvy shook out a rug from the opposite house; it was still only the middle of the afternoon.

Rebecca sighed. 'You know, Jenny, I have worked so hard on this house, before you came, trying to get it right. Trying to get *myself* right, to be a good wife, as Mr Ruskin says. But I find that I am wrong for it somehow. Alexander only hates me the harder I try.'

'You are not wrong for it, madam! I don't see how you can be. I think perhaps ...' Jenny turned away to the bed again to straighten the sheet. 'It's no' but a period of adjustment. I am sure Mr Palmer will come back to you, husbands usually do.'

Rebecca sighed again. 'Aye, perhaps you are right. I had not expected it, not today.'

'Your feet look awful sore, madam, even behind your stockings. Shall I fetch some cream?'

'Oh yes, that would be grand, Jenny, thank you.'

But when she was alone Rebecca felt her heart grow low, almost into her stomach. She cast her mind back over her marriage. What detail, what deed, signified that Alexander was lost? Why, only six months ago she had thought herself happy. During their brief engagement Alexander had taken her to a coffee shop and it hadn't mattered that the cruet stand was broken, or that the paint had been peeling, or that the waiter had slapped down their mugs hard enough to spill them, because his knee had been pressing into hers under the table and above it he had leaned forward and almost taken her hand. Rebecca had taken the press of him as complicity, a sign of a shared future.

'My real work,' he'd said to her, rolling the *r*, and she'd noticed how the woman at the next-door table had sent him an admiring look, 'is not in the pharmacy dispensing medicine, but in the laboratory above it.'

'In the laboratory?' she'd said, dipping her head to her cup.

'I intend to invent new medicines up there. And with them I will make a name for myself. Who knows, I may even become a member of the Royal Society of Chemists! That would be a very fine person to be married to, don't you think?'

'Oh yes! Like Mr Bird,' she'd said.

'I don't think Mr Bird is a member of the Society, even though, it's true, he is a chemist.'

She'd laughed then, embarrassed. 'I only meant that Mr Bird invented his custard in the laboratory above his pharmacy, and now it is sold all over the world.'

'And now he is rich, you mean to say. Yes, I dare say money will flow from my inventions, and we shall be rich, if you like.'

And Rebecca had dropped her eyes to her cup again and stirred her coffee. For he had found her out: she *would* like to be rich; that was why women married – some of them, was it not? Being rich wasn't a sin.

'Illness is nothing more than a body out of kilter,' he'd continued. ''Tis a wrong to be righted and it's my business to put the body back in balance. Similar to algebra. Do you know algebra?'

Rebecca had nodded her head, a little vaguely. Her governess had not mentioned it.

'If I can get my formulation right, I can get the body right, and even the mind, too, if it is depressed, say, or overwrought.'

But perhaps, after all, the press of his knees had only signified that the table was too small. There was to be no shared future, not now that Alexander was with another woman. Even now he could be prigging Evangeline in the back of the pharmacy, her green skirts up around her waist, his bowler hat knocked from his head and rocking on its top beside them.

Jenny came back, pushing open the door with her foot. She was carrying a tray with some food on it: a mackerel with blackened skin and cold potatoes, and the lotion she had promised for Rebecca's blisters.

'Oh Jenny, thank you. That is thoughtful. I am hungry, awful hungry, now that I see the food.'

'I thought you would be. Shall I set it on the table?'

Rebecca nodded. 'But do not go, not quite yet. I don't think I am ready to be alone. Won't you sit with me while I eat?'

'I still have the fire to light,' said Jenny. 'I hadn't the time earlier.'

'No need for that now. Won't you sit?'

So the girl sat on the edge of the easy chair and blushed, and put her hands between her knees, and watched Rebecca eat.

'You must be hungry also,' said Rebecca.

Jenny shook her head.

'But I think you must be. Will you have some? Look, you have given me a heap of potatoes I cannot possibly finish. And that mackerel is big enough for two.'

'Oh no, madam – I couldn't!'

'If you mean that a maid ought not to eat with her mistress, never mind! There is no one here to see.'

The girl looked, and frowned. 'If you are sure. I don't think Mrs Bunclarke—'

'Never mind Mrs Bunclarke. Eat – please.'

Jenny picked up Rebecca's fork and began to eat, shyly at first, biting the tip of the fork with her teeth, and then more boldly.

'We are alike, aren't we, you and I?' Rebecca said.

'Are we?'

'We have both come here almost as strangers, and do not know quite where we are.'

'Aye, madam,' said the girl, 'perhaps.' A lock of hair had fallen forward over her face, the colour of sand, the same colour as the beaches she'd left in Argyll. Perhaps her home had stained her somehow.

'Are you happy here?'

'Aye, madam, as happy as can be.'

Rebecca did not know if she meant she was as happy as it was possible to be, or as happy as it was possible to be under the circumstances, having left her family two days' journey away, and the croft where she had lived all her life. 'You must be homesick. I will not take it as an insult. I am homesick too, though I know not what for!' She thought of the house she had left, which was not hers any more, but sold to pay her father's debts: empty, cold, full of ghosts. Her father had died in it so recently she had fancied she could still see the edges of him if she came suddenly into a room.

'Sometimes I am homesick, aye,' said Jenny, pushing her hair back up into her cap. 'But most of the time I am glad to be here. I never thought I should leave the croft and come to Edinburgh. There are enough carriages here to fill up the whole world, I think! Somebody is always about, even at eleven o'clock at night. At home, darkness falls, and that is that.'

Rebecca smiled. 'You are unusual then. But I am glad for it.'

Jenny glanced out of the window, as if to check she was still in Edinburgh. Darkness had not yet fallen but the heat had gone from the day. 'I'd best be off,' she said, rising.

'No need to go just yet!' Rebecca's eyes fell on the newspaper, neatly folded over, that Jenny had put on the tray.

'Aye, I thought, seeing as Mr Palmer did not come home ...' said Jenny, following her glance.

Alexander always read the newspaper first, over breakfast, but today he'd not had the time. Once Rebecca had taken it before he had read it, and got some grease on it, and he had been angry. Red spots had stood out on his cheeks and she had thought for a moment – though of course he would never – she thought for a moment that he would strike her.

But Alexander would be home late tonight, he had told her as much … prigging.

Rebecca took up the paper carefully. 'Thank you, Jenny; that will pass the time very nicely. Only, p'raps I will wipe my fingers first.' She rolled each finger on the napkin. 'Shall we take a look at what is happening in the world, what do you say?'

'Oh, yes please,' said Jenny, who had got up only because she thought she ought, and had no wish to return alone to her little room at the top of the house.

'Oh, look there: *The Edinburgh Seven Petition the University.* I have been following them with interest.'

Jenny squinted down. 'Oh yes?'

'Just imagine it, seven women in amongst thousands of men!'

'Oh yes!' said Jenny.

A cart rolled by outside, its driver very angry. 'Shall I turn over?' said Rebecca.

'If you like, madam,' said Jenny.

'I mean, have you finished?'

'Finished? Oh no, madam, I cannot read.'

'Oh! Oh yes, of course. Well, I can read for both of us.' Rebecca spread the paper in front of them. 'And, if you should like it, p'raps I could teach you a little, shall I?'

Jenny looked doubtful. 'But what use is there in reading, for me?'

'What use? I think to know about the world. Or to read the railway timetable. Or a book, for fun.'

'But I have no time to read.'

'Well, if I, if I lighten your load, what do you say? P'raps the grate does not have to be blackened every week. And if the silver has not been used then there is no need to get it out and polish it.'

'But if Mrs Bunclarke sees me sitting idle—'

'I shall tell her you are not sitting idle but learning to read.'

A dog howled from a yard nearby, shut out or in. Rebecca turned to the front of the paper. 'Now, come here, look, this is the first letter: A. It goes up and down just like a wigwam. The normal type of *a* looks like this, see.'

'There are two sets of letters for every sound?' said Jenny. 'Why?'

'Capitals start off sentences, and names, but never mind them now. Let us keep to the more usual version of *a*, here.'

They went through the first five letters of the alphabet, trying to find them. After that Rebecca read aloud from the article, pointing out the letters whenever she came to them.

'*The Edinburgh Seven Petition the University. It is a particular feature of our modern age that our female friends now take up cudgels and clamour to be allowed into the hallowed precinct so long belonging only to men. In our city of Edinburgh, seven women are knocking on the door of our university and …'* Look, there is an *a*, see how it sounds, *ah*, as in *hallowed.'*

'You mean to say that it has two different sounds? *A* and *ah*?'

'Oh dear! I think I am not teaching it right. One is the sound of the letter, the other of the letter when it is in a word. Let us stick to finding the letters for today, shall we?

'Seven women are knocking on the door of our university and, demanding entrance, for the study of medicine. We beg to point out to our readers—'

'There is an *a*,' said Jenny, pointing to *demanding*. 'I see it! And there, and there. For so long it has all just been scrawls on a page, or a shop front, I have not been able to find anything in it, but look, an *a*!' She put her fingertips to her chin in a steeple and grinned.

'Good, now can you find a *b* here? Have a look, I will read: *'We point out to our readers that these women represent the first women of all Mankind to beg matriculation at a University. Soon will come a time perhaps when our species ought more properly to be known as Womankind, if our elders will not faint dead away!'*

'Imagine that!' said Jenny. 'Women learning to be doctors. Do you think it right?'

'It would be like visiting Africa, or somewhere else where everyone is different. But I think women might want other women to attend them if they are ill.' Rebecca's doctor had been almost deaf, his ears blocked up with sprouting hairs. Her mother had made her visit him during her menses, because she had fainted. He had made her strip naked, to see if her womb was distended.

'Can you find a *b*?' she said.

'Is that it, there?'

'Beg. Quite right, bravo! B has this sound: buh.'

'There are the Pyramids,' said Jenny, pointing to a photograph halfway down the page. 'I love stories about Egypt. Will you read that one?'

'Egypt!' Rebecca shifted uneasily. 'Are you sure? It may be very dull.'

'Oh no, I love the sphinxes, ever since I was a child. Won't you read it?'

Rebecca swallowed. 'Very well then. *The long labour of the Suez Canal is almost at an end, carried on in spite of Great Britain's laudable objections to the working conditions of the Muslim Lascars, which has been found to be deplorable.* Look, another *b*.'

'There is a *b*, and a *c* in that word. What does it say?'

'Forced.' Rebecca found her hand was shaking.

'But where is the sound of kuh?' asked Jenny.

'Well, the *c* has a *kuh* sound and a *suh* sound. I'm afraid I am not doing very well for you, Jenny! It is hard to remember the rules when I learned them so long ago.'

'But you are, Mrs Palmer. I am so grateful to you. Look

now, I can see the shape that is an *a,* and a *b,* and a *c.* 'Tis like, I don't know, panning for gold in sand. Will you read on?'

'Yes, of course.' Rebecca put her hand on her chest to rub away the anxiety. She could not let the girl down, when she had promised to teach her to read.

'Even the infidel ought not be expected to carry extortionate loads of rocks on their backs in the burning sun all day. Thousands have already died under the execrable circumstances of forced labour, which was little more than slavery. Though Britain has put an end to this practice, sanctioned by the French, many more men are expected to die before the canal is finished.'

Rebecca put down the paper. If her hands shook any more she would crumple the sheets and Alexander would discover her. 'No sphinxes, I am afraid, and I find myself tired, all of a sudden! We can continue tomorrow if you like, for I am glad to teach you.'

Jenny blushed. 'Of course, madam. I don't wish to put you to trouble. Would you like help with your gown?'

The maid stripped her mistress of her gown and her petticoats and her corset and her chemise, until Rebecca was as bare as a twig. She shivered and put her arms over her breasts.

'Thank you, Jenny, just put my nightgown on the bed there and I will get into it.'

Even now, in summer, the sheets had a chill to them if there was no fire in the room. She was trembling only down to the chill, only that.

Rebecca had thought that by marrying Alexander she would be a house with a room in the middle of it that would be locked. She had hoped that if the room were locked for long enough she would forget it was even there, and not miss it. That would, she thought, be a fair price to trade for a dark space shut up in the centre of her. But if she was trembling over a foolish little newspaper article, perhaps she had not guarded it well enough.

Rebecca had expected to sleep the night through, because of her exhaustion, but some hours later – in the middle of the night, it seemed – her eyes flew open. It took her a few moments to understand that someone was in the room with her. She sat up, bunching the bedclothes in her fist. His skin was dark, she could only make out the hollows of his eyes and cheeks.

He had come back at last!

No, no, not him, of course not. She rubbed her eyes.

Her husband. Breathing through his mouth. He had come back, yes – only from the pharmacy, and from Eva. Her heart, jolted awake, started to beat against her chest and she put her hand to it, like a woman surprised, in a painting.

But would he smell of Eva, taste of her? Or had Eva thwarted him in some way, that he was now coming to her?

'What time is it?'

'It is late.'

It was too dark to see the hands of her clock. But the darkness had paled now that Rebecca's eyes had been open for a moment. Through the gap in the curtains she could see the sky lined with light, as if drawn over with a pen with silver ink in its nib.

'I do not know the time, Rebecca, why do you ask?' Alexander sat down on her bed and pulled at his shoes. He got one off and it dropped to the floor with an animal thump.

'Where have you been?' she asked.

'At the pharmacy, and then with John Badcock.'

'For all this time?' She hated the querulous tone her voice had taken on.

But he was struggling with his buttons, and did not hear it. 'We were toasting our success. Help me, would you?' He sat back heavily on his hands.

Surely if he had gone to Eva he would not now be coming to her! Not a man of nearly forty. She turned to him and unfastened his top coat. The night air still clung to his hair. Now that she had taken off his coat she could feel his chest under it, not big but unyielding, and she faltered then, her breath catching in her throat.

He was her husband, after all, and one that many women would die for.

Alexander went to lay his coat on the back of the chair. Now he turned to his jacket, which he managed himself, and his collar, and his waistcoat, and laid them all on top. The back of the chair, in the half-light, looked like a pair of ribs which, the further Alexander disrobed, grew more and more like a living thing, watching them both.

At last he stood there in his pulled-up socks, his undergarments and his vest. He sat down heavily on her bed, chaffing the skin of her thigh with his weight. She wriggled away awkwardly to the other side of the mattress, though she could not get far, it was quite narrow and bounced her towards him, as he fell back.

Now, though, as they lay there side by side, their ribs rising and falling, Rebecca's mind jumped about. A snatch of the song that the band had played, how the sun had glanced off the puddles. The china shepherdess on the shelf at the foot of the bed had no sheep. She had not seen any sheep in the china department.

Without turning over, her husband placed his hand on her breast. His fingertips pressed against her ribcage and the palm of his hand put pressure on her nipple through the thin fabric of her nightgown.

Rebecca ought to have bought some sheep! The pretty little shepherdess twisted her head back under her bonnet as if she were looking for them.

Alexander let go of her breast, propped himself up on his elbow and started to pull the bedclothes down in a series of jerks.

'Shall I?' said Rebecca, also propping herself up and trying to help him. The blankets had been tucked in too tight. But he shook his head, and with a final pull he threw them all the way down past Rebecca's feet.

The air was chilly. She longed to be back under her bedclothes. But her white voluminous gown was revealed now in the brightening morning, like some giant grub. Her feet, at least, were self-composed, the toes of each of them companionably angled towards each other. They almost seemed not to belong to her. The cream Jenny had brought had eased the redness, which was as well, because Alexander was touching them, squeezing her instep as he had done her breast. He still wore his vest, as bright in the dimness as the hair that curled out from under his arms was dark. He bent forward and put his lips to the middle of her feet, and then his teeth, biting into them as if into a ripe pear.

Rebecca gasped. Alexander ran his hands up her ankles, circling the bone with his fingers. Then he pushed her nightgown up her legs, his fingers palpating her thighs, moving inwards, moving and rubbing, circling and dabbing, his breath coming faster.

Rebecca closed her eyes, the strangeness of air circulating between her legs made her think of being outside. She was lying on the lawn, she knew by the way it curled out from the house that it was Gabe's lawn, with her legs exposed. Pray God their mothers would not see them! Fingers were touching her thighs and stroking and at each touch pleasure sprung upwards to tug at her between her legs.

Rebecca sighed and turned towards him. She wished he would kiss her. She reached her hand to the back of his neck and tried to guide his face across to hers. She pressed the length of her body against his body, feeling, below the crush of her nightgown, the bones of his legs against her own and the hardness of him poking into the soft skin of her stomach. She began to move against him, to rub at the ache that was growing between her legs. She wanted to pull him into her, and he wanted the same thing—

Alexander stiffened. Had he spent already, into his drawers? But there was no sound, no grunt of release or embarrassment, no wetness against her nightgown.

Rebecca kissed his cheek, trying again to bring his mouth to hers. But he arched away. Rebecca stopped moving and opened her eyes, searching for his face, but could not find it.

Alexander detached his hands, rolled his shoulder under him and sat up.

'What is it, my love?' she said. 'Did I do something wrong?'

His back, held straight, radiated displeasure.

'Will you come back?' she said, more falteringly.

He turned to look at her then. His face was determinedly impassive, but something at the corners of his mouth suggested disgust. 'You ought not to be so eager.'

Her stomach fell. She pushed the nightgown down.

'It is not right – in a wife.'

'But I thought ...' she stammered out. 'I did not know. I

am sorry! Won't you come back and I will be different? I can be, I think. I can be whatever you would like!' And she really thought, in that moment, that she could.

But all he said was: 'It is too late.'

Rebecca wrapped her arms around herself, feeling the air cooling on her skin. Alexander was already retreating into the dimness, merging with the shadows. He only stopped to pick up the clothes from the chair, piece by piece, until the ribs of its back were revealed once again and she was alone.

CHAPTER 3

By the time Alexander returned home, around the middle of the morning, Jenny had already been up for six hours. She had polished two pairs of his shoes to a high shine, so that if Alexander chose, as he sometimes did, to hold them up beneath the chandelier before going out, their points could be clearly seen in the toes. It was hard going, the kind of work that would usually fall to a manservant, but the Palmers had none. Her knuckles were ribboned with cuts.

Then she had set to work cleaning the ceiling rose in the parlour, first with bread to remove the grease, and then with soap and water. After that she had scrubbed out the soot from inside the gas lamps, and then – well, at eleven o'clock she was sitting before the fire in the kitchen drinking a mug of tea.

She heard Alexander say, out in the hall: 'I need a new shirt. Call Jenny.'

'Yes, husband, let us change it,' said Rebecca. 'Did you stain it in the laboratory?'

'Lionel left the chemicals out, when I have asked him over

and over to clear them each night. But never mind that. Where is Jenny?'

Jenny paled and set down her mug and went out into the hall. 'May I talk to you, Mrs Palmer?' she whispered.

'What?' said Alexander. 'I cannot ask for a shirt in this house without whispering?'

Jenny's hand fiddled with the frill of her cap. 'There are no more clean shirts! Mr Palmer is wearing the last one.'

Now Rebecca paled too. 'The last one?'

By the time Jenny had come to use the goose iron on Mr Palmer's shirt her arms were worn-out. She had heated the iron on the stove in the kitchen but by the time she had stretched out the shirt on the ironing board it had gone cold. So she gripped it by the neck with a stab of homesickness, wishing she were with a real goose, back on mother's farm, not a goose iron, and set it by the fire to warm.

But now when Jenny came to press the shirt flat, instead of the snowy whiteness she was expecting, the iron had created a path of muck in its wake – she had forgotten she must never heat the iron by the fire – it was caked with soot.

She had rushed to the sink to put a scrubbing brush to the shirt, but nothing would shift it. Jenny had not had the time yesterday to put any other shirts in the tub and washboard because Mrs Bunclarke had called her in to help tear the feathers from a pheasant.

'Speak up, won't you? I am waiting for a simple thing,

merely a clean shirt! No use whispering it all to my wife,' said Alexander, beginning to undo the buttons of his waistcoat.

Jenny tried to stammer out her explanation. But as she spoke Alexander grew still. As still as stone, or a rock.

'So am I to expect that there is no clean shirt in the house? Nothing for me to wear?'

'No, I am sorry, sir!'

'And what, do you think, I should do then?' He took a step closer to the girl. 'If I go back into the pharmacy like this it will look very bad. It will look as if I cannot control my household, and leading from that, as if I cannot control my shop. This is your fault.' He turned on Rebecca. 'Since *you* are the person who employed her. You ought to have known she was no good.'

'She *is* good!' said Rebecca, looking over at Jenny. 'She is a good girl and a good worker and I don't see how she can be blamed—'

Alexander's fists clenched and unclenched. 'Jenny is clumsy, with no experience whatsoever. She has ruined our dining-room table.'

'What?'

'There is a stain there, the shape of the Isle of Skye. Wine, I presume. It has taken off the varnish. I look at it every time I sit down to eat.'

'I am sure I did it myself. Yes – I remember I did, with the wine, yesterday evening, when you did not come home. Could you not have worn an apron?'

'Oh, do you now tell me what to do, woman? In front of the servant girl?' Rebecca shrank away, even though the flight of stairs where it unspooled into the hallway separated them. 'Do you know that I only wear an apron upstairs in the laboratory, and not when I am downstairs in the pharmacy? Do you know that? Ach, to be surrounded by women! I ought to have stayed a bachelor. You can go, you stupid girl, get out of my sight.'

Jenny turned on her heel and ran to the back of the house, the palm of her hand pressed over her face.

Rebecca's head was pulsing with pain. She longed to lie down in her bed. 'I am sorry, Alexander,' she began. 'I know how you insist upon order—'

'You put it as if it is a preference of mine, when the world would not have got as far as it has without organization. Rational thought. Though of course those are masculine attributes. Females lack such order, which is why I now have to go to work in a soiled shirt.'

Two gilt mirrors hung on opposite walls of the hall, Rebecca had thought them pretty. Now she could see the back of Alexander's head, with its full head of hair, multiplying itself into infinity.

She turned away then to go upstairs, though her heart was so full it made her whole body heavy and the front of her slippers dragged against the stairs as she went up. She had not reached the top when she heard the front door bang in a way that gave Alexander's wrath full expression – one of the lighter oil paintings leapt on its hook like a struggling fish – and Rebecca felt a corresponding hurt shoot up the side of her cheek.

In that first moment of pain she had the impression that the slam of the door had caused it, that an arrow of air had shot straight into her face. Rebecca grabbed onto her cheek and sank down where she was standing, her knees striking the Turkey rug. But the pain in her face kept going, it was not an arrow, it was something from her. She bent forwards, letting her forehead touch her lap.

The pain. It was all up and down one side of her now. A high scream forced itself out of the back of her mouth that sounded, even to her own shocked ears, like an animal caught in a snare.

She could not tell where the pain ended and she began. Her nerves had been hit by lightning. One side of her body was on fire with it.

Alexander must have come back in, for now he was crouching somewhere near her ear. 'What has happened?'

'The pain!' she said.

'Where is it?'

But, as suddenly as it had come, the pain withdrew, leaving a tenderness in Rebecca's cheek, a tingling along her side. Only her kneecaps throbbed. 'I am recovered, I think. It has withdrawn. Ring for Jenny.'

'Can you stand?'

'I think so.'

'Then let me help you. Here.' Alexander wiped his thumb across his lips, and behind it he almost seemed to be – what was it there? Rebecca looked again to make sure, though her eyes still pulsed. Yes, it was a smile.

Alexander caught her looking and dropped it as sharp as a stone. 'It was a violent pain that receded suddenly, is that so?'

Rebecca nodded, her hand still holding onto her cheek.

'In the cheek only or through the whole length of your body?'

'In the cheek – I think – though the pain was so bad it seemed to spread everywhere whilst it lasted,' she said shakily. The smile – what did it signify? Could he hate her so much?

But Alexander had taken a step back, better to look her over, husband and pharmacist in one. 'It is an attack of neuralgia, I believe. More often it is limited to the face, but occasionally the pain spreads elsewhere. It is more common in women for some reason; it may perhaps be an hysterical reaction.'

'Hysterical?'

'Or sometimes neuralgia can occur for no reason at all, as in your case.' His mood seemed quite changed, even though he'd not been able to rub the stain from his shirt, it sprouted from behind his waistcoat in a purple arc. 'You ought to rest. No need to ring for Jenny, I will take you to your room. Come now, wife, take my arm. You may lean on me as you like.'

They went along the corridor, Rebecca leaning on her husband quite hard, her other arm wrapped around her side, in terror that the pain would come again.

'I will let you in on a little secret now, shall I? I have made quite a discovery. It came almost by accident, as most discoveries do.'

They had reached the door of Rebecca's room, and went in. Alexander helped her off with her shoes and her dress.

'A marvellous cure! For coughs and the easing of breath primarily, and the symptoms of tuberculosis, but we think – Mr Badcock and I – that it will have numerous other applications.'

'But …' stammered Rebecca. 'I thought you said such medicines were snake oil.'

'You are talking of Brandreth's Pills and the like,' said Alexander. 'But this, *this*, is not snake oil. It was chance, and only chance, and I am not afraid to admit it! I was led by someone, or some*thing* – something divine, perhaps – on that afternoon. Mr Badcock and I suspect that perhaps this new medicine can cure all ills, physical *and* mental. Say now, would you say that the worst of your problem is that your pain *may* return, and not that you are in any physical pain?'

Rebecca's hand flew to her cheek again. 'Perhaps, yes.'

'Well then, my cure is the perfect thing for it.' Alexander settled her back on her pillows and smoothed her sheet under her breasts. 'We shall be able to employ a manservant, and a coachman, and four horses. Would you like to try it?'

'A cure for everything?' said Rebecca.

'I cannot see anything that my medicine would not cure.'

'Well, then – yes. I should like to try it.'

He patted her on the hand. 'Good. Very good. Rest now, and I shall send Lionel over shortly.'

CHAPTER 4

Jenny had fled to the kitchen. Mrs Bunclarke was there, muttering over her jelly moulds, but no one else would come in; not Mr Palmer, not even madam.

Jenny sat down on the wooden chair by the door and rubbed her knuckles. She thought about giving herself over to crying, but she had not cried since her mother had beaten her, many moons ago.

'Ye'd best get on wi' that, there.' The cook gestured to the fireplace with its great blackened pans hanging from it.

Though her time was not her own now, she could not be stopped from thinking. So as Jenny brushed out the hearth in the kitchen she thought about the great fire that covered the whole of her home with its heat. Her sister had the charge of it and knew somehow when it was at its weakest, and would rush back over the hillside no matter what she was doing, to stoke it up.

'And then there's the silver,' said Mrs Bunclarke, pointing towards the dining room with her thumb. 'That will all need a polish.'

Jenny could not remember what it was that polished silver: lemon juice? Vinegar? The cook gave a great sniff. Jenny dared not ask her. She thought of Lionel. He had smelled sharp, when she got close to him. Sharp and fresh.

Mrs Palmer had shown her the silver in the whirl of her first week, and how to clean it. But her mistress had looked so uncertain, and had stammered out her instructions so fitfully, Jenny had not taken it in.

Jenny dipped her rag in vinegar – she'd taken a guess – when she had heard the front door slam, and then the most terrible scream.

Mrs Palmer! He had hit her with something, something like a poker.

Jenny ran to the door and put her face to it. 'Oh dear God!'

Even the cook had stopped her chopping and come to the door. But as suddenly as it had started, the screaming ceased.

'Well, that is marriage for you,' remarked Mrs Bunclarke. 'Always takes a bit o' getting used to.'

'I must – I'd best go to her!'

'You'd best not, not till Mr Palmer has left her.'

God only knew the power of Mr Palmer, how he had made his wife cry out like that without touching her.

So when the doorbell rang a little while later Jenny answered it very timidly, thinking it was Mr Palmer. But it was not he – thank the Lord, it was Lionel. 'What do you want?' she said, regretting her shortness at once – it came from surprise.

Lionel rocked forwards onto his toes and whipped off his cap. 'I knew I'd see ye here. We met yesterday.'

'I remember, aye,' said Jenny. Lionel was not handsome, not exactly, but he had a shine to him. His hair-oil glinted with reflected sunlight and his skin was scrubbed clean.

'I've brought something for Mrs Palmer from the pharmacy.'

'I see,' said Jenny, her heart falling a little. 'Come in, then, will ye not?'

Lionel pinked at that and took heart. 'And,' he said, reaching into his pocket, 'I brought you something, too.' He held out a piece of soap. 'I made it myself. Rosewater and glycerine.'

'That is kind,' she said, taking it, and putting it to her face to hide her embarrassment. 'It smells lovely.'

'I do not need to take up Mrs Palmer's medicine to her straight away. I mean to say, p'raps your mistress could wait a few moments?'

It was raining again, summer drops that spattered fatly against the long window panes. Jenny looked up the stairs at the door to Rebecca's room. 'I have not heard her cry out again. But I think she might be in pain still.'

Lionel lowered his voice. 'And that is the subject of my concern. I am sorry for being so bold. But I saw yesterday how much you admire your mistress, and I thought ...' Lionel ran his hand through his hair. 'Perhaps you saw that I admired you, too.'

'Oh! I did no such thing!'

'And I hoped I could talk plainly with you. No, no, not like that!' Jenny had put her hand up to her face again. 'About Mrs Palmer.'

'Well,' said Jenny, 'I would do anything to help Mrs Palmer. I expect she could wait, for a moment, if it is important.'

She thought of Mrs Bunclarke sighing and sniffing over her gravy. They could not go to the kitchen. Could she take Lionel up to her room? No, it must be wrong, though she hadn't a bedroom, or a boy at home, to know what was done or not. 'Let us go out back,' she said eventually. 'But Mrs Bunclarke must not see us.'

So they waited until the cook had gone to the pantry and crept through the kitchen, Jenny had her finger to her lips. They stood under the eaves to the side of the house with the rain dripping down in front of their noses. Lionel rolled a cigarette and offered her one.

'Oh!' she said. 'I don't—' But p'raps city girls smoked all the time and she half held out her hand, but he had taken her answer as a no, and put the case back into his trousers before she could take one.

He would think her a sap, a bog-dweller. But he said nothing, only drew on his cigarette until its tip glowed. The smell of the cigarette was not unpleasant, but it was not like the smoke she knew, from burning peat. The smoke from his mouth reached into her hair under its cap, curled into her ears, her nose.

'What do you know of Mr Palmer?' he said at last.

She said, before she could stop herself, 'He is cruel, I know that.'

Lionel drew in his breath. 'Do you know it already?'

'Anybody would know! His shirt, just now—'

'Yes. It was me who—'

'I heard, yes, you left the chemicals in the wrong place, was it?'

'Aye, aye, close enough.'

They both nodded, and caught each other's eye, and smiled a little.

Jenny said: 'And he has made Mrs Palmer ill like this, and cry out worse than I have heard anything, any animal caught in a snare, only by slamming a door – some magic he has on her. And he is unfaithful! At least, she says it is so.'

'She says it! To you?'

'Ought she not to?'

'I don't know!' He blew out more smoke. 'I'm sure you are easy to talk to.'

'What does that mean?'

'Only that … you are easy to talk to.'

'Aye, I am, at least that is what the sheep always told me.' She burst into laughter and just as quickly covered her mouth with her hand. She ought not to laugh, not with Mrs Palmer ill upstairs. 'I have not had much company, before I came here.'

'I would like to be your company, if you will let me.'

Jenny smiled and tried to hide it by covering her teeth with her lips.

Lionel threw his cigarette down and they both watched it get rained on, its tip quickly turning to ashes.

'Mrs Palmer thinks she is a cuckquean, you say?'

'A cuckwhat?'

'She thinks she is being cheated on.'

'Aye, with that woman in the green dress, at the opening. You know her, I think.'

'Evangeline?' asked Lionel. 'I do know her, aye.' A blush crept up his cheek above his collar. 'But what has Evangeline to do with it?'

'Mrs Palmer feels she is making her the cuck-whatever-it-is. I tried to tell her otherwise.' Jenny stared out across the garden to the back of the house behind. Somebody's washing was getting wet in all the rain. 'But what do I know? I only know what sheep do, nothing about men.'

'I don't think I have seen a sheep with the preferences—' Lionel coughed. 'With the desires of Mr Palmer. Have you—' He coughed again. 'Have you noticed anything peculiar in the house?'

'What peculiar? If you mean the paper-hangings—'

'No, no nothing like that.'

Jenny made an arc with the toe of her shoe through the dirt. 'I think everything is peculiar in the house, though I only know my own house to compare it with. What else am I to expect?'

'Anything, I don't know, out of the ordinary.' Lionel leaned towards her and stroked the back of her hand with his thumb, just once. She did not draw back. 'You will know, when you see it.' Lionel ran his hand over his hair. He could not meet her eye. 'But what I said about company ...'

'Aye?'

'Will you let me be your company then, to the park, one day next week?'

'Really? To the park?'

'Aye, or to Arthur's Seat – if you would like it.'

'Oh yes, yes, I should like that. I miss the grass from home. Underfoot is all so hard around here.'

Lionel grinned. Now that his swagger had rubbed off, like a bit of bad gold, she saw that he was only just past being a child, like her.

'Tuesday I will have the afternoon free.'

'Right then. Good!'

Mrs Bunclarke came to the back door and sighed and sniffed. They held each other's gaze, knuckles pressed to their teeth, choking back laughter.

'I had best get this medicine upstairs,' whispered Lionel.

'What is it, this medicine?'

'Mr Palmer has kept it a secret. For all his faults – I know he has many – he is a good chemist.' Lionel put his hand into the pocket of his coat and drew out a blue bottle with thick sides, small enough to fit in the palm of his hand, and held it up to the light. It was just like hundreds of others except for one thing: it was not stamped with the name of the maker, for the maker was Mr Palmer. 'I think what this bottle holds inside must be more powerful than the size of it suggests.' Still holding the bottle he caught hold of her finger with his own and drew it towards him. With his other hand he quickly brushed her cheek.

'See you Tuesday.'

'Aye, till Tuesday then.'

Rebecca pushed herself upright on her pillows. 'What is it, Jenny? Why do you smile?'

'Lionel came to bring you this.' Jenny held out the blue bottle.

'I didn't think my medicine would make you so pleased— Oh, I see now, it is Lionel that has made the change in you.'

'Lionel?' Jenny put her hand to her face. 'What change has he made?'

'Your cheeks have some colour to them; look, see.' Rebecca pointed to the glass opposite that held both their reflections. Jenny was flushed and smooth; Rebecca was wan, her hair coming loose from her plait, lines etched between her brows. She closed her eyes.

'We talked, madam. I don't think it is wrong to talk, or is it?' Jenny fiddled with her cap again. It still felt strange to wear it.

Rebecca laughed. "'Tis not wrong to talk, Jenny, even here! There's a great deal wrong in Edinburgh, but talking isn't one of them. And Lionel is a good boy.'

'Do you know him, then, apart from as Mr Palmer's apprentice?'

'His sister used to work for my father, who made shoes. I don't remember if I told you that – he had a factory, which was really just a large room, with ten girls in it. But they made fine ladies' shoes; they were just beginning to be known before my father died.' Rebecca sighed and pulled the sheet up to her chin. 'Lionel was only a wee boy then, he used to come in and wait; he always had his socks pulled up as high as they would go.'

Rebecca had suggested Lionel as an apprentice to her husband, sure that Alexander would say no. But instead he had laughed, and said that he knew of him already – and he would do very well.

'You know him?' Rebecca had been surprised.

'Through an – ah – mutual acquaintance. He has three sisters and a father dead so he will be a good worker.'

'Well, there is a sister who works—'

'A woman's wage, aye. That is not enough.'

Lionel had finished school five months ago. His mother had lost her job in the clock shop and Lionel had not been able to apprentice himself anywhere in the meantime, and now time was ticking away. The house had had a sour smell to it when Rebecca had visited, and his mother's features were sharp.

'He always wants the best, my Lionel,' his mother had said. 'He spent all my wages on a good shaving brush, though he barely has any beard to speak of.' Though she'd smiled at him fondly as she said it.

Rebecca put her hand to her cheek.

'Has the pain returned?' asked Jenny.

'No, though I am afraid it will. Has Lionel made a plan with you?'

Jenny straightened Rebecca's blanket and tucked it in, then she gave Rebecca the bottle. 'Only to go to for a walk. But here is your medicine. Lionel said that Mr Palmer was most particular. Take all that is in the bottle, he said, even if no pain has returned directly.' Jenny put a hand to her cheek where Lionel had touched it, so that for a moment both mistress and maid held the same pose.

Rebecca took off the stopper and tipped a little of the contents into the palm of her hand.

'Salt?' said Rebecca. 'What is this?'

'I don't know, madam. Lionel said to take it dissolved in some flavoured water, here.' She held out a glass with a little orange juice squeezed inside.

'Look there, it dissolves quite quickly. P'raps it *is* salt after all, that Mrs Bunclarke might use on the beef!'

But it was not sea salt. Though it tasted bitter it did not, at first, seem to be anything at all. Rebecca lay back. She could not now tell whether she felt pain or anxiety or a mixture of both.

But in a little while, so gradually that she was not aware of her fretfulness slipping away, a pleasant feeling begin to congregate in the region of her chest. The warmth of it tethered her to the bed, and in turn held the bed to the floor, and held the floor to the foundations of the house. Rebecca understood that she had lived her life up to this moment like a balloon filled with helium, anxiously bobbing here and there and never finding a place to rest. But now the bones of her chest hummed with a mechanism that seemed to be something like a cog, heavy and fixed and connected to the bigger wheels that she could feel turning somewhere towards the centre of the earth.

She regarded the hectic plasterwork of the ceiling rose without involving herself. The curtains spooled on to the floor without accusation. She let her eyes come to rest on the rug, the paper-hangings and the rosewood table poised on its spindly legs. They were all perfectly themselves. Now when she thought about the argument and the slamming door, and even Evangeline, she found she could run through it all without feeling her heart constrict.

Her eyes were transparent and her eyelids, as they dropped, as fast and heavy as stones in a pool, were transparent too. Behind she saw through them into another world, which was not like the usual drift into sleep at all, but fierce and teeming with instant life.

She sees her home, her childhood home, with her mother and father still living. She is on the beach, pulling back seaweed, turning over rocks, tilting her head to be out of the way of the sand fleas that jump up from under. He is with her. He is always with her. Their heads touch as they bend to inspect the hollow left by the rock. They are looking for crabs, the little bright coloured ones that hide there, to put them in Crab Castle.

Their families live in two houses that are close. Hers has a black slate roof, grey stone, bow windows on either side of the front door. The symmetry of it lodges between her eyes, as right and compact as a die. His house half faces hers, half faces the sea, and is made of stone the colour of the sea on a winter's day. Ivy reaches up the walls in irregular waves.

Rebecca opens her eyes and the vision vanishes. What pleasure it is to conjure up her childhood home in such detail! Usually when she tries to remember such things, even her father's face, the features waver and blur. But now everything is sharp.

The slant of the sunlight suggests that it was the middle of the afternoon. She taps her head, but there is no more pain. No pain, no fear of pain. She ought to rise, but it is so peaceful just lying here looking at the dust motes in the beam that she decides against it. Has she missed lunch? Rebecca cannot remember having eaten it. But she has no hunger, no hunger at all.

She is neither hungry nor thirsty, nor is she in pain. She needs nothing, wants nothing. It is the end of desire.

Rebecca lets her eyes drift shut again and she falls deeper, deeper. Down here Gabriel is taller and thinner in the cheek. He has just come home from school and she has rushed onto the driveway as soon as she heard his carriage on the gravel, thinking to embrace him as she usually does, but something about him stops her.

Instead, she says: 'Will you come to the beach? It is such a fine day.'

But Gabriel shakes his head.

'What? Not to the beach?'

He shakes his head again. 'I don't know if I like to play' – he gives a short self-conscious snort at the word play – 'at the beach any more. I turned fifteen, you know, at Charters.'

Rebecca takes a step back. 'I know you are fifteen! I am also fifteen! Did you not get my birthday letter?'

'Oh, yes.' He scratches vaguely at the pimple on his chin, already raw. 'Thank you.'

He is always changed when he comes home. Rebecca has got used to his ears, or his nose, or his mouth changing shape, but this time it is his voice. A man's voice coming from a boy's body. And even something more; what is it? Rebecca stands on the driveway, the wind bothering her hair, no coat on, trying to work it out.

'Why do you sound *English*?' she asks at last.

He flushes, the blood rising easily to the surface of his pale skin. 'I do not!'

'You do so! English, English!' she chants, not knowing what else to do other than to tease him as she did when they were children, though she knows it in a moment: childhood is gone.

'Well, it can't be helped then, how I speak.' He shrugs; she thinks it is with nonchalance. 'Charters is in England. P'raps it is for the best.' He signals for his trunks to come down from the carriage and turns to go indoors.

'Oh my!' Rebecca claps her hand to her face. They had used to mock Scottish boys who pretended they were English. 'But that is not your voice!'

He has started to walk towards his house; she notices the bones at his hips, his legs that have grown longer. She sees that has driven him inside. 'You sound stupid,' she says, to keep him.

He turns. 'Is it stupid to sound as if I am part of the most powerful country in the world, and the best?'

'But,' she stammers, 'I thought we *were* part of it.' She is uncertain, though; the governess she shares with four other girls at her schoolroom is not well educated.

'It is not Scotland that people talk of when they talk of Britain, it is England. I don't think there are many Scottish generals, or queens, or—'

'There are philosophers, I think—'

'I don't mean here in Edinburgh. I mean out there, in the Empire! The Empire is our greatest jewel.'

He turns to go inside then anyway and Rebecca goes to the beach on her own. With his new voice and his sentences that sound as if he has read them in a book, she does not know who he is.

She is on her own all day. He comes to the beach the next day, though she had not asked him. He sits on a rock, on a promontory, looking out to sea.

'You look as if you are thinking of poetry,' she says, meaning it scornfully.

He gives a little nod, as if to imply, perhaps, that he is.

'Or rather, you look as if you *want* to look as if you are thinking of poetry.'

He flinches. Then he says: 'We are studying Lord Byron this half at Charters.' He picks up a rock and flings it into sea.

'Does *Lord Byron* mean I must make Crab Castle on my own, then?'

He turns to her and says scornfully: 'Do you really still want to build Crab Castle? You know all the crabs escape.'

'They do not!'

'They do so! The gaps in the wall are too big, you know it!'

Rebecca is furious. They never admit that the crabs, small enough to fit on Gabe's fingernail, could escape. They had taken great pride in the building of the walls, selecting the stones and fitting them together. If they saw a crab inching its way out they would pretend not to have seen anything and call to the other for more stones or seaweed.

'They do not escape!' She runs over to his promontory and gives him a shove. He falls sideways but as he falls he grabs hold of her by the hair. She shrieks, he curses. It is a shock, up close, to see here and there stubble on his cheek, and the sharp new bone of his brow and the smell of him, an earthiness that comes through the smell of the sea, as land does.

He is different, not only from how he was before, but different to her, in a way she had never noticed.

They lie together, awkwardly tangled. Her head stings where he has pulled it. 'Get off, you wretch! Is this something they taught you at Charters too?'

'No! Though they do,' he swallows, 'they do ask me about you.'

'Me? What do they know of me?'

'Only what I tell them. That you are a stupid girl. They say girls do not like the same things as boys, that you will want to get married soon enough if we spend any more time—'

'Married?' Rebecca is astonished. But she *has* thought of it, during the lonely months he has been at boarding school. They were idle thoughts, stupid ones.

'And,' Gabe runs his tongue over his lips, 'would you?'

'Would I what?'

'Want to get married.'

'No! You're mad as hops.'

They can hear the sea slapping up against the rock. 'Would you?' she says.

'When I am at Charters,' he says carefully, turning his head away, 'I think of you, as much as any girl would think of a boy, though I try not to. During all my lessons of Lord Byron, and Robert Burns, and in Chemistry and in History, I think of you all the time until I would do anything to be rid of it.'

They have grown still. His cheek is flushed.

'Do you?' Her heart has begun to beat hard, it feels like terror.

She feels him now, his hips against her hips, his hard bones pushing against her soft ones. Slowly he brings down his mouth and covers hers. It is surprising, stifling, gritty. She is about to pull away when, by mistake, she tips her tongue to his. A shudder runs through him. The slime of it does not feel right, their tongues are minnows in a rock pool. She nearly tells him this and nearly laughs. But then his tongue, now she has discovered it, runs over her lips, and then she does the same to him, as a game at first, only then tremors run out from her lips all over her face and then over her chest, and pulls it in tighter and tighter until she can hardly breathe with the kissing of him.

'And now you must marry me,' says Gabe, when at last they pull apart. 'My friends were right. I think we have to now.'

CHAPTER 5

'See now how she slumbers,' said Alexander. 'She is murmuring something.'

'And how she tosses her head from side to side. No doubt she is dreaming of you,' said Mr Badcock, running his fingertip along the back of Rebecca's hand. 'For what else do women dream of but their husbands?'

'Tea sets and Turkey carpets, I dare say!' said Alexander. 'But how do you think the medicine does?'

'She sleeps very deeply; perhaps you gave her too much.' Mr Badcock turned Rebecca's hand over and pressed his fingers to her wrist. 'Her pulse is slow.'

'That is to be expected, it does not mean the dose is too much.'

Mr Badcock leaned in and put his ear close to her mouth. 'Her respiration is shallow.'

'That is also to be expected. Be careful, John, else you will wake her; see how she stirs.'

Mr Badcock dropped his voice to a whisper. 'But I did so want to see for myself the effect. The effect of the first time! She is slumbering certainly, but ...'

'But it is not the usual kind of sleep, I know. Anyway, that is only part of it. She will wake and the medicine will still have its hold on her. Come,' said Alexander, standing up. 'I do not want her to wake and see you. She will wonder why you are here.' He signalled to the window.

The two men went to sit down at Rebecca's card table.

'Did you read the paper?' said Alexander.

'What, the *Scotsman*?' said Mr Badcock.

'No,' said Alexander, picking up the newspaper. 'Ach! What is that doing in here?'

'Not much news in it, I dare say.'

'Enough to fill a woman's head.' Alexander pursed his lips, folded up the *Scotsman* and put it to one side. 'I meant, have you read Mr Davy's paper?'

Mr Badcock spread out his fingers on the table and inspected them. They were very clean and fat. 'Yes, I read it.'

'The research is not current, of course, but the experiment was the first time the fields of chemistry and personal experience were brought together, I believe. Many have attempted something similar since then, but I think that Mr Davy's has still not been bettered. By measuring the amount of nitrous oxide he consumed, in a laboratory, he made an attempt to describe the human condition.' Alexander poured himself a glass of water from the windowsill.

'Although to immerse oneself in an airtight box, stripped to the waist, inhaling nitrous oxide until Mr Davy lost consciousness does not follow a reputable scientific method,' said Mr Badcock.

'Yes, it does smack of hedonism. Nevertheless, his conclusion is what interests me: *Nothing exists but thoughts.*' Alexander tapped his finger on the table as he said each word. '*The world is composed of impressions, ideas, pleasures and pains.* And that, John, is where our future lies.'

'And this here ...' Mr Badcock gestured to Rebecca, who twisted in her bed, and sighed, but still did not wake up. 'This here seems to confirm it. Who knows where she is now? But that she is perfectly content, I don't doubt.'

Alexander tweaked off the head of a little wild rose that was sitting in a vase on the windowsill. 'If it were possible to bathe an individual's brain in a vat of contentment, like this,' he dropped the rose head into his water glass and set the glass on the table, 'it does not matter what external things befall him – or her. I may cause a commotion over here,' Alexander slapped the table with an open palm. 'But if the brain is surrounded by – water, in this case, see how the little flower stays still. Even now see.' Alexander shook the edge of the table. 'There may be a few ripples, but nothing compared to what is happening outside.' He took hold of the glass and began to slop it about. 'Not until I cause quite a commotion does the flower begin to suffer.' The head of the rose went lower and lower into the water, the beads of liquid on its petals sitting like heavy jewels.

Jenny entered the room only a moment later but by then the rose had almost sunk to the bottom.

'Careful now, Alexander,' said Mr Badcock.

'Oh, sorry, sir, Mr Badcock.' Jenny made him an awkward nod over the pot of tea and biscuits she carried. 'I didn't know you were in here. I came to see if Mrs Palmer was awake, if she was hungry.'

'She is not,' said Alexander.

Jenny looked at the windowsill. 'Would you like another glass? I'm not sure you can drink from that.'

'No need,' said Alexander with a shake of his head. 'You may go.'

'Your maid is very young,' remarked Mr Badcock as the door was pulled to. 'Barely past menarche.'

'Young and inexperienced.'

Mr Badcock stroked his beard with the pad of his thumb and stared at the closed door. Then he turned back to his friend. 'But we are drifting, if I may say, dangerously close to heresy! The solipsists believe the same thing, that nothing exists but thoughts, and they are heretics. If only one's mind can be sure to exist, the external world and other minds may, as the solipsists say, be simply a figment of one's own mind. And God also might be a figment of one's own mind, which, of course,' Mr Badcock raised his eyes heavenwards and pressed his fingertips together, 'is the worst kind of thinking.'

Alexander frowned. 'I am sure you exist, John, for I can see you here praying to God. But say this: a man may wake up one day and feel happy, and wake up the next and feel as if he cannot go on, though his life remains exactly the same. Or, to take another example: two men may lose their sight. One man quickly adjusts to it and continues to lead a useful life, the other falls into despair. What does that tell us? That the mind is all! If we can control the mind, it does not matter the circumstance.'

Alexander's eyes were dark and his face pale. In front of him Rebecca stirred and opened her eyes. Both men stilled as if they had been put in the ice house: Alexander with his fingers spread out as if he were pressing an invisible box, Mr Badcock in the middle of idly pulling the petals from another rose.

But Rebecca's eyes only gazed unseeingly ahead for a moment and then fluttered shut.

'I ought to go,' said Mr Badcock, pushing his chair back quietly. 'But what a stroke of luck, dear boy, hmmm? This neuralgia!'

'Indeed. It has the natural look to it. Though the right opportunity would be bound to present itself sooner or later.'

'Oh?' Mr Badcock looked at his friend sharply then brought his hands together quietly in what would have been a clap. 'I see it now! This is why you married her, hmmm?'

'Whatever do you mean, John?'

'She is handsome enough, though you could have got handsomer.'

'Every enterprising man needs a wife, John.' Alexander smiled.

'And you could have got one before, you had plenty of opportunity!'

Voices sailed up from the street and it seemed as if Rebecca would wake again, but she only murmured and turned onto her side.

'But I did not need a wife before now,' said Alexander.

Mr Badcock gave a low whistle and shook his head. 'Most impressed, Alexander, hmmm? Yes indeed. And she has no parents to speak of either, which fits the bill.'

'Her father, poor man,' said Alexander, 'fell down dead in his factory. Over-work, I believe. Left her nothing but debts.'

'You can't have everything. Not everything. Otherwise perfect, yes?'

Alexander gave a low laugh, looking at Rebecca as he did it. 'Well, John, you have discovered me! Rebecca is perfect in nearly every way, what of it?'

'Oh dear boy, I thought you could not surprise me any more, but I must say, hmmm? Such dedication to work!'

'Work *and* science,' said Alexander gravely, his black figure at the window almost blotting out the light.

Mr Badcock pulled the door of Rebecca's room closed behind him and crept out along the corridor. Rebecca was sighing and fidgeting; she would be bound to rouse herself soon. What fun

Alexander could have with her after a dose of his medicine, if he so chose! And that could be another application of it, yes? Why, they could brand it under the heading: *A Man's Best Friend*.

All was quiet, which was good for his purpose, but was it too quiet? Pray God she was not in the kitchen, hidden away like a little trinket in a muck heap. Mr Badcock stole to the door and put his ear to it. The cook was muttering, but to whom? No, he could not hear a reply. Only muttering over her pots, then. He let out his breath through puckered lips.

Mrs Bunclarke need not bother with Mrs Palmer's supper; she would have no appetite this evening. He ought to suggest that she not make so much, when it seemed to be costing her so dear. But then if a cook did not cook, what use was she? Another idle woman in need of her medicine.

Mr Badcock crept to the parlour, making hardly a sound, marvelling at his nimble feet. It was too quiet down here, though, and empty of course. The door to Alexander's study was also closed and silent. No one in the dining room either, just the grandfather clock, the sun and the moon ticking round on their orbits.

Ah, but what was that? A sound coming from upstairs: something being moved, perhaps? But what perfect timing, she must be waiting for him! Though he mustn't frighten her, she was bound to be timid, she was fourteen, fifteen at most. Though those country girls let all sorts have them, he wouldn't be surprised if she'd been spoiled already.

He had caught a glimpse of Jenny's large curved calves walking up the stairs as he'd stood in the hall taking off his coat and now he could not get the image out of his mind. The way she'd glanced back at him as she went down was an invitation. Nice little Annie, and Alice too, hadn't they worn just the same expression? And they had been most welcoming. They had both been saving for something, he forgot what, but the extra money had come in handy. No doubt young Jenny was saving for something too, and had taken a fancy to him to help her buy it.

'We have Mr Darwin to thank, do we not, dear boy?' he would tell Alexander, if he were interrupted. 'We men are but slaves to our sexual appetites.' Though perhaps Alexander would not be too pleased, if he did happen to interrupt him with his maid; better to be circumspect.

He reached the end of the corridor. The linen cupboard was ajar – she was in there, of course, putting away the sheets! He could push the door shut, for a joke, to hear her shriek, just as Alexander once had told him his mother had used to do to him. Only his mother had kept the boy in for several days at a time, as he remembered, without food. Alexander had seemed quite cut up about it.

But Jenny was not in the linen cupboard. She was in the spare room, upholstered all in blue, polishing a candlestick of all things! He could have laughed out loud. Underneath his drawers he felt his prick stir. 'Why are you blushing, Jenny?

Did you expect me?'

'No, sir, it was the shock of seeing you in here! Have you lost aught?'

'No, I have not lost anything at all. It is what I have come to find,' said Mr Badcock, taking a step towards her.

Jenny stopped polishing and dropped her hands to her side, keeping hold of the candlestick. 'What have you come to find, sir?'

'Oh, Jenny!' Mr Badcock smiled. 'Can you not guess? I think you can. Did you not lead me here to you?'

'Lead you, sir?'

'Why not call me John, hmmm? I saw you looking at me earlier on the stairs, when you lifted your skirts.'

'You are wrong, sir.' Jenny tried to back away but after one step she was already pressed up against the fireplace. 'You are mistaken, sir. I did no such thing!'

'Why, then, are you blushing even harder? Look now, your cheeks are quite red. Is it I who is making you blush? I think it is.'

'What do you want?' Jenny stepped away from the fireplace and tried to get past Mr Badcock but he blocked her way and grabbed her by the arm.

'Oh, do not be afraid, Jenny! I will not hurt you. Just stay with me a while, just a moment. I only want to talk, yes?'

'Talk, sir, about what?' Jenny looked down at Mr Badcock's hand where it gripped her.

'Oh, I don't know. What would you like to talk about?'

'I don't want to talk. Will you let me go?'

'Say, I don't know, romance?'

Jenny tried to pull her arm away again. 'Romance, sir?'

Mr Badcock's voice grew harsher. 'Now, Jenny, no need to repeat everything I say, like a parrot. You know why I am here.'

'Just to talk, sir, was what you said. Let me go!'

'Well, yes, that and a little kiss, hmmm? A little kiss, then I will be away.'

'A kiss? No! Mr Palmer will be along in a moment and discover us.'

'He is occupied, no need to worry about that.' Mr Badcock wrenched the candlestick from her hand, better to be safe, and put it back on the mantel. Pray God she would not make him work too hard. It was a hot day and he was already starting to perspire. 'One kiss, what do you say?'

'No, sir, I'm sure I won't. I don't want to do it!'

She *was* making him work, and yet he did like a woman with a bit of spirit. The pursuit gave the conquest spice. He wrestled with her for a moment until his pego got stiff. 'I'd give ten pounds to be in bed with you for an hour. You haven't had a prick up you before, have you?'

At the word 'prick' Jenny gave a violent start and managed to wrench her hand away. She ran for the door but Mr Badcock got there first and stood before it. Both of them were breathing heavily.

'I have seen your legs when you showed 'em to me—'

'I did not!'

'On the stairs now, come, don't be a coquette, hmmm?'

'I didn't! I didn't!' Jenny stood before him, her breasts going up and down. She was saying yes, even as she denied it!

'Come now, give me a kiss and I will give you a sovereign.' Mr Badcock tried to grab her round the waist, but she would twist away so, and her waist was too stout to get a good grip on.

'Let me go to the kitchen! What a beast you are!' said Jenny.

'Come and open the door, my dear, and you will run against this.' Now he let her look at the bulge in his trousers. She would soon get as lewd as he!

But Jenny, stupid girl, turned her head away and would not look. Well then, let him try another way. He felt in his pocket and brought out the gold coin, it gleamed in his palm, even brighter than the afternoon. She would not resist *that*. He took a handkerchief from his waistcoat and mopped his brow. 'What do you say, dear? Shall we sit down?'

But in the end he had to drag her to the bed. Which, after all, was better than her going willingly, she was the more likely to be a virgin. And he hadn't had a nice little virgin since the servant girl of the Fowlers'. She had put up a good fight too, just like Jenny was doing, though by the time he had finished with her she was quite as lewd as he.

'There is the sovereign, then. That will buy you things, hmmm?' He was sweating but his handkerchief lay on the floor in the scuffle. He dare not get it. A drop of sweat from his brow landed heavily on her dress.

'I do not want money. Let me go or I shall scream!' said the girl.

He pushed her down on the bed and lay half over her, feeling her lovely thighs give way beneath his own. Her cap fell across one of her eyes; her hair had come loose and was streaked across her lips in a most provocative way.

'If you scream, Jenny, it is your reputation that shall be ruined, not mine, yes?'

But the door had come a little way open and, though his ears were ringing with lust, Mr Badcock could hear footsteps coming quite deliberately towards them. Damn it! He increased his grip on her arm. 'Move and I will hold you tighter still,' he hissed.

Jenny ceased to struggle, though she still took great gasping breaths through her reddened lips – still provoking him, even now!

The footsteps drew closer. They might, Mr Badcock thought hotly, pass them by. No one would come to the spare room, save the maid, or someone pursuing the maid. His head was pounding, and his prick, bother it, was wilting! Never mind, he could agitate it again soon enough.

But no, the steps stopped outside the room. Mr Badcock held his breath. Jenny stopped panting.

The door swung open towards them.

But it was not Alexander. It was only Lionel, whose mouth, the stupid boy, fell open like a yokel at the sight of them.

'What do you want?' said Mr Badcock. 'Can you not see we are busy?'

'I heard a cry, I thought Jenny—'

'You thought Jenny *what*?' Though Mr Badcock found he could not keep his hands on the girl whilst the boy stood there, like a fool, in the doorway.

'I thought Jenny was hurt.'

'Well, she is not.'

But as soon as he took his hands off her Jenny leapt up and ran to Lionel. Her cap had fallen off onto the bed and it lay there, at the head of the ruckled and creased sheets, as if the ghost of her was still there.

Lionel must have seen it too, for the set of his face got very stubborn.

'Why are you here, boy?' said Mr Badcock irritably, but dammit if he was not flushing himself, his face growing hot just as if he were guilty. He ought to have thought to open a window. He stood up and tightened his belt and walked towards his handkerchief.

'I have come to fetch Mr Palmer to the pharmacy,' said Lionel.

'I will have you sacked if you breathe a word of this, Lionel, to anyone, hmmm?'

Now it was Lionel's turn to flush. But before he could threaten them again they turned and ran, just like a couple of children. He could hear their footsteps running down the hall. Running – as if there were anything to be afraid of!

Their footsteps came down so hard on the paving stones Jenny thought Alexander would come out of Rebecca's room to see what the commotion was. But they got through the hall and into the kitchen, and the door with its bit of green baize nailed up to hide the glass banged shut behind them.

'What have you two been up to?' said Mrs Bunclarke. 'No good, I expect.'

'Are you all right, Jenny, are you fine?' asked Lionel.

'You ought not to bring boys in here, Jenny, this is not—'

'And you can go to hell!' said Lionel, turning on her.

The cook dropped her pan on the floor and a greasy liquid spread out from it. 'Oh, look at that, my stock!'

'I am sorry about your stock,' said Lionel, looking about for a mop.

'Five hours in the oven that was, and now nothing to boil up for the soup!'

'But let Jenny sit down, won't you, Mrs Bunclarke? She has had a shock. Come now, Jenny, here by the fire. I will bring her some tea myself and she can drink it here in the kitchen. Please, Mrs Bunclarke, would you leave us, just for a moment? There is nothing untoward.' Lionel swallowed on the word. 'Look, I only want to comfort her.'

'I have had a shock, being spoken to by a boy like you!'

said the cook, rubbing her nose. But perhaps she saw Jenny's face, red and without its cap, and Lionel's pale one, because she left her pan and went through the back door to the garden.

Jenny's eyes were wet but she pressed the flat of her hands into them and scrubbed them away. 'Lionel, thank God you came in time! I should have been lost.'

'Don't say so, Jenny,' said Lionel, wanting to pick up her hand but letting his hand only hover over hers.

'It is the truth.'

'Well, it did not happen. And he, who is always in church, going on about the sins of prostitution and the like, while behind closed doors he ...' Lionel shook his head. 'The disgusting old sod.'

'But I think it is my fault.' Jenny rubbed her forehead. 'Mr Badcock said I meant him to come to me. And I must've, without knowing it!'

Lionel shook his head. 'No!'

'He said I showed him my leg; I didn't mean to, but I think there must be something bad in me that he should find me out.'

'No,' said Lionel again. ''Tis all him that is bad. He has only rubbed his badness on you like ... I don't know ... a snake rubbing on you and shedding his skin.'

It was the wrong thing to have said – Jenny shuddered again and pressed her knuckles into her eyes. Then she shook her head and went to the sink and washed her hands with the cracked bit of soap, turning her hands over and over under the stream of cold water until they got red with cold.

Lionel shut off the taps and handed her a tea towel. 'Won't you sit down again by the fire? Warm yourself up.'

'At home we had a minister who taught children lessons from the scriptures, and used to get the girls up on his lap to read from St John. The longer we stayed on his lap the more bread and sugar we got. And I had no sugar at home, nor any cakes or biscuits. And I sat there the longest of us all whilst he … tickled me. It did tickle too, and I didn't mind it, especially the sugar. And now Mr Badcock has found me out.' She rubbed her nose.

''Tis not so, Jenny! I'll bet Mr Badcock does that with any maid he comes across, the filthy letch, as he cannot get a woman the normal way! Do not let him ruin your mind; you are too good for it. And as for the minister, he should have been reported. You are too good, Jenny, that is why you get taken advantage of. I saw that straightaway at the pharmacy.'

Jenny stopped rubbing and let her hand drop. 'Did you? Do you really think so?'

'I know it. I am always right about such things.'

Jenny straightened. 'Perhaps this is not so unusual. Not such an unusual happening that it must floor me. Mr Bad—' She faltered and could not finish his name. 'He has done it before, as you said, to other maids. I must think my way past it.'

'I am glad to hear you speak that way.' Lionel brushed her hand quickly. 'You are still cold; look here, draw nearer the fire.' He moved a log so that the embers underneath it glowed brighter and they leaned in together, towards it.

CHAPTER 6

If Alexander seemed cruel for no reason on some days, on others he was kind and solicitous, and the draught made it all easier to bear. On the afternoon he took Rebecca to the Gymnasium north of the New Town, he seemed positively gay. It would be a show, he told her. And it was. They stood near the Great Sea Serpent in its pool of water being powered by hundreds of men rowing around and around, splashing and yelling good-natured jibes to one another as they went, and he hardly flinched as the water, which must have been holding the dirt of a hundred factory workers' feet, splashed over his jacket.

'Exercise like this does not seem a chore,' he said, stepping back one pace, 'but it succeeds by keeping the workers away from the less healthful pastimes of drinking and gambling.'

'Have ye only come to stare, or will ye be showing yer wife how tay do?' shouted out a man dressed only in a vest. Hair sprouted out from his armpits and his arms bulged as he pulled his oar.

Rebecca expected Alexander to blanch and pull her away, but it seemed he was determined to be festive. 'Och aye!' he said, in a broad accent. 'I'll be showing her, dinnae you worry aboot that.'

Great hoots of laughter followed that, and Rebecca looked to her husband anxiously. But he was smiling, only smiling, and they turned to look at the men flying past on their giant trapeze swings, just like brawny circus performers. After that Alexander had a go on a see-saw as long as an omnibus and lifted his hat to Rebecca as it reached its highest point far above her, as high as the birds.

But as she stood with her face lifted up to the white sky, staring at the uncharacteristic figure of her husband flying up, there, a couple of rows away, she saw, with a jolt of her heart into her mouth, was Gabe. She knew him straightaway by the bones in his wrists and the great round arc of shoulders, sprinkled with reddish hair, though his face was turned away from her.

She pressed her knuckles to her lips. He was back! Not three feet away from her husband! Would she greet him? No – she could not, not with Alexander by her side.

'You are very pale – what is the matter?' asked her husband when he got off.

Gabriel had got off on the other side of the see-saw, but she could not turn away, not yet, not until she saw his face.

'Is it the excitement?' he asked.

'Yes, just that.' Rebecca stared ahead, twisting her neck.

'You look as if you have seen a ghost!'

But it was not Gabriel after all. Now that the man was coming towards her she saw that he was quite different. She could not tell if she was relieved or dejected. 'Yes, a ghost,' she said.

'But you are perspiring!' Alexander put his palm on her forehead, damp with his own exertions. 'We best make our way home.'

And when they got there Alexander made her up a small draught to ease the worst excesses of her excitement. Women's temperament, he told her, could not bear as much as men's. As she sunk into her chaise, the sky darkening at her window, she thought he was probably right.

By coincidence Rebecca had finished doing up Albany Street at the same time as the pharmacy was finished and she had organized her own little opening for a few days later. Her friend, or acquaintance rather, Violet, known for her good taste, had come to inspect the house and make her pronouncement.

But if Alexander's opening represented a beginning, Rebecca's represented the end, she thought dismally, as she sat in the parlour staring at the paper-hangings. She had not got it right, not at all.

How she had pored over dish covers, ottomans, fish knives! And then, after she had settled upon one type of fish knife, which would scoop up the cod just so, she saw an advertisement in the newspaper that told her that there was a more impressive one, whose handle was the body of a fish itself, and she knew she had chosen wrong.

Her periodicals had told her that brightness was a good thing in wall decoration, which is why she had chosen these orange curlicues flouncing round a central yellow ball. At the time the pattern had seemed to offer the right mix of wit and merriment. After all, as the periodical said, good cheer could hardly be expected to survive in an old-fashioned room of browns and greys. But now that the afternoon sun fell on her wall the garish colours made her head hurt.

'Are you all right?' asked Violet.

'A little tired, thank you,' said Rebecca. 'Would you like some more tea? I will ring for some.'

'I'm sorry I could not come to the opening of the pharmacy,' said Violet. 'But dear Henry insisted we see his mother.' She made a face.

Violet had only just come back from her honeymoon in Madeira. Her husband had some interest in geology and the weather there was temperate all year round.

'Did you bring anything back?' Rebecca asked. 'A memento?'

'Oh yes, my house is full of them. Fans, painted plates, articulated fish. Although Henry would insist on bringing back *plants*. It was all I could do to prevent him making a pet of a lizard! He said the wretched thing didn't exist anywhere else, that it was a reason to believe Mr Darwin.'

'And do you believe Mr Darwin?' Rebecca noticed for the first time that her friend's cheeks were covered with a filigree of blond hairs. Was that supposed to signify something – was it appetite?

'Do I?' Violet laughed. 'Why, I have never thought of it much either way! But you are married to a man of science, so you must have an opinion.'

'The evidence of Mr Darwin's adds up, more for the side of the monkeys I am afraid to say, though I wish it did not.'

'Oh dear, I dare say you are right, but I'm afraid I don't like the look of Mr Darwin; and Mr Huxley is worse, just exactly like an ape himself! So I am prone to disagree with them both.'

Violet dabbed at the corner of her lips with her napkin. Two fat flies whirred against the window pane, blundering on until they trapped themselves between the glass and the silk curtain. Rebecca stood up, meaning to open the window and let them out, but, before she could, Violet put down her napkin and said in to the silence: 'It was the funniest thing!'

Rebecca turned. Violet did not look amused. A frown of uncertainty passed across her face. 'I think I can tell you the story as we are both married women now,' she said.

Rebecca remembered her crepuscular bedroom, Alexander's face in the dawn light. 'The story?' she said.

'You may find it humorous. They have no wheels on Madeira you see; they travel about on a kind of sledge, with a boy running ahead flicking water on the stones.'

Rebecca smiled, to be nice. But Violet had not got to the amusing part yet.

'We decided to go bathing, and that was how we got there. The sea quite *glittered*. Like a jewel. And not cold at all, not like Scotland. Dear Henry said it never gets cold in Madeira.'

'How picturesque.' The orange of Rebecca's paper-hangings was the colour of a foreign sunset. Her own honeymoon had been spent on the Isle of Skye. Not too far away, at Alexander's suggestion. They didn't want to spend the whole time travelling.

'Only there were no bathing machines – did I say that? And as we came down the path, my slippers seemed to have grease on their soles; I had to hold on very tight to Henry to get down. I was looking forward to bathing: my bathing dress was so light compared to the ones we wear here. But we turned the corner and, well, you'll never guess—' Violet broke off. The door opened.

'Can I bring you anything, madam?' said Jenny.

'Thank you – the tea is running low, could you bring us some more?'

'Should I wash out your cups first, madam, for the leaves?'

'No need – here, just take the pot.'

But on her way to the door Jenny, perhaps catching the press of Violet's mouth, caught her shoe on the leg of the chair. A spot of tea leapt from one of the cups onto a pale silk cushion and spread quickly outwards to become a stain.

'Oh, madam, I am so sorry!' Jenny blinked. 'Shall I scrub it?'

'I've heard gasoline is the right thing for taking stains off silk,' said Violet. 'Have you any?'

'Gasoline? What is that?' said Jenny.

'I am sure it will come out without the use of gasoline. The stain is not so big; just wash it in the usual way. And if it doesn't, there are plenty of other cushions.'

'Yes, madam,' said Jenny, clasping the cushion under one arm, balancing the tray and the pot with the other.

Violet sat forward, as if poised on a ledge.

'I am worried about Jenny,' said Rebecca. 'I think she may be homesick. She has grown so sickly in the past few days.'

'Girls like that are always homesick. My maid was terrible when she first came to me. They get over it. But what was I saying?'

'Your bathing trip,' said Rebecca. 'With Henry.'

'Ah yes!' Violet's eyes darted from side to side. 'You'll never guess.' She swallowed. 'Three men, Portuguese, bathing in the sea, at just the spot we were aiming for. But they had no clothes on. At all!' A blush rose up her cheeks but Violet seemed compelled to carry on. 'And as we came down they all got out of the sea, and ran towards their clothes, which they had discarded, in a heap.'

Rebecca saw the naked young men wriggling out of their clothes, laughing. She put her knuckles to her chest and rubbed her skin.

'And *one* of the men,' Violet caught her lips between her teeth, 'one of their, their man's *parts*, was quite the biggest thing ... like a horse's, if you have ever seen that! I mean to say, it slapped at his thighs as he ran.' She clapped her hands to show how.

'Oh Violet!' Rebecca turned. 'Why are you telling me this?'

'I don't know!' The blush stained deeper and spread down towards Violet's neck. 'Because, well, as I said, you are married. We are both married. It might amuse you. And,' she went on, 'I thought you might know, I mean ...' She swallowed. 'Is it normal? Because Henry ... well, Henry tried to turn me away, of course, from the sight of it. I think he may have put a 'kerchief over my eyes, but I could see through it quite well. But I wish I had not seen it now after all.'

'Why?'

'Because I cannot help but remember it! And it is wrong to remember such a thing, especially, you know, in the night, and Henry knows I am thinking of it sometimes, when we ...' Violet swallowed again. 'And he becomes angry. I mean to say, for several nights afterwards he would not undress in front of me, even though it was our honeymoon.'

Rebecca leaned over to put her hand on Violet's knee. All these things gathered from every civilization, and underneath it all there were quims and cockstands and parts of animals. The silk curtains made by worms, the heart-shaped ivory boxes carved from an elephant's tusk, even the ashtray was made from the outside of a horse's hoof.

'Oh Violet, I don't think it can be wrong to think. Perhaps you ought to push it from your mind when you are with Henry, that is all.' Rebecca bit the inside of her mouth. 'As I ought to, with Alexander.'

'Do you, with him? I can't imagine it!'

Rebecca looked through the window; a mother was dandling her baby in the window of the opposite house. Violet must have seen it too.

'When we have children time will not weigh so heavy as it does now. I will forget all about this and I dare say I will look back and think how stupid I have been.'

'But should you like to see the house?' Rebecca asked her. 'It is why you came, after all.'

'Oh yes, I should love to. I have some space that needs filling in my own parlour – though I'm sure I don't know how, with all the shopping I have done!'

When they got to the hall the long windows spattered with a sudden squall. Violet had to raise her voice over the tick-tack of the rain hitting the glass.

'This beautiful gasolier; where did you get it? I have long wanted one just the same! And I do so like this Turkey carpet! They can be gloomy, but this one here has bright reds in it.'

'Oh, a shop on Princes Street, I think, just by the drapers ...'

And then Violet had a number of other queries: why had she decided upon the Worcester dinner service rather than the Spode, and where had she found the puzzleballs there on the sideboard, and who had sewn her dining-room curtains?

Before she could answer, Violet had another question. 'What distinguished paintings. Who are they?'

Rebecca pinked. She had bought them at auction: men sitting wide-legged on the back of horses or leaning purposefully on sticks. Alexander's father, she understood, had been a kind of street-seller when he had been alive. Though superior to the usual kind, for he sold his own inventions, he was still not the kind of person to pose for an oil painting. He had had a little success with a liquid that promised to clean everything: laundry, hair and carpets, with just a few drops. His mother was alive but Rebecca had never met her – she had not come to the wedding, nor written to congratulate her. Alexander had told her she was too old to travel.

'The man and the horse I bought at auction,' said Rebecca in a spirit of penance, hating herself for being a fraud. 'And the rest of them—'

But Violet caught sight of a room that they had not seen, with its door shut. 'What's in here?'

'Mr Palmer's study. I have done it in a dark green the colour of pine trees. For his concentration: he spends a great deal of time working in there.'

'But cannot I see where your husband spends his time? How lucky you are to be married to him.' Violet flushed a little. 'I think he is very mysterious. Oh, but look! The door is ajar, not closed altogether. I am sure I would never go in, but couldn't we peek around? If I am to get the full tour I want to see the *masculine* side of the décor.' Violet had her hand on the doorknob and gently with the other hand began to prod at the door.

'I don't think we ought,' said Rebecca. 'He forbids me to go in. Women have no place in his study, it is for intellectual rigour.'

'Oh, I'd just like a peek!' Violet pouted. 'Couldn't I?'

'We ought not, he forbids it!'

But Violet was pushing open the door with her finger and inching her head round, just enough to—

'Violet, do not go in! If Alexander finds out you have been in there …' Rebecca tried to pull her back. 'He will find out and then he will …' He would hit her, with an open hand. He would say prying was a regrettable side to the feminine character, but that was no reason why she could take liberties, and Mr Badcock would nod and they would both look sad and pitying but behind it their eyes would be hard.

But Violet had given the door a last push and with a sigh it swung open. Heavy brown curtains. Green walls. A tapestry hung on them: a hunting scene, a deer being pursued by hounds, which Alexander must have chosen for himself. Everything neatly and sharply angled: the rug to the window, the pen to the pile of papers, the chair to the desk.

But there was something else – what was it? That pale shadow there, on the desk? It did not fit. No, it was something like a misshapen animal, silver, red and panting.

'What on earth is a *shoe* doing on the desk?' Violet laughed, a high-pitched kind of laugh, and then Rebecca saw – it *was* a shoe but still, the animal feeling persisted. For it was a shoe distorted by bad dreams. The heel, the red thing, rose up and up at an impossible angle – how it would hurt to wear it! Only the tip of the toe had room enough to touch the ground. A hoof. And then, as she went in towards it – she was drawn in, they both were – she saw the number of straps, gaping open like tongues.

'I say, Rebecca!' Violet's blue eyes flew open like a doll's. 'Oughtn't that to be in your closet?'

Before she could stop herself Rebecca said: 'But it isn't mine!'

'Not yours?' said Violet in a voice that even though it was shocked, still held some excitement. 'But why does Alexander have it in his study?'

'I don't know,' said Rebecca.

'P'raps Mr Palmer was planning to surprise you. Is it your birthday soon?'

Rebecca shook her head. She could not take her eyes from the shoe. Whomsoever wore it must be turned into a goat. It was Eva's, of course! But that her husband should bring it back to the house afterwards, and put it in his study … How could Eva walk about in it? Nobody could walk in such a thing? The pain would cripple her after a few steps. Her father had begun to make higher heels at the end it was true, but *that* … It was like something very old, from China, or medieval times, an instrument of torture, not to be walked in, to keep women indoors.

Not meant to be walked in.

And if not walked in, was it only for tupping?

Were there such shoes, just for tupping? She had not known of it. But the thing that she had not known existed had just now been wrenched into being, and there it was, on Alexander's desk.

Rebecca's stomach sunk. It was for tupping Eva, of course. Eva who was beautiful, who held herself in check, who was not shameful.

Violet's voice skittered away again in a rush. 'I think Alexander must be planning to surprise you. How exotic! I think dear Henry might never recover if I brought it home.'

Rebecca backed towards the door. Was there any sign that they had been in? A crease in the carpet, the heaviness of the air disturbed? It *was* disturbed, but surely the air would redistribute itself and settle back down by the time Alexander came home.

Jenny's voice at her shoulder made her jump. Her coming must've been muffled by the carpet runner.

'Madam, I think the tea is growing cold in the parlour.

Should I bring it up?' Rebecca saw Jenny's gaze go past her and to the desk and her hand come up to her mouth.

'Why would you bring up the tea? It should only spill. And I don't know if it was you who left this door open but it ought to be kept shut at all times,' said Rebecca, pulling it closed with a bang.

CHAPTER 7

Rebecca found her maid in the parlour, picking up the china teacups with her swollen fingers and clattering them onto the tray.

'I am sorry I was short with you. Perhaps you can guess why.' Rebecca tried to smile but her stomach would not come back up.

'The shoe do you mean, madam?'

'I was angry, but I ought not to have spoken to you in that way. It must be Evangeline's, of course.' Her failure as a wife was one of imagination, Rebecca saw that now. P'raps all husbands had such things on their desks! Although dear Henry seemed not to.

'I don't know whose it is, but it looks very uncomfortable,' said Jenny, her lashes lowered over the saucers.

'Aye! I wore shoes one quarter as high to the opening and my blisters are still not healed.' She thought of Evangeline's card, under her hairpins in a box on her dressing table. 'You look tired, Jenny. Should you like to sit a while? I have time for another lesson if you should like.'

Jenny looked doubtfully at the green velvet chair; it still held the imprint of Violet's behind. 'Oh, a lesson! I don't know. I don't think I feel right for it today.'

'Come on, it may help us to forget our own worries.' Rebecca opened the paper.

'Very well, then, thank you, madam.'

'Well then, let us see. Where is the *a* here?

'*It was expected that as a result of Western Education the Hindoo would of necessity cease to believe in the extravagancies of Hindooism and that he would, as a general rule, be brought to believe in and embrace Christianity.*'

Jenny hesitated over the word *and*, finally pointing to the *d*.

'Almost, but the *a* has no stalk above it.'

'But I don't see why one squiggle should mean one thing, and another squiggle, another. There is no plan behind it.'

'No, there is no plan. It is just agreed upon, that is all. And it is harder to learn now you are fifteen. But let us continue, I think it is only through repetition that it will go in.

'*Experience now, however, has most plainly shown that although an educated Hindoo does cease to believe in the absurdities of Hindooism, yet he does not, in general become a Christian—*'

Rebecca broke off. Jenny held her head in her hands. 'But what is the matter? Is it for the plight of the Hindoos?'

Jenny shook her head. 'Come!' Rebecca drew the younger girl towards her.

After a moment's resistance Jenny rested her forehead on her shoulder. She spoke quietly. 'I am afraid if I tell you, you will send me away.'

'I would never send you home, not unless you wanted to go.'

'It is Mr Badcock.'

The answer was so unexpected that Rebecca could not, at first, take it in. 'Mr Badcock?'

'Oh, it is no matter! I shouldn't tell you.' Jenny struggled and attempted to rise.

'Where are you going?' said Rebecca, pulling her arm.

'Do not hold me!' cried out Jenny.

'I am sorry, Jenny, I only meant—'

Jenny leapt up and ran to the window. ''Tis only that I was taken back for a moment – to him.'

'To Mr Badcock?' With his eyes that were glints of granite in the folds of his face, that roamed around as if they were seeing under her clothes. 'Oh! To Mr Badcock! I begin to understand.'

'He said I provoked him. And then he came to the blue room, and he tried to give me a sovereign ...'

'Oh dear! Did he did he manage to ...'

But Jenny shook her head.

'Thank God! Then there is no danger of a child. But, oh! I will speak to my husband.'

'No, madam, you must not! Mr Palmer will tell Mr Badcock and I shall be blamed for it.' The skin at the base of Jenny's neck grew mottled. 'They will agree with each other, and then they will agree to send me away. Then I will not find other work, and will be turned out on the street.'

Rebecca stared at Jenny and then across the ottomans and hard-backed chairs she had placed around the room. 'You are right,' she said finally. 'My word will count for nothing. But there must be something I can do!'

'There is not. I think it happens often.'

'Oh Jenny, but it is not right! How sorry I am to have brought you here.'

Outside a couple walked by, they were discussing whether it would rain or not as if it were an argument.

'Lionel stopped it,' said Jenny. 'He saw Mr Badcock and would have fought him, I think. I hope it does not cost him his job!'

'For that, Mr Badcock would have to tell Alexander why he ought to lose it. And I don't think he will.'

Outside, the woman had won the day. It would not rain. Their voices were fading off.

'Will you go and rest? I will talk to Mrs Bunclarke on my way out, about the tea things,' said Rebecca.

They had almost reached the door when Rebecca added: 'Oh, there is one other thing. I am going to visit Evangeline now – I must do it. Only, Mr Palmer likes me to be in the house at this time of the month. Not to exert myself. He is very particular on the matter.'

Jenny nodded and pulled on her ear.

'I ought to be in my bedroom, lying down. I will be home before him, but if for any reason he comes home, as he sometimes does, and asks after me, could you tell him I am sleeping?'

'But I am going out myself, 'tis my afternoon off – you said I might.'

'Oh yes, yes, of course. No matter, I will be home. I will make sure of it.'

'We are only going to Arthur's Seat.'

'Lionel is taking you to Arthur's Seat?'

'Aye, for a walk.'

'I am glad of it! You must – promise me that you will – you must enjoy yourself!'

Rebecca looked so determined on the matter that Jenny faltered. But, 'Aye,' she said obediently, 'I will.'

And so the two women left the house, walking together down Albany Street until they reached Leith Street. It was windy and the breath was swept out of Jenny's mouth as soon as she opened it. As she rounded the corner of Calton Road her heart was thumping uncomfortably, though she could not tell if it was the weather or the sight of Lionel, standing at the corner, his hands pushed deep in his pockets, that did it.

They greeted each other with a nod. Jenny's cheeks were flaming and she turned away from him so that he would not see it, and they walked on together. It seemed an age until they got to the slopes of Arthur's Seat, and all the way the only words spoken between them were about the wind and if Lionel's cap would blow off or no.

But when they started the climb Jenny's heart lifted a little. It reminded her of the hills of Argyll: there was a wildness to the springy grass and the bare rocky outcrops, though it was just next to the city. At each step more of Edinburgh was revealed, until they were looking down at the pointed spires and then the Water of Leith and finally beyond that to the mountains.

At last they reached a hillock that made a natural resting place, and there was nothing to do but stop.

'Sorry tay get you all the way up here,' Lionel said.

'I'm sorrier for you,' said Jenny, watching Lionel go to a patch of grass and rub mud from the tip of his shoe.

'No bother!' he said, smiling. 'The view is grand, though.'

'Yes,' said Jenny. 'It is! I have never been up here before.' Her face still pointed towards the view but her mind was to him: his cheek, the side of his cap. The wind blew the smell of him towards her, sweeter than grass.

'Aye, a grand view,' said Lionel again. A kestrel circled overhead. 'Have you ... are you ...? I mean to say, have you been bothered again?'

'By Mr Badcock, you mean?' Jenny shook her head, with her eyes on the view. 'If he is at the house I keep to the kitchen. He cannot get me there. He hasn't threatened your job?'

'Mr Badcock takes no notice of me. He struts around the pharmacy and winks at the ladies and I am there, behind the counter, hating him, and thinking of you.'

'You did enough, Lionel, I'm sure.' Jenny turned and at the same moment Lionel turned and their hands touched behind their gloves. Jenny smiled and breathed out in a half-laugh. 'How windy it is up here. It is blowing my thoughts clean from my brain, I swear!'

'But how fetching you look in it,' said Lionel. 'It is putting the colour back into your face.'

'Aye, that'll be the broken veins,' said Jenny. Then her smile fell away again and she looked grave. 'You said to tell you if I noticed anything strange. I did – I think I wasn't meant to – though it may sound senseless to you.'

'Aye?'

'A shoe. There now, you think I am stupid for telling you! But it was not Mrs Palmer's shoe, I could tell it by her expression. And it was with a heel – I have never seen a heel the same, nothing like. P'raps it is common enough in Edinburgh, I don't know, but Mrs Palmer was awkward, and she slammed the door on it quickly enough.'

Lionel put out the tip of his tongue and ran it over his top lip. 'You must go home,' he said quietly. 'Or somewhere else. I do not want to lose you but …' He swallowed. 'That house is not the place for you. Can you not find work out in the countryside?'

'What, for a shoe?'

'Not just a shoe – Mr Badcock too.'

'But I thought you said men like Mr Badcock were common enough, that I mustn't let him trounce me!'

'Aye, but he has taken a fancy to you—'

'I can avoid him. Now I know what he is about I can take precautions.'

'There must be another position in all of Edinburgh!'

'Why? Why do you say I must leave?'

Lionel pushed up his cap. The rim of it left a red line across his forehead. 'You know how easy it is for a girl like you to drop off the edge. Maids, servants who ... who lose their honour – through no fault of their own – and end up in worse kinds of work. The pay is better, but I don't think they are happier for it. You know what I am talking about?'

'Aye. Prostitution. But I cannot leave. I cannot leave Mrs Palmer. Not now. Another maid would not be able to do for her as well as I ...' Jenny turned to the view again and let two strands of pale hair blow across her cheek. 'And now she spends half her time asleep I think she needs me more.'

'She needs you less, it sounds like!' Lionel sighed. 'I have seen this before.'

'You have seen everything before, and yet you are the same age as me! What have you seen, then?'

'Maids who will do anything for their mistresses. When their mistresses care not a jot for them.'

'Well, Mrs Palmer does care. She is teaching me to read. Though I am not learning well. But I have learned all about the Hindoos and the women who would be men.'

'Women who would be men – what are they?'

'They are women who want to be doctors. Mrs Palmer says it is a good thing.'

'I see! I thought you meant ...' Lionel blushed and worried a tuft of grass with his toe. 'Well, something else. For there are such women, you know.'

'Are there?'

'Aye. But I am glad you are not one of them. I like you just the way y'are. I suppose I should be grateful to your mistress, for I've no doubt you should leave Albany Street and leave Edinburgh all together, but I must admit I am glad that you will not.'

CHAPTER 8

When Rebecca got out into the wind she found it prevented her from going as fast as she would like. She'd had, at the last moment, a compulsion to stuff the shoe into her carpet bag. For all the shoe's horror, it was not big: the height of the heel meant it was compressed into a kind of solid thing, almost a cube, and it disappeared from view quite easily. She had the idea of thrusting it in Evangeline's face.

Rebecca did not want to go down North Bridge and straight past the pharmacy's window, so she walked down Market Street and into the Old Town that way. She had not visited the Old Town for some months; it was always a surprise to feel the change in atmosphere. Here the streets were not as straight as they were in New Town. They stuttered with differently angled, differently sized houses and lurched into the alleyways as if they were drunk. The stone steps that led one alley into another were not smooth like Rebecca's steps in New Town but sagged in the middle if they were made of softer stuff.

Blackfriars Street was not in the slums, not quite. But from where she was, at the top of it, she could smell the acrid smoke that the slums always seemed to give off. Several filthy children clustered in doorways and eyed her as she passed, the chilblains on their toes shining angrily though the grime of their feet.

Number nine, then. It did not look to be in such a state of disrepair as the others nearby: there was glass in the window, the bricks were not as blackened.

She rang the bell. The two dogs curled on the steps must've been used to visitors for they paid her no heed. She rang again. Now one of the dogs gave a great sigh and settled its nose under its tail.

P'raps she had the wrong address? No, this was number nine, though the number had been partly obscured by soot. Evangeline must be out, then.

Rebecca rang once more. The other dog got up, circled round and round, and dropped down again, its head facing the other way.

Well. She would come back tomorrow.

Rebecca had made her way down the steps and was halfway along the street when the door opened and Evangeline came out.

'Oh, Mrs Palmer – do come back!'

Rebecca turned. Evangeline was without bonnet or petticoats, or gloves. Her dress was unbuttoned at the top, as if she had pulled it on in a great hurry.

'I was asleep; I have strange habits, I am afraid. You did not send ahead! But I am awake now. I am glad you have come.

Will you come up?' She wore the same stretched look that she had had before, as if she had been pulled too tight and might at any moment break in two.

Now that Rebecca had turned to leave, she wanted anything else but to turn around again and go inside, even though she had come all the way down here.

But she must, alas. There was nothing else for it.

When they went inside Rebecca looked around for a drawing room or a parlour to be shown into, but Evangeline led her through the hall and pushed open a door at the very end of the corridor. It seemed she lived in a lodging house.

Rebecca's first thought was that Evangeline had been the victim of a burglary. The table had been pushed unevenly towards the centre of the room, and the smell! Rotting fish, or some other sea thing. Rebecca took out her handkerchief.

'Oh dear,' said Evangeline. 'Yes, that fish belongs to Kitty Kat.' Eva took up the bowl with a skeleton of a fish half in it and flung it through the window. She opened the other window and flapped her hand through it. 'This must seem dreadful to you, I think. I have let it get away from me. I have been …' She paused and took a gulp of air. 'I have been ill. And you surprised me – though I am glad you did! I haven't had time to tidy anything away.'

Rebecca looked about the room for signs of Alexander, at the hairpins next to the sink, the books stacked on the chair and fallen off it, the saucer rimmed with dried milk. But she could not imagine that *this* was where Alexander came to tup. They must have somewhere else.

She stared at Eva's face, as if she might see a clue in it, a trace of her husband. Eva was half-turned away at the stove, a kettle was on it, steam was coating the glass with condensation. The paint was peeling on the sill from all the tea that must have been boiled there. But Eva only frowned at the kettle, which was coming to a shrill boil. She grabbed hold of the handle but there was too much water in it and dropped it back down with a cry. Some of the water came spilling from the spout onto the hem of her dress and the floor.

Eva cradled her hand next to her chest and hopped about. 'Oh dear, my wrists are so weak! And now I have wrecked my slipper. And my toe too, I think!' She raised her skirts and stared down. 'Water is terrible for satin.'

'Wait a moment,' said Rebecca, her heart beating fast. 'I know something about shoes, my father was a sweater's hand. Let me look.' She crouched down and held out her hands for Eva's shoe.

Eva leaned against the table. She drew up her skirts further.

Eva's slipper was worn at the heel and dirty at the toe and – long. Very long. There was no way that the shoe could belong to her.

Rebecca rose to her feet. Laughter rose up in her chest. But she must not laugh, else Eva would think her mad. Instead, she covered her mouth with her hand and smiled into it.

But Eva looked at her, her brows drawn. 'I see you have noticed my slippers; they are dirty, I am afraid. I dare say you think me very slovenly. I was not always this way! I—'

'No, it is not that!' said Rebecca. How could she have ever thought that Alexander would be having an affair with this Eva, who caught at her hair and chewed it, whose nails were bitten, whose hem was caked in mud? 'I think your slippers are perfectly fine!' Now she was sounding foolhardy. 'I think, I don't mind about the state of your rooms, not one bit.'

But Eva's brows furrowed still further. 'You are being polite. Or sarcastic.'

'No, I merely—'

'I have not always lived like this, you know. I grew up in a parsonage, in Perthshire.'

'Aye, I'm sure you did and I—'

'It had six bedrooms. And the lawns ran, let's see, as far away as that building there.' Eva gestured to a blackened building quite far away through the back window.

'Really, I have no judgement at all.'

'But Father was a parson, you see,' Eva continued as if she had not heard, picking at a dry piece of skin on her cheek. 'And a parson's wages do not stretch to eight children. By the time I was born there was a hole in the roof that the rain came through, and the damp growing up the parlour wall had mushrooms on it. When I was ten Father died from a congestion of the lungs and later I came to Edinburgh to become a governess. Only you know what sort of work that is, neither fish nor fowl.' She shuddered and looked up at Rebecca again in a kind of appeal, her eyebrows up into her hairline, and again Rebecca had the feeling she had seen Eva somewhere before. 'The children were devils.'

'A governess; are you trained for it?'

'Oh, you do not need training to teach girls! I got it all out of a book. I think growing up in the damp is why I am so sickly. Do you think it can be?'

'Are you sickly?'

'Oh yes! Most terribly.' Eva picked at one of the charms that hung from her bracelet. 'I have fits – melancholy fits – and I don't know what to do with myself. Then I wish myself dead. It is hard to seek work feeling like that. I've run into the sea, you know, and thrown myself in. Once I swam far enough out, certain that I'd never get back in, I was sure that would do it. But a boatman hooked me up and took me to the shore again. He even charged me for it!' She squeezed her face together, as if she would sneeze. Instead, she laughed. 'Ah well! You have not come here to hear about me. I have not followed the proper paths of conversation! It comes of living away from society, as you can see.'

Watching, Rebecca felt something go out of her, towards this pale, fretful woman, who was not, after all, so different to herself. 'As do I, Eva. I live far away from society! I think my maid is my best friend. And she is fifteen, I am eight and twenty – nearly an old maid. Or I was, before I married.' She blushed.

Kitty Kat leapt up onto the sofa and pushed his way under Eva's hand. 'I am the same age. But do you not recognize me?'

'I do! But I cannot place it.'

'After the governess's position I got a job as a sweater's hand. For your father.'

'My father?'

'We talked of bridge. You were going to make up a four, with your father's friends, only—'

'Yes, I remember it now! Only I hate bridge and was only going grudgingly.'

'Because your father wanted it. Yes – and I said—'

'You said that you hated the game too, that there was nothing more boring. Only you said it in a low voice, so no one else would hear. I remember, and we laughed, didn't we?'

'I was not with your father for long.'

'No, for the next time I came to his rooms a new girl was cutting. And I thought you had gone somewhere that paid better. Are you a cutter still?'

'Oh no, I get by on my savings.' Eva rubbed at the edge of her teacup with her thumb.

'What a coincidence!' said Rebecca. She could not resist looking at her carpet bag. 'I remember it clearly now, even though we only spoke a few words! It was several years back.'

'Yes, a coincidence.' Eva looked down at her tea, which was getting cold. 'Did you take your father's death very hard?'

'Not as hard as my mother's. When she died I was lost, and father too. That is why he worked so hard, I think.'

'If he'd lived he would have been rich.'

'But he had not a head for business. He paid too much for new machinery and when he died he was greatly in debt.'

Eva leaned forward and touched her arm. 'We are both orphans, then, and we are both the same age! It is a good recipe for friendship.'

Kitty Kat scratched away at the threads that hung down from the side of the sofa; Eva scooped him up under her arm and went to the window. 'Oh, you devil! You will ruin everything. Out you go. And see you don't come back with a poor dead bird!' She pushed him through the window and tried to shut it but Kitty Kat slid through her grasp and ran to Rebecca, his tail swishing with fury. 'Oh dear! I cannot control him, not at all. Perhaps that is the nature of cats. But be careful of your bag, he will claw it if he gets the chance. Should I keep it safe? I think I should put it up there, on the shelf.'

'Oh no! I mean to say, I don't want you to—'

But Eva had already crossed the short distance to the bag and was bending over as if she meant to pick it up.

'No please, there is no need,' cried Rebecca, snatching it away and feeling herself flush. But she had grabbed hold of only one of the bag's handles so that lifting it and swinging it out of reach had the opposite effect: it gaped open.

From inside the shoe gleamed and glimmered darkly, visible to them both.

'That! What are you doing with that? Oh, oh!' Eva staggered back and fell against the little table, sending its legs scraping against the floor.

'You know it? It is yours, then!' said Rebecca.

'Mine? No! It is not mine.'

'But you know whose it is!'

'Yes,' said Eva. 'I know whose it is. But why do you have it – why have you brought it here?'

'I found it. In my husband's study. And I thought it was yours. I feel very foolish telling you. I thought you were his mistress.'

'His mistress?'

'I know the shoe is not yours – I saw it straightaway. But – oh please, Eva – you must tell me whose it is!'

'You do not want to know.' Eva shook her head and looked to the ceiling. 'I wanted you to come here because I thought I might protect you. Now I see that it is too late! I thought that I might be able to make up for the wrongs I have done. But you have brought *that* here, and it is too late.'

'What do you mean, too late?'

But Eva only shook her head. 'And you love him? I think you do.'

'Alexander?'

'Your husband, yes.'

Rebecca paused, with her hand to her throat. 'I don't know. I ought to.'

'But …' said Eva. 'Does he hurt you?'

'We have not been married six months and already he is unfaithful.'

'Not with this, this affair. I mean, in other ways.'

Rebecca remembered the way he had gripped her, she thought of his clenched fists. 'Not yet,' she said slowly. 'Will he? Oh Eva, tell me what you know of him!'

Eva blinked twice.

'If you mean to protect me you must tell me!'

But Evangeline only shook her head again. 'I cannot tell you. You will know everything when I show you the owner of the shoe. If you are still sure you want to see her. But it will take time to set it up.'

'How long?'

'I cannot say. Two weeks, maybe three. I cannot say.'

It was Rebecca's turn to shake her head. Then she saw the clock. 'Oh, but I must go home! Alexander will be back soon.'

'Well, then,' said Eva. 'I will send word.'

CHAPTER 9

Rebecca went as fast as she could, though people turned to stare, not in the Old Town, for there they were used to women running, but as soon as she got up into the New Town. So she slowed to a trot, through the kind of dusk that poets write of: the thrush singing and the air scented by jasmine. She was sweating by the time she came in sight of the front door. She pulled off one glove and grasped the key and tried to get it in to the lock. And then, from behind the door, she heard her husband's voice.

'Where is she? You must know. You are her maid, and I think, know most things about her. She confides in you too much.'

'She is in her room,' said Jenny.

Rebecca twisted the key and began to speak as she walked through the door: 'I told Jenny I would be resting only then I decided to go out.'

'Out? And at this hour!'

'Just – to take the air. It is a lovely evening.' Rebecca looked back, as if for confirmation, at the lime tree, ruffling its leaves in the breeze.

Alexander smiled, showing his small white teeth. 'Strange

that a maid should not know her mistress's whereabouts.'

'Not really, I think. She has been out herself, for it is her afternoon off.'

'You took a bag with you,' said Alexander.

'I thought I might need to take something, in my condition, even for a short walk.' She clasped the carpet bag tighter under her arm.

'Such a large bag seems unnecessary.' He stared as if he could see through the sides of it. Rebecca spread her hand, the thread of the carpet hot under her palm.

'Do you not know what happens if you over-exert yourself?'

'Yes, you have told me—'

'See how your breath labours? Menstruation is a disease and someone with a disease ought not to leave their bed. You have not the blood to support it.'

And now Mr Badcock stepped into the hallway from the parlour, nodding his head and smiling. 'The future of our race depends on it, hmmm? Even you, Jenny, yes, even the servant class, if they are British, are good daughters of Albion and must take care in the same way. Do you, Jenny?'

'Do I what, sir?'

'Do you take care of yourself?'

'I – I haven't long started it, sir.'

He moved towards her. 'Speak up, I cannot hear you!'

'She says she has only just begun to be a woman,' said Rebecca, moving to put herself between Jenny and him.

'Even more important then! Oh Jenny ...' He took a step to the side so he could still see her, his hands drumming on his belly. 'If you exert yourself in your menses, either physically or mentally, say by reading – though I expect you cannot read, can you?'

Rebecca and Jenny glanced at each other. Rebecca gave a tiny shake of her head.

'No,' said Jenny.

'Let us into the parlour, John,' said Alexander, growing impatient, 'for I have business with my wife.'

'Why don't you go to your room, Jenny?' said Rebecca, adding under her breath, 'And lock the door.'

'A good girl that, Alexander, eh?' said Mr Badcock, smoothing his beard.

'Too young,' said Alexander shortly. 'And too idle. You have put me off my stride, John.'

'Your stride, Alexander? Your stride is a very good one. Very direct, as I always think.'

'Well,' said Alexander, 'you have put me off it. I do not think the reproductive organs of servant girls are important. They breed like rats.'

'Well, *who* or rather *what* do they breed, eh? More of themselves, that is the answer. Low types. The race needs to be raised up.'

'Someone needs to clean the grate, John, and would you rather it be my wife?'

Rebecca had still not had a chance to put down her carpet bag. Sweat stuck her dress to her ribcage.

' I don't think it has been blackened this week. Look here.' Alexander ran his finger across the fireplace. 'I think the maid is idle.'

'I don't know about that,' said Mr Badcock.

'And the Turkey carpet has not been beaten for over a month,' Alexander carried on. 'It holds the dirt of all of Edinburgh in it. I will beat it, since you and the maid lack will, and the strength. Where is the stick?'

'Beat it now?' said Rebecca.

'Where is the stick?'

'But it is nearly dark!'

'Come now, Alexander,' said Mr Badcock, with a smile on his face. 'What's this?'

'I can do it with a broom handle, fetch me that.'

'A broom handle?' said Rebecca, her heart starting to thump.

'The house is full of dust. The fires are not lit. Get me the broom.'

When Rebecca returned to the parlour with the broom Alexander had rolled up the Turkey rug and put it under one arm. 'Come, John,' he said. 'Here she is.'

'But the air has a chill to it!' Mr Badcock cried. 'I do not want to go outside.'

'You may find it – amusing.'

'You are not known for your humour, Alexander, as I am,' Mr Badcock said. 'Let me see, then. But I must fetch my scarf.'

Outside darkness had almost fallen and windows up and down the street flared with brightness. Alexander unrolled the rug with a snap and began to haul it over the spikes of the railings. But it was awkward, the spikes caught on the nap and it would not go on.

'For God's sake,' he said peevishly, dropping the rug and holding his hand to his chest. 'I have caught myself on the iron. The paint is flaking.'

'It can be dreadfully sharp, if you should happen to get a flake of it under your nail, yes?'

'This is woman's work! Get the rug in place, will you, wife?'

Rebecca bent down and tried to pull the rug over the spikes. It would not come. One last bird, confused by the lamps, still sung out. 'Like this?'

'No, said Alexander. '*Over* the railings, not hanging like that.'

'I had a note from my banker today,' remarked Mr Badcock. 'I have put the greatest part of my fortune into this venture, as you know. He does not approve, but I told him that it was *bound* to be a success. Yes?'

'I hardly see how it can fail. I have never been more certain.'

'Like this?' said Rebecca. Sweat blossomed down the sides of her dress where her corset gripped her.

'Further over. The two sides ought to be even.'

'Yes, yes; that is what I told him. We shall all be rich!'

'That will do,' said Alexander. 'Now, John, do you see how to beat a rug?'

'You will show me, I think, yes?' He clasped his hands.

Alexander raised the broom high over his head and brought it down. His bowler hat tipped backwards with the effort and a cloud of dust rose from the rug. Mr Badcock pulled his handkerchief from his sleeve and sneezed into it.

The crack bounced backwards and forwards between the houses like something solid. Surely it would bring everyone out of their homes!

Alexander brought the broom handle down again. 'And you continue to beat it until it is clean,' he said, wiping off his brow. 'Rugs are like wives in that respect.'

'Hee hee, dear boy, I see your purpose now. Only—'

He brought the stick down again. *Thwack, thwack!* The violence of it flattened Rebecca against the wall. P'raps it *would* wake somebody, and they would come out and complain, and Alexander would have to stop.

'Only I do wish I had not got so dirty in the process. See now, I am going to sneeze again.' Mr Badcock gave another hiccough into his handkerchief.

Rebecca shrank further back into the shadows. Her breath rose around her in clouds.

'It is lucky I am strong. For this rug is quite the worst I have ever come across.'

'Yes, yes; oh very good!' Mr Badcock said.

'But I will go at it again, because it needs it, would you not agree, John?'

'Oh yes, yes!'

Alexander worked at the rug, putting his weight into the task, grimacing, narrowing his eyes. Rebecca found she was shivering. She tried to move back towards the house, but Alexander saw it and called her forward.

'What are you doing back there? When all this is for your benefit!' He brought the stick down with another grunt. 'I must say I am enjoying this more than I thought!'

'The benefits of exercise, Alexander, can never be underestimated.'

Alexander smashed it down again, but this, at last, was too hard. 'Look now, I have broken the broom handle. You had best order another from the hardware store tomorrow. You can run to that, can you, Rebecca?'

Rebecca licked her lips. 'May I go in now?'

'I am tired. You may bring the carpet in and set it back in its usual place. Let us go inside, John, I need some refreshment.'

But all the beating had pushed the rug so firmly onto the spikes that no matter how hard Rebecca tugged, it would not come free. She felt like weeping. She tried pulling on it from every angle, until her hands burned, but it was too big. Eventually she sat on the step and put her head on her knees.

A minute passed, maybe more.

The door opened again. Rebecca jumped up with a start. 'Oh, Jenny, thank God, it is only you!'

'What has happened? What did he do?'

'Will you help me, Jenny? I must get the carpet off the railings.'

Jenny nodded. She did not ask why it was on there.

'My husband's idea,' Rebecca swallowed, then sniffed, 'of a joke.'

They worked together to free the Turkey rug; between them both it came off all right. Then they rolled it up and took one end each. At the door Rebecca listened out for the men. They were in the parlour; she heard the sound of another drink being poured.

'Bring it in here please!' called Alexander. 'And roll it out. Now we may walk upon it without dirtying our feet.'

The wood was slippery and it was hard to get the rug straight in the silence with the men's eyes at their backs. It slid about on the floorboards like a live thing.

'A little to the left, Jenny, I think,' said Mr Badcock. 'A little further towards me.'

'I can do it on my own now, thank you, Jenny,' said Rebecca.

'Yes, that will do,' said Alexander. 'For it is time for your medicine, wife. Do you feel the need of it?'

'Medicine,' Rebecca said. 'Yes, I have need of medicine. I am feeling weak.'

'And this,' he held out the blue bottle, 'shall make you strong. Let us go upstairs. You are in your menses after all.'

CHAPTER 10

Rebecca settled herself as quickly as she could, trying to calm her breath and the beating of her heart. She had run to put back the shoe where she had found it and hidden the carpet bag back in her room, but when Alexander came in he had his own black bag in his hand, and he set it down now, to unfasten it.

'The neuralgia has not returned?'

'The remedy you gave me quite cleared it up.'

'Yes, it is a powerful remedy, as I told you.'

'But it has worn off.' She thought of Gabe then, and his freckled arm, and longed for it.

'That is to be expected,' said Alexander. 'Even the best remedies wear off. Is there an ache at the womb's neck?' He pulled up his sleeve and palpated her stomach.

'Yes. And I feel dizzy.' Both were true, and easy to say.

'And in your mind, how are you?' He looked at her. His cheeks were flushed, his hair was dark, his lips were red. He was very handsome.

Rebecca bit her lip. 'My mind has been better.'

'Continued use of the medicine would do you very well, then.' Alexander shook out the salts onto his scales. 'A smaller dose this time, I think, as the pain is not as acute.' He took out the smallest weight and adjusted it until the scales hung evenly, then tipped the salts into a glass of water.

Rebecca reached out for it, the ruby in her engagement ring catching in the light.

'Now, now! It is not all dissolved.' Alexander agitated it some more and held it before his eyes. 'There. Now you may have it.'

This time the taste was worse for the water was not flavoured and struck at the back of her throat. But the wrongness to her would soon be made right, so she drank it all down.

After the first rush of warmth into her chest Rebecca lay back. The space between physical and mental had melted away: the feeling in her body corresponded *exactly* with the feeling in her mind.

Oh, but the release of anxiety, 'twas better than anything! Only now that the rippling-out darkness smoothed out from the centre of her did she realize what she usually endured. If only her skin did not itch so, and the very tip of her nose! She had made it raw with scratching.

Never mind.

Never mind.

Never mind.

Down she sinks, and further down.

'We have been down here since morning. I am hungry! And I think they will begin to miss us.'

'There is nothing unusual about spending the day together on the beach. Stay a moment longer, please.' Gabe puts his head to one side and blinks up at her.

'Ah, all right then!'

'And kiss me, just here.' He points to his nose.

She leans forward. 'There, your nose is wet! I knew it. Y'are a dog.'

'Aye,' say Gabriel, 'say it again.' He tickles her between the ribs.

She gets her knee up and pushes him away, gasping. 'Now I will have you!' She pushes him back and sits across his chest. He breathes up and down hard on purpose and she feels as if she is riding a whale.

They are in a space between two great rocks. Far away the sea rushes onto the beach and off again in a great many layers of sound. It is chilly and damp and seaweed clings to the walls.

'I saved a boy, did you know? Look, I have the scars to prove it,' he says, holding out his arm.

'Those marks there – that look like dots?'

'They are not dots! They go very deep. They are the marks that pins make when they are stuck in wax and thrown. They were not meant for me, they were meant for Fontmell—'

'Fontmell?'

'A poor wee boy, always bullied. But I put out my arm, and stopped them. Do you see how deep they go?'

'Y'are very brave, Gabriel,' she says, laughing at him. But he is cross and turns away and she must chase him and kiss him again to bring him round. She is not surprised to find that his lips taste of the sea. His tongue, as she takes it into her mouth, is cold. Even though she has kissed him like this before, his moustache is fuller this time and it tickles her. Though it is not wiry but soft, as soft as a girl's hair. She pulls back to stare at him, as if by staring she can see through him, beyond his bones.

But he still looks to be the same Gabe as ever – though he is flushed and his reddish hair is sprightly with sand. His breath is as hot, it warms her face. As he gets closer her heart grows tighter, and then he puts his lips on her bottom lip as lightly as the wind skates from a seagull's wing, but even so she thinks her heart will get crushed by it. Softly he draws her lip into his mouth and sucks on it. She opens her mouth to put her tongue on his – to play, she thinks, a game. But when their tongues meet they start to kiss in earnest, their mouths open, each one's hand on the other's breast.

Rebecca is surprised to find muscle where a few months ago there had been only bone. She wants to feel his skin. She draws back and fumbles with his waistcoat until it flaps open. But when she looks up at him he is smiling.

'What are you trying to do, freeze me to death?'

Overhead the ragged laugh of a seagull.

She falters. 'I only meant to … to touch you.'

But, 'Here then,' he says, and undoes buttons of his shirt quickly and then his collar and looks about for a place to put it.

She takes the collar from him and throws it on a rock, where it curls again. When she turns back she finds she is afraid to look at his face, afraid that something will be revealed in hers. She looks instead at his ribs and his chest, with its little bit of hair, and the size of him blots out everything.

Now he comes to her and starts to unbutton her gown, only his hands are shaking so much that he manages only three or four buttons before she puts them down on either side of her waist. But her own hands are shaking almost as much and she cannot force the tiny hoops over their mother-of-pearl buttons, they are held in place just as surely as an anchor. Gabe pulls open a few more, one of them comes off and falls away lost into the sand, but he must still unhook the eyes from her corset and she must pull away from him to let him do it and now the thought strikes her again: how strange to be getting undressed here in between the rocks that have the air of a haunted house! And she almost falters, only now he has her corset unhooked at last and she can breathe in the air in great green gulps. But she feels too free, and is about to put her arm about her waist, until he pulls up her chemise without bothering to unbutton it and plants his hand underneath it on her bare breast.

And she realizes that the only familiar thing here is Gabe.

She wants him to touch her, not softly, but to knead her and press on her. She kisses him again, hard, and pushes against him. He pushes his tongue into her mouth. His hand cups her breast, then pulls and tugs at one nipple, then the other. His thigh presses and presses between her legs.

She is liquid, she is water; she wants to throw her skirts over her knee and feel him there. She wants him to put his hand inside her. She sets up a rubbing against him, for she feels as if she is gathering up and must burst. She tries to show him how, what she wants, only he does not understand, or her skirts and her petticoats are too heavy and he cannot reach her.

'There! Just there!' she cries.

'Where, madam?'

'There, oh there!'

'What is it you want?'

'I want—' Rebecca is not confused as she would usually be on waking from such a dream. She is only disappointed. After her maid is gone out she may close her eyes again and go back.

'I want a glass of water, please, if you could.'

'Will that be all?'

'Yes. Yes, thank you. You are so thoughtful, Jenny dear!'

The door closed and Rebecca lay back with a sigh. Her eyes were black sea stones, her cheeks were as big as caverns, her brows were as wide as the sea.

She need not have worried about having nothing to do after the house was finished, not with this medicine! So many women, so many wives, would drink these salts down and be the happier for it.

CHAPTER 11

The days began to shorten and the wind brought the first autumn leaves down from the copper beech across the road. Rebecca found herself looking forward more and more to the moment when Alexander shook out the white crystals onto the scales. Sometimes she went with her husband to the pharmacy, where she waited as he retrieved the medicine from his laboratory upstairs. On other days she had her draft just before breakfast from a supply he kept in his study, and some mornings, if she had a headache, say, or felt the onset of a cold, she could hardly bear to wait.

However had she managed without her medicine? It was, as he never tired of telling her, beneficial to her in every way. It cured all manner of aches and pains, coughs and difficulties of respiration, and more than that, as he said, it cured her mind. She was not bored, or restless, she did not pine or sigh. Her medicine made her strong, as strong as a heroine.

And so, in the mornings, up to her room she would go, in a sweat of anticipation, and lie down on her chaise to wait for the draught to take effect. And then the warmth that was as much a feeling as a thought: nothing mattered very much after all.

But once, when Alexander was late with her draught, Rebecca surprised herself with thoughts of the exact opposite colour: nothing was easy, she was a trapped bird whose feathers were black. And she knew then that the other way of looking at things was a delusion.

But then Alexander came hurrying up to her room with her draught and the smoothness of it soon eased its way into her very cells. It had a physical property which seemed to keep hold of itself as it disseminated around her body, turning every part into a version of itself. Ironing away her creases and drying up her sweat and bearing her away to a camel whose nose was as moist as velvet, and then to a place of shadows and chatter whose words she could not understand, and then again to Gabe, who was very pale and clear, and lying with his head propped on his arm.

'I can see that you are absolutely *rotten* at embroidery,' he says. 'That flourish there.' He points to the corner of her handkerchief, which has fallen onto the grass. 'What is that? Branch or flower?'

'Neither! It is a *curlicue*.'

'I still cannot read your handwriting, or your needle writing, or whatever it's called. Why ever have you got a *B* there in the corner?'

'It is an *R. RM*. Rebecca Massey.'

'Of course, I see it now. Rebecca Massey. That is your name and I won't forget it. P'raps I could keep this, to remind me of it?' He dangles the handkerchief from one corner.

'Not when the embroidery is so bad! I don't want my name blotted. *BM* could be any number of things. Baby Monkey. Black morning.'

Bland Munning, Back Manning, Ban Man. Her name drifts away from her into a spell in which every word had weight and meaning.

But she had not sewn BM onto her handkerchief. She had sewn RM and that was not her name any more. She had drifted away from her name, her home, into a new name, a new home that was not a home. A home in a shoe and she a little old woman.

'I should say this is American cotton, judging from its soft-ness.' Gabe picks it up and drapes it on his face. He puffs it out with his breath and lies still so that it looks like a shroud.

'And it smells of you, Rebe,' he says, still beneath it. 'Rose-water and leather; you have been at your father's workshop again, haven't you?'

He sticks out his hand and gropes around for her face, his palm reaching her chin, his fingertips at her lips.

'And cow, of course, for you cannot have leather without the poor wee cow; and grass and earthworms, I think – is there a hint of earthworm there?'

Rebecca draws his fingers into her mouth and bites them. He tears the handkerchief from his face then and springs up, towering over her with his great wrist bones and feet large enough to set sail in.

And she is an old woman in a shoe. And he is sailing away, that's what he meant to tell her, of course. The handkerchief had been a way of easing into it.

'American cotton is done for, you know, and there won't be any more nice handkerchiefs,' he says.

'The Civil War, aye.'

'Aye.' He folds her handkerchief into smaller and smaller squares. 'And there must be a new place for us to get the cotton, otherwise the industry shall be finished. And that place seems to be Egypt.'

'Egypt? You mean, land of the Pyramids?'

'Yes, Egypt.' His look is strange, and when she catches it, a horrible realization begins to creep over her.

'You mean ...'

'Father is sending me.'

'To Egypt? No!' She stands up.

'Aye.'

'Oh. To Egypt. How far away ...?' She cannot think.

'A week's journey, perhaps.' He reaches for her. 'I don't – ever since father told me—'

'How long have you known?'

'For two weeks ...'

'Two weeks? And you have kept it from me?'

'I didn't know how to tell you.'

'And when are you leaving?'

'In another three ...'

Rebecca spins away from him. 'So there is no time! And if you had told me straight away, we could have been married and I could have come with you. Rather than being left here.' She throws her arm around the grey sea, the grey sky. 'You always talk of being married, Gabriel, but we are not, still. I am becoming an old maid! And now you are leaving, to Egypt!'

He tries to come to her again but she pushes him away.

'I do not want to go, Rebecca, my love, know that! But you know what Father is like. He insists, Rebe! And p'raps he is right, there will be no money if someone does not go, and he is too old, and he trusts no one else but me. He says he has found a new plantation there, in the delta. And I think it is no place for a woman, and no time for a proper wedding, I should like to do it right ...'

She lifts her head to stare. 'How do you *know* what is right and wrong for me? You have never been there. I am sure there are plenty of women in Egypt!'

'I will be back in six months. Nine at the most. It would be no kind of life for you out there!'

She catches her breath. Looks at him again. 'But you *want* to go! It is not a trial for you. That is why you have waited so long to tell me.'

'No, Rebe!'

'You do! I can see it in your look. I can see it.'

He sighs then and stares at the ground. 'I do not want to leave you, Rebecca. You must know that – I love you! But – p'raps I *do* want to go, you are right – I am curious – and p'raps there is some good I might do there, in Egypt … More good than here, at least, hidden away in Edinburgh.'

'And I am to be hidden away in Edinburgh then, instead.'

'The reason,' he says quietly, 'that I have not asked you to marry me – properly, I mean – is that …' He swallows, his great Adam's apple like a cork in the sea. 'I do not want to be here in Scotland working for my father's business – I must strike out on my own, I think, to prove myself! Only then can I come back and be a husband.'

'I have no say, then,' says Rebecca.

'There might be something I can *do* about the world. The Egyptians are very poor, and Hindoo, and p'raps, though God knows I am not very religious, Britain is a great force of good in the world. We ought to bring to the poorer regions our sense of order, and morality.'

'Ambition is men's way of excusing selfishness,' she says.

'There is nothing wrong with ambition, I think, as long as it propels Mankind forward in the right way.' Gabe's face has transmogrified smoothly into someone who Rebecca understands to be Alexander. 'Or womankind, if there is such a word. Which of course there is not!'

But sometimes the spirit of the draught gave her energy, and Rebecca rose up from her couch and put on her cloak and visited Eva. As they strolled together in the park, or rambled up and down the streets of the New Town staring in at people's windows, or sat side by side at the window in Eva's rooms reading their books – they both had a taste for Mr Collins – the spectre of the shoe receded, until Rebecca hardly thought to press Evangeline on the matter.

It was on such an afternoon, they had known each other a month or two, that Rebecca discovered something surprising. The sun was pouring in through Eva's little window panes and making her dozy. She must have dropped off because as she came to she found Eva looking at her with a peculiar expression.

'I fancy,' said Eva, staring harder at Rebecca's eyes, 'that I have had a doze like that. And now I see that your eyes show the marks of it. Your pupils are constricted, are they not?'

Rebecca turned to the looking glass. They were, she had not noticed. That was to say – she had noticed something was different about her image in the glass, something impersonal. But she had put it down to the armour the draught gave her, the way they had of firming her up. But now she saw that her eyes in the glass looked back at her without her really being in them.

But Eva knew, for when she pointed out her own eyes in the glass, she had exactly the same! They were like two dolls with glassy eyes, standing close together, their sleeves pressed flat against the other's arm and Kitty Kat weaving about their feet.

When they saw it they laughed. 'I thought as much,' said Eva. 'You are taking the new medicine!'

'And you too? How queer!'

'I think we are privileged. 'Tis better than laudanum, do you not think? And far more effective.'

'Laudanum – for the relief of backache, and so on?' Rebecca had seen the tins stacked up on the counter. 'But I did not know this was laudanum!'

'Not laudanum, no – 'tis better, as I said. They haven't a name for this medicine yet. They say it will take away the hunger for my drops that I had before.'

'Hunger, do you hunger?' asked Rebecca. She had always thought of her medicine as the end of hunger. But, perhaps after all, it took away all hunger except for that of itself. 'But, I do not want to end up like a Fensman or a Chinaman, living only for my pipe!'

'I do not think it is the same thing,' said Eva. But as they regarded each other in the looking glass a furrow appeared between Eva's brows. 'I hope it is not.'

Rebecca reached across and smoothed Eva's brow with her thumb. 'You are right. We are not from China, and the Fensmen are well known for being lazy and falling asleep on their hoes. I would not be without my draught. My days go easier, and my husband is easier. If every woman knew that there was a prize to be had just by taking down a solution of those crystals, though the taste is not quite nice, why, they would be able to bear anything.'

Knowing that Eva felt exactly as she did, that Rebecca could fall into a doze on her armchair and not be asked why she did it, that in short, they were together in all their thoughts and feelings, was enough to make Rebecca reach over to Eva again and kiss her on the cheek.

Eva put her hand at the spot. To Rebecca's reflection she said: 'But I sometimes wonder if I could stop it, in spite of what Mr Badcock says.'

'Stop your draught?'

'I had a hunger for laudanum before, it grew terrible, and Mr Badcock has given me this as a cure. But I don't know ...' Eva trailed away. 'I did try to go without, for a day, only Mr Badcock was concerned, and insisted I take it. He said it was not good to stop it all at once.'

'Oh Eva, I am sure that it is for the best. Something that gives such a feeling of goodness cannot be on the side of evil, can it? And besides, we are together in this, and can help each other.'

Eva let out her breath. Her lips were dry: 'Oh, you are right. Of course you are right! It is all for the good.'

'That must be why Alexander pulled me away from you, at the opening – for the sake of the draught. They do not want us to know each other. Do you think so?'

'Perhaps. I hope so! It is some sort of secret yet, until they patent it.' She pulled at a piece of skin on her lips. Then she brightened and inclined her head. 'What do you say we take a walk?' There was a patch of blue at the top of the glass. 'Look how pale we are! We could do with the air, I think.'

CHAPTER 12

7 May, Biahmu

My Dear Rebe,

You will think I have been a long time writing to you and I can only wonder when you will get this letter, but all I can say is that I have been in Egypt for two months and miss you dreadfully! Nobody here speaks any English but there is a fellahin boy in the town who does and who will take a letter for you to the agent, my dearest.

All the fatigue of the journey was worth it, to arrive and see a line of camels, if only you had been here to see it with me. The sun is of a kind we never see in Edinburgh – it blazes away in the bluest sky and it gives everything the solidest shape. Scotland is green but I see now that it is a country painted in watercolours. The green here is garish; the palm trees, the crops, the fields of berseem are all a brilliant emerald in the sunlight, then fall away to something greyer in the evening. Night does not come as it does in Scotland, at least in the summer, creeping slowly and quietly. Here it is noisy with insects and braying donkeys and turns all at once into darkness. Once the sun is gone the smell of dung seems to rise up.

Oh my darling, do not mind me talking of dung! We can talk about anything, can't we? Only dung is a feature of life where I am now, just as it is on the streets of Edinburgh. And how I long to be back there to see your face. The camels and the gamoose and the donkeys and I dare say the children too, all drop it along the dusty paths that lead into the town from the fields. Only instead of boys to fetch it up as they do in Edinburgh, here the women and girls turn it into something resembling pancakes but which is rather fuel for the fire.

I can hear you asking me, Rebe, in that voice you reserve for such questions, about the cotton fields. They are as long and white and I dare say voluminous as I imagined and they will make Father rich, I suppose, though the owner must sell them to him first.

And I haven't yet seen the Pyramids, my own darling, to tell you about them. Some people come from Britain but I think the journey not worth it to see a pile of stones.

But, as to the main point, I had hoped to do some good, that was the purpose of all this. That was why I left you tearful and alone on the station platform, and how I chastise myself a hundred times a day for it! There is *certainly much good that needs to be done here. Babies crawl naked in the dust with their faces hard to make out, there are so many flies massed about. Old people more skeleton than human. I have not yet got to the Suez Canal but they say that conditions there kill hundreds of men. I have been doing the rounds, helping where I can.*

I was taken to see a Bedouin marriage ceremony Tuesday last. The legal part of the ceremony they call 'marriage by twig' and it consists of a green twig being stuck in the groom's turban for three days – though it is as binding as any of our rituals and a church is nowhere to be seen.

How I wish you were here, dearest, and I could put in a twig for you. And it would be that easy, if we chose to live here.

I never caught a glimpse of the bride for she was inside the birza the whole time we were feasting. But all through the evening I had the strangest idea that it was you! I couldn't shake it. And when the bridegroom went in, accompanied by all the shrieking cries from the women and thumping from the men, it was all I could do not to thump him.

I had had too much drink, I think. But the idea persisted, still persists. The married women here wear a burqa from nose to chin with pieces of gold sewn on so that you cannot see their faces, only their eyes. Sometimes

I see a woman whose eyes look like yours. I think you are hiding from me, or following me, or both!

I will never be free from you, and I don't want to be. We ought to have married as you said and then you would be here with me. Because this place has crept its way into my bones too.

I received your last two letters with great joy. But to hear you talking of unhappiness cuts me to the quick! I am sorry you are lonely, Rebe, and only wish I was there to wrap my arms around you like I always used. Is there nothing you can take pleasure in? Could you help out your father again? You need an occupation. You are one of those women, the new type, who need an activity. And yet you underestimate yourself and tell yourself you can do nothing.

Write to me of home and how the place looks. I frequently wonder whether the wall round the oval pond is as it used to be, or have some stones fallen off it? And also the yew hedge whether it has been kept clipped or is untidy. I wish I could take a turn at it, I think I should enjoy just such employment now rather more than I did when I was at home. Just to sit on the lawn and talk as we used makes my heart ache to think on it.

Ever your <u>most</u> loving,
Gabe

The letter had suffered many readings in the early part of its life, and none in the latter. Rebecca fancied, even after two years kept hidden away behind her lavender bags, that it still retained a smell of some kind of sweet thing that didn't grow in Edinburgh; flower or dung, she could not tell which.

At first she had thought he had moved, or was coming home. But he had not come home. She had grown so dizzy from the waiting that some days her father had sent her to bed. And then the waiting was just a habit, and the letters, when they turned out to be from her aunt and not from Egypt, did not make her heart fall so hard. After her letters had grown desperate and pleading, and she would have got them back if she could, she had met Alexander outside Church's shoe shop on some business for her father just after his death. He had recognized her and had taken off his hat and kept her for twenty minutes or more. Each time she moved forward, or took a breath to say, *Well, I probably, I ought to be, I should be, I really ought to be getting along*, Alexander started another conversation. He wondered how they had not met before, living so close by. And in that wondering, managing to convey surprise, at himself, that he had lived so long and managed to miss her. Rebecca had been astonished to find herself so suddenly chosen, and by someone as handsome as this.

It had seemed the answer to a prayer that she had thought but not exactly spoken.

CHAPTER 13

Rebecca had fallen asleep in the parlour and when she awoke she had the idea she had been asleep all day. The house was quiet, no sign of the servants, nothing left for her out on the dining-room table. No matter, she was not hungry. She would go up and read *The Moonstone*, then. Rebecca went up the stairs in bare feet and paused at her door. She could hear someone in her room – Jenny, no doubt, putting things away.

But when she stepped in further she saw it was her husband, not Jenny, hunched in the bottom of her dresser, which was odd because he usually hated to slouch, his face stuck down into something. Rebecca could not see what, his body obscured it. There was something so private in the shape of him that she did not greet him, did not make a sound.

But – what was he doing? Rebecca bent forward until her whalebone pressed into the soft part of her belly … and there past his shoulder, beneath his face … were her shoes. He had his face buried in one of them, the ones she had worn on the day of the opening. The little pale buttons had been wrenched open and his palm was pressed against the sole.

She gasped a little, before she could remember not to. But Alexander did not hear. His own breathing must have taken up all of his ears. In, and out. In and out.

She had discovered him in the act of – what? Something private, but … in *her* room, with *her* shoe, not that … thing, that other girl's shoe. P'raps it meant he had come back to her! That the marriage would be tolerable after all.

Rebecca crept back downstairs to the parlour and sat on the sofa, turning page after page of *The English Woman's Journal*. The articles passed by her eyes in a blur: 'Married Women's Property Act … recipe for blancmange … poem for summer'. Even the *Journal* did not advocate divorce.

Five minutes passed, then ten. When he came down there was nothing in her husband's face to suggest that he had just been in her closet. His lips were not twitching, his hair was oiled and combed. 'You are awake. Are you feeling refreshed?' he said.

'Yes – quite. How long have I been asleep?' She would visit the kitchen and tell Mrs Bunclarke to cook Alexander's favourite dish, if it was not too late to send Jenny to the butcher. And bread, if the baker had any, to put in the Potatoes à l'Allemande. Oh, and apples, for they had nearly run out!

'Long enough,' he said. 'Were you tired?'

'I was plagued with bad dreams last night.' Gabriel, of course, but turned to clockwork and falling apart in her hands.

'As I thought, for the salts were just the same as always. But what are you doing with that?' He pointed to the periodical.

'Oh, this?' Rebecca flushed. 'I borrowed it from the library.'

'The library ought not to keep such things. It is full of sedition and ideas that will foment public unrest. Look here, I will tear it up for the fire, to save Jenny the trouble.'

'Do not tear it!' But it was too late. The whole thing was quickly up in flames. Now Rebecca would have to explain the periodical's disappearance to the librarian, who had only let her take it as a favour. Best to buy a new one herself.

And after all, the evening had gone off tolerably well. The candle-light was flickering just as it ought, sending light skittering over the table and over her husband's face. Alexander had pushed his chair back from the table, just as he ought, and was leaning back with his hands laced behind his head. Conversation, which had not been much, had died away, just as it ought.

Though the haunch of venison had been perhaps a little short at the fire. Rebecca had put Mr Francatelli's cook book straight into Mrs Bunclarke's hands but the recipe called for four hours on a spit and it had not started turning until past teatime. Rebecca only had a few forkfuls. The potatoes were a little sour, too much vinegar to them, but the Charlotte of Pears was good. Rebecca spooned the cream onto her plate and peeled off two of the syrupy sponge fingers pressed around the sides. Alexander, who had drunk several glasses of wine, only cut himself a small slice, dissecting two of the fingers in half and eating them in four sharp bites.

Rebecca too had had several glasses of wine. She hoped her husband might be looking at her as she ate, the candlelight seemed to suggest it, and the sponge fingers as she put them forward-facing into her mouth seemed to suggest it too, but he was staring at the guttering candle, drumming his own fingers lightly on the table.

Rebecca let the cooked flesh of the pear fall apart in her mouth. 'Shall we go up?' she said.

Alexander frowned, looked at the clock. It was his custom to go up at ten o'clock.

'Only, I am a little tired,' she hurried on. 'Not tired, so much as, perhaps the effects of the wine ...'

He nodded then, looked back at the clock and nodded again. 'If you are weary then very well. Let us go.'

At the top of the stairs Alexander stopped and turned to her. His lips were even fuller in the gloom, like a woman's. He leaned forward. Rebecca thought he was going to kiss her, and she pursed her own lips in readiness, but as he came near he turned his face to the side. There was a faint abrasion from the day's growth on his own cheek as he turned, enough to make her shiver.

'Goodnight then,' he said.

'Goodnight?' she said, on the in-breath.

'The wine,' he said, 'was making you drowsy.'

'I find I am not so tired, now that I have left the table!' In her confusion she looked down at her shoes. She had meant to save this for the bedroom, but he had forced her hand. She pulled up the hem of her dress and pointed her foot.

Her cheeks burned – he would dismiss her, tell her to stop.

But Alexander followed her gaze and looked down. 'You complained of those shoes. I thought you would not wear them again.'

'I find I am used to them now, they are so soft and the shape they make of my foot is so pleasing. Do you not think?' Her breath caught in her throat. Seeing his look she grew bolder and pointed the shoe up at him.

'Yes, indeed,' said Alexander, his eyes fixed on her foot, his turn to flush. 'I always thought it.' They stood in the middle of the corridor that led away in each direction to their rooms, between the two gaslights.

Rebecca remembers what followed as a kind of dream. They both turn away from his bedroom and towards hers and he lays her down on her bed. The satin coverlet is slippery under her fingers.

'Oh, Alexander!' she cries out, as he draws off her stockings. She has the time to throw her arms behind her head, her forearms pressed up against the chill silk of the bed hangings . She closes her eyes. She fancies she might resemble a painting, done in rich brushstrokes, though she can't recall the name of the painter.

Finally her feet are bare and her toes, one by one, are

being fanned out. Alexander is kissing them. He takes the smallest toe into his mouth – a damp cave – and sucks on it rhythmically. Her leg tingles and she felt a twinge higher up, between her legs.

He moves onto the next toe. A cave with an animal in it, with a mouth that sucks. She has not realized before that her toe and her neck are connected by a nerve that runs all the way up her body. Thank God she has plunged her feet this morning into a bowl of cold water and rubbed her heel smooth with a pumice stone.

The next toe. The tip of his tongue darts over the length of it. The electric sensation crosses over to ticklishness and she tries to pull her foot away, but he grips the middle of her foot with both hands.

'My darling! Will you not come further up?' She tries to tug him upwards so that she can kiss him, but he moves onto the next toe, exploring the nail of it (thank God she had filed it not three days before!) and fluttering up and down its length. And then – even in the rhythmic fluttering moistness and excitement Rebecca can sense a doggedness, a need to finish the sequence – the last, the biggest toe.

He tongues the pad, she worries for a moment about its toughness, but he takes the whole toe into his mouth like the others. Rebecca squirms, the toe is too big, too wet, and the rest of the toes still damp. There is a draught where the window does not push up to the frame.

'Should we get under the covers, dearest?'

He makes some indefinable reply, even though the toe has popped out of his mouth, but now his lips are crushed into the thin skin of her ankle.

She props herself up on her elbows and looks down, hoping to encourage him upwards. But he is already naked from the waist down! She had not noticed him go away from her and come back, but there are his trousers, folded on the back of the chair. He is two people now: one very proper in a shirt and waistcoat, the other, from his buttocks downwards, covered only in a sprouting of dark hair. She tries to haul him up again but again he resists.

Rebecca stares up at the folds that made up the canopy of her bed. A spider had made her web across the corner of it, too high for Jenny to get to. The button in the middle of it reminds her of the crown of Alexander's head, with its thick hair spiralling out. The thought of it makes her dizzy and she turns her head.

'Dearest!' she cries again. At her feet Alexander is increasing the pressure of his mouth and fingers and – some other part of his flesh. He has moved up the bed a little and the weight of his body bears down on her calves. He begins to thrust, as if he were going to make love to her – but – he was in the wrong place, she cannot move him – and then – he gives a gasp – Rebecca feels her ankle become not damp from his kisses, but wet, wet all down one side.

Rebecca pushes herself up again. Her heart falls away. 'Are you? Have you … oh dearest!'

Rebecca rubs her ankle on the sheet. Her husband stands up. Tomorrow she would have to change the sheet, or tell Jenny to do it, though she would wonder why, having just been changed yesterday.

CHAPTER 14

The next morning she felt the effects of the wine she had drunk. Her mouth was dry and even though she had been asleep for many hours she felt as if she had not slept enough.

When she came to the dining room Alexander was already at breakfast, eating a kipper. The smell of it made her turn her face away. But Alexander was in a good mood. 'How are you feeling today, wife? Are you hungry?'

'I think p'raps the wine was too strong, last night. I think a draught would cure it.'

'Have you plans for today?'

Alexander quite often wanted to know her day's activities. He usually received a litany of chores and reading lists, when most often she had spent her time with her new friend. But today, because she was distracted by the dryness of her mouth and the throbbing at her temples, she said: 'I am going to see Evangeline.'

'Evangeline?'

Rebecca blinked. 'I did not mean Evangeline. I was only thinking of her. I meant to say Mrs Bishop.'

'Evangeline?' Alexander carefully placed his knife and fork together. 'How do you know her?'

'We met at the opening of the pharmacy.'

'But I sent you home.'

Rebecca screwed her eyes shut and shook her head. 'I mean, we met on the street, at a later date. She was on her way to the pharmacy, and she said she knew you, and we struck … we struck up an acquaintance.'

'An acquaintance?'

'Only of the mildest kind! Not any kind of friendship.'

Alexander started to tap the nail of his longest finger on the table. 'So I am to believe that you met her once on the street, and then?'

'And then nothing!'

'But I told you not to talk to her. Did I not?' *Tap tap* went his nail on the wood. 'And yet you have disobeyed me.'

Sweat trickled down Rebecca's ribcage. It was past time for her medicine. She would have liked to ask him for it. 'I will not see her again.' Though the thought of that was terrible.

'We should have opened the pharmacy quietly, with no fuss, I told John as much. But he had to have fanfare!' Alexander pushed back his chair. 'Everything you say leads me to believe that you are lying. I think you have seen her more than once. Even visited her rooms. Have you?'

'No, no, I have not. I swear it!'

'Let us call Jenny, then, shall we? To ask her how you have spent your time these last few weeks.'

'There is no need, you will embarrass her!'

But Alexander had already set the bell jangling and Jenny must have been close by for she opened the door almost at once.

'Ah Jenny,' he said, very low and even, although a muscle jumped in his cheek. 'How has Mrs Palmer been amusing herself these last few weeks?'

Jenny looked at Rebecca. She shifted her weight from one foot to another. 'I don't know, sir. I don't know her movements.'

'But has she been out, say?'

'Out?'

'Of the house?'

Jenny looked at Rebecca again, a flush spreading up her cheeks. 'No, she has been inside, sir, in her room. Reading.'

'And you are sure?'

'Yes, sir, I am sure.'

'Why do you colour, then?'

Jenny put her hand up to her cheek. 'I – I do not know.'

'She colours, husband, because you make her colour!'

'She colours because she is lying, because you told her to lie. I can see it in her face, plain—' He laughed. 'Plain as day, I was going to say, but I ought to have left off at plain.'

Rebecca stepped forward to put her hand on Jenny's sleeve.

'Well, you two make a fine pair – and with Evangeline it

makes three.' He shook his head. 'Women cannot be trusted. I have always said so. Two liars under my roof, but you have made a mistake, Jenny, for it is *I* who pay your wages.' He shook his head again. 'You are dismissed.'

Jenny said nothing, but put her hand before her mouth.

'Pack your bags.'

'Pack my bags, sir?'

'Do not punish Jenny, she has done nothing wrong. It is me. Only me!' cried Rebecca, gripping Jenny harder.

'And you call *lying* nothing, do you? I suppose you may, as you lie to me so easily.'

'Please, sir, I have nowhere else to go!' Without a reference, she could get no other position. Except, as Lionel said, on the streets.

'You had best pack now, if you are to be gone before luncheon.'

'But where will I go?'

'Let her stay! I will not see Evangeline again, I swear it!'

'No, you will not.'

Rebecca bit down on her lip and pressed her fingertips to the corner of her eyes. She must not cry, not in front of Jenny. But Jenny herself was crying, she bit her lips to stop them trembling but she could not stop the tears which overflowed her eyes and fell down her cheeks.

Rebecca turned to her husband. 'Will you let Jenny—' Stay, she would have finished, but something flew past her ear and landed on her cheek with such a noise that she staggered backwards.

Her face had split in two. She cried out, or Jenny did. She put her hand to her cheek and fell against the wall. The noise was still an explosion in her ear.

Jenny ran to her. 'Are you all right, madam?'

Alexander said: 'Have you learned not to lie, do you think? Or do you need another one? 'Tis nothing that a boy does not learn at school, when he is ten years old. But women are like children, so p'raps after all, you may learn something.'

Rebecca said nothing, only backed towards the door. Alexander turned to Jenny. 'You'd best pack now, if you are to leave before luncheon,' he said once more.

The bell sounded. The boy had come to carry Jenny's case to the station, already! Rebecca started up, she must say goodbye, properly if she could. She went into the hall and looked upwards. The sound of Jenny's crying from behind her closed door came down to her in muffled staccato.

But it was not a boy; it was a man of fifty at least, with a dirty apron tied round his waist.

'I came to the right house, then? There is nought wrong with this door as I can see.'

Alexander came out of his study. 'The lock on it has grown sticky,' he said. 'It needs replacing. I want it taken out and a new one put in. What have you got?'

'At the stall there's more,' said the man uncertainly, looking towards the stairs.

'One of these will do,' said Alexander, picking up a lock. 'Whichever you think best.' The spots had died away from his cheek, he spoke calmly.

Alexander bent over to inspect the contents of the man's bag. Rebecca could only see the back of his jacket pulled smooth. A carapace. And she, a weak thing, scrabbling for purchase. 'What's this?' she said. 'I did not notice the lock grown sticky.'

The locksmith held up a heavy black lock. 'This will fit your door, and I've a key for it here.' The creases of his face, she noticed, were filled in with pale specks that were not dust but iron filings.

'There must be some mistake,' she said.

The man looked at Alexander. 'I was called,' he said.

'By me, to fit a new lock,' said Alexander.

'But we've no need!' Rebecca said stupidly.

The locksmith scratched his cheek. The barrel of the lock dangled from his other hand.

'I shall keep the key for it, to prevent you from going out,' said Alexander.

The locksmith took a step back. 'I don't know—' he said.

'If you will not do it, I shall get someone who will,' said Alexander.

Rebecca wanted her medicine. Alexander must know he was late with it; he was always so particular about the time and the dose. 'I ought never to have visited Evangeline without telling you, I understand that now! I have learned my lesson. But won't you listen?'

'Listen to what, wife?' Alexander rubbed his chin with his hand as if he were someone who had every intention of being reasonable.

'It is impossible! I think you mean to punish me, and I am punished.' Rebecca put her own hand to her cheek. It felt as if it had been held to a fire.

The locksmith stood and gaped at them.

'A wife's first and every thought should be with her husband. Not against him, not deliberately defying him,' said Alexander.

'Yes, yes! But this – how will the tradesmen get in?'

'Round the back as they always do.'

'And do you mean to change that lock too?'

Alexander glanced to the back of the house. 'If I must.'

'And what of your friends? Mr Badcock?'

'I will tell Mr Badcock of the arrangement. Only I will have the key, and the new maid, I suppose. It is an unusual arrangement, but he will understand.'

'But what about my friends?'

'If you mean—'

'No, not Evangeline! But Violet,' she snatched at the name. 'She is meant to come this afternoon.' Thank God she was. 'What will happen then?'

'Who?'

'My friend, Violet. You have met her, at … you have seen her, when we were engaged.'

Alexander rubbed his chin again. In the commotion he had not yet gone upstairs to shave. 'Violet. I remember her.'

'Yes! You talked together, on the sofa.'

'She was asking me about soap, pale hair.'

'How will Violet visit me, if I cannot open my own door? We do not want to appear too irregular!'

Alexander put his hands in his pockets and seemed to consider. At length he drew out a shilling and gave it to the locksmith. 'My wife has convinced me of her contrition. I dare say she will not cross me again.'

The man shoved the locks back in his bag without looking at either of them, chiming his keys together in his haste to be out of the house.

'Let me measure your temperature. I have frightened you.' Alexander collected his compact thermometer and opened its leather case. 'Open your mouth now.'

The bulb was cold on her tongue. She wished it were her draught. The taste in her mouth was bitter, as if she had had it already. These switches in Alexander's temperament always confused her.

'You know, dear,' Rebecca stammered, when he took out the thermometer, 'I think it may be past time for my medicine.'

'Yes.' He glanced at the clock. 'Two hours late. Let me see how you do.' Alexander took up a notebook and sat down close to her. 'Your eyes are lachrymose.' He put his fingers to their outside edges. 'The muscles seem fatigued.' He wrote something down, then put his fingertips on the inside of her wrists and took her pulse. 'Slightly raised,' he said. 'And yet a decrease in vital energy in general. Would you agree?'

Rebecca nodded. She felt as if she might never get up.

'But your temperature has fallen,' said Alexander. 'Unusual under such circumstances. Do you feel cold?'

'I am shivering,' said Rebecca, showing him her arm, which was pulled into goose bumps. 'I don't know if it is with cold.'

'I will get your medicine. Though after the adventures of the morning …' Alexander looked up to the ceiling and made his calculations. 'I think I will weigh out a few milligrams more.'

And now Rebecca wept, with relief and sorrow and fear. The tears were easy to make.

CHAPTER 15

Violet stood outside the house on Albany Street with her hand on the bell, hesitating to pull it. Her last visit had ended so awkwardly, with that strange shoe up on Mr Palmer's desk. But perhaps Alexander was inside. She thought she could see him moving about behind the stained glass. She took off her glove, wet the tip of her finger and smoothed down her eyebrows with it. Even though she was pale, her eyebrows often sprung out of place. If Henry noticed, so would Alexander.

But when she did ring, she found the door flew open straight away and Rebecca was standing right behind it. She seemed very pleased to see her. But how changed she was! So thin, even more than fashion demanded. Men wanted a thin waist, but they also wanted a curved arm and a rosy cheek. Rebecca's cheek was not rosy though her eyes alone shone with a strange kind of health. Perhaps she had put drops of lemon juice in them.

'I am so glad to see you! Your visit is most welcome. Come to the parlour.' Rebecca took hold of her arm and led her to the easy chair nearest to the fire. But she put herself in a hard-backed chair all the way across the room next to the door and kept looking through it in a way that prohibited easy conversation.

'Are you expecting somebody else to call?' asked Violet at last.

'Oh! No, only my maid. She is going – on a trip. I must speak to her before she leaves.' Rebecca fingered her sleeve.

'Somewhere nice, I hope.'

Rebecca nodded, but her look was vague.

'Is your husband at home?'

'He is about somewhere.' Again Rebecca looked to the door.

'How lucky you are, to have him around and not always at work. Dear Henry is always out paying visits, it is the elderly who rely on him most, I think. They call him up at any time of the day and night. I hardly see him, though I must not complain, when he is out curing people.'

'Oh yes?'

'Shall I ring for tea?' said Violet after another silence. 'I'm fairly parched.'

'Tea, yes, I shall get you some. Or, rather, I shall ask Mrs Bunclarke to do it. For I am without a maid, you see, for today.' Rebecca got up.

Violet's wrists were not strong enough to carry the tray, Henry said, and he was right. She *couldn't* manage a great many things, even when she thought she could.

The grandfather clock ticked on into the silence, it began to wear on her nerves. Perhaps Alexander would come and take tea with them. She reached to her velvet bow and straightened it. But now she could hear Rebecca outside in the hall, and the maid who was going on a trip.

But what sort of maid went on a trip? Maisy only had half a day off a week, and she was perfectly happy. And Rebecca was not talking to her maid in the way one usually spoke to servants. Was she *sobbing*? Violet had thought about not coming at all – she didn't know if it was quite respectable. Because surely the shoe on Mr Palmer's desk signified an *affaire de coeur* with someone, though Violet could not find out with whom. But in the end she had decided: yes – she ought to come, she must not let gossip stop her, she must be noble.

'Let me find a pen,' said Rebecca from outside. 'There is usually one there in that pot – yes, there it is – and oh – the notepaper is in the parlour. Wait a moment …'

She came in, smiling tightly. She seemed to have forgotten all about refreshments. 'Please forgive me, I have something to attend to,' was all she said, as she crossed the room to her desk and opened the drawer.

Perhaps in a gloomy light Rebecca might look fashionable, after all. Her skin was very pale, and her eyes with their hollows would seem romantic, and the thinness would be confused with weakness when, in fact, Rebecca moved with a jerky kind of purpose. She took out some paper, took the pen from its holder and crossed the room again. Ink dropped from its nib onto the carpet and spread out in uneven blossoms, and Violet would have said something about it, only Rebecca had gone out again before she could.

'How sorry I am to see you go!' Violet heard, just as easily as if Rebecca had been in the room.

''Tis not your fault,' said the girl.

'But it is! And I will always know it. If I had not been so foolish ...'

Perhaps the maid had got herself in trouble of the worse kind though her face was awfully plain. Perhaps – Violet's hand went to the base of her neck – she had even succeeded in tempting Mr Palmer himself!

'Look – it is hastily written, but it will do, I think, to get you another position.'

'Thank you, madam – yes – you are very kind.'

'But you are all these things I have written here, and more.'

'Don't say it, madam.' Now the maid was sobbing too! 'I don't like to leave you – what will you do?'

'I shall be fine. It is you I worry about. Where will you stay tonight?'

'I have some wages saved up.'

'No, you must not use up your money on that! Take this.' Another muffled sob, hard to tell from whom it came.

'Make sure and look for another position, start tomorrow! Do not fall into despair.'

Violet sat with her hand to her mouth. The girl could not have tempted Mr Palmer to stray, else Rebecca would not be so upset. What then? She had been slovenly perhaps. The house was not at all clean, old newspapers lay open on the side table and dust gathered on the mantel. Mr Palmer must have let the maid go for her laziness, only Rebecca had got too attached. It did happen between some ladies and their maids.

But Mr Palmer was surely right. A man does not want to come home to a house in such disarray.

When Rebecca at last came back her face was blotched and she rubbed at her nose with her palm – without even a handkerchief. And she had not brought tea.

'Is everything all right?' asked Violet.

'I am sorry,' said Rebecca. 'I had to let my maid go, unexpectedly.'

It was hard to get a conversation going after that. What would be appropriate? The house and its decoration, health, weather, shared acquaintances. None seemed possible in that room with its horrible paper-hangings.

'I can recommend you another maid, I dare say,' she said after a while.

Rebecca nodded and rubbed at her nose so hard Violet fancied she could hear it squash. But she could not have been out in society, not acting like that!

'Have you been out? There is a new exhibition on down the road. I haven't seen it myself. Gainsborough.'

'I have not seen it,' said Rebecca.

Violet gazed fretfully down at her nails. It was too soon to leave. She could plead a headache. She did have one, almost. Her nails always disappointed her. She often found herself chewing on them, with no memory of putting her fingers to her mouth. If there had been a few seconds gap between the wanting and the doing perhaps she could have stopped herself, but she never caught it. She only become aware of chewing on her finger whilst in the middle of a conversation with Mrs Anstruther, say, and then caught the broken shard of nail lying on her tongue. It made her hands ugly: clumsy and rounded, like a child's drawing of hands. But no matter how much Henry spoke to her about it, she could not stop biting her nails. His anger made it worse if anything.

But she would not do it now! She touched her hands to her head and breathed in quickly. 'I think I ought to go. I have rather a headache.'

Rebecca nodded. She did not even say, 'So soon?'

But as Violet was rising to leave Mr Palmer came in.

'Ah, ladies,' he said, making a small bow. 'Rebecca said you were paying her a visit, only I did want to see for myself!'

Violet stood at her chair, her calves pressed back into the frame.

'Is the maid gone?' Mr Palmer said.

Rebecca nodded. 'Violet was leaving too. She has a headache.'

'Although,' said Violet quickly, 'perhaps it would be rude to leave just as you have arrived!' She felt herself blush.

Mr Palmer smiled, just as she'd hoped, and sat down near her with his hands on his knees.

'A headache, you say? Is it severe?'

'Oh no, not too much.'

Now that Mr Palmer was here, conversation flowed quite well, even if Rebecca took no further part of it. He was solicitous as to her health, just as a pharmacist should be. Then all the topics were covered that Violet had considered, and abandoned, earlier that afternoon, but now in a way that seemed quite natural – at least as natural as it could be when a man such as he was making small talk. Last time she had seen him he had hardly spoken.

Half an hour later Violet rose to leave again. Rebecca seemed tired, exhausted even, her head on one occasion falling forward over her chest. It would be rude to stay under those circumstances, even though she wished she could.

Mr Palmer rose with her. 'I shall see you out.' He nodded at his wife. 'Do not worry about Rebecca, she did not sleep well.' But when they got to the hall he drew her to one side, saying he wished to show her something in the dining room. Alone, and at such close quarters, Violet felt herself become dizzy. She found her breath was coming rather hard. 'Is it this that you wanted to show me?' she said, pointing to a flecked paperweight at random.

'That? No, I am afraid I got you in here for a different reason, Violet, forgive me.' Mr Palmer smiled. 'I must apologize for Mrs Palmer. She is tired and,' he shook his head a little and cast his eyes to the floor, 'since I know you are a close friend of hers I feel I can be truthful.'

'Oh. Yes! What is it?'

'I hope you will not find it awkward, what I have to ask you,' said Mr Palmer, lifting his eyes to hers. They were quite blue, bluer than her own, even, and her own eyes were always remarked upon.

'Awkward, what?' Her hand flew to her chest.

'I have been worried about Rebecca recently. I am sure you have seen the change.'

The change, thought Violet in confusion, was on account of him, wasn't it? She thought of the shoe on his desk. Was he going to confess to an *affaire*? 'Yes, yes I have,' she said. 'She is much thinner.'

Mr Palmer drew his eyebrows together. 'And I love my wife, of course, very much! As you love your husband.'

'Dear Henry,' she said, though her shoulders drooped. 'Yes.'

'Though I always thought he had a prize in you. We men are unworthy beasts!' He stepped a little closer to her.

'I don't know! I wouldn't say that!'

'We are, but luckily you women take us all the same. And that is why we love you.'

'Do you?' she stammered.

'Oh yes,' he murmured. 'We are slaves to your kind. Anyone who says different is a fool.'

'Are they?' P'raps he may kiss her! In here – already!

'Which is why I would do anything for my wife.'

Violet's heart fell. She stared at the paperweight in confusion. 'Ah, yes.'

'Forgive me if it is inappropriate—'

Violet lifted her eyes to him again.

'But perhaps you would keep an eye on Rebecca? For me.' He smiled. He must have some chemist's toothpaste, she had never seen teeth so white. 'I would not ask, only you are such close friends, and I know you to be a kind and caring sort of girl. It would set my mind at rest.'

Violet looked to the paperweight again. 'Watch out for her, in what way?'

'Perhaps if you were to find the time to pay us a few more visits, say. Of course, I would ask Mrs Bunclarke to prepare a good luncheon for you, on the days you did come. No need to send your card and so on. To see how you think Rebecca is faring.'

'I don't know that we are *that* close.'

'And I shall see you when I can, to hear her progress. You are welcome at the pharmacy any time – or, perhaps we could meet once a week, in a park say, somewhere that raises no suspicion.'

'Once a week?'

'Or more. Just between us.' Mr Palmer inclined his head.

Violet's heart beat harder again and a blush rose to her cheek. 'I should like to meet in a park. I mean to say, I like parks, and the summer is turning. One should make the most of the weather, don't you think?'

It was a strange request, thought Violet as they went into the hall, but no stranger than the other goings-on in this house. She *was* a kind girl, as Mr Palmer said, quite the kindest she knew. It was nice to be noticed for it. And the way he had caught up her hand, just for a moment, as she opened the door had given her a great deal to think about.

CHAPTER 16

14 January, the desert

Dearest Rebe,

I have found my cause! For which please excuse me, my darling, for not writing before. The Bedouin have taken me to the canal, I wonder if you read about it in your newspapers? I think you do because the British here, I am glad to say, are on the side of God. I think the British cause must always be on the side of God (and the French of the Devil) and that is what makes us so great – do you agree, Rebe? I can see your brow furrowing as you read this but wait, just wait, until I explain.

The conditions of the men building the canal at Suez are worse than you can imagine. The French have <u>forced</u> the Egyptians to work for them – they are little more than slaves; if you could see the desperate faces on these men, Rebe, you would see things as I do. All in the burning heat they are compelled to dig and dig and dig – with their bare hands, many of them, without even the help of a spade, their fingers blistered and suppurating – and *forced to pay for their own food and drink, which they cannot, and so they are starving to death and parched.*

I went to the Suez disguised as a Bedouin – how you would have laughed to see it! My face rubbed all over with burnt wood and then wrapped in their style over the mouth and head with a piece of cloth – but in this way I dare say I saw more than any other white man. The Egyptians are ragged, utterly destitute, whilst the Frenchmen stand on some hillock or another dressed entirely in white linen conducting affairs as they see fit.

I must tell of this, so that you will understand how it is. I saw one man die in front of me. He stood up from his work, wiped his brow and fell down dead. I looked straight into his face as he fell – oh Rebe, I'll never forget it! He looked as I saw a deer once, in Scotland, brought down by hounds. Resignation and silence, and that was it.

The Frenchman cared nothing, he sneered, as Frenchmen will. I think hundreds must have died that way, in front of him. He motioned for the man to be picked up – he was a bag of bones, there is no way to put it better. I saw him later piled into the corner of a railway carriage waiting to go God knows where. Just sitting as if he were alive with his legs splayed out in front of him! His eyes were still open, nobody had thought to shut them, and they were covered all over with flies.

I must do something, Rebe; I cannot return until

I have. The Bedouin are engaged on a plan with the British to – well, I <u>cannot</u> say what to do, for it is all deadly secret and you must not mention that I said even that. I ought not to have written it but I have no will to start the letter over again. Do not tell anyone, promise me, Rebe. But write to me, soon! Still send to the same address, though I move from one place to the next with the Bedouin now, I will find your letters, I promise.

   Since then it has been my greatest pleasure to go about with blackened skin disguised as a Bedouin, in flowing robes and headdress. They have a word here: Kayf. The best translation for it is the feeling of being intoxicated by life itself and following on from that the <u>dissolving</u> of the self. I think I find it then. I hardly know myself – all my old ways of thinking drop away. I have been learning their language, and their customs are becoming ever less strange. Indeed, it is <u>our</u> customs that sometimes now seem the strange ones, though they have <u>you</u> in them, under the rain and mist and drizzle. Here in the desert it seems impossible that such weather exists – I have only your word for it, my own darling. And how I wish I had more – your arms, say, or your lips.

   But at some moments, when I am not sick for home, and you, I mean <u>if</u> I manage to throw that off, for the merest heartbeat, say at dusk walking about listening to the Moslem prayers and tang of the mimosa plant in the *heat, I can forget <u>myself</u>. I wonder if that is perhaps one way to live, if it were possible? Such a throwing off of shackles! A freedom in it that I had not known. I mean not to live a life of passive impressions but can instead dissolve myself in the cause.*

My dear love, I cannot write any more, the heat is taxing my powers of description and the flies continually land on my writing arm. I await a letter from you more than anything in the world.

With fondest love, my own dear Rebe, and a kiss if you will bear it, kisses and more, I am <u>your</u> own dear love,

Gabe

Fondest love, and afterwards, nothing.

Kayf: did it rhyme with belief or was it shorter, like strife? But Rebecca understood it now, however it was said – the medicine had given her a sense of it.

She balled the letter into her hand and crushed it, letting her eyes fall shut. She ought to destroy the letter, but she found herself too tired. It was old, the paper was thin and the ink soon smeared in the sweat of her palm.

A few days later Rebecca was surprised to open the door to Violet again.

'Oh,' said Rebecca. 'Did you forget something? Or did we have an appointment?'

'No, I – I only thought to see how you were. I was passing,' said Violet, blushing hard and tucking her chin into her collar.

'I see. Thank you – should you like to come in?'

'Well, I was passing,' said Violet again, peering past Rebecca's shoulder. 'Are you alone?'

'I am,' said Rebecca, opening the door. But as she turned to go inside she caught sight of Eva, out on the pavement, lifting her hand up to waist height and making her a little wave.

Evangeline, come to the house? She was pleased to see her, God knows, but she had not arranged it, and if Alexander ever found out—

'Oh, who's this?' said Violet.

'This? A friend. I don't think you have made her acquaintance.'

Violet's cheeks, which had been beginning to grow pale, were flooded again. She looked at Rebecca in astonishment. 'Is *she* coming *here*?'

'Do you know her, then?'

But before Violet could reply, Eva was upon them, only giving the other woman a hurried 'hullo', and stepping up towards the door.

'I am afraid I have not warned you of my coming, Rebecca, and now you have someone else!'

Violet's face, still in its heat, managed to grow sour.

Eva said: 'Your husband is at the pharmacy, is he? I thought he would be out.'

'Have you each other's acquaintance?' said Rebecca, nodding at Violet.

'No,' said both women.

'I have seen you, I think,' said Violet.

Now Eva started. Her eyes widened. 'Have you, where?'

'Oh I don't know! On the street. Edinburgh is a small place.' Violet fiddled with the tips of her gloves. But they were saved by Kitty Kat who fled between them all and into the house.

'Kat,' cried Eva. 'You ought to be a dog, I swear it.'

Inside the cat had pulled himself up on the flagstones, his legs splayed, as if he had not meant to come in after all.

'Oh dear!' said Eva. 'He is so disobedient, I am afraid I cannot get him to listen.'

'I do not mind him,' said Rebecca. 'Let him stay.'

Violet pressed her lips together and gazed at the cat as if he might provide an answer.

'Thank you, Violet, for your kindness. Drop by again, won't you?' said Rebecca.

'I will,' said Violet. 'Tomorrow, perhaps? Or the day after.'

'I look forward to it,' said Rebecca.

But after she closed the door she said to Eva: 'I don't know why she comes round at all. We have nothing to say to each other.'

'Well, I have something in particular to say to you!' said Eva. 'Alexander is gone, you say?'

'Yes, until this evening. But let us go up to my room – just in case.'

'Yes, let us,' said Eva. 'I could not bear to be discovered. But what terrible paintings! They do not suit you at all. You bought them at auction, I suppose?'

They went in to Rebecca's bedroom, Kitty Kat at their heels, turned the lock and sat down together on the bed. The counterpane was hanging off and the sheets were flung carelessly aside. Jenny had always kept the bed tidy. And where was she? Rebecca had not heard.

Eva sneezed. 'Kat has taken to sleeping on my pillow. I wish he would not.'

'No, he has great deal of fur,' Rebecca said, pushing her hand down his back.

'But look what I have to show you. It is something – do not be surprised – that I hope will cure me, at last,' said Eva.

'Cure you? Are you ill – why did you not come over sooner, if that was the case?'

'Because …' Eva yawned so hard that tears squeezed from her eyes. 'Perhaps you share the malady.'

'What – is it catching?' Rebecca thought of smallpox, scarlatina.

Eva heaved a sigh. 'Mr Badcock said these salts would cure the hunger for my drops. Only I find they have made the hunger worse. I think there is some mistake. He says it is some mistake in me, that I have a weak character. I think he is right! But I cannot help the craving.' She sighed again. 'But Mr Badcock has given me something else. He says it will cure the hunger for it, for ever, because it does not go in by the mouth. I wanted to share it with you. For we are the same, aren't we? Sisters, almost.'

Evangeline brought out a brown leather case from her reticule, polished and smooth. 'Mr Badcock, just three days ago, gave me less, much less, of the salts, to see if I could do it. He said I ought to cut down, he told me that my hunger was too great.' She ran the pads of her thumbs over the surface of the case. 'But I could not hold out! All the time knowing I could soothe my aches and shivers with a draught of laudanum, the temptation was too great. So I went out by the Cowgate and found a very low-down place that would not mind that I was sweating through my dress. I drank it there in the street, though it made me retch!'

'Eva—'

'How angry he was, when he came! I had never seen him so angry! And the drops had not even made me well again. But he pressed his face close to mine – his breath smelled foul. And his cheeks were quivering—'

'Oh Eva, does he—'

'I must not go elsewhere, he said! How much had I taken? I told him – twenty drops – or more. Though I could not be sure, my palm had been moist and the dropper had slipped from my grasp, and I wanted so much of it. For laudanum is not nearly as strong.'

'What did he do? Oh Eva, tell me he did not touch you!'

'He – he kissed me. On the cheek, where I was expecting a slap. And then he kissed my ear.' Eva shuddered. 'And put his tongue into it. His breath was hot.'

Rebecca went to her and put her hands on Eva's, still on the leather case. Both were cool and smooth. 'And no more?'

'I fell into a swoon – I don't remember. When I came to I was sitting in my chair, and my dress and stockings were on just as they had been, although I was bruised about the thighs and the ribcage. I don't know. Mr Badcock had left.'

'If there is comfort to be had, that is a meagre one – that you don't know.' Rebecca sighed. 'Would that I never had to see him again! But he is Alexander's friend – his only one, I think. And would that I never had to see Alexander either.' She stood up and gazed down at the street. 'But I am his wife. He hit me – slapped me full in the face – for seeing you! And threatened to imprison me in this house.'

'Oh! Does he not know? Does he forbid it? Yes, I see now – how stupid I have been!' Eva pulled at a piece of hair. 'I did not mean to put you in danger – that was the last thing I wanted! He hit you, you say?'

'Yes, in front of Jenny.'

A pin had fallen from Eva's head, she stooped to pick it up and poked at the back of her hand distractedly. 'This is it, then. The beginning! Oh, how I meant to save you from it.'

'But how could you save me? I have married him, it is impossible you save me. No one can.'

'If I could have got to you before the wedding, but I did not know you then.'

Rebecca gripped her by the shoulders. 'Eva, I am hit. Many husbands use force with their wives, I think. Husbands are allowed to do with their wives as they please! But we have our medicine. That makes anything bearable, do you not think?'

'You are sure Alexander will not return?'

'He is gone to the pharmacy. He will not be back till after dark. He is orderly in his routine. Unless ...' Rebecca remembered the shirt.

'Unless?'

'Unless something unexpected happens – an accident, say.'

'An accident?' Now Eva looked more afraid, her hand up in front of her mouth. 'What kind of accident?'

'A shirt, say, that was dirtied! Eva!'

'A shirt, you say.' Eva shivered and shivered again. 'I think someone has walked over my grave! It is time I took you to the place, to the girl who owns the shoe. You will see for yourself. If you see her, if you know, then that might protect you where I cannot.' Eva coughed, and coughed again. Her eyes were streaming.

'The medicine,' said Rebecca. 'You have a need of it.'

'I will take you, very soon, in a matter of days! Though it is not easy. You will have to wear a mask. I hope you can rise to it! But I cannot think on it now.' She coughed again. 'At least with the medicine I never have a cough. Do you find the same? It is miraculous. Mr Badcock says your husband has made another breakthrough, he has made the medicine in a different form. Liquid this time.' She brought out a bottle from her reticule with shaking hands. The bottle was plainer than the one that kept their salts, but otherwise similar. 'I think he means to sell it everywhere, in different forms. Mr Badcock says it is a medicine strong enough for heroes, I think he was thinking of Greek ones.' Eva was talking quickly, shaking the bottle as she spoke. 'I told him it should be called heroine, as he has made it for us.'

'I have not seen it made this way,' said Rebecca.

'It is because your hunger is not as great. I have only tried it once before I brought it here. I thought you might like to try it too … We could try it together. Mr Badcock has left me enough for three doses, but I am sure after this I will be able to cut down, so you may have one of them without him noticing!'

Eva set out the leather case again on her knee. As she slowly lifted the lid, Rebecca saw at first only a ruched and gleaming bed of pink silk. Was it a necklace she had there, made of diamonds? No, whatever was inside was too insubstantial for that. Even the dim light of the afternoon passed straight through it. Eva took it out and held it up as she would a prize. It was a syringe. Rebecca had read about its invention here in

Edinburgh by a doctor, but she had not ever seen one herself. It was beautiful. The syringe perfectly proportioned, its barrel was glass, demarcated with black lines, which tapered down to a silver nose and further into a long silver needle, which in turn narrowed slowly down to the sharpest of points. Its plunger was made of carved ivory.

'There are women who make a cut in themselves to drop in the morphine,' said Eva. 'But this is much better. I think there is no danger at all.'

'I seem to remember that the doctor invented his syringe for injecting morphine into the site of pain – for neuralgia. I had neuralgia once – there was nothing more painful. P'raps many women get it – have you had it?' Rebecca picked up the needle and very gently rubbed the tip of her thumb against it. It had a far sharper point than a darning needle, yet it was made to plunge into her skin in the same way that the other plunged into a ball of wool. She shuddered, and in shuddering she caught the tip of the needle under her skin. A single bead of blood oozed out of the pad of her thumb.

'Neuralgia? No. Never mind that, the tip is so fine, it will heal.' Eva took the syringe from her and shook up a bottle, not blue, but black. 'I think he means to sell it everywhere, in different ways that will suit everybody. There now ...' She drew the plunger carefully back. 'Ten lines up. That is what I must take. Oh, I long for it, only, you know, to ease my aches, and pull back my tears!' The liquid filled the glass barrel now, not dark as it had looked in the bottle, but pale, as clear as water. 'But the feeling, as it disperses, is much more sweet than the salts.' Eva hitched up her tartan gown and unhooked her stocking, rolling it down to her knee. Her thigh, the colour of milk, had three blue bruises on it, each one the size of a halfpenny bit.

'Does it hurt, going in?' asked Rebecca. Eva held the point of the needle at the largest part of her flesh, up near her hip.

'Mr Badcock did this the last time. But it is impossible for him to visit my rooms twice a day, though God knows he tries. It is simple, there is nothing in it, he did it easily enough, though it stings ...' Eva narrowed her eyes and pushed the tip onto the skin of her thigh. The flesh around it dimpled. She pushed in a little more, drew in her breath.

'Ah, there now, there we are! Just keep it steady!'

'It looks as though it might hurt,' said Rebecca. 'It does not seem natural.'

'It does not hurt over much,' said Eva, slowly burying the tip of the needle into her flesh. 'It simply goes in like this' – her hands were shaking – 'and a little further – there!' The needle was all the way buried, and now it looked as if it were part of her, a metal obtrusion. The wind rattled the panes and flung the first leaves of autumn against it, but neither of them looked up.

'Can I ...? Is there anything I can do to help you?' Rebecca asked. For whatever she claimed, her friend was pale and sweat stood out on her brow. But Eva made no reply, only carefully brought her other hand over her leg to the barrel, catching her lips between her teeth as she pushed it down.

The liquid flowed down. Eva sighed out. When there was nothing left she pulled out the needle and sat back. Her eyes were still dark, her pupils still took up the whole of them.

'It does not hurt,' she said through white lips. 'At least, not as much as you might think. Very quickly the benefits flow out from it. And that thought helps with the discomfort.'

Rebecca shuddered. It was not right to be penetrated so. A bead of blood had sprung out of the place where the needle had left, as big as a ladybird, and then a beetle, and then it ran over as a beetle might and fell down onto the counterpane. Eva saw it and dabbed at it with her sleeve.

'I will get something for it, in a moment. But can the syringe really cure the hunger, do you think?' asked Rebecca.

'The men say it. They are men of science; they must know what they say.' Eva pushed the hem of her gown down and sat fidgeting at the edge of the bed.

'Is there pain after you have taken the needle out?'

'Only an ache, nothing more. But it is the waiting for the effect that is harder!' She kicked the side of the bed with her heels. 'After I am rid of the hunger I mean to save up, and after a few years, two at the most, I will have enough to start a small concern of my own.'

'A shop?'

Rebecca thought Eva had been cheered by the thought of it because she brightened. But it was not that.

'Ah now, I start to feel it at last. It spreads out, yes out …' she said, rubbing at her chest with the palm of her hand. She closed her eyes and let her hand drop. Her eyelids fluttered.

Rebecca's medicine did not work as well as it once had. Hadn't her original dose doubled, or more, on some days? But she felt just the same. Even the best moments – about half an hour after her morning dose – could sometimes be frayed around the edges, and she hardly ever had a sleep like Eva was having any more.

But, as if she knew what Rebecca was thinking, Eva snapped her eyes open again and sat up. The effect was just like Rebecca's childhood doll, when she used to sit her up for tea, only the doll had clear blue eyes fringed with thick lashes, and apples for cheeks. Eva did not have any of those things, except for the colour of her eyes, which were blue and inhuman looking, now that her pupils had constricted. 'But you must try the syringe – that is why I came to you!'

'I – I have had my medicine!' said Rebecca. 'Alexander keeps me exactly to it – you know as much.'

'And is it enough?'

'I think … I think I will ask him for more.'

'But that is how the hunger gets its grip on you! This way you will be cured.'

'I do not want to be cured, in that way!'

'Ah, you are afraid,' said Eva, letting her fingers paddle at her lips.

Rebecca plucked at the coverlet. 'It is so violent; as if you were stung by a monstrous bee.'

'But we find a bee's sting in nature, why should we not find this? Only instead of poison there is pleasure ...' Eva fumbled for her stocking, got it onto her foot and up to her ankle, then her hand slackened and her eyes, before she could say any more, drifted shut. Kitty Kat, perhaps knowing such things, barged into her foot and rubbed his back along the side of it, purring loudly. 'But I still long to stop,' said Eva, her eyes flickering open. 'I think if I cut down a little each day I will be clear of it in a week, perhaps two. And after a few years, I will have enough to start up my own concern. A shop ...' Eva's eyes again fell closed.

'Yes, yes,' said Rebecca, dismayed. 'So you said.' Her friend was drifting, drifting away. 'But why,' she said loudly, to wake her again, 'must you be clear of it? Haven't you always said the medicine is a friend to us? If every woman knew, I remember you saying that, what *we* knew, no one need be unhappy again.'

Eva sat up and scratched fiercely at her nose. 'But can you not see? It is drying me up, from the inside out! I cannot laugh, not truly laugh, nor cry neither. It is a kind of half-life that I live. Do you not feel it too?'

Rebecca hesitated. 'Yes, I *do* feel it – but – it is better this way, for me, I think. My husband – my life – are more tolerable.'

'But not for me! I am sorry, dearest Rebecca. Only – I want to give up! It makes no difference to you, does it?'

'You must do as you want, of course. It does not matter about me.' The medicine was her only source of comfort, her rock in the middle of a stormy loch. And Eva had been her friend in it. P'raps she could try this new way, not to stop, but to dream again, as Eva was dreaming now. Eva's lips were murmuring and her hand was fluttering, she was talking to someone – someone else – behind her eyelids. She would try it. She would wake Eva and have her fill the syringe once more. But another look at the clock told her it was late; Alexander would be home within the hour. She must wake Eva in any case, but to tell her to go. She dare not risk it, not today. But tomorrow, early, she may ask.

CHAPTER 17

But the next day the streets were treacherous with leaves. Every time the wind blew, a new bustle fell down; sweepers could not keep up with them and great piles gathered untouched under trees. Rebecca was going out, on her way to Evangeline's, when she slipped and almost fell on the edge of such a pile that had turned to slime. To right herself she put out her hand to the pavement and twisted her head back and thought she saw – but it could not be – thought she saw Gabriel.

Rebecca rubbed her eyes with the heel of her hand. She was not dreaming! Her gloves were filthy, she would not dream that. Her nose itched. She would not dream that either, would she?

All the youthful vigour had gone from his face and she hardly recognized him. He looked, what? Forty years old, when he was not yet thirty! His hair, once so golden red, was now run through by streaks of grey and grease. Pallid skin, the colour of porridge. His moustache had been joined by a short beard that was dirty too. Deep lines ran from his nose to his mouth.

He had started to walk on, leisurely enough, but because of his height his strides were long and he was already almost at the corner. Rebecca turned away from Eva's house. She would follow him to see if he was an apparition.

And because she could not be certain she was not dreaming, she followed him at a distance, quite calmly, her heart cool and her hands swinging at her sides. Though she could have been at his elbow and still been unseen, for he turned neither left nor right, neither stopped to inspect anything nor chatted with anyone.

Up Leith Walk they went, the two of them, keeping to the pavement, for the tramlines were getting ready to be laid in the street. Everybody else was on the pavement too and there was a crush; it was easy for Rebecca to follow along behind, unseen.

After a while the houses gave way to weeds and she saw up in front of her a ragged boy with a pail in each hand. Gabe overtook him, still striding on, but Rebecca paused when she reached him. 'Where are we?' she asked.

'Can you not tell?' the boy said, pointing his nose up. There was a stench in the air. His buckets were filled with dog leavings.

'Oh!' she said. 'I see. Thank you. I've not been round here before.'

'No one who does not work here comes. You are lost. Go back the way you came and turn left. That is the way to town.'

'Thank you,' said Rebecca, reaching into her purse for a coin, 'but I am on the right path.'

'I don't need that,' he said, 'for a bit of conversation.'

'Aye,' said Rebecca. And it was true, the boys like him who collected pure were well paid.

What was Gabriel doing in the tannery district? She went on, following the boy, and the stink hit the back of her throat and made her eyes water. Perhaps it was only now that she realized she was not dreaming. The trees and bushes all drooped as if the smell had a weight to it. Someone had lined the way with mint and Rebecca snatched up a few leaves and crushed it beneath her nostrils, but it did not help.

At the end of the lane was the tannery itself, housed in an assortment of dank sheds. Rebecca turned into the first one she came to. Several of the windows had broken panes and cold air feathered in through it, setting the light from the lamp glancing over the uneven rafters and wooden pillars that supported them. The plash of the wheel turning in the water, the trembling yellow light and the smell of fermenting faeces made bile rise in Rebecca's throat once again and she leaned against a pillar, pressing her mouth with the back of her hand.

Where was he? The wheel concealed another man, a giant, his sleeves rolled up past his elbow in spite of the chill to reveal a forearm as big as another man's thigh.

'Have you ...?' Rebecca began. 'Do you know of a man here called Gabe? Gabriel, I mean?'

The man inclined his head. 'In the lime yard.'

Gabriel did work here in this awful place, the boy had been right. For how long? And why had he not come to see her? Outside were more puddles, her toes were soaked through and stinging with lime. She went towards a rasping sound, wrinkling her nose against the smell. It took her a moment to realize, in the stench of it all, that the rasping sound came from a skin with the fat being scraped off it, and that the man with the knife stretched between his two hands was Gabriel.

'Gabriel – oh!' she cried out before she realized what she was saying.

He looked up. Stared at her. Looked away, frowning, then stared at her again. The yellow of his skin turned first white and then red. He looked back down at his work as if he did not know where else to look and made as if to carry on, but one end of the knife slipped from his grasp and he dropped the other wooden end of it onto his toe. He picked up his leg and hopped. 'Is it you?'

His voice had not changed, not really.

'Of course it is me!'

'You are so different.'

'You are different, I hardly recognized you! I followed you all this way, not knowing.'

Outside the boy whistled and clattered his pails.

'You should not be here,' Gabe said.

'I thought it was you, only I could not be sure. Nowadays I – well, never mind. Where have you been?'

'I have written you a letter,' he said, with a helpless gesture.

'When? I never got it.'

'I don't … I haven't … sent it. I was planning to—'

'You haven't?'

'When I had got it right.' Gabe looked down at the bony gleam of his hide.

Rebecca coughed without bothering to reach for her handkerchief. 'If you knew how I waited for those letters! If you—' She coughed again. 'What happened?'

Gabe looked down. 'I have ruined it. It was the shock of seeing you—'

'Not the hide! Though I don't,' she swallowed, 'I don't know what you are doing here, of all places. Of all the places to find you!' She closed her eyes, shook her head. 'What happened to *you*, I mean, in Egypt?'

'To me?' Not taking his eyes from Rebecca's face Gabe let the knife clatter down on the stone, making them both jump. 'Me? I wanted to write to you, to explain it. I don't think I can tell you here,' he let his eyes go round the room, 'in all this. Because I want you to know, I wanted to tell you, to make you understand, that I never stopped thinking of you in all that time. To make sense of it! Oh Rebe, you know what I mean.'

'I do not know what you mean. Not this time. I have spent more than two years waiting for a letter! And now I find you here, and you have not visited me … even still … even though you are in Edinburgh.' Her eyes stung and tears fell from them before she could blink them away. 'Why did you not write to me? You could have been dead!'

He kept his eyes on her face. 'I am sorry. It is not enough, just to say that. I know it. But … I am sorry. I lost … hope. I lost you.' He is crying too, she sees.

'I am married, you know.'

'I know.' Gabe let his hands hang at his sides. His fingers clenched and unclenched. 'That is why I have held off coming to see you. Though I have followed you once, twice … 'Twas stupid, I know, but I wanted to see you. I hope you are happy.' Next to his lip there was a scar she had not seen before, the length of her fingernail.

'Happy?' Rebecca gave a disbelieving laugh. Gabe must have seen something in her face because at last he crossed the space between them and made as if to touch her, to embrace her, but at the last moment he stopped his hand so that it only grazed her sleeve. 'You are not happy! I knew it. Rebe, what has happened? I know I have no right to ask. Are you ill?'

Rebecca wanted to step back and forward both, to sag against him. She did neither, only took in the strangeness of his face. 'I don't know.'

'Do not cry. Oh Rebe, do not cry! What can I do?' He worked his lips and tried at last to smooth away a tear but she jerked away.

'Do not do that! Who are you?'

'I am no one, no one. How right you are to ask it! But I care for you …' He shook his head and almost seemed to smile. 'I love you still. That is who I am.'

'You cannot say that to me!'

'I say it with no claim at all, I ask for nothing back. But if I can help you, only tell me!'

'It is too late. Years too late!' She turned her shoulder to him. 'I have things in my life that you know nothing about, and never shall.' She is almost glad, almost proud, at last, to say it, though God knows it is madness to be either. 'And I don't think anything can help me now, especially not you.'

She has waited for him, feeling as if she were nothing, feeling as if she did not exist. She had made him everything, she had made him as big as the giant in the next shed. Now he was in front of her, he was just a man, and a strange-looking man at that.

Perhaps she had grown used to the regular features of her husband after all.

'Just – please – I must know – are you dying?' he said.

'What? I don't – do not be stupid! I haven't consumption, or anything like that.' She scrubbed her hand across her face again.

'I have made you unhappy, broken your heart perhaps, and I cannot forgive myself for that.'

'You did, I admit it. But I have fixed it again! I am very well. You do not need to worry.' She needs, suddenly, to breathe.

'Send for me – any time of the day or night! Only send a boy and I will be there. Promise me, Rebe.'

'You are too late,' she tells him again. Then she is outside, taking great gulps of foul air.

CHAPTER 18

Tomorrow she would ask Alexander for another dose of her salts. An evening dose, for by this time her morning dose had worn off entirely. The want of them made her restless. The restlessness started in her joints, in her elbows and knees, and travelled upwards to her heart, to her mind, until she could not bear to sit still.

She could not read, could not write, could not play solitaire. Could not sew her tapestry, nor darn her stocking, could not, in short, do anything.

Rebecca went again to the window and drew the curtains apart with a lurch. A brougham clattered past, its own windows impenetrable. Then the street fell silent again. Not the weather for walkers, and too late. Except, who was that? A boy, who came round the corner at a run. A ragged boy, his shirt showing through the holes in his jacket, his trousers several inches too short. What was he doing out so late? He ran up the length of the street, appearing and disappearing under the flood of the street lamps, his head turned to the houses on her side, looking at the numbers.

Rebecca pressed her forehead onto the pane. It was cold and made her neck shiver, but she wanted to see him run. Closer he came, until Rebecca could see the dirt on his face.

He disappeared under her house and she waited for him to turn up on the other side. But instead the doorbell rang out noisily into the silence, so loud it seemed everyone on the street must hear.

He must be carrying a message. For her! Rebecca's first thought was Alexander – there had been an explosion in the pharmacy! She ran swiftly downstairs on bare feet, pulled open the door.

The boy's breath clouded the darkness. He snatched his cap off and reached into his pocket. The notepaper was creased by the heat of his hands. 'I've to give this to, Mrs Palmer. That's you, in't it?'

Rebecca nodded.

'I'm to wait for a reply.'

She stepped back into the house a little, leaving the door open, in case the contents of the note made her cry out. But the writing on the front of the envelope was not Alexander's, or even Gabe's. The neat hand held a trace of the governess: Evangeline's, then. What news had she, so late in the evening?

Rebecca tore open the envelope, in her haste cutting a thin line of blood into the side of her finger. She sucked on it as she read.

Dearest R,

You asked when you first came to visit me to be shown the owner of the shoe. Come then, tonight.

You think you know what is in store, but I must warn you, in the strongest terms, prepare yourself! I have grown accustomed to men's predilections – but p'raps you have not.

Tell the boy you will come and I will see you in an half an hour on South Bridge, just past Mr Carraway's, the tea dealer. Look for a brass plate advertising a cordwainer and wait outside it. We will go in together.

Your loving friend,

E

Rebecca folded up the note and pushed it into her pocket. 'Tell Evangeline – the woman who sent you to me – I am coming.' Then she flung on her cloak and snatched up her keys. As soon as she got onto the street she realized she had caught up two sets of keys in her haste, they clanked together in her reticule, but there was no time to return them. If Alexander should notice … But he would not; no matter.

She had also forgotten to clip on her pocket watch, but she arrived at South Bridge certainly less than half an hour after she'd got Eva's note. There was Mr Carraway's, with its boxes of tea, and there was the cordwainer's, its sign shining out from its dingy brick surround, the thumbs of a hundred men had rubbed it to a shine.

No sign of Eva, not yet.

Rebecca must walk or else explode. Someone had up-tipped a cart of sprouts. Someone else had been selling bloaters. At the turn in the road a woman screamed – and now there would be crying. Rebecca turned back towards the cordwainer's – she could not bear to hear it. But there was not crying, only a man's voice, low and pleading. Rebecca put her hand on her chest and tried to breathe; she longed again for her medicine. Not having it made her start to sweat, although the night was chilly.

She did not hear Eva come up; her voice at her shoulder made her jump. 'Rebecca? Are you ready?'

She turned. Eva's face was the colour of distemper, her eyes were ringed with dark circles. Her lips were dry, cracked; she chewed on them.

Rebecca tried to smile. 'Ready? I don't know! This is not how I expected to spend my evening!' She had meant it lightly, as a kind of joke, to ease the strangeness of it all, but Eva grimaced.

'Let us go in.' Eva grasped the knocker, which Rebecca now saw was too heavy and ornate for a usual shoemaker's; it was some kind of snouted animal with wide-open eyes. Eva brought the nose of it down on the plate twice, then twice again.

One minute passed. Two. Then came the sound of footsteps shuffling towards the door. Slowly, slowly … the maid must be very ancient.

Rebecca had lived and died before the door, at last, creaked open.

But she was not ancient, this girl, she was young. She wore a man's black cap and a high black collar, and a man's britches, but her mouth gleamed with gold, like a pirate's, and her hand rested on the silver bulb of a walking cane. Rebecca had heard such women whispered about, but she'd never seen one for herself. Did she go about as a boy in the daylight too? Rebecca must have seen them without knowing, walking in the street, say, looking as if they were young men yet to shave.

How Alexander would hate them if he knew!

The boy – the girl dressed as a boy – gave them a nod and a gleam of her teeth. The corridor was very close and very dark as they went in; Rebecca stumbled and put her arm out. Eva gave her a shove. 'What is it? Do you want to turn around?'

Rebecca shook her head, both to clear the fog from it and to say no to Eva.

They went on until the corridor opened out onto a large room with high ceilings – an aristocrat's old home, like all those in the Old Town. A row of pillars extended down the centre of the saloon, ornamented with black wax candles, guttering in a breeze that only they could feel. The girl pointed to an old silk divan, grubby at the front. 'Sit there a moment, we are not ready for you yet.' Her voice was high, she made no attempt to lower it.

'Your fob watch!' Rebecca said, as she was turning away.

She smiled then and, for an instant, looked more like a girl. 'Do you like it?'

'It is very fine – I have looked for one just the same.'

She gave her a bow and a wink. 'Pure silver,' she said, and banged her cane down smartly.

Eva elbowed Rebecca in the ribs. 'You must not talk to him – to her!'

'Why not? I have never seen such a person before and she is so handsome. Do you think she goes about as a boy always?'

'I don't know! Or, yes, I think she does, that one. She prefers it. But there are rules here. Just … be quiet.'

Rebecca sat still then, as still as she could, for her heart was jumping around in her chest. Now she began to see about her more clearly. The place was filled with furniture and tapestries: Spanish mahogany tables polished to an ebony sheen, blood-red carpets with Persian patterns. On the wall: murals, painted in reds and blacks, except for the white orbs that the hissing gasoliers gradually brought to life – breasts or buttocks or cheeks. She became aware that there were others in the great room, hidden away on couches, chairs, even sitting on cushions. Men, of course, of every kind. She saw yokels with dirty clothes; they must have come up from the countryside. How would they hear of such a place? Rebecca supposed that news of it must travel, from mouth to ear. A drunken confidence. And more urban types: swells with silk kerchiefs in their top pockets, inky-fingered clerks still in their work clothes, swankeys with their polished boots. Rebecca had always thought that pleasures of this kind were taken by men who were tipsy, ribald, yelling encouragement to each other. But these ones sat, looking quite cast down and dishevelled. The only sound was the hiss of the gasoliers and the slow step of the Tom as she opened and shut the door. Or – Rebecca's eyes were used to the sombre light now – they were not *quite* cast down. Wasn't there something theatrical in the angle of their heads, in the nature of their sighs? They were all watching the several doors and the staircase that led off from the room, with – Rebecca realized it now – a hunched kind of excitement.

'Do not gawp. I ought not to have brought you! Now you have seen the place, you can imagine what goes on! Must you see it with your own eyes? For once seen, you cannot un-see.'

'I am come too far to leave in the anteroom!' She grasped Eva's hand and felt the bones move beneath her fingers. 'Who is that?' She pointed to the enormous painting behind them, of a woman whose wisp of a silken dress accentuated her pointed breasts, whose red hair tumbled onto her shoulders. Her breasts were bared and she leaned over a man curled up on his knees, his face twisted with terror, or laughter.

'Do not point, you will bring us to notice!' Eva glanced behind her quickly. 'She worked here, her name was Mary.'

'Mary? She does not suit it.'

'She went by Esmeralda,' Eva whispered.

'What has happened to her now?'

'She has been saved, I heard. She found God. Here now, get up.'

Rebecca looked for the Tom, she must have made them a sign, but she stood near the door and only made them another little bow and a smirk.

'I know the way, come.' Eva led her past the men – one of the swells could not keep up his dejected attitude and followed them frankly with his eyes as they went – and into another corridor. Down here the place was not silent at all. The doors all had a thick velvet piece of material hanging down over them, but even so she could hear a snapping sound, as if a branch had been broken, and then a sharp cry.

She heard a man's voice: 'Oh mistress, mistress, I'll never offend my mama!' Another thwack. 'Oh my dear nurse, beg me off!'

'No, sir,' the woman's voice was stern. 'I am desired to see you well whipped. I'll whip this backside of yours till I strip every bit of skin from it!'

Rebecca bit down on her lip. It was a house of flagellation – there had been a scandal about the same in the newspapers not three months ago. P'raps it had been this one. But she must calm herself! It was not she who was going to be whipped.

They went in through a door that looked like the rest; it might have been the main bedroom in an ordinary house. It was *still* a bedroom – of course, as sumptuous a bedroom as it had been in the days of the aristocrats. In the middle, a large bed, with tall silken canopies. In the panelled alcoves were classical paintings: Leda, Europa and the Bull. The humans with their animal partners were rendered very lifelike.

And propped up in front of the footstool, a wooden board with a golden crest written with the word PATENT, which cordwainers used. It looked very out of place. The board was padded in glossy pink satin, with a hole in the middle. The hole, as Rebecca knew, was for a lady to thrust her leg through and still remain concealed behind the board, to preserve her modesty.

In the grate the fire snapped and popped. Rebecca put her hand over her breast to try to quell the beating of her heart.

'You must take this,' Eva said, and gave Rebecca a mask, like the ones worn at the Venetian carnival. It was made for revelry but there was something else, a subdued malice in the expression of it.

'We must not be seen, at any cost!' said Eva, pushing it at her.

Rebecca put it in front of her face. Behind it she could be anyone; she could be no one. It smelled of unwashed necks and something sweeter, another woman's scent. What type of woman had been behind this mask before her? Who could come here who had not been driven to it?

'Other girls,' said Eva, as if reading her mind, 'from this house, usually, if they are free, come to watch, if that is what pleases a man. It is to increase his disgrace, us being here.'

Rebecca shuddered then and drew her arms around herself. A little of her strange excitement drained away. She thought of Jenny. Perhaps she had ended up in a place like this. Or this place! God forbid it. But it would not be unusual. Oh, she ought to have done more for the girl! But what could she have done? Again she felt her own impotence, and now she felt something like rage.

'Eva, do you know all the girls who work here?'

Eva had her mask before her face and regarded her with its sinister expression. 'No, not any more.' Her voice was muffled. 'Keep your voice low, it is about to begin.'

'But do you know if a girl, quite plain – but you know her, my maid—'

'No, no, your maid is not here!' Eva put her fingers behind her mask and picked at her lips. Rebecca saw she *was* trembling a little, though she seemed to know all about the place, and was trying to hold it in. 'Hush now, look, they are coming in!' She inclined her head towards another door that Rebecca had not noticed, it was hidden in the wall at the back of the room. Someone was coming in.

It was a girl with alabaster skin wearing a toga; she looked just like a Roman goddess. Her hair was done up loosely and ringlets, which had been tonged, fell down around her neck. She held a bow and arrow – Artemis, then. She gave hardly a glance to Rebecca. She might have blinked at Eva once or twice, or it may have been part of her performance. Though the conceit was broken by her feet, which should have been in sandals, but which were clad in a pair of shoes with monstrous heels. The same, the *very same* – of course they were! – that had been on Alexander's desk.

Such a pair of shoes on such a girl! On such legs, which were revealed by the toga as she walked to be smooth and bare and rounded. The toffer made a great show of walking in her shoes, grinding them down so that the wooden boards creaked and protested under the heel.

Behind the goddess came a man, up until now almost hidden by the swirling toga. He shuffled, cringed, looked at the floor.

With a sickening bolt of recognition Rebecca saw – Alexander!

But he was at home. Wasn't he? He would have come back from the pharmacy by now, and ought to be eating the plate of fried lamb that Mrs Bunclarke had left out. Rebecca blinked behind her mask, wanted to reach behind and rub her eyes. She had such a strong sense of the other spectral Alexander eating his dinner that she could not align herself to this real one, who was getting down on his knees in front of the board.

Rebecca turned to Eva, letting her mask slip just for a moment, and showed Eva her eyes, which were rounded with surprise, and her eyebrows, which had shot up into her hairline.

Eva shook her head and motioned with her hand – *up, up!*

Rebecca put her mask back up. She shrank back into the wall. She must look ahead, though she would rather do anything else.

'Hurry now!' the toffer barked out. The silence had been thick and the strength of her voice made Rebecca start.

The person who seemed to be – must be – her husband flattened himself on the floor.

'Wait!' the toffer said. 'Unbutton your trousers and lower them. And your undergarments too.'

The space between Rebecca's face and the mask had become hot, stiflingly so. She wanted to tear it off, she needed air, she was halfway from her seat when she felt Eva's hand on her thigh, pushing her back down.

'We must stay, else he will suspect something is wrong,' she hissed.

Like a play unfolding backwards, in which the end is known before the beginning, the scene in front of them inched slowly towards its inevitable conclusion.

The toffer strode over and gave Alexander a little kick, letting her toga fall open to reveal a thick triangle of curling hair. Not Artemis then, at all. Her body was like poured cream. She must, thought Rebecca distractedly, be very well paid.

'Lie down!'

Alexander made a snuffling sound and lay on his back. Rebecca saw that his face wore an expression just the same as the humans in the paintings: ecstasy and humiliation. But he was still in his pharmacist's clothes! At least, his jacket was off, but he had his waistcoat still buttoned up and his shirt still on, though the collar was loosened. And his breeches were on too, but unbuttoned, with his cock sprouting through the middle, bent upwards towards his waistcoat, its tip a surprising pink.

Rebecca was an eye, another eye. She would turn it on the girl, not her husband! The husband she did not recognize. Her breath came heavy behind her mask.

The girl must have been about one and twenty. Her lips were painted with carmine and her cheeks were pinched red. Her eyes sparkled with brandy, or something else, Rebecca could not see the size of their pupils in the dim light. She wore an expression on her face of rebuke, as if to a difficult pupil.

'You are not low enough. I shall make you lower, now see if I don't!' She put her shoe in the middle of his chest and pushed down. 'Do you see?' She pushed down harder until all her weight was upon him, then she swung her other leg to meet it so that she stood upon him. He gave a groan, of lust or pain.

The toffer wobbled a little but managed to walk down the middle of his chest. Then she stood again on one leg and one shoe pressing down on Alexander's body, lower and lower, until the sole of it was on his cock. She rubbed her shoe up on down on the veiny underside of it and Rebecca saw it twitch.

The air in the room grew thicker. 'Oh!' Rebecca gasped. Eva turned her head minutely towards her and shook it. But Alexander had not noticed. Rather, he had hardly looked at them at all. Rebecca wanted to tell Eva: *But Alexander cannot abide uncleanliness! And now here he is being caressed by the bottom of a shoe.* But all she could do was shake her head back at her friend; the sides of the mask grated against the sides of her cheeks.

'That's enough,' said the goddess, after some more frottage. 'Now get up – do not dress! *Undress* rather; yes, that is right. Quickly!' Alexander kicked off his breeches and was pitifully revealed in his socks and garters, his cock redder than ever.

'You may get over there.' She indicated the board. 'On your knees. It pleases me to be served, and you have not served me enough this evening.'

This whole time Alexander had uttered not a word, but now he said just one: 'Yes.' He said it long and low, with a hiss at the end that made Rebecca shudder.

The board. Now she understood. The board with its pink upholstery.

Alexander shuffled on his knees to the front of the board.

The toffer strode, as best she could – one of the heels tipped to the side as she did it – to the back.

'Closer! Closer still! Do not look at me!' The shuffling and adjusting seemed to go on for an age.

The toffer took off her shoe and pointed her toe, and slowly, first the big toe, then the others, and then the arch and heel, pushed them all through the hole, which, Rebecca realized now – exactly resembled a puckered arse hole.

The toffer clenched and unclenched her foot and turned it about on its beautiful ankle, her bow and arrow propped up against her chair. They were the same as the ones a little boy might use, Rebecca saw now, quite cheap and bought from a market.

Alexander, on the other side, received the foot, licking his lips.

'Now, now, you may not clean it, you disobedient boy!' she said, as his tongue lapped between her toes. 'Put my shoe back on. For I am to go to a ball and I must look my best!'

The fire and oppressiveness of the room and all the heavy furnishings and sumptuous fabrics combined to make it terribly hot. Rebecca longed to run to the window and throw off her mask. She felt the press of the bench against the back of her legs, and sweat. She lifted first one thigh up, then the other.

'You may clean the shoe. The shoe is dirty, the foot is not.'

Alexander snuffled gratefully and bent his face to the sole of the shoe and began to lick it.

And suddenly, Rebecca would never know why, the whole scene struck her as ridiculous. A leg coming out of an enormous arse! As if a cow were birthing a human! Rebecca gave a hiccup and Eva jerked upright. And – her husband, a ludicrous figure! To think she had ever been frightened of him! She snorted. Oh, if only his customers could see him now!

Eva turned. Her frizzed fringe above her sinister mask did not go at all, it gave it a comical effect. Rebecca gasped and clamped her lips closed, biting them between her teeth. Her shoulders started to shake.

'What are you doing?' Eva hissed.

But Rebecca could not answer. Hilarity was beginning to cluster in her belly. Eva let her mask down and shook her head more vehemently.

But it was too late, Rebecca's eyes had begun to water and her cheeks were burning with hysterical mirth. She gave a louder snort.

In front of them Alexander and the toffer turned. Alexander frowned, and suddenly he looked more like his usual self, as if he had been disturbed at his desk, only his cock sprouted there—

And it was that which made Rebecca finally burst out with a shout of laughter and – she could not help it – she dropped the mask from her face.

Alexander's astonished gaze met her own for two, three heartbeats, perhaps more. And then, the laughter dying on her lips, Rebecca pushed herself up and away from the bench, and grabbed onto Eva's arm. Eva, in her shock, had let her own mask down – Alexander must see them both, though Rebecca looked only to the door, and ran through it, pulling Eva with her.

CHAPTER 19

The feeling of lightness pursued Rebecca all the way back
through the corridor, past the closed doors with the smack of
the rod coming from them, through the great salon with the
waiting men and out onto the street. So he had seen her! That
was for the best, was it not? And with everything stripped
away, they were free to have a new kind of relationship. Not
the usual sort of husband-and-wife drear. He could be free of
her, and her of him. They need barely see each other!

But at the rag and woollen shop her mood darkened. Her
husband would never let her go free. Now he would keep her
even closer. And how would he punish her? Surely witnessing
his shame would lead to a worse beating than the men were
getting in the bawdy house.

They slowed to a walk. The run away from the bawdy
house had not coloured Eva's cheeks at all, though a sheen
of sweat lay over her face, making her look as if she'd been
polished.

'I am sorry!' cried Rebecca. 'I don't know what overcame
me.'

But now Eva turned to her with fury. '*Sorry?*' You are sorry?' She shook her head. 'You have put us both in danger! And you are sorry.'

'It was only, simply … I mean to say, the occasion was so strange, it seemed to be another man there all together, and then, thinking of Alexander sitting over breakfast so stern, and seeing him like *that* … It seemed comical all of a sudden.'

'It is not comical to me,' said Eva, her mouth set into a line. 'God only knows what he will do; he is not a man to be crossed. As you yourself know! Added to that, there is Agnes.'

'Agnes?'

'The girl you have just seen him with. She will be furious. She won't get paid tonight, I'm sure, and she let us in there for a favour. And p'raps word will get out, and it will be written down in one of those horrible guides that she cannot be trusted.'

'It will not come to that, surely! P'raps I could make it up somehow, could I pay her myself?'

'You? How? What money do you have? Would you take it from his pocket?'

It was true. She had nothing, it was all Alexander's.

Things did not now appear humorous at all. It had started to rain, a thin insistent drizzle that made the black streets blacker. Drops of it fell from Eva's hood onto her eyelashes.

It was not only Agnes' night she had ruined. Her husband

knew that she still associated with Eva, after he had forbidden it. Though what could he have to say about it now, after this evening? They had both been found out. She shivered.

'I have used up my new medicine for the day. I wish I had not,' said Eva, passing the back of her hand across her eyes. 'How I wish I had not! I ought to have saved some. Alexander said he would come, this evening, to give me a drop more, but he will not now. P'raps he will never come again, nor Mr Badcock neither.' Eva's voice rose. 'And then what will I do? Where will I find it? For no one else has the same, not yet. He's to send it round the country, he says, after the patent, but, oh that may be months off!'

'What about the drops? Do they not help?'

'Drops?' Eva laughed harshly. 'Drops do not help, they are too weak! Oh, I ought never to have agreed to show you.'

'You did it for me, Eva, you remember, and I am grateful.' The rain came down, coating Rebecca's cloak with a heavy dew. Her skin prickled and itched, she felt as if she were on the verge of an illness – the influenza, p'raps. How lovely it would be to feel warmth again, that kind of rightness, in her belly, that only the medicine gave!

Eva looked so dejected, and it was all her doing.

'We could go to the pharmacy,' she said. 'I know where the medicine is kept – the salts, I mean. The new kind would be there too, if it were anywhere.'

'But the shop is all shut up for the night. We could not

break in, like a pair of common thieves. Alexander would know, and then it would be worse.'

'He will not know,' Rebecca took Eva's arm, as if they were two ladies on a stroll, 'because I have the key.' She opened her reticule and felt about inside. 'I picked up a spare one for the pharmacy in error. It has been jangling about all night.' She pulled out a single key, hanging on a leather strap, long enough to open the doors to a palace.

'What would Alexander say?' said Eva, her eyes great holes in her face.

'That we must not.' Rebecca could not get the image of Alexander as she had last seen him out of her mind. Perhaps it was the same when someone died. 'But he will never know, will he, if we are careful?'

'Oh, Rebecca, do you think we could?' Eva's fury had thawed and her face now showed only longing. 'I had been dreading the night, for I cannot sleep, you know, not if I start to feel the sickness. And now ... now things are worse still. But, if we can get into the pharmacy, and have our medicine, there might be some respite, do you think?'

Eva spoke brokenly, but her pace began to quicken. The soles of Rebecca's shoes were thin – she had not thought to change into her walking shoes. The paving stones of South Bridge were uneven and piled up with horse dung and straw, she felt it all. 'You knew,' she said, 'all this time, that Alexander frequented that brothel.'

'Yes. The judges and politicians who visit and show their arses to the rod, you cannot imagine.'

'But how did you know it?'

Eva's voice crept along like a beetle to match their pace. 'Can't you guess? Have you not, even by now?'

Rebecca tried to fix her eyes on her friend but the gloom seemed to gather round her and obscure her, and her eyes would not stay still long enough for her to see her face. 'You work there yourself.'

'Not any more. But once, not so long ago.' Eva sighed. 'Now I get by on my savings, as I said, and what Mr Badcock gives me.'

'But you were a governess!'

'In the bawdy house, aye.'

'In the house.' The air was sharp in Rebecca's nostrils. 'I see, I see it now. And *that* is why Alexander forbade me to see you.' Rebecca's heartbeat seemed to push the sweat out of her pores as she spoke.

'I could not tell you earlier, I thought you would cut me, and I could not have borne it. But ...' Eva took her arm away and hugged it to her. 'I suppose you will cut me now.'

'Eva, no, I will not cut you. Of course I will not! How could you have thought it?'

'Everybody I once knew has cut me,' said Eva.

'I will not. How could I? I only wish you had told me earlier.'

'Oh Rebecca you are a true friend!' Eva put her arm back into Rebecca's and they walked on. Around them the windows of the old houses showed blank, except for one, which still had a line of washing hanging from it like broken teeth. 'You cannot know what it means to hear you say that.'

They went carefully, for there were no street lights here, only pools of darkness and greater darkness. A light flared briefly in a window and went out.

It was hard to see what they stood on; the stars were all obscured by clouds. They passed a rag and wool shop and another that only sold string. A rat ran across their path, shrieking. Then they crossed the bridge that arched over the slumbering railway carriages and linked the Old Town with the New Town and came onto the North Bridge, their breath coming faster now that they were so close. From here it was the work of only a few minutes to get to the pharmacy.

Rebecca had not seen the place in darkness before. The liquid in the carboys, so bright in the daytime, at night were all as dark as arterial blood. They looked like strangely shaped people hunched in the window.

Her hand was shaking as she drew out the key and turned it in the lock. But Lionel must have oiled it recently for the key slid into place and turned in the lock with three soft clicks. The door was not so quiet, though, it shrieked on its hinges as if it knew what they were about. At any moment Rebecca expected to hear a shout, and footsteps, and a constable. But p'raps the noise had not been so great; it only seemed so in the quietness of the night. And what of it, in any case? She was the pharmacist's wife.

There were no lights anywhere, it was the deepest part of night, perhaps three o'clock. Rebecca was used enough to the darkness to feel her way across the floor and open one of the drawers. She had seen Lionel stop a match girl a few weeks ago, perhaps there were some matches still. She used her fingers to feel about ... a few coins, some string ... And yes, one match, the last one, and a piece of rough paper curled around it, to strike against.

She went over to the gas lamp. Her hands were still trembling. But the match was good, dipped in enough gunpowder to make a large flame, and the lamp took, at first dimly, then flaring into brighter life.

'Where is the medicine?' asked Eva. 'All the bottles have the same liquids in this light.'

'P'raps it is amongst those jars.' But there seemed an impossible number of them. Rebecca went up and down the shelves as she had so often seen Lionel do, reading the labels that were not obscured by dirt: *Oil Eucalypt, Eau do Cologne, Acid Sulphur...*

'It won't be in the jars,' said Eva irritably. 'Do not waste time. It is always in the smallest glass bottle. I bet Alexander keeps it upstairs in the laboratory. Where are the candles?'

'In that drawer there.'

Eva pulled it open and pushed things about. 'Only candle-ends in here,' she said. 'Are there no new?'

'No new, Alexander will not run to it.'

'Never mind!' Eva took up a stub and held it to the gas, and swore, and snatched her hand back, but the flame wavered into a brief life. 'There now, I have it. Are you coming?'

But as they went up the stairs, with the stuttering flame and the rattling window and the shadows that loomed and died over the benches, Rebecca was gripped with the certainty that she should not be there. All around her lay evidence of feverish labour: large glass jars were connected by rubber tubes to small glass jars, the residue still spattered around the inside. Pestles lay inside their mortars, glass funnels were stacked together on the bench, up on the table a stack of notebooks, whose pages were covered in equations, crossed over and scribbled upon. And there, in two rows running down the middle of it, were the small square-sided black bottles, all with stoppers in them. They were without labels but Eva recognized them at the same time as Rebecca; she gasped and snatched one up.

No blue bottles, with her salts in them, anywhere.

Eva stopped trembling and brought the bottle to her mouth and kissed it. 'Let us go downstairs, there is more light!' She was already turning away and clattering down the staircase. From her reticule she brought out her leather case, as before, and opened it. She moved quickly towards the light bracket and leaned against the wall underneath, one foot propped up on its toe. She pulled up her tartan skirts and her petticoats and leaned on it to keep it from falling. She rolled her stocking down, as before. The upper part of her thigh was spotted with scabs.

Rebecca could not help the thought that sprung into her head: Eva looked like a three-penny upright, for any man to have up against the wall.

But it was not a man that Eva wanted. She filled up the barrel of her syringe with the liquid as dark as venal blood, shook it up and squinted at it against the light. A small bubble rose to the needle end; Eva pushed on the barrel until a fine plume of liquid squirted through it.

She set her teeth and plunged the needle into a part of her thigh that was still unbroken. This time, it seemed to go in easier, or p'raps she was more used to it.

'Ah,' she said. 'Now, now it will come.'

Rebecca turned away. She did not want to see her friend gasp and slump down, her eyes rolling back in her head. Not when a thirst for her salts had been awakened.

From the first moment of suggesting it on South Bridge, Rebecca's cells had realigned themselves so that every part of them was pointing towards relief. To be denied, once she had expected then, was terrible. Her joints grew irritable and her skin puckered up in painful shivers. Somebody pointed the tip of a feather up and down her spine.

And then, Eva, who had seemed so cold and desperate and strung with anxiety, sunk down on the floor with a great sigh. Her head fell forward on her chest and her lip sagged.

Rebecca opened all the drawers on top of the counter. Nothing – only papers, pencils, an India rubber. She got up on the ladder and moved things around on the shelves. It was maddening: there was opium in tins, in twists of paper, and dissolved in bottles of laudanum for the relief of every beggar and actor who might come in, but no salts, none at all.

Well then, she would have to have drops. She began to pull the cork from a bottle of laudanum, but she was trembling so hard that it fell from her grasp and bounced – but did not break – on the wooden counter top.

Eva raised her head and wiped her mouth on the back of her hand. 'Have you not found your salts yet?'

'No,' said Rebecca, 'I have not. And I can't endure searching for them any longer. I have found drops, that is all, and opium. I will take them.'

'You cannot have drops, not after salts! They will do nothing for you, not unless you drink three bottles at once. And the taste of that would be terrible, and make you sick, and then you would most likely not get any benefit at all. No, no, you must do it my way.'

Rebecca had thought of a twist of opium, she could find a match somewhere, and then … light it, and smoke it. But how, with what – did she not need a pipe? She had not seen it done.

Drops then, no matter if she got sick. But p'raps Eva was right, the drops were so weak, she might be left in just the same way as she was now, and she had nothing to flavour the water. She said: 'Your way, is it better than the salts? Does it quite take away pain?'

'It is better than love. And it will take away the pain of love too, good or bad, no matter.' Eva held out the syringe, it still had a tiny drop of blood on the end.

'I do not know ...'

'You hunger, I can see it. And this will take away the hunger!' Eva's eyes were glassy. 'You will feel well – better than well. Better than you have felt in your life.'

A bee sting. Rebecca had been stung by bees. P'raps it was bearable, then, especially when the other side of it would be so pleasurable. She was sweating into her bodice and her head was pounding. But all her problems would be wiped away, with just one sting of a bee.

'If you help me with it, then I shall try it. It does not hurt too much, you say?'

'Not too much. You will be glad you did.'

Eva opened up her leather case again and looked for the syringe.

'It is there, in your hand,' said Rebecca.

'Ah, yes.' Eva's stocking pooled round her ankle. Her calf was even thinner when it was bare, and lined with fair hairs over her shins.

Rebecca's heart thumped at the sight of the needle, poised to enter her. But first Eva plunged the tip of it into the bottle and drew up the liquid. 'There must be no air in it, for that is very dangerous. That is what Mr Badcock says.' She pushed the plunger down as she had done before.

'Look away if it troubles you. Then you will not flinch so, and I will be able to stab.'

'Stab?'

'I mean, it is a poke, merely, a scratch from a thorn, nothing worse.'

'Let me – wait! Wait a moment.'

'Why?'

'Till I catch my breath.'

Eva blew upwards, but her fringe was too matted with sweat to fly up.

'I will have this one, then. I have made it weak for you, so it will hardly affect me. I think I have need of a little more, in any case.'

'Are you sure you ought? The men are so particular with doses, and to do two at once—'

'I need it twice as much after this evening. And I think after one dose the other will not hurt so much going in.'

'It might knock you unconscious.' She paused and added: 'Then you will not be able to help me.'

'Nonsense. If I sleep, then rouse me, as you always do. There is only the littlest bit in here.' Slowly, slowly, as if she were in a dream, Eva was already passing her hand over her thigh again, with a peaceful expression. She hardly looked at where the needle was going in. She did not grimace, instead her face was blank, perfectly blank. Only by the movement of her thumb did Rebecca know that she had stuck the needle in and was pushing down the plunger. It was very quiet in the pharmacy. A mouse came out, sat on its haunches and cleaned its whiskers.

'You know,' said Eva, her voice already far away, 'the men have made a trap for me, and even knowing it, I cannot escape.'

'The heroin?'

'It was part of the plan they had for me, and for you, all along! I don't know when it started quite, but ... I have seen some papers.'

'What, what papers?'

'Mr Badcock brought them, by mistake. Your husband's handwriting. When he saw that I saw he snapped his bag shut. Never looked more like a turkey with all its red chins ... I will try to show you, though that would be hard – I must tell you rather. But promise me ...' Her voice faded.

'Eva! Do not sleep! Tell me now.'

But when Eva started speaking again she said slowly, 'We are all trapped, us women. We are none of us free. But at least we know it, you and I, and we might do something about it, mighten we, together?'

Eva had white flecks at the corner of her mouth. Her breath smelled of stale wine and something else, more sour, from the depths of her. 'I have some money saved up, and you, you could take what you could carry from the house ... we could, could we not, just go, far from here. To England, perhaps, where we are not known. And then the men would not be able to find us. We could start a concern of our own, selling men's undergarments.'

'Undergarments?' Rebecca looked at her friend to see if she was in jest, but Eva's head sagged forward again. 'Eva! England, what now?'

'Yes, this minute.'

'We cannot go tonight. ' Rebecca looked at the sky. The darkness was leaching away, the tops of the houses had begun to pick themselves out against it. 'Why, it is nearly morning. We will not have the time! This kind of plan needs time.'

Eva sighed slowly. 'You are right. I was a fool to think ... only ... ahh, here it comes now, what dark wings!'

'I only mean, we must think on it more. We cannot run away dressed like this. The men would have us in the madhouse, wherever we got to! And what about our medicine, how would we have it?'

The mouse put its front paws down, they were more like tiny little hands, and ran towards the door.

'Say, in a week. I think in a week. I ought to be able to survive that long. Eva!'

Eva had slumped forward again, her head almost touching her knees, her hair hanging over her face.

'Eva, wake up!' Rebecca shook her. Rebecca had been right, she had been knocked unconscious! She shook her harder. 'Eva!'

Very slowly, as if she was acting, Eva fell over on her side towards her.

'Eva, come now! I said you ought not to have done it again.' Fear gripped at Rebecca's heart. Eva was very heavy. Spittle ran from the corner of her mouth. And – her eyes were open! Could they be open if she were unconscious?

'Eva!' she shouted, scrambling up. 'Wake up! Wake up!'

But now that Rebecca was not there to support her, Eva crashed to the floor, her head slamming on the tiles.

'Oh! Eva, you have hurt your head! Evangeline! Eva!' Rebecca tried to find her pulse – was that the place? P'raps it was not, for there was nothing there. Nothing in the other place she tried, or the next.

She put her cheek in front of Eva's mouth to feel her breath. Nothing.

'Do not die! Not now!' Rebecca shook her again at the shoulder as she lay on the floor.

This was not happening. This was not real. She was dreaming – still dreaming.

But now she touched Eva's lips, which had a bluish tinge, and her eyes, now that she was close to her, were like no living thing. They were like the eyes of her old great-aunty, that she had seen when she was a child, before her mother had shut them with coins.

Rebecca snatched her hand away. 'No!' She would not do it; she could not close her eyes, for it would mean that Eva was really dead. But she could not stay to see it, those blue eyes as unseeing as stones.

Rebecca got to her feet, hardly knowing how she did it, still staring down. Although her heart was slamming in her chest her feet were clumsy. She knocked into the counter with her hip as she turned away and made for the door. She could not remember which way it opened and she stood there, pulling and pushing and telling herself she was in a dream. She turned to look at Eva, willing her friend to have got up. 'Eva!' she shouted again, to wake her. But from here Eva looked worse: she had fallen at an awkward angle with her arm beneath her and her head twisted up.

Rebecca turned back to the door and with a wrench got it open finally and went out into the night.

CHAPTER 20

But when she got out she found it was not night after all. The clouds were streaked with pink and the houses loomed over her as grey as gravestones. Men were setting out their stalls and turned to stare at her, and leer. One of them stood in front and pushed his face so close that Rebecca could see the corner of his chipped tooth, and asked her price. She must have given him a terrible look, for he shrunk back.

She had not given a thought to Alexander. If she saw him, what should she say? But as soon as she got in the hall she could feel at once that there was nobody home; and she saw with relief that his coat and hat were not on the stand. Only a letter there, addressed to her, in childish handwriting.

Still at the bawdy house then, or somewhere else?

And what wife in a thousand would be glad to know that, except her?

She was tired and longed for her bed. She climbed the stairs, tearing open the letter as she went.

Dear Madam,

It started, for there was no date and no address. *I thought you would be glad to know I am back at home in the croft, and I thought I would write and tell you it, as I have learned now to write – all thanks to you!*

I miss Edinburgh and those in it but it is for the best, I spose,

All fondest,

Jenny

Well, there was one piece of good news. Now perhaps Rebecca would sleep. She put the note aside and lay back to try it, only her sheets felt as if they were made from wool and itched her at every point. She turned and bunched her pillow up under her head. Yet how could she sleep when Eva lay dead? She should have moved her, hidden her somewhere! But she would have been seen, wouldn't she, dragging her outside, and suspicion would have fallen on her, and besides, Eva had been so heavy.

Tears came then. Rebecca turned on her other side and wiped her nose with the pillowcase. The side of her cheek that faced the ceiling was drenched in sweat. But she was not warm, she could not get warm. Her feet were as cold as the pavement outside.

She thought of her salts. She must give them up – she saw that now. But not yet – not today. She must sleep, and they would get her to sleep. Alexander *must* keep a bottle here. No matter if she met him coming in! He could hit her, kill her, she cared not.

If only Eva were here! Tears fell down her face and her nose ran with the same colourless liquid, as if all this water did not belong to her, as if it came from somewhere else.

Then she threw off the covers and went into Alexander's study. Nothing in the drawers or the shelves but books: *Common Objects of the Sea Shore*, *Scientific Dialogues*, *The Playbook of Science*. And a great many pieces of paper, covered over in Alexander's hand.

She went into the parlour. The flowers were brown on their stems, the apples had wrinkled in their skins. The salts would not be in here, but Rebecca still looked on the mantelpiece and on the occasional table, just in case.

His room then, his bedroom, though she recoiled from going into it, it smelled so persuasively of him. She was starting up the stairs again with legs that felt as if they may never walk again, when the bell went.

Eva, come to tell her she was up and about! She had been wrong, she was no doctor. Oh, Eva! Rebecca's heart beat hard into her throat and she ran down to the door. Eva!

'Yes, Eva,' said Lionel, for she must have said the name out loud. 'I have just found her, in the pharmacy, she is dead!' Lionel was white all over. He spoke as if he could not believe his words.

Rebecca let herself fall against the door. 'Oh!'

Lionel was rubbing his fingers together over and over, he was not wearing gloves, he must have forgotten them, the sound of it was like paper. 'Where is Mr Palmer?'

Now she must be careful! She must not admit that she had been there, that she knew already. 'I have not seen him. He is not in the house. Have you sent for the inspector?'

'Yes, I think he will be there by now. I came for Mr Palmer. I think ...' Lionel's lips began to tremble. 'I think it will be very bad for custom.'

'Come inside, won't you? Come in.'

They went into the parlour. The paper-hangings gave the illusion of sunlight, but otherwise it was covered in dust. How long since she had sat in here? She could not remember.

'I think I ought to get back, for the detective, and Mr Palmer.' But Lionel only carried on fiddling with his fingers and bent his head. 'I cannot believe it, I still cannot believe it.'

'Why is she dead?' said Rebecca, her words sounding unbearably loud.

Lionel rubbed at his forehead. The red line that was usually on it was not there, he had come without a cap. His hair, full of oil, fell in locks over his face. Rebecca thought of the mouse in the pharmacy and its tail.

P'raps she would be reminded of this night, by anything she saw, for ever.

'First Jenny, and now this!' Lionel rubbed his fingers.

'Would you like some tea?' Rebecca asked. Tea would be the usual thing.

'The door of the shop was already open. I thought we had been robbed. That is what I thought as I went in. Drawers were opened, a bottle was on its side. And then' – he shook his head again – 'I saw her. Just lying there! Quite unnatural. Her face was bruised and her eyes were open and her skin ...' He shut his eyes and shook his head. When he opened them again he pointed with a shaking finger to the ivory box. 'Her skin was the colour of that. I thought at first that harm had been done to her. Her stocking was off as if someone had tried to ...' He swallowed. 'But it was not that. It was the medicine. Her syringe was rolled away, not too far. I think she took too much.'

Rebecca sat with her hands on her lap and stared at him. Did Lionel know where the salts were? She would ask him. He would wonder at it, but if she had ever needed them, she needed them now. He would understand.

But Lionel was crying, wiping his nose on his sleeve. 'Evangeline always speaks ...' He swallowed again. 'Spoke so highly of you.'

Rebecca bit her lip. 'I did not know you knew her so well.'

As he rubbed his eyes fiercely with the palm of his hand Rebecca remembered again how near to a child he was. 'You were her ... her visitor?'

Lionel flushed. 'Years – more than a year – ago. Of course

she has given it up now.' He blinked. '*Had* given it up. Oh, I must speak of her in the past tense!'

'Let me fetch you a handkerchief.' Rebecca fetched her reticule, opened it.

'Thank you.' He buried his nose, then dabbed at his eyes and his cheeks and his forehead. He must've caught the corner of it for he pulled it away and looked at it. 'Did you embroider this?'

'Yes.'

'*RM* – is it yours?'

'Yes, Rebecca Massey, my name before I married. Mr Palmer says I must get rid of it. But I don't embroider any more.'

But Lionel had fallen to twisting the handkerchief into a rope. Tears stung Rebecca's eyes again. Outside, birds were noisily singing.

'She was a friend to me,' said Rebecca.

'And to me,' said Lionel. 'Oh, do you think Mr Badcock had a hand in it? She was afraid of him, said she had found something that made her more afraid.'

'I don't know. She wanted to leave – to run away, she said!' Rebecca put her sleeve to her face. 'And p'raps she might've if I had, we would have, but the hunger. And then it was too late …'

'The hunger for the medicine that was meant to take it away! She was getting deeper in to her medicine even as she tried to pull herself out. I told her she ought not to use the syringe, it is not natural, it's not right, I told her that. But she would not listen.'

'I know.' Rebecca saw her friend again, on the floor. She trembled. 'But what of the detective, what will he do, do you think?'

'Nothing, I expect! She is of no note.' Seeing Rebecca's expression he added, 'To the detective, not to me! Or you. I mean to say, she was a … prostitute, at one time, a fallen woman, and now she has died, an accident of her own making – as they will see it. Laudanum addicts die all the time.'

'He will not notice the syringe?'

'I don't think he will care a jot.'

Rebecca crossed her leg over her knee and rubbed her foot. The cobblestones had made it ache. Only a few hours ago she had been with Eva and now she would always be counting the days, and months, and years, back to last night. The slipper fell from her toe with a slap.

Lionel stared at it. 'But I don't think it was the fault of the medicine only,' he said. 'The shoes were what started it.'

'The shoes, with the heels?'

'Heels? Aye.' Lionel fell silent.

Rebecca closed her eyes. 'She took me to see the shoes … to see the girl, I mean – Agnes – last night.'

'Last night?' said Lionel surprised. 'She must have gone to the pharmacy after.'

'Aye.'

Lionel spoke quietly. 'At your father's factory Eva met a girl who was working in a ... house, with the birch.' In spite of his pallor Lionel blushed a little. 'She suggested that the high shoes she made there could add to her costume for the night, and Eva saw money in it, more money than she could make in a month at your father's.'

'My father's shoes?'

'They had the tallest heel, according to Eva—'

'Yes, but they were nothing like ...' Rebecca faltered.

'Your father stopped selling them to her when he found out what they were used for, and then she must have got them made somewhere else, for they had got popular at the ... house by then.' Lionel crossed one leg over another.

So Alexander had chosen her on her father's account! Some kind of whim, or private joke. Their first meeting, he had known who she was. What else had they talked of? Shoes ... Rebecca's insides fell as she remembered it. She had thought it remarkable that he could recall so much about women's fashion. He had looked down at her own shoes, hadn't he, even then? Finely made, of course, by her father. And now – horrible thought – p'raps his bowler hat had been covering a cock-stand, or the stirrings of one!

But it was Evangeline who had really paid for it all. 'Is that how she met Mr Palmer – at that house?' Rebecca asked.

'Aye. It is notorious, they say. I never went there! But the house,' said Lionel, staring at his hands, 'did not agree with her. Her skin was thin, she was delicate. You know yourself how she was.'

'Aye. Delicate.'

'And sometimes, as is the custom there, she held the birch, other times she was under it – which one it was depended on the man. I heard only snips of this more lately, as she drowsed, but it bothered her greatly. As Eva told it, sometimes she would wear the shoes along with the rod, but sometimes it was just the shoes. Men liked to see girls wear them, and walk upon them.'

'Walk upon – do you mean, all over?'

'Up and down the back, and given the rod. There were men who paid for the same.'

'Mr Palmer,' said Rebecca, her voice not above a whisper. She pressed her hand to her chest to hold down the nausea.

Lionel blushed and shook his head. 'I couldn't say.' He took up a cushion and set it back down again. 'But the house is notorious. Only there are so many politicians who visit it, it was not closed down. Other girls might not have minded the place so much.'

'Yes – she always took things hard.'

'And one night – and this was what tormented her the most; she would drift away and still dwell on it over and over again … One night a girl had her spine crushed, or bent, and it was Eva who'd done it with her heels, for the pleasure of …' He ran his tongue over his dry lips. 'For the pleasure of a man.'

Rebecca's heart plummeted. 'Oh!'

'She could not forgive herself, as the girl ever after could not walk without a stick.'

'She never told me!'

'You are Mr Palmer's wife. How could she tell you?'

'And it was my husband who suggested she take the medicine,' said Rebecca. 'To cure her!'

'He said it would cure all her ills, and he was right, for a while. But then—' Lionel turned his face away and buried it in the back of the sofa. 'I had better go,' he said, muffled. 'They may need me there. At the pharmacy.'

'But Lionel, you know all this, and you still stay in Mr Palmer's pharmacy?'

Lionel turned, with the faintest trace of his old swagger. 'Of course I will stay. Till I have learned all I need. It is a good business, for the making of money. There would be plenty who would have my job if I were to leave.' He ran his hand through his hair. 'After a year I will be able to open a business for myself.'

Rebecca shook her head. 'Eva, Eva said the same. She had hoped to save enough to leave her business and now—'

'Now she is gone, because of her medicine, which was meant to soothe her and bring her back to the world, not carry her out of it.' Lionel stood up and smoothed down the front of his trousers. 'Mr Palmer told her to stop your friendship, but she would not, even though he threatened her. She said it was the only pure thing she had in the world.'

''Twas not pure,' said Rebecca, shaking her head. The afternoons fugged with heroin. The sludge in their blood setting them out on feelings that were not theirs to feel. Rebecca pressed her knuckles into her eyes. A white blizzard took the place of her friend and obliterated her.

But if they had managed to feel something for each other despite all that, it did not matter, did it, the circumstance.

CHAPTER 21

The two of them parted in the street, Lionel towards one pharmacy, Rebecca towards another. It was not far to Mrs Shrivenham's pharmacy, but she paused outside the bow window and stared in. Mr Badcock had mentioned the place, notable for being run by Mr Shrivenham's widow, as if the place would be all at odds. But inside everything was familiar: the same rows of bottles and drawers, the same polished wood counter, the same tins of opium stacked up on top, as her husband's. Her heart gave a lurch at this. One of them was being handed over, even now, to a farm labourer, who was at the head of a great queue of people waiting to be served.

Rebecca wanted nothing more than to be free from her salts. And she wanted nothing more than to take them again. Every part of her body demanded it. And – this was harder – her mind whispered that she would never be happy again, not truly happy, without her medicine. And then, when she looked out over the bleak and desolate landscape of her life, she saw it was true.

The thought made her tremble and step inside. She had a

ticklish cough, that much was true, and she had need of soap. She could ask for that first.

Mrs Shrivenham was behind the counter, licking the lead of her pencil. She looked up.

'Mrs Palmer, good morning.'

Rebecca started. She felt so like a ghost that it was strange to be talked to.

'Have you come in here to spy?'

'Spy?' said Rebecca.

'For your husband's pharmacy!' Seeing Rebecca's face she added, 'I am not serious.'

'I was passing this way. I am not well. I have a cough.' Rebecca drew her handkerchief from her reticule and coughed into it.

'A pack of Allcock's Porous Plasters, that would be the very thing. Anthony! A packet of Allcock's Porous Plasters please, for Mrs Palmer.'

'Yes, Mrs Shrivenham,' said her apprentice.

'For we have Mrs Palmer in here and we must show her we know what we are doing! You need to warm it up, you know, Mrs Palmer my dear, and put it on your chest. It eases the cough that way, by pulling it up. But you know all this! How is Mr Palmer?'

'He is well.' Rebecca's eyes were watering. She blinked. 'I cannot sleep, either, when I am coughing. I may need a draught.'

'I think you ought to be in bed, Mrs Palmer, I should say. You are very pale, my dear.'

'In bed, yes. But I cannot sleep.'

'You could take … now, let's see …' Mrs Shrivenham tapped the end of her pencil on her upper lip. 'You could take some of Mr Brandreth's Pills. My customers like them; they cure everything, so they say. An explosive effect!' She laughed.

'Have you any laudanum?' Rebecca held her breath – the lady would look again at her pallor, and refuse her.

But Mrs Shrivenham only said: 'Oh yes, laudanum, that would help the cough, and the pain too.'

'I think I might need more than one bottle.'

Mrs Shrivenham did look at her then, a quick glance, but if she had seen anything in Rebecca's face she let it pass. 'Three will be enough, will it?'

Rebecca nodded. And now that she had relief so near at hand – she had noticed this before – it was as if she had already drunk it down. Her mood lifted. And catching it she felt guilty, that she still lived while Eva did not, and could feel anything at all.

Anthony reached up for the bottles, standing on his toes. Rebecca leaned forward over the counter. 'Does Anthony mind being given his orders by you?'

Mrs Shrivenham smoothed out her apron. 'He has no choice. It is this way, else he is out of a job, and you can see for yourself,' she indicated the shop, full of people, 'he would be stupid to let the position go.'

How lucky Mrs Shrivenham was that her husband had died! But the woman gave a start. Rebecca realized she had said the words out loud.

'I would not say that! Dear Alfred was a good man. But,' Mrs Shrivenham lowered her voice, 'terrible at business. The ledger books, when I came to them, did not add up. Did not add up at all.'

'But have you been taught arithmetic?' The drops were next to her hand now, and the plaster too, wrapped up in brown paper, as if they were a gift.

'You can teach it to yourself. There is nothing to it. Anthony, the gentleman there! He has come in for his *Cigares de Joy*, for his throat. On the top shelf! To the left.' She turned to Rebecca again. 'But the Royal Society will not let me in to their club. There are not many of us lady pharmacists, I only know of Mrs MacDonald, and she got her shop when her brother died. Anthony, look there, the orange peel, you have broke it apart. Your hands have no subtlety in them.'

Anthony's round face coloured. 'Yes, Mrs Shrivenham.'

Mrs Shrivenham had her pharmacy. Eva could have had her undergarment shop, then. Though it was impossible to imagine her friend behind the counter in the same bright way as Mrs Shrivenham.

'You have gone a bad colour, my dear,' said the lady. 'Would you like to sit down?'

'No – thank you. I had best be on my way.'

'Send my regards to your husband, won't you, my dear?'

On the street Rebecca looked for a step to sit upon. But there was a little patch of green that passed for a park, with a bench upon it, that would do.

She ripped apart the brown paper and pulled the stopper out from the first bottle, and drank the whole thing down. It tasted very bitter. And she felt nothing, no effects from it at all. When she caught the smell from the second bottle she coughed and retched until she spat. Eva had been right. But she put it to her mouth and drank down a quarter of it anyway. Her chest heaved with the taste of it; she leaned forward over her knees and spat again. The last bottle rolled from the package on the bench, picking up speed as it went, and splintered onto the stones.

She could have cried. She forced down another quarter of the bottle and sank back on the bench. After a while she did feel a little better, a little warmer. These would be her last drops. She was certain of it.

Rebecca lay back on the bench and fell into a fitful sleep. She dozed as a sea turtle does, grappling between two states, darkness and light, water and air. Time passed in a thousand pieces. She roused herself and saw Alexander and had a conversation with him. And then she realized she had only been speaking with spirits, or demons, and then she sank back down again.

A moment later, or so it seemed, she was roused by a gentleman in a top hat who spoke to her most insistently.

'Madam. Madam! Are you well?'

Her mouth had wool in it, her eyes had grit. She nodded, drew her cloak tighter round herself and made as if to sleep again.

His expression changed. 'I don't think you should sleep there. Have you no home to go to?'

'I – have not.'

'Well then, let me take you somewhere. A home, for people such as yourself. A warm bed. Porridge.' He stood over her, obscuring the light.

'No! Thank you. I do have a home. Only my husband is at work, and my maid is … on her holidays. And I have forgotten my key.'

'Does your husband not have a key? And who locked it, if you did not?' The gentleman tried to get a look at her hand, to see if the finger bulged with a wedding ring behind her gloves.

'He has no key. And my maid …'

'Why don't you come along with me? Come now, I know all about women such as yourself,' said the man.

Rebecca turned her head. 'Oh go away, won't you, and leave me alone!'

'That is no way to—'

'It is none of your business why I am here. Go away, I tell you, otherwise I shall scream!'

'Now, now, calm down. I only meant to help you. I think you don't know what you say.' But he was backing away.

'I shall scream!' said Rebecca again. The man shook his head at her, his sorrow turned to scorn.

And then she slept again, or half-slept. The difference between night and day, waking and sleeping, was nothing. And if dreams carried as much weight as wakefulness did, who was to say which one ought to be called reality?

There was Alexander's voice again, coming persuasively up the stairs. She must confront him, she must go down. 'I saw you,' she meant to say, 'and you saw me. I know what you did to Eva. She is dead because of you. Let that be an end to it, our marriage, and pretence.'

He smiled. 'There can never be an end to our marriage, you must know that.' He spoke with force, getting closer to her with each word. 'I still need a wife. If you thought so you are much mistaken of shoulton earshots carparta shin.' He kept speaking but now only the tone was understandable, not the words: insistent, assured, persuasive.

CHAPTER 22

When darkness fell Rebecca went home. Even though she had
spent the afternoon half asleep, she was still more tired than
she could remember. She could fall down in her bed and sleep
for nights and days.

She would sleep and then think what to do.

But as soon as she stepped inside she heard the men, talking
in the parlour. A great weariness overtook her. Where would
she go, then? She had nowhere. She must creep up to her
bedroom unnoticed and sleep and then think what to do.

'I have arranged everything. We may continue, we may
continue, hmmm? After all our work, that is the important
thing,' said Mr Badcock.

'We may, and we must,' said Alexander. 'I have already some
important information stemming from it. But it is ever more
important that Rebecca comply, that I keep her close.'

Rebecca put her hand to her throat and turned her head.

'And if she does not comply, I mean, if she is not a good
subject, we will have to end it. Which would press us most
terribly after all our work, hmmm?'

'We will still be able to speak in front of the Society, I think.'

'Oh yes, whatever happens, still that, yes.'

Rebecca must go out again, anywhere. But in her haste she clattered the chair against the wall and before she could get to the door Alexander was there, standing in front of her.

'I have been expecting you all day,' he said. She looked for a trace of the man she had seen last night. He looked drawn, he mustn't have slept either, but that was all. 'And now you are going out again.'

'No – I am going to my room.' She tried to get to the stairs but Mr Badcock skipped over and now they both stood in front of her.

'Come to the parlour for a moment – only a moment, hmmm?'

'But I am tired,' said Rebecca. 'I do not feel like talking.'

Mr Badcock took hold of her arm and pulled her towards the parlour. 'Come now, hmmm? And join our celebration. For we have heard today that our paper has been accepted to be read at the Royal Society. The Royal Society!' He rolled out the *R* wetly on the tip of his tongue. 'Home of Joseph Black and any other chemist of note. I think it will mark the beginning of our fame. Do not struggle, we only mean the best for you. You are grown quite wild! Hasn't she, Alexander? Quite wild.'

'You see now what I have on my hands,' said Alexander, a muscle jumping in his cheek.

'I think the death of a friend is one of life's very worst tricks,' said Mr Badcock. 'I think we must make allowances for her, Alexander, today.'

'And yet Evangeline should never have been a friend. Not at all. But what I cannot fathom is how Evangeline came to be in the pharmacy.'

'Was she?' Rebecca stammered out.

'You know she was. Lionel told you.'

The clock ticked slowly round, and Rebecca's heart ticked with it, only she felt as if hers might stop. 'Evangeline wanted to get better. She thought you would make her better. She said the heroin might be the cure, *you* said it might be the cure!'

'Come now, whores die for many different reasons.'

Tears stung at the corners of her eyes. 'Will there be an investigation?'

'Oh no, constables do not bother much with fallen women. He came and he went.'

'She is dead, poor thing,' said Mr Badcock. 'And do you mind?'

'Do I mind? She was my only friend, despite it all!' Now the weight pressed into her heart and caused a sob to escape from her mouth.

'Yes, but what *quality* is it, your grief?'

Rebecca pressed her face into the seams of the sofa. In the silence she could feel Eva looking down upon them, watching.

'You long for your medicine,' Alexander continued, when she said nothing, 'and that brings tears easily. But I think that the salts are not strong enough.'

She started. She had seen him at the bawdy house and he meant to punish her.

'No, the salts do nothing against it,' said Mr Badcock. 'Even though the salts have been your friend these past months, have kept you on – how to say it? – an even keel. An even keel! You have not toppled, not toppled at all, on the contrary, you have steered a largely straight path.'

'*Largely* straight,' said Alexander, rubbing his chin. 'Though not *entirely*.'

'In terms of mood and—'

'*Not* behaviour, but I think we can fix that, yes, 'tis so.'

She jumped up from the sofa. 'I must go to my room!' But Alexander's hand gripped her arm and he pushed her back down.

'I don't think it worth giving you the salts, my dear,' Mr Badcock continued, as if she had not spoken, 'when we have something much better.'

'But she knows it already,' said Alexander. 'Evangeline must've told her. And yet you do not seem pleased! Does she, John? She does not seem pleased, though I work night and day for it, for *her*, and for all of her sex!' Alexander let his eyes close and in his face, just for a moment, Rebecca saw an image of the man she had seen at the toffer's. Then his eyes opened again. 'But I cannot expect gratitude.'

'Perhaps the death of her friend works on her still.' Mr Badcock moved towards the side table upon which lay a smooth brown case, just the same as Eva's.

It *was* the same as Eva's. They must have picked it up from the pharmacy floor. Fear gripped Rebecca as hard as her corset used to do. She put one hand to the fireplace and felt the chill of the marble as a kind of burning. P'raps, if she could only keep the men talking, they may forget themselves for long enough for her to run at the crack in the door and get through it.

'She knows the new way, and she does not like it! But she will, soon enough, hmmm?' Mr Badcock went on. 'Just as Evangeline did.'

'I know,' she said, her voice faltering. 'Your medicine will change the world.' Her breath was coming hard. 'A marvellous cure!'

'The needle, John!'

'Ah yes, the syringe.' Mr Badcock snapped open the lid. 'Far more efficient.'

'Roll down your stocking,' said Alexander.

'I won't!' They meant to kill her. Kill her for what she had seen. She shook off Alexander's hand and leapt up from the sofa, knocking into Mr Badcock, who grunted in surprise. The door was only five feet away, she could see the hall through it, and beyond, the front door, and beyond that, freedom! But the heel of her shoe caught on the rug and brought her knee and hands slamming down onto the wooden floorboards. She hardly felt it, for Alexander got to her a moment later, and pinned her down with his knee.

'Come now, wife.' A little thread of spit hung from his mouth as he worked to hold her. 'I don't know why you struggle so. It is only for your own good. You have not the temperament to take on the blows of life alone. Haven't you said so yourself? And by the by, I found a letter, an old letter of yours. I forget whom it was from.'

He had not forgotten, she could see it in the jump of his jaw.

'A derivative name of some kind. A married woman ought not to keep such a letter. It would give people the wrong idea, if they were to find it. And I have a little bird in my grasp. I know what you have been up to.' Alexander still held her with his knee. Dark hair was growing on his cheek, the only sign of the night he had been through. And a twitch near his eye, which gave the illusion of a sudden grin.

Well, she would die then, just as Eva had done. 'Fuck you and fuck you too!' she spat.

'Oh I say! I think she may be losing her mind, hmmm? Do you think it?' said Mr Badcock.

Rebecca turned on him. 'And you! You are nothing but a letch and a goat.'

Mr Badcock's jowls fell. 'Come now,' he said more grimly, 'I think she may be mad after all. Fill her up with the syringe now, won't you?'

'You almost ruined my maid, and would've too, if Lionel had not come by.'

'That was japes, old boy, nothing but japes, eh?' Mr Badcock spoke to Alexander.

'Japes it is to force yourself on a virgin girl hardly past puberty? What a tiny prick you have, by all accounts!'

Mr Badcock paled and for a moment his grip on her slackened. 'What words! Foul words, where did you learn to talk like that?'

But Alexander had paused. 'Is this true, John? Because such things lead to rumours and if a man's home is not respectable—'

'Not true at all! She is lying to cause trouble. The syringe, Alexander, for God's sake. Shut her up, shut her up!' Mr Badcock's grip tightened on her leg, his nails cutting through her stocking. Rebecca kicked at him and succeeded in landing a blow in the fat of his belly with her knee.

'You will not shut me up. You are both the worst kind of men God must have put on this earth! For we have not talked of last night, have we, husband dear? At the bawdy house – the house of flagellation, the one that all the newspapers wring their hands over? That is *your* true home! And that is not respectable, oh that is the last thing it is!'

'Whatever is she talking of, Alexander?'

'Nothing, she is growing insensible! She is foaming at the mouth, look there. All this foul language is a sign of her falling away into madness – but I think the new medicine— Stop her kicking, I say, John—'

Mr Badcock did not know! 'Ask him, ask my husband, how he likes to spend his nights! With his head in a shoe, a shoe that is more like a quim, and his arse in the air!'

'What?' said Mr Badcock.

'Eva took me to see my dear husband, at the house of flagellation, where he got his prick out and he was just as pathetic as a worm and as dirty.' Rebecca struggled again. 'I will show you, I found the same shoe in his study, if you do not believe me!'

'No need to bother with the stockings in this case, I think,' Alexander pulled up her skirt to her hips. The cold air slapped against her thigh.

'What? Prostitution?' said Mr Badcock.

'No matter, John, now. Leave it alone. Disarray is what she wants and why we must silence her. Hold her tighter!'

Mr Badcock, breathing hard through his teeth, forced her thigh straight with both his hands and knelt on her other leg, which she still tried to thrash about. 'It will help you if you keep still, hmmm?'

'Leave off!' Alexander slapped her round the face; her cheek struck the floor on the other side. He had the syringe in his fist and raised it up.

At that moment Rebecca brought up her knee – Mr Badcock's arms were flabby after all – and landed a great blow to Alexander's chest. The point of the syringe jabbed into his hand. He loosened his grip.

'Goddammit, she has done me an injury!' A bead of blood oozed its way from Alexander's palm. He paled. 'I am hurt. Hold her now!'

Rebecca got an arm free and reached into her hair and drew out a pin. She brought round her hand so fast that Alexander had not even the time to defend himself, he had only time to let out a shriek, a yell, a curse.

'What have you done?' he cried, dropping the syringe and holding onto his neck. Mr Badcock clung grimly to one thigh but he was staring in shock at his friend, who was on both knees now and moaning as a trickle of blood ran down his neck.

'Alexander – are you wounded?'

Rebecca span and twisted and in a few more thrusts shook herself free.

'Get after her!' Alexander said through gritted teeth, holding onto his neck with both hands.

Rebecca picked up her skirts and ran, sending the door banging back on its hinges, through the hall and to the door. She wrenched it open and got out onto the street, the air freezing on her bare skin.

Behind her came a shout, but she did not turn round to see. She only ran, fear driving away her exhaustion.

CHAPTER 23

Where should she go? Not towards the Old Town. Somewhere out of the New Town. Only keep the house on Albany Street behind her!

Another shout, of rage and venom. She turned around now – she could not help it. Mr Badcock stood on the steps, the colour of a poisonous berry. He saw her and raised his arm towards her and shouted again. 'You whore!'

A woman on the pavement put her hand to her mouth.

She must run. Run!! Pick up her skirts and run! She must not trip, not stumble – only go.

Mr Badcock stepped onto the street and came after her, waistcoats flapping.

She must not mind the people who stopped and stared. She must not go her usual route, south, towards Eva. She must lose him in the backstreets.

Up the street, to the end of it and sharp round the corner. 'Help me!' she gasped out, to someone, a man in a top coat, coming towards her. But he frowned, only frowned, staring at her bare head, her sweat, her pallor.

'She is not in her right mind!' shouted up Mr Badcock, coming fast behind. 'Detain her, I am afraid she will do herself an injury!'

The man made a grab for her. 'Escaped from your nurse, have you?' But she ran around him and twisted away, stumbling over a loose stone, pain shooting up past her ankle.

She got to the second corner and looked to the left and right. She cannot ask for help – she will not be believed. He will get her and drag her back to the house.

'You think you can outrun me, you hussy?' Mr Badcock wheezed. 'You are a women, no woman can outrun me!'

Rebecca looked again, to see how far away he was. Ten feet, a little more. His arms swung over his stomach as he ran and his fob watch hit him in the belly at every stride.

'Stop that women, she is mad! Stop her!' he cried out between breaths.

An old man bent across her path to leer. 'Alas, my running days are past me. What's she done?'

Rebecca's feet were bad. She was still in the same pair of shoes that she had snatched up last night, made for the house, her toes had almost pushed their way through the front of them and she had a patch at her ankle that grated with every step. That alone was enough to make her weep, but, as well as that, the laudanum Mrs Shrivenham had sold her had not been enough. Sweat fell off her in sheets; her bodice was soaked through.

'Don't know why you're chasing her. Looks too cheap to bother with!'

'Catch her for me, will you?' shouted Mr Badcock.

'Not likely. Wouldn't like to dirty my hands!'

Rebecca had left behind her the familiar part of Edinburgh; now she ran, though her lungs burned with the effort of it, down a wide street with evenly planted trees that she had never come to before.

'Go on, dearie, run, whatever it is you've done to him,' said a woman, leaning against a tree, dressed twenty years younger than her face showed. 'I shall stick my foot out for you.'

'He wants to kill me!' Rebecca managed to get out.

'They all do, my dear. They all do!'

Rebecca forced herself on a few steps more and then looked back. The woman had done as she promised, Mr Badcock was not sprawled on the floor, but his pace had slowed and he was cursing. Rebecca put her hands to her side and pressed.

'I'll have you for that!' he cried, but the woman laughed and spun away from him.

'I doubt it, dearie, unless you've a shilling to spare!'

Mr Badcock coughed without covering his mouth. His face was mottled with red and white. He started running at her again. He was like a mechanical automaton Rebecca had seen once in a museum, wound up to his fullest.

Now the road gave onto another, bigger one, busy with carriages and wagons. A young man on a velocipede shouted out, 'Disperse, let me through!' The pavement was busy with people – anyone could stick out their hand and grab her.

She must cross this road and find a smaller one, lose him that way! But how? A man in a brougham poked his head out of the window and stared, his moustache stiff with surprise. He seemed about to pull his horse up and come back for her, but she ducked into the crowd, and when she dared look again he had gone.

But Mr Badcock was still behind her, his beard covered in spittle.

There must be a break in the traffic! Where, how could she get through? The noise so close to the edge made her want to cover her ears. Nothing but cabs and carriages and horses as far as she could see.

Now then! It must be now! Rebecca cast herself off, as if from a tall building, behind the wheels of a black-sided carriage, picking up her skirts as far as her knee. From one side of her, a whinny, a jangle of a bridle, a horse's white eye. 'What in God's name?' the driver shouted out, but the rest was lost in the mêlée. She swerved, her heart beating out of her chest. She had got to the middle of the road, traffic streaming past either way.

She wavered there for a breath. She had known a boy who was killed by a carriage, crossing a road like this. A dog cart jangled by. A brougham, she caught a glimpse of her reflection in the sides. No wonder people stared! If Mr Badcock were to catch up with her here they would both be dead.

She plunged in, hardly caring or seeing how she went. A four-in-hand, the horses' hooves striking on the stones, went in front of her, perhaps the wheels went over her skirt, she could not tell, for she was jolted forward and into the path of a pony cart. The driver, a swarthy man with a great beard, hauled his little pony round until she whinnied. But now Rebecca had a space, a thin one, and she threw herself onto the other side, stumbling on the pavement's edge and falling onto it.

She looked back for Mr Badcock. She could not see him.

P'raps he was killed. She hoped for it, but the traffic went on unimpeded, so he couldn't be.

She drew a great shuddering breath. But she must press her advantage; she dreaded to hear his gasping wheezing threats just behind her ear. On she went, the sore on her foot burning, her toes bleeding. She plunged down a side street but as soon as she was on it she longed to be out, for if Mr Badcock followed her here she was done for. She turned again, and quickly again. He was not here.

Now, at last, she slowed. There was no one behind her on this road but a child playing with a hoop. Rebecca saw that she was out of the centre of Edinburgh and into a plainer part of town where there were gaps between the houses and grass grew between the paving stones.

She leaned against a stone wall and took off her shoe. Now that her heart had slowed she wondered if she could walk at all. Could she risk going in her stockings? She no longer cared who stared at her. But it was too cold, too muddy, and there was a damp in the air that was not only down to the drizzle.

It was the sea! How had she not known it? She was more than halfway to her old home.

Or, as she saw it now, more than halfway to Gabriel's house. And miles away from anywhere else.

She had left the house without her reticule. No money then, to find a room, or even to buy herself a pie!

What then? Could she beg for a coin? Or earn it, in an alleyway? Or steal, from that baker's there ... that seemed to be the least painful way forward. They would not miss a roll of bread too much. Not yet, not yet. She would wait until she was desperate.

Where to go? Every house she gazed in now seemed to express an ordinariness that was lost to her for ever. Women standing by their fireplaces, servants polishing brass, cats arching their backs on the windowsill.

But what had become of Kitty Kat? Poor thing! He must catch his own mice now, though he had always been good at that. He would miss Eva as much as she did. She felt the longing to see her friend, to tell her what had passed, as a physical thing that clustered in her chest, and she staggered against a wall, and almost fell.

She rubbed her nose. She had not got gloves, there had been no time. She put her hands inside her cloak to cover them. The sea was near, it would be calming to look on, the sight of the blue spread of it would clean her mind. She went on, slowly now and limping. But when she got to it, the sea was just as grey as the sky, the pebbly beach washed up with yellow foam.

Her old home was very close; she could even see the corner of it, just the same as ever. And Gabriel's house, too, stood as it had always stood, with its neat pointed gables and whitewashed stone. She had got here without knowing it, without admitting to herself that she was going there. And she ought not to be surprised that the houses stood the same; a little more moss had grown over the wall perhaps, but it had not been so very long since she had left her father's house. If days had passed like years for her they had not for the stones and the trees and the gardens. But – she saw it now – she had nowhere else to go.

But Gabe would still be at the tannery. She would have to make polite talk with his mother! And about – what? Her murderous husband, her dead friend? Gabe's mother doted on her garden and wore her hair pulled back into a plain bun. No, she would have to wait here on this wall, or walk about on her sore feet.

But the maid opened the door of Gabriel's house anyway, and came towards her. 'You cannot stop here! Be off with you, we've nothing for you.'

'Arabella, it is I, Mrs Palmer. Rebecca Massey!'

The maid stepped back startled. 'Miss Rebecca? I beg your pardon, Mrs Palmer – I did not recognize you! What has happened – are you hurt, or ill?'

'Could I wait a while, for Mr Gabriel to return? I have something in particular to ask him. I need not cause you any trouble.'

The look on Arabella's face changed. 'You had best come in, then. Mr and Mrs Parsons are away visiting a relative; they are quite often away now, as perhaps you know.'

'I did not know it,' said Rebecca. She did not care for Arabella's look, which had grown disapproving.

'They got into the habit of it when Mr Gabriel was away and have not got out of it.' The maid paused, her hand on the door frame. 'Mr Gabriel does sometimes not return until late. P'raps you ought to return then?'

Rebecca picked up one foot and rubbed it on the back of her leg. 'Arabella, I am desperate, as you see here. Won't you let me in?' Wives ran away from their husbands, didn't they – she could not be the first to do it. There had been a case of it just now, in the aristocracy, only the wife had been called mad and committed to an asylum.

The maid pursed her lips but she let Rebecca in to the parlour with its view of the grey rocks and the grey sea without saying any more. Rebecca sank onto the easy chair. It was good, after all, to be out of Albany Street, out of the New Town. To look through the window and see the same view that she had seen since she was a child. It was good to let her head fall back on the cushion, and when she closed her eyes she still saw the sea swelling behind them.

Sometime in the middle of her sleep she felt herself lifted and tried to struggle, for she thought it was Alexander come to get her, but in the depths of it she recognized Gabe's voice, and she let herself fall again, and was put into a bed with deep pillows and a soft mattress where she again fell away into blackness.

CHAPTER 24

When Rebecca woke up she knew not who she was, or where she was, or when it was. And she would have liked to stay that way for longer, only there was Gabe's face above her, drawn together in concern.

Then came the longing for her salts, back in Albany Street. And after that, Evangeline. Her flight. Alexander.

'Rebe! What has happened? You *are* ill, I knew it.'

'What time is it?'

'Four o'clock.'

'In the afternoon?'

Gabe nodded.

'I have slept all day! Should you not be at the tannery?'

'I sent them a note.'

She sat up. 'Is there a pharmacy nearby?'

'What do you need? I will ask Arabella to fetch it.'

'My feet are aching and full of blisters. I ran a great deal yesterday in shoes that were not made for running, you see them there. I need some laudanum for the pain. Will you tell her?'

'I will tell her.' Gabe got up.

It would be the last time, she was certain of it. Rebecca drew the sheets around her and tried to smooth the hair from her face. She must smell terrible; she must look horrible. She ought not to be here.

When he returned she said: 'I am sorry I came; only I had nowhere else to go. My husband ... his friend Mr Badcock came after me, they want to do me harm, but I ran away, and I could not think of anywhere else to go.'

'You have no need to explain anything to me, dearest Rebe. I am glad you are here.'

Rebecca wiped her nose with the back of her sleeve. 'I only want a place to stay for a night or two, and a little money. I am ill, Gabriel, my husband has made me so.' She pushed her hair away again. She had been put to bed still with pins in it, it had not been brushed or put into a plait and it fell all over her face. 'That is not right. I have made myself so. Or – circumstances, that is it. Circumstances have made me ill.'

Gabriel looked at her, but said nothing. 'Is there a cure?'

'I must get myself away from Edinburgh for a while. A week, or more. That is the cure. I must be out of the city and then I hope I will get better.'

Gabe took hold of her hand with both of his and put it to his forehead. 'Oh Rebe,' he said, with his head still down. 'I have been out of my mind with worry since I saw you last! Let me go to your husband and tell him you are not coming back.'

'Oh Gabe, no, that is not the way. You cannot rescue me as if I were one of your boys at school! If you went to Alexander, he would find me out and they would come for me. I am his wife; it would be my word against his. No, let me get away. Will you help me get away?' Rebecca sat up and pushed against her bedclothes. She was sweating.

'Of course I will, Rebe, do not trouble yourself. But where will you go? You will not stay here? You ought not to travel too far.'

'I will go to Jenny, who used to maid for me. Will you get me some paper so I can write to her? She will understand, I think. She lives far away, in Argyll, in a croft. She was always talking about sheep. I don't think there is anything for miles around. I will be safe there.'

'But what will you do? Are you sure you will be able to recover without a doctor? A croft is bound to be damp and smoky. Are you sure it is the place to recover from whatever ails you, Rebe? You are so terribly pale.'

'Gabe!' Rebecca said. 'Stop fussing! I must go there, 'tis the only way.'

Gabe drew back his hand. 'I am sorry, Rebe. Only to see you like this, when I have for so long imagined you ...'

'Differently. I know. I felt the same, when first I saw you. But let me be! You left me alone for two years, and I learned to make my own decisions. Wrong ones, I admit it, but I am trying now to do it differently.'

Gabe looked down at the blanket. The back of his hand was freckled all over. 'Yes, I left you alone, and I shouldn't've. I've no right – I will do anything you ask, of course I will. Argyll, you say?'

'Oh Gabe – I am sorry. I swore I would never see you again, but I found myself here, by accident it seemed, in such desperate straits, and you said if I ever needed anything—'

'Hush, Rebe, whatever it is you want, I will get it for you.' He lifted his hand and touched his thumb to her nose. The gesture was so childish that Rebecca blinked and had to turn away.

'I will have to first get to Glasgow, and then another train to Inveraray. And afterwards a trap. I will have to hope the letter arrives safe, and that she does not mind to have me. I don't know what I will do after that! But I cannot think of it now. Has Arabella returned?'

'Not yet.' Gabe smiled. 'I have a few shillings saved up and I will gladly lend it to you, all of it. I think it will cover the journey, and food, and pay your way at the croft, for they cannot have much.'

'Thank you, Gabriel. I can't pay it back, not yet, not ever p'raps.'

'No matter, no matter at all! But, Rebe, will you let me go with you, at least part of the way? You will have to stay the night in Glasgow. Anything might happen!'

Now Rebecca smiled, though she was so unused to smiling that it felt unnatural. Then it *was* unnatural, because she remembered Eva, and felt guilty for smiling at all. 'You talk about Glasgow as if it were Timbuktu. The Glaswegians do the same to us. I don't think it is so very bad.'

'So you always said. I have heard terrible things.'

'Oh Gabe!'

'All right. I am sure they are fine people. But let me come with you! It is not safe for you to travel alone. Besides, you are not well. And – I will worry. I want to know that you make the journey there safely.'

She might rush off the train to buy laudanum, if the sickness got too bad. Rebecca pushed her hair back behind her ear. 'Aye then, until Glasgow.'

'And now let me draw you a bath, my dearest Rebe. To have you here under my roof, even in such desperate straits!'

'Oh Gabe!'

'And did you know, Father has had hot water put in? It is astonishing – straight out of the taps!'

They set off the next morning, just as light was coming through the weave of the woollen curtains and illuminating them. Gabe had found a case for her and had put two of his mother's dresses in it, and a shawl, some bonnets, a pair of gloves, a bar of soap, several books, pen and paper, and half a sovereign in a purse.

Rebecca sat back in the carriage, glancing through the window as they went through the city. Several times her hand flew to her cheek, but it was not Mr Badcock, only someone else with the same kind of topcoat, or bulk, or manner.

She must go, go to the wilderness, with only one fixed thought in her head: to be rid of her salts, her drops, any of it, at any cost. She must not think of the return, and what she would do then.

The last bottle of drops had helped little, and only pushed back the worst of her sickness, but the effect would wear off soon, even on the journey. For they had reached Waverley Station now and Gabe was steering her through the crowds towards the train. Though they had seemed to set out in plenty of time the whistle blew for the train straightaway and all around them people surged forward. So she was carried on, whether she liked it or no.

She held onto Gabe's arm, more for guidance than anything else, and they boarded a second-class coach, Gabe throwing up her bag to the man who was fixing the trunks on the roof just as if it were nothing. They took their place beside an old man in a kilt and a boy with a sack between his legs that would not fit above, and a young couple about the age of Jenny and Lionel. Rebecca turned her wedding ring round and round her finger underneath her glove. Her bonnet felt strange on her, and her shoes, that were both Mrs Parson's. She could have been someone else.

The porter strapped down the last bit of luggage above them and the carriage swayed and creaked, then the whistle blew again and the coach gave a great lurch and began to move. The young couple fell into each other and the girl giggled and pinked. Rebecca would have fallen out of her seat if Gabe had not thrown out his arm and saved her. The girl giggled again, taking them for lovers, or marrieds, but Rebecca could not meet her gaze. She turned her head away and stared through the window.

They were soon out of Edinburgh and into the countryside, a soft rainy mist pulsing down the outside of the windows and obscuring the views. She was out of the city, so easily, and Alexander and Mr Badcock left behind. But she was not out of their grasp, not yet. And here was green, and here were trees, and bracken, and all the time the train drawing her further away.

Soon the man in the kilt fell into a slumber and began to snore, lolling his head against Gabe's shoulder. But Gabe did not seem to mind; he sat very still and gazed out at the watercolour view. Probably the trains in Egypt were much worse.

The boy with the sack got off and the girl leaned her head against the boy and they both closed their eyes. She and Gabe had not exchanged more than a few words since they'd got on, hours ago now. Rebecca's skin had begun to creep, and a tickle had lodged itself in her throat, making her cough again and again into Mrs Parson's kerchief.

Darkness was already falling as they drew into Glasgow, though it was not yet five o'clock. But when they got to the station hotel there was only one room left. The clerk at the desk, seeing their crestfallen faces and thinking that they were a couple who could no longer stand each other, started to suggest somewhere else, not more than ten minutes off. But Rebecca, who had been buffeted and jangled all day in the train, shook her head.

'There is a daybed in the room?'

The clerk said there was.

'Let us take it, Rebe, and I will sleep on it,' said Gabe.

But when they climbed up the three flights of stairs Rebecca wished she had dragged herself to the other place. They both stood in the centre of the room and stared at the bed, with its red coverlet. There was hardly room for anything else. It reminded her, for a moment, of Eva's bed, with its red blanket, though Evangeline's always hung at an angle. She ought to be here with Eva instead! Rebecca had run away after all, but had prevented Eva from doing it.

She passed her hand in front of her eyes and half-fell against the bed.

'You are tired,' said Gabe. 'Will you lie down?'

'I was remembering my friend, Evangeline. Who died. I miss her, though we were always … always drifting about.'

'Died? I'm sorry!'

'Yes.' Tears slid from the corners of Rebecca's eyes. 'I ought not to be here, when she is dead.'

'Do not say that, Rebe. She would not like you to, if she

was your friend. Rest your head, like you always used to, just for a moment.'

Rebecca let herself be drawn in and put the side of her head on his chest so that she could hear the distant whirr of his heart.

'Why did she die?'

'An accident, of her own making.' She said nothing more, and he did not press her. Outside a boy gave a piercing whistle, and then a cry.

'That lad is awful loud,' said Gabe. 'I think he is selling hot wine outside. Shall we get a cup?'

So they went down and bought a cup from him, but the wine sat like vinegar in her stomach and made her queasy. 'How unlike Edinburgh it is! Everybody seems to want to be somewhere else. Can we go inside, into the coffee room? We could order some supper.'

The other diners at the hotel were men of industry or groups of English travelling up to the Highlands. The waiters danced around, whisking their towels and placing plate upon plate on the white tablecloths. It should have been a cosy scene, but the sickness was upon her, and everything Rebecca looked at filled her with gloom. The men of industry were supercilious, the English were noisy and nasal, and Gabe was looking at her too often, and frowningly.

Even so, she set upon her mutton chop and the potatoes and carrots in butter, and the gravy. When the blancmange came, held up next to a waiter's ear, she ate up her bowl so quickly that Gabe offered his too. The cream and the sugar and the strawberries together were as good as anything she had ever eaten.

But after she sat back and wiped her mouth with a napkin the awkwardness came back. Upstairs lay the room and its big red bed. But downstairs were the English and the men of industry, drinking wine, growing more grating by the second.

'Shall we go up?' said Gabe at last, and Rebecca was forced to say yes.

Gabe waited outside the room for her to undress, and she shed her clothes as fast as she could, leaping into bed and pulling up the sheets to her neck.

'You may come in,' she whispered.

He opened the door, an awkward smile hovering about his lips. Rebecca could not bear to see it. She turned her head on its lumpy pillow and stared at the flock paper-hangings. She heard the fumbling of his buttons coming undone and his sigh as he settled himself onto the daybed.

'You will be cold, Gabe. Your feet are always cold.'

'I have slept on worse, do not fret about me.'

'You are kind to come with me. I could not have borne it alone, after all.'

'Hush now,' he said.

But his feet and the bottom half of his legs stuck out over the end of the bed and he had only a thin grey blanket to sleep under. Nevertheless, he closed his eyes tight against her gaze, so she reached up and dimmed the lamp.

Gradually the noises outside fell away. Rebecca stared on into the darkness. She longed for her medicine. She longed for it so hard she fancied she could almost taste it. Again and again she drank it, imagined its spreading out, felt every care put away.

And then she longed for sleep, but it would not come. After a while she threw off her covers and went to the window. But it was past ten o'clock, no pharmacies would be open now, even in Glasgow. Her elbows ached with irritation, as if insects were shaking out their wings. She stretched out her arms, and shook them, and shook out her feet. She sighed, once, twice, three times. Her bed, with its tossed-about covers, regarded her balefully. The window rattled and a blast of cold air came through. She ought to stoke up the fire again.

Then a great and sudden racket came from outside, as if something metallic had been knocked from a carriage. Glasgow never really quieted, as Edinburgh did. She went to the window but there was no sign of the carriage. She had half-expected to see ships' panels littering the road on its way from the railway to the docks.

'What was that?' Gabe sat up. Perhaps he had only been pretending to sleep.

'I don't know. Something from the railway yard, perhaps.'

'Let me stoke up the fire.' He got out of his daybed and crouched in front of the fireplace, his woollen nightshirt stretched over his back as he worked to coax up a flame, the sound of the bellows heaving in and out. One flame leapt up, then another and Gabe sat back.

'You are still cold,' he said.

'No, only … well … I am hot and cold both.'

Gabe came over and rubbed her arms, put a hand to her forehead. Rebecca squirmed away.

'You have not a fever,' he said, looking at her with narrowed eyes. The glow from the fire made him look younger again, as he had looked before he left.

'In Egypt,' he began, 'a great deal of hashish is smoked. There is not the distrust of pleasure that there is here. It runs along the same lines as *kayf*.'

Rebecca stayed silent. She did not want to admit that she had read his letters over and over until she knew every line.

'I smoked it too, for a while. I think – well, it does not much matter what I think – but at first it made the world so much brighter, and then it became a consolation for – well, for the terrible things that kept me away from home.' He paused. 'I had to take myself away from Cairo, into the countryside, much as you are dong now. And then, when at last I gave it up all together, I craved nothing more than another cigarette.'

He had guessed then, at the reason for her illness!

'But hashish is a great deal easier than, say, laudanum, from what I hear.'

In the darkness, Rebecca's cheeks grew red. 'I have been weak. I have ended up like all those other women dreaming their lives away and now I am a slave to it. But my husband has made a new medicine – much greater than laudanum. I did not realize it was the same thing at first. He gives it to me. I expect you will hear of it soon, it is to be sold in every pharmacy round Britain.' From the next room somebody coughed. As if it was catching, Rebecca raised her hand to her mouth and coughed into it.

'Are you suffering, Rebe?'

'Not as greatly as I have done, when you left,' she said, before she could stop herself.

Gabriel sat with his hands clasped between his legs and his head bowed, pressing the side of his body into hers. Though she willed it not to, she felt herself grow warm where he touched her. She felt the texture of his skin, the warmth of his breath, the spring of the hair from his head, the point of his elbows, the sweep of his eyelashes, the particular width of his thigh – all of it – just there by the side of her, radiating heat, when the rest of her was frozen.

Just as the salts dimmed every pain and quelled every hunger, the lack of them had the opposite effect: her skin was on fire, tears slid from her eyes, she felt melancholy and crazed and hilarious all at once. She hungered, not only for food.

'You were the only reason I returned,' he said. 'Otherwise I would still be in Cairo, and die there.'

Rebecca shut her eyes. Points of flame still danced behind her eyelids. 'Why did you not take me, then? You knew I would have gone.'

'I thought I would prove myself, and come back to you better. I thought ...' Gabe sighed. 'I thought Egypt would be no place for a woman. But everything I thought was wrong. And that is what I have learned.'

Rebecca sneezed, which set up a tingling all over her body. She had not realized that the lack of her medicine would cause desire to flame up all over her.

'It is what I have longed for these two years, to be with you. But now that you are here in front of me ...' said Gabe, keeping his eyes on her.

The deepest part of the night had passed. A bird, fooled by the burning of the street lamps, had started to sing. Didn't she know, too, what it was to lose herself – and wasn't she, too, paying the price?

'Oh Gabe, I have hated you for so long! I thought I had put you away for ever.'

'And now?'

Slowly, as if in a dream, Rebecca reached for him and pulled the thin fabric of his nightshirt towards her. His hand came up and stroked the back of her neck. It set all the hairs on her neck and arms on end and pulled her nipples up into points.

She sighed. When she shivered he wrapped his arms tightly around her back and pressed his cheek into hers.

'I am not in my right mind,' she said. 'I feel as if all the skin had been flayed from my body, and my mind feels as raw.'

He said into her hair, without releasing her, 'We have this. Only this moment. And if I never am to see you again I will remember it.'

'I have hated you for so long. But now I find …' She moved forward an inch, then another. Their lips met. Gabe's were not so full as Alexander's and she could not get the feel of them at first, not until she felt the point of his tongue come out to touch her own, slippery and alive, and she pulled back, her breath coming hard on his cheek.

When they kiss again it is easier. Lips on lips. Tongue on tongue. His hand comes up to draw her face in, further in, until she grows dizzy, and will drown in it. She takes his other hand and puts it on her breast. The material of her nightgown is so thin that it does not feel as if it is there at all. His rubbing there sets up a line, a connection between her nipple and the place between her legs, tugging at her, pulling at her, until it is almost pain.

She takes his hand and puts it where she aches. His breath catches in his throat. He strokes her, flutters his fingers. Still they kiss but she is breathing so hard she has to draw her lips away.

Now they lie down, awkwardly, not wanting to lose contact, he on top of her, she struggling to free her legs and get them out on either side of his. 'How heavy you are!' she whispers into his mouth.

'And you, and you …'

She wants to feel him inside her. She takes him and puts him at the place. But now he seems to hesitate.

'Are you sure? You are married, and I—'

'Oh Gabe, do not stop now! Not now!' She gets her hands onto his buttocks and pulls him in to the centre of her, and then he does not hesitate any more, but moves against her, and slides, and moves, she is wet and dissolving into nothing but this. She builds to a greater and greater ache, she can feel him breathing into her ear: 'Oh my darling, my love.' He moves against her, so sweet, and so sharp until the point tips over and runs out and she is lost.

They lie together then, her breathing coming back, and with it, all of herself, until the weight of him grows too much on her where it presses against the floorboards and she presses him away.

He seizes her nose and her temple and kisses her again on the lips, softly. 'How I missed you,' he says.

She shivers, a final time. 'Let us go to bed now,' she says. But she cannot sleep, not until the dawn starts to press its way through the blinds and it is almost time to wake up.

CHAPTER 25

It was past noon by the time Gabe handed Rebecca onto the train bound for Inveraray. As he stood at the door he said quietly: 'People will think we are a married couple – oh, kiss me now before you go!' They kissed until Rebecca's heart was beating again, his hand winding into the hair under her bonnet. They kissed until a woman came up behind with a *humph!* and they had to break apart to let her on.

'Do you have to go, really? Could you not get better back in Edinburgh?' he said.

'At your parents' house? Sweating and trembling and having to explain why? They know me well enough to see that I am not my right self, and, oh Gabe, I could not bear that! For them to know what I am come to …' Rebecca let her forehead rest on the collar of his jacket; it prickled, but the prickling was a comfort somehow. 'It is bad enough that *you* know how weak and foolish I have been.'

'You have not been weak! Foolish perhaps. To marry that fiend.' He rubbed the back of her neck with the pads of his thumbs, she could feel where his skin cracked apart. He whispered: 'I only wish I did not have to let you go.'

'Excuse me,' said a young man holding a leather case, 'let me past, please!'

'Go to your carriage,' said Gabe. 'I will come to the window. We have a few more moments.'

Rebecca found a coach that was empty save for an old lady in a black cap behind her newspapers. She set down her reticule, pulled down the window and stuck her head through it. 'Gabe, here!'

He half ran, half skipped to her, snatched up her hand and pressed it to his mouth. Then he grew grave. 'Can you write to me, from the croft?'

Rebecca put her hand on his face. 'Yes, Gabe, I will write. And yes, I will miss you, most dreadfully. But I think, I am afraid, that even after last night,' she blushed and glanced at the old lady, but the old lady did not look up, 'things cannot be as they used to be between us.'

'Oh!' Gabe flushed. 'I know it. At least, I ought to have known it. I think I hoped ... But perhaps I would not have wanted it so, exactly as it was before. I was stuffed full of arrogance and pride.'

'Oh! The tannery, I understand it now – it is your way of making atonement! Is it?'

'Rebe, only you would have guessed that! A poor kind of atonement, most likely worthless, but it is good for my humility.'

'Your humility! Oh Gabe, you always wanted to be humble! And yet concentrating on it only made you more arrogant.'

Gabe flinched.

'I don't say you are still arrogant now. I don't say the tannery is the same, only, do you remember that boy – the boy that was bullied at your school? I forget his name.'

'I do not see how Fontmell is the same.'

'You were so proud of those scars, you could not wait to show me.'

'I know, I know, but it was better, wasn't it—'

'That you got the scars rather than the other boy they were aiming at, yes, it was.'

'But wasn't it? Fontmell was so small and thin and bullied most atrociously, and those pins thrown at him like that, I think they would have driven him out.'

'Oh Gabriel, yes, I am sure you are right. And a good deed is still a good dead, no matter what.'

The whistle blew then and the guard began to move along the train slamming doors. Rebecca took up Gabe's hand again and spoke quickly. 'Whilst I am gone can you find me a room in Albany Street, where I can look out at my husband's house? I must get in there whilst Alexander is at the pharmacy. I must find something that my friend Evangeline told me about before she died. Can you do it?'

'Anything, Rebe, I shall be glad to! And I am happy you are not returning to him, at least! Thank God for it, darling.'

The train was moving now, and he running alongside, twisting his fingers in her own, until the noise and the smoke grew too much and the tips of their fingers were pulled apart by motion.

Then Rebecca leaned her forehead onto the window and cried.

'Never mind, lass, you'll see him soon enough, I expect.' Rebecca started. She had forgotten the lady was there.

'I shan't!' Rebecca let herself say. 'I don't expect I shall ever see him again, at least ...' Not in *that* way.

'Did you have a row? Every marriage has its arguments. I was married for fifty-five years and we had an argument every day, round about noon usually.' She wheezed with laughter. 'And my husband lived until seventy-five!'

Rebecca nodded. 'Around noon, how did you manage it?'

'He got hungry then, I think that was the reason. A good argue puts the backbone into a relationship, I'm as sure of it as I am of this strap here.' She leaned into the leather strap as the coach creaked round a bend.

'It depends,' said Rebecca, turning her head to the window again, 'on whom you argue with.' Her breath quickly steamed up the view. Her toes were numb. She put her new reticule onto her lap and opened its clasp. Her nose was dripping, but surely Gabriel had not thought to put in a handkerchief.

But there it was! With violets embroidered in one corner – she had seen it up the sleeve of Mrs Parsons often when she was younger, she must have embroidered it herself.

Beneath the handkerchief, she saw it immediately, a letter, made up of several pages and folded together carefully; Gabe's writing. He had written lengthways and widthways on the same thin sheets from the station hotel. The words seemed to give them density.

Rebecca tore open the envelope, her hands were trembling so hard that she almost ripped the paper inside along with it.

You are my own, I feel as if I shall die if I can't have you for ever. But as you lie sleeping here I must hurry to explain, as I could not last night, explain what has kept me from you for so long.

I told you I learned nothing – that was not quite true – I learned that I was nothing. Nobody. But now you are here I am somebody – or – we are somebody perhaps, somebody new. Even for one night.

I must explain. Oh, I lose time just by looking at you, and how fitfully you sleep, and even so, how beautiful you are. It is strange to write this in a hurry, that I have written twenty times or more out in Egypt. Often I got as far as to give it to the boy to take to the post – and then I sent another boy after the first to retrieve him. And the longer time went on, the harder it was to write, until the thought of it weighed me down and I could not even put pen to paper.

She *had* slept fitfully and had not noticed Gabe writing anything in all the times she had roused herself, but perhaps she had not woken up, only dreamed she had.

'Bad news, lassie?' said the old lady. 'You look awful pale.'

Rebecca put her hand to her cheek. 'I don't know if it is good or bad.'

'Ach well, a visit to the countryside will right that, plenty of wind to burn some colour into your cheeks, right enough.'

I must explain!

I left hoping to make my mark on the world. And in the cause that the Bedouins took me to, the plight of the men at the canal, I thought I had found a way to do it.

Did you hear of the rebellion, did it come to the newspapers here? I think it must have, and you would have read it.

Oh Rebe, it was marvellous! The Bedouin are the most fearsome warriors you ever saw. They lent me a horse, a skinny creature, but fast, fast as a wave breaking. And they lent me a costume to match their own, not like the riders here wear, but light swathes of fabric wrapped all around which seem to blend into the wind. Writing about them again I see them so clearly, as if they are real and Glasgow is not.

They took me to see the men who worked the canal, who were slaves, or part of a forced labour camp, which means the same.

It was deep in the night, we had to go quietly to the men who slept at the canal's side on the bare ground, else the French would be alerted. Our orders from the British: to arm the workers ready for morning, to overthrow the French and bring an end to their slavery!

The sun's rays were already lighting up the eastern horizon, and the light fell in such a way on the dunes that everything seemed suffused with meaning. My heart began to beat violently, for, in my imagination I felt I had been called upon to do something for mankind! I thought that we were on God's side. We were doing what was right.

The Bedouin had given me a sharp spear, and as we crept along we armed the workers with more. But the men were starving and weak, and some could barely walk, let alone fight. So it was up to the Bedouin to take on the French, as soon as there was enough light.

You are still asleep, thank God, and I can still feel you, the memory of your face and your body ... that there should be <u>that</u>, and this, which I am coming to, in the same world ...

Rebecca put the letter on her lap and pressed her cheek to the window. She felt again the breadth of him, the hollow at his collarbone that she could put a fist in. The old lady had fallen into a doze, her cap fallen down almost over her eyes. The train leaned round first one bend, then another.

In the chaos of the fight a man – a boy, really – got struck down. He was one of those Frenchmen paid to keep the Egyptian labourers working, who whipped them sometimes, and refused them food. I should've hated him. The boy must've had a spear to his side because he cried out and clutched onto it and blood spilt out from between his fingers. What blood! I never knew blood gushed like that out of a man.

I must tell it, because in telling, you will understand why I kept away.

I often thought, afterwards, if the boy had not died at my feet, would I have come home and thought it all a great success?

I tried to help him. I tried to stem the blood with my hands but there was too much of it. His face got so white, Rebe. It was exactly like the marble on your father's mantelpiece. I thought of that, as I watched him die. What a stupid thought! I know only a little French, but he was calling for his mother, over and over again. Maman, Maman!

I must stop a moment and watch you. I am not the only one who has suffered, after all, and I have written so hard that my hand aches with it.

He must have written all through the night! Perhaps she had heard his pen scratching away and mistaken it for bed bugs. She had not had good dreams.

The Bedouin are hospitable, it is their way: they must feed and shelter any visitor to their tent for three days and nights. That was one of the things I most loved about them and so different to our pinched manners! But the British officers made a sport of their hospitality, they would go to the Bedouins' tents for some trifling reason, and sit, whilst the Bedouin slaughtered their lambs, and their chickens, and baked their bread, to feed them. All the time the British men sneered at them behind their backs.

One night the men were drunk on gin. I heard one of them, Snakes, say that they ought to give the whole thing up and go home. And the other said, 'Don't you like it here, Snakes, in all this land of plenty?' When they had stopped laughing Snakes said, quieter: 'Britain doesn't give two figs for the plight of the working man. Why, we have used forced labour a thousand times, on any railway you care to mention. Only difference is, the French have got at this canal first. All this is just jealousy. Men have died for jealousy.'

'Everyone knows that,' the other said.

But I hadn't known it! It came as a shock to me, Rebe, as you know it would have.

I know I did wrong to stay away without telling you, and I have hurt you, and Mother and Father too. But I made my own enquiries, and Snakes was right, and of course work started up on the canal again soon after, just as bad as before.

Everything I had thought of myself, and my home – you above anyone know how highly I had regarded both! Everything fell away. I went back to Cairo and took lodgings in a very poor part of town. I longed for the oblivion that I had had when I was with the Bedouin, living as one of them. I let my hair grow out and my beard, and then, because it was easier, I wrapped up my hair with a turban and afterwards, though I hadn't meant to, I found I could pass as an Arab again.

Only this time it was because I was a shadow.

I learned some Arabic. People started coming to me with bits of work, translations and the like, and in their eyes I saw myself as someone else. My life in Edinburgh no longer seemed real; each day I left my old life further and further behind. The hashish helped the days to pass, and I fell into a routine that seemed normal to me: a little work in the mornings, and in the evenings sweet tea at my local ahwas. The afternoons I passed with the help of hashish. I was largely alone and talked to no one except the men at the ahwas, who were my only friends, though they did not know what to make of me, I think.

In this way the weeks passed, until they passed into years.

And now at last I am back here, with you, in Glasgow! You are right, Glasgow is not as bad as they say. I still feel strange, gazing at you, and again everything is different, only this time it does not matter. I would be a fool to hang onto what I know, for life is made up of strangeness, is it not, Rebe? We are both strange, and we have met there.

You will wonder why I came back after all, when I did. It was quite a little thing that started it, I will tell it you quickly, for it is getting light.

I was quite unrecognizable, or so I thought, and drinking tea in my ahwas one evening. A lady traveller came in – she was not such a rare phenomenon, many come to see the Pyramids – but women were never seen in my ahwas. But as she was foreign they let her pass, and she in turn did not seem to mind their stares. She was used to it, I dare say. But somehow in the course of it – I will never know how, she recognized me as one of her own. She was from a small town in Perthshire! We fell into conversation and spoke a great deal of home. I found the damp, the weight of the buildings, the smell of rain, all coming back to me. I broke into tears there and then. She thought I was cracked! Of course, I was crying for you – for what use are buildings and drizzle if they do not have you in them? The lady, with her talk, had brought back a part of me I had thought lost. And it followed on that I must set sail, immediately, for I saw straight away that I had been away too long.

And I left on the next steamer, and I am here.

How you are tossing about, my darling! I think you will wake soon, I must—

Rebecca turned over the page. But there was no more. She must have woken then, and not seen him. But now she thought on it, she had only stared down at her own legs, which were kicking about, to see if they belonged to her.

Well, she had his reason now, after waiting so long for it. She folded up the letter and put it back in her reticule and waited again, this time to watch how she felt.

But she only felt as if she must leave her seat and walk about. Her legs still had an itch to them and she longed to stretch them. She only felt as if she must yawn, and put her arms up to the ceiling, and yawn again till her eyes watered.

She only felt as if she must endure these next few days, else fall back into the grip of her husband, and then she would never feel again.

And Gabe – and last night – she must put from her mind, though if she put her nose to the gap just above the button of his mother's gloves she could smell him still.

CHAPTER 26

As the train steamed into Inveraray Rebecca saw that her note had arrived: Jenny had come to meet her, her face shining out through the gloom.

'I thought you'd prefer it if I was here. It's only an hour's drive but it can be awful lonely in a bad frame of mind!'

They embraced. 'Oh Jenny, it is good to see you!'

'But you look bad, Mrs Palmer. Thank God you have got away. Have you come to get yourself better?'

Rebecca hadn't said as much in her note. But of course Jenny knew; she must have known all along. Rebecca could weep – had she been the only one who had not been able to see what was coming? 'Did you hear of Evangeline?' she said.

'Aye. A bad business. I am sorry for you, Mrs Palmer, right sorry.'

'Please call me Rebecca – after everything, let us not be formal!'

'Rebecca, then.'

They climbed up into the dog cart and squashed up together by the driver. And what a comfort it was to feel Jenny's body pressed alongside her own up in the trap, and to have her draw the blanket tighter around her as the mist came down and drifted around them all as the little pony clattered along.

'I am glad you returned home. I had dreaded that you were out on the street, or somewhere worse.'

'Yes, I am here. But would that I were in Edinburgh still.'

'Why did you not stay – could you not?'

'With your reference I thought it would be easy. I got an interview with a lady in the New Town, but Lionel came to me and told me I should not go.'

'Did he not want to keep you close by?'

'Oh yes, he wanted nothing more. But Mr Badcock had asked after me at the pharmacy. Of course, Lionel refused to tell him where I was, but he worried about it. He worried Mr Badcock may find me out, or spread rumours to my new employers. And so we both decided I would be better off back here.'

They had left the town and its two markers of society: the huge castle with its iron railings, and the low-lying prison with its iron bars. Almost immediately the road narrowed until it was no more than a grass track leading over the hillside. And now they were trotting along inside the belly of a cloud; the tartan rug pulled over their legs was not thick enough. Rebecca's skin pimpled and her clothes rubbed against it like sandpaper.

'Your teeth are chattering! Look, have my portion of blanket.'

'No, Jenny, I cannot – do not give it to me. Look now, you have made me cry.'

'Do not cry, Mrs Palmer, I thought you had come to get away from that.'

'Rebecca, I beg you!' Rebecca rubbed at her eyes. 'I am crying because I do not want you to get frozen on my account. I think I bring you nothing but trouble.'

'Do not say it! I will always help you, I am happy to do it.'

The driver was looking at them both frankly, taking in Rebecca's good cloak and bonnet with its woollen flowers sewn by Gabriel's mother, and Jenny's dirty coat and skirt that had been patched twice at the front. Seeing it Rebecca bloomed with sweat again and every fibre of her dress seemed to press harder onto her skin and made her want to throw it off. It seemed they were going very far, towards nowhere. The enormity of what she had to go through struck at her.

'From the city, is she?' the driver asked Jenny.

'Aye.'

'Come to get well?'

'Aye.'

'Dare say she spends her time indoors.'

'Aye,' said Jenny.

'Lot of diseases they have there, right enough,' he said.

P'raps it was not too late – they had not left Inveraray so long ago. Rebecca grabbed Jenny's arm. 'Could we ... could we go back, d'you think? We have not yet gone such a great distance and there is something I need from one of the shops back there.'

But Jenny turned to her and stared. 'We have come too far to go back now. We have everything we need back at the house.'

'But I think we must! Oh Jenny, can I not visit the pharmacy there? I should not be above a minute. I have forgotten something I need.'

It used to be her giving the orders, and now it was her taking them. Rebecca squirmed further into her seat and told herself that she was stupid, and a worm, and unfit to crawl across the face of the earth.

'You have come here, Mrs Palmer, to get better. I think you should. I think more drops would only delay it.' Jenny squeezed Rebecca's arm.

Rebecca felt a sob rise to her throat, whether of gratitude or desperation she could not tell. And this too – Jenny knew Rebecca's mind, what was inside it.

The driver slapped his reins on the pony's back and turned to gape at her again, his eyes glinting through his mass of beard and hair. 'What's the matter with her?' he asked Jenny.

'She hasn't brought a thick enough coat. She is cold, that's all.'

'That'll be as she's from Edinburgh.' He slapped down the reins again and the trap lurched forward. 'Probably no used tay being out o' doors over-much, is she?'

Jenny spoke quietly. 'I have told Mother that you are here

on your husband's business, and you had a romantic notion about staying in a croft, as some of the English do. I had to tell her something, but I have left it vague.'

Rebecca nodded, too miserable to speak. It *had* been a ridiculous idea, hadn't it? But she had been desperate. She had fled, she was still alive. She let herself lean into her friend's shoulder while the trap bounced and jerked them forward into the mist.

At last they pulled up outside a single-storey stone cottage, its white stones fading into the whiteness all around. Rebecca pushed off the blanket and stumbled down from the cart. A woman came out of the door without a cap, Jenny's mother. Rebecca swallowed and raised her hand and tried to smile. The ground, just there on the boggy path that led to the house, looked good enough to lie down on; she would have done it if she could have borne the mother's look.

She must get in the house and – what? A bath was what she longed for, but they would not have it. Get out of her clothes, then. Lie down.

Mrs Campbell was frowning. Rebecca stumbled forward. 'Good afternoon. I am Mrs Palmer. Thank you so much for opening your house! I am afraid I have been taken ill on the journey. It is such a long way and I am weaker than I thought. But it is so kind of you to have me for these few days, while I rest, between … business.' Her voice shook.

'My mother speaks only Gaelic,' said Jenny. 'I told her you have been looking at the pharmacy in Inveraray, for your husband's business. It is a good one, known for miles, though I dare say she wonders why you have come so far.'

Jenny spoke to her mother, and then to Rebecca. 'I was reminding her of Mrs Macdonald's goitre that everyone thought would kill her, and the chemist there gave her something to put on it that made it drop off in a week. Perhaps that will convince her!'

Mrs Campbell wiped her hands on her apron. Was there suspicion in the woman's gaze? Then Rebecca could go to the hotel, back in Inveraray, it would be better. 'I don't mind staying in a hotel; I think I am putting you to too much trouble!' she said. If the pharmacy was as good as they said then she could buy her drops there without problem and retire to the hotel. Gabriel had given her enough for it.

But Jenny must have heard the eagerness in her voice because she said hurriedly: 'Not too much trouble, Mrs Palmer, we already have the bed made up.'

And they had. When she saw it, Rebecca felt even more the madness of her position here: the bed was nothing more than straw pulled together with string and topped with a woollen blanket. Yellow shafts poked out through the wool. The house itself was only one small room. There was another bed of similar arrangement by the side of it, and a fire belching out dense smoke in the middle that filled the whole place.

'Where do your sisters sleep?'

'Mother and Mhairi and I sleep here.' Jenny pointed to the bed. 'The others have gone to Canada.'

'To Canada?'

'It is better there than here; they have all emigrated. Rhona has a husband already and the others hope they may find one.'

The idea of it made Rebecca feel a moment of gladness – a new life – it *was* possible!

'Mother still feels it awful hard,' Jenny went on.

'Have you any money?' said a voice near the fire.

'Oh yes, money!' Rebecca started. She had meant to give it to Jenny's mother, outside. Most of the crofts had gone long ago, evicted by landlords who burned them to the ground and left the crofters on the hillside to die. The ones that were left had to struggle.

'Mhairi! Don't ask like that – it is rude.' Jenny turned to Rebecca. 'Mhairi does not ask for it for herself. She likes to count it, and sort it, and arrange it in rows, whenever we have any coins. Which we do not, so often! But it stops her from her weaving, and we need her weaving to live by.'

'But I meant to pay you – I mean, pay my way,' said Rebecca, blushing. 'I must, I insist upon it.'

Now that her eyes had got used to the light, Rebecca saw that the little croft was not as gloomy as she had first thought. It was true that the walls were bare stone, with gaps in it through which wind darted, and the roof was wooden. Every so often bits of peat fell through the rafters from above. But a good dresser took up most of the top wall, with stacked tin plates and cups. A single chipped china mug hung from a hook in the middle as if on display. Spindly wooden furniture of different dimensions made up the rest, except the loom. A short shelf was nailed above the bed, with two books upon it, and a piece of soap that looked to be new.

'That soap, is it from the pharmacy in Edinburgh?'

'Oh yes,' said Jenny, blushing. 'Lionel gave it to me.'

'Sent it to you?'

'No, gave it, some weeks ago.'

'But it is new, it is hardly touched!'

'It is too good to use. Every time I think I might be dirty enough, I think 'tis a pity to waste when the water is so cold. And besides, the soap was a gift.' She frowned, and then smiled.

'It is only two days' journey that separates you – could he not visit?'

'It may as well be two years!' said Jenny. 'I cannot leave here for even a day, not at the moment, when money is so short. But p'raps one day I shall return. I would like to. Not as a maid. In some other profession.' She tugged down her shirt and pointed to the shelf. 'See those books there? They are mine. After you started me off, I found I could not pass by letters in the same way that I used. I wanted to read, so I have taught myself, more or less. There is an old lady who is glad of the company, not too far from here – she helps me. I find there is some pleasure in it after all, and 'tis thanks to you.'

'I think reading is a gift that all us women should have. I thought that about my medicine once.'

'But I can see you drooping, Mrs Palmer, it has been a long journey. Would you like your bed?'

'Perhaps I could lie down, just for a moment.'

Rebecca was gladder than she thought she could be to lie down on her lumpy mattress and rest her head on her pillow that made her sneeze. Even so, she felt sure she would never sleep. The straw was full of creatures, she could hear them rustling about under her head. But after a while the murmuring voices and the rustle of the sheep that stood in the next door shed lulled her into an uneasy slumber, where her skin crawled with straw insects and her eyes itched.

When she awoke the soup was ready and she drank it down, and another bowl, until she dared not ask for more. Then she lay down again under her blanket and stared at the fire. Her nightgown smelled of Gabe. It ought to comfort her, but it only made her feel more alone. Her toes were numb and she pressed them into the back of her knees to warm them, and must have slept again, because when she looked again the fire had died back to its embers and was giving out a low hissing sound.

Now Rebecca felt wide awake. She must get up then; she could not lie here itching. She pulled her blankets over her shoulders and went outside.

How cold it was! The shape of the loch, which she had not noticed in the fog, pricked through the darkness. A heron was standing motionless near the shore, its legs disappearing into perfectly black water, its beak tucked into its feathers. There was a rightness to it that pierced her heart.

Last night had only made the missing of Gabe worse. And Eva was dead and lying in her coffin, alone – and she had a husband whom she hated – and who wanted to kill her – and – where was comfort? Her father? God? And here she was, in a bog, at the end of the road, behind a clump of bracken, just as insignificant as that insect there crawling along a frond.

Tears fell straight out of her eyes and onto the stones. Nothing there, no one to see it, no tree to grow watered by her tears, no one to bear witness. She sobbed harder until her nose ran and she had to scrub at it with her palm, only her palm was streaked with muddy sand, and scratched her skin, and made it worse.

No God but the heron, and the curlew calling out over the water. Stones pressed into her knees and bog pressed into her feet. Far away a gull screeched, it seemed a confirmation of her aloneness, and she cried again.

Finally she sat back.

She would have to face the day. There would be chores to be done, she could help the family; it would pass the time. And now, Rebecca was surprised to notice, she felt a little better.

She got back into her pallet of straw and watched the morning creep in through the stone walls. As soon as Jenny stirred, Rebecca got up again and washed her face and in between her legs from a pail at the back of the house, and asked what she could do.

Mrs Campbell went off to the shore to collect kelp. Mhairi sat down to her loom. So Rebecca, just as Jenny had used to do for her, set to brushing the floor, and heating water over the fire, and setting the beds straight. After lunch she sat and watched Mhairi weave until her head lolled. After her tea she went for a walk and when darkness fell, she slept, fitfully.

And the next day the same. And the day after that the same, only now Rebecca felt a little strength returning to her limbs. She did not feel as if she would rather lie down in front of the brush and be swept away herself. She did not feel as if she would rather fall into the bed as she was making it. Rather – this struck her as she was setting another of Mhairi's rows straight on the hearth: a shell, a seed pod, a thimble – she felt a rising and quite unlooked-for joy. The oppression had lifted from her crown as a black hat might lift away, and now she felt this new thing – happiness! So fierce it buzzed in her ears.

She went over to Mhairi and gave her a kiss. But the girl flinched.

'I'm sorry, Mhairi, only I don't think I have felt this well in all my life! I ought not to have forced myself on you. Here, let me.' Rebecca bent down and pushed the clam shell back into place.

And as she felt stronger, her thoughts turned to Alexander. Could she go into his pharmacy and let out the leeches, and tip out the salts, and mix them with ammonia, and scratch up his counter, and cut up the orange peel and swap the lozenges for the pessaries? It felt good to think of it.

But it was not enough. It would only annoy him and she needed to do more than that. She needed to destroy him. But how? First she must find whatever it was that Eva had found just before she died; perhaps that would spark a plan.

CHAPTER 27

'You look better, much,' said Gabe, pulling her towards him. Into the hair just behind her ear he added: 'But you need a bath, a hot one.'

It was true, she smelled of chemicals, she had noticed it herself, as if she had been too long in Alexander's laboratory. She had sweated the sickness out but somehow it clung to her still.

'But I care nothing for your cleanliness,' said Gabe, drawing her back to look at her face. 'Kiss me again!'

Rebecca looked about her. 'I cannot – we are in Edinburgh now! But is there a bath in the rooms you have got for me?'

'A shower-bath, yes. The rooms are not fine, they are rather dirty, but they are near to your house and have one good long window looking out onto the street, where you may just about see your front door, if you crane your head.'

'You smell better than I, for once,' said Rebecca. 'What has happened – they have invented a violet bath for the hides rather than a pure one?'

'Would that they could! No, I have left the tannery. I thought I would look for another kind of work. I thought, if

I was to ever see you again – I know we cannot be together as we were in the hotel – but I mean see you at all, it would be better if I did not smell of dogs' leavings.'

'Ha! Well, I cannot pretend to like you better when I have to hold my nose.' She laughed and they turned and began to walk away from the noise and steam of the station, his hand lightly touching her elbow. She was dismayed to feel her heart beat harder at the touch, it was a waste of blood to feel that way.

'You read my letter?' He stared at her, chewing on his lip and frowning. The gesture was so familiar that she had to turn away. But Gabe mistook the movement for anger, or something like it. 'It held nothing for you. I was afraid it would not! I ought not to have tried to explain myself; it is another form of selfishness, to want to.'

'No – do not think that! I am glad you wrote it. We feel the same – and I understand now, I think, why you stayed away.'

Gabriel waited, still frowning, still chewing on his lip.

'But it does not change the fact that I am married to Alexander.'

Gabe sighed. 'Amongst the Bedouin it is easy to divorce. A man need only say to his wife "I divorce you" three times and it is done.'

'And if a wife wishes to divorce a husband, what does she do?'

They walked on. 'She can only run to her father's tent,' said Gabe.

'And what happens to her, afterwards? Is she cast out?'

Gabe nodded.

'I thought as much! And I suppose he keeps the children, as he does here. And all her property, as he does here.'

'You are right, Rebe,' said Gabe. 'Though things are changing, do you think?'

'A little. Too slowly.'

After a while they came to the streets that Rebecca knew so well – there was the ash tree she had watched bud and leaf, there was the house where the dog was always barking from behind a closed door. But it all now seemed, to her eye, quite different. The tree was bare, its leaves stuck wetly around its trunk. The dog was quiet. Shutters were being raised and doors were being slammed.

'I think we should part now, Gabriel. In case anyone should see. I must creep in alone.' A dread of her lonely and unfamiliar rooms came over her. 'Thank you, Gabe, for the rooms. And the money.'

'But he cannot hurt you, not when I am near. And surely you do not fear scandal?'

'No, but I still fear *him*.' A shiver, like a memory, ran through her. She could not stay in these rooms for ever. What would she do then? Well, she must see.

Gabe drew her to an alley and kissed her hard on the lips,

his other hand pulling her in at the small of her back.

'Let me go!' she said. She could not bear it. She wanted to be away from him, to think.

But when she drew back Gabe had tears in his eyes.

'It is hard to let you go again, when I have just found you!'

'I know, I know. But we must.'

Her rooms, when she came to them, were plain, as Gabe had said. A narrow bed, a stove much like the one Eva had had. The floorboards were cheap pine dyed darker to resemble oak.

If only she could have told her friend that it was possible to leave the medicine behind! Even though it had run through her and changed her in some way, at the level of her cells. Another rush of loneliness ran through her and she turned towards the window and stared out.

How strange it was to see everything from a different angle! From here she could see old Mrs Pringle sitting at the window, playing solitaire by the light of her lamp, as she must do every night. And Mr Todd, striding up and down in his living room, shouting angrily at his children. Whenever she had chanced upon him on the street he had been all politeness, and his children silent.

Number 19 was in darkness. But there, sitting by the railings outside, was a poor wet cat, his fur pressed down onto his bones. She would have hardly recognized him! Without putting on her cloak or bonnet Rebecca quickly ran down and over to the other side and scooped up the cat under her arm.

'Oh Kitty! Weren't there enough scraps for you down there in the Old Town?' Rebecca bent and scooped him under her arm. She rubbed her hand across his back. 'You are too thin! Nothing but bones. Oh dear Kitty Kat, I will take care of you for as long as I can! Only, I do not live here any more, you see, dear Kat. Come with me across the road, over here, see now. And do you miss Eva very much? So do I. But if you stay with me perhaps we will find those papers. Then I might have a better idea of what to do.'

Rebecca slept badly, dreaming of fighting her way through a thick forest. When she awoke it was still dark and Kitty Kat was curled on her chest, his tail draped over her face. She longed, with a keen pain, for her medicine. If it could be as it was the first time, when she could take it innocently! Life had been simple: no other choice, no other course of action, but to have her medicine, and then wait.

She would never believe she could have grown so nostalgic for such a time. Now there were too many choices, and fear, and anxiety.

Laudanum, perhaps … the nearest pharmacy …

Rebecca put her palms to her temple and pressed them together. Not today. Not now. She must hold her nerve.

She waited then, by the window, for the street to wake up. Air came in through it and cooled her tea faster than she could drink it. Her emotions came over her as strongly as a child's: she was near to tears when she heard a boy whistling 'Bonnie Heather' in the street. A patch of blue sky brought a lump to her throat. Then the first men left the houses, and the first housemaids came to the steps and shook out the rugs. It was not yet nine o'clock.

Pray God Mrs Bunclarke had stayed at the house and she could get in! But she had not been away so very long, not so many things could have changed, could they, except for her?

It was too early to visit the shops. Even so, there was a woman from the New Town coming down the street, alone. Though this woman had not the stride of someone bent on shopping, she was more furtive, and vague: her feet slip-slopped along the pavement. She had the fair hair of a fashionable woman, but there was something awry.

She reminded Rebecca of Eva – Rebecca half started up – but Eva was dead, she was being foolish. The window was not clean enough, that was all. She spat into her palm and rubbed the glass with her sleeve. As she squinted down again she saw that the woman was Violet.

But what would Violet want with Alexander? Perhaps she had come to visit Rebecca, not knowing she was away. She'd had a habit of visiting her at odd times in recent weeks. But Alexander himself came to the door; Rebecca caught a moment of him as he stood there: she knew his eye, but not his beard, which had grown in.

How thin Violet looked, how unwell! But how her face lit up, to see Alexander. It was he, then, that she had come to see, not Rebecca.

Poor girl! She must warn her, she must get her away. But not today – she dare not risk it.

Twenty minutes passed. Thirty. Then Violet came out again, in a dazed kind of way, and set off towards the New Town. Soon after came Alexander, pausing on the step to brush something from his jacket. He blinked rapidly, surprised to find himself out of doors. His beard was patchy, as if he had not meant to grow it after all. He went in the direction of the pharmacy, and turned the corner.

Rebecca pushed back her chair; her legs were stiff. Kitty Kat leapt down from her lap with an angry thud. Rebecca drew on her cloak and tied on her bonnet and pushed her hair up into it, smoothing the wisps behind her ears. 'Now, Kitty, you stay here. Look, here is a little milk. There now, do not follow me, I shall be back soon – I hope. And if I am not, look, I will leave the window open just a little. If you get desperate you can push your paw through the crack there. You will have to take your chances on the street, but that will be better than starving to death!'

Rebecca closed the door in the cat's face and crossed the short distance to her house. She had not her keys and must pull on her bell, as if she were a visitor. Her heart was beating hard.

At last, here were footsteps, in no hurry at all. But what if it was Mr Badcock, staying here in her absence? She must turn back and watch a little longer! But the door had been pulled open, and Rebecca, who had been sure she would see Mr Badcock's great jowls saw, instead, the lesser ones of Mrs Bunclarke.

But if Rebecca felt relief, the other woman felt surprise.

'What are you doing here?'

Rebecca put her hand to her throat to stop her pulse beating. 'I have been to my aunt's.'

'Do you have an aunt?'

'Oh yes, poor thing, she has been quite incapacitated. And no daughters to take care of her, so I have been busy,' said Rebecca. 'And actually, I am only visiting, just for the day.' The hall was just as she had left it – what else did she expect? Only now, everything in it reminded her of her medicine.

She turned towards the cook. 'I have come back, Mrs Bunclarke – it is rather irregular, I know – as a kind of surprise for my husband. It is for his birthday, did you know?'

Mrs Bunclarke shook her head. She had a drip hanging from the end of her nose but it took her an age to reach inside her sleeve and pull out her handkerchief. 'He never told me. He ought to have, if he wanted something special.'

'Nothing special! At least, I am organizing something in particular for him. He thinks me still with my aunt, and I would be very grateful if you would not mention my visit here.'

'He never told me,' she said again. 'Will you be having lunch?'

'I do not think so, no. For I would not like Mr Palmer to return and find me out!' She tried to keep her voice light, but there was a catch in it.

She would not untie her bonnet, in case she needed to flee. Her cloak she took off and put on the chair near the door. Then she ran upstairs, pulling herself up the banisters, to Alexander's bedroom. Her breath was coming fast. It was hard to search for something when she did not know what she was looking for. But there was nothing in his drawers, nothing in his bed, or under it. Every surface was clear, nothing to see, hardly anything in the room at all.

Back out then, to the corridor. Nothing on the marble table, nor on the little shelf above it. Think! Where would Alexander keep a set of papers that he did not want anyone to see? She had thought it would be in his bedroom, but, as she went back downstairs, more slowly this time, she realized: in his study, in the same room that she had found the shoe. He did not expect anyone – any woman – to go in there.

The house seemed to know she was trespassing; it creaked and groaned around her. She pushed open the door, half-expecting to see the shoe there again, in its wrong element. But there was no shoe. Only Alexander's notebooks, which she had seen a thousand times, in the same place as the shoe had been. Notebooks, bound with tape at the spine, faded marbled covers. He was always writing in one or other. Could Eva have meant them?

She walked towards them, pulling at her lip. This was too easy. But then the men would not expect women to want to read such notebooks, densely written on and annotated in the margins. They would not think of hiding them. P'raps Mr Badcock had even taken them to Eva and left his bag open for her to see. She pulled the first towards her.

But it was only notes for the pharmacy, records of things bought and sold. Rebecca put the book back, sliding it onto the papers underneath in her haste to be away. But the papers were poorly held together and tumbled down, fanning out on the floor.

In bending down to pick them up Rebecca caught sight of the writing on the first side, still close and cramped and festooned with crossings-out.

We applied 15 drops of laudanum to Patient E after a violent shock of the heart owing to an occurrence at her place of work.

Patient E? Now Rebecca's hands were trembling so hard she thought she might never be able to read more. She put the sheets back on the floor and leaned forward with both hands.

Before she ingested the drops she reported a good deal of nervous energy concentrated about the solar plexus.

After one hour we came to her again and she reported a change in her person, namely, the strength and turbulence of her agitation had subsided. To this had succeeded a state of being uncommonly serene and tranquil. When Patient E was questioned about the previous injury done to her person she recalled it only in the mildest terms: 'emotion recollected in tranquillity', to use Mr Wordsworth's phrase.

Rebecca blinked twice, three times. Ran her knuckles across her lips. Turned over.

In this case we calculated that P was equal to 30 (Where P = Pain), owing to physical and mental anguish following on from an incident at the bawdy house. Accordingly we gave her 18 drops in the morning.*

It was Eva. He had made a study of Eva. And, her heart turned itself over – Alexander, with all his probings, squatting down by her side, after she had had her drops – he must have made a study of her too.

One hour later Patient E reported a great warmth and general unusual glow about the chest, in direct opposition to her anxieties of the previous 12 hours.

And across the margins: ** *30 drops of laudanum will be found to be equal to one grain of heroin salts.*

Rebecca turned to the next page, her breath coming quickly. In the kitchen Mrs Bunclarke moved pans about and dropped one, and cursed.

Owing to the nervous nature of women, and the extreme susceptibility of the female race to stimulation both positive and negative, we find that heroin is the best method to regulate the weaker half of our sex. Many who have been unproductive members of society may be cured! It is not too great to claim that we may perhaps hold in our hands the formula of happiness.

That was what they had wanted all along! They had wanted Eva and her subdued. Unable to laugh or shout, or run away. The shoe was part of it. The very last shoe any woman could run away in.

The great benefit of Patient E is that her life is such as it is provides a great many events, each of differing magnitude, and hard to tolerate by the patient herself, owing to her fallen nature and her nervous constitution. That is where our experiment can flourish!

Eva! Poor dear Eva. She had found this, had perhaps known it all along, but even so could not escape.

Note: For the measurement of pain, both mental or physical, we have assigned both the Non-Verbal Pain indicators designed by Mr Hunter, and Mr Lesseques and Mr Hayman's Symptom Assessment System, where 0 is no pain. See Blue book for further description.

Where P = 3, a worry or anxiety, we found H = 1 grain on average. We also, through repeated experimentation, have come up with a formula of a 1:3 increase of P to H depending on severity.

More of this, equations and annotations and corrections. Rebecca turned to a further page, which had spread out towards the door, her eyes passing over it all bit by bit. She was growing dizzy; she must rest her forehead on the papers and close her eyes, and then go on.

These pleasant sensations were not new, they were felt but to a lesser degree, on ascending some high mountains in Perthshire. (NB This means the brain contains within it its own salvation! One day could we not train minds to produce the chemical analogous to opium for themselves? But – alas – there is no money in it.)

Perthshire – that was she! She had told Alexander, when first he had given her the medicine, in the first flush of her feelings. She had enjoyed, back then, the attention he had given her, which she realized now, her heart falling, always came one hour after her draught.

Patient B is of a malleable disposition and will make an excellent subject for the study. However, one difficulty with the patient lies in the necessarily docile life that a wife must lead. To which, on the first occasion, I was lucky enough to apply to her the most strenuous emotion a wife can feel – that of her husband's infidelity. NB Does it not being true, by which I mean, true as she thought it to be so, compromise the experiment in any way? I think not, due to her belief of its being true.

Although the main part of our experiments lies in the direction of suffering and mental difficulties and their alleviation, it may be worth exploring their opposite, to see if a draught can subdue an excess of pleasurable emotion, which also may disrupt the feminine character and indeed often has. To that end, Mr Badcock has suggested I take Patient B to the Gymnasium for an outing, to observe the effect of well-formed men on her disposition, and then to make her docile again with the draught. NB This will be an invaluable experiment for husbands of all kinds!

Rebecca drew back with a breath. Had she been watched even then? And how would Alexander find her now? He would expect her to be crushed, upon reading this. But she was not crushed, she was angry. She felt the anger as a swelling and engulfing tide.

But something nagged at her; something was not right. Why had Alexander and Mr Badcock come after her with a syringe and tried to kill her?

Because she had seen him in the house of flagellation. Because he knew about Gabe.

No. She pinched the skin between her eyes. No – it made no sense.

If she was Patient B then would they not want her alive, for more tests?

They had come after her only to subdue her. The anger had come from their fears that she would not be subdued.

But Rebecca had underwritten Eva's death, had she not, in – oh, countless ways? She ought to have run away with her when she asked. She ought not to have let her take the second injection. She ought not to have … *they* ought not to have let the days go by together drunk on their medicine, at all.

She sighed, smoothed her eyebrows apart with the tips of her fingers and stood up, meaning to go back to her rooms. But she had got up too fast, the blood rushed away from her head and the ground swam before her eyes. She staggered forward onto Alexander's desk, knocking it with her hip bone.

She held her breath. But the cook still banged down her pots on the sideboard in her usual way. But in knocking it she had dislodged another set of papers that lay beneath, bound together tighter, that she had not seen.

There on the front page, written very neat:

Talk to be Given before the Royal Society of Chemists: The Formula of Happiness.

Or: *An Attempt to Correct the Feminine Problem with Reference to Heroin (the Aim Being to Establish a Working Formula).*

Rebecca sat down again and pressed her hand to her head. She glanced at the clock. Alexander ought not to return yet. She crept into the dining room and poured herself a glass of water. She must read all of it. She must know what the men would say about her and Evangeline, and perhaps if she knew it she may end up with a plan – a proper plan – after all.

But not here. She picked up the papers very carefully, as she had once done the newspaper. She would have to pray Alexander did not miss them.

CHAPTER 28

It took her the rest of the morning to read them – why were men's papers so long? And further into the afternoon to think on them, as her feet grew cold and her legs numb and the cat swarmed round underneath the table. But by teatime Rebecca knew what to do. Kitty Kat was hungry and she needed candles, for the light was already failing, and firewood and paper and a pen.

Well then, she could do all the tasks at once. First, Rebecca went to her little table with its uneven legs and wrote out a note:

> *Gabe, I have found the papers. Will you go to the Royal Society and find out when Alexander is speaking? I have forgotten it, but I must know the date.*
> *Your friend,*
> *R*

Quickly round the corner then, in case her husband or Violet should return unexpectedly and see her on the street, and find a boy to take a note to Gabe. She would have to hope he was there at his parents' house, not out looking for work. She hurried towards the High Street to the little shop that sold paper of every size and colour.

'I am not looking for paper with roses on, or any other flower,' she said to the man behind the counter. 'I need plain writing sheets, of the kind men use, if you have any. And a hole in them, if you would be so kind as to make me one, just there in the corner.'

On to the stall that sold only string – for she had nothing, nothing at all of her own – to tie the sheets together. And then to the ink and pen shop, to buy the cheapest pen they had, which would have to do, and some more expensive ink, so it would match. Lastly to the fishmonger, for some fish heads for Kitty, which, even though the fishmonger wrapped them in five layers of newspaper, still smelled very bad. The wet worked its way through them all onto her dress as the package bumped along her thigh on her way home.

'You must thank me for this, Kat,' she said as she dropped the package on the floor. 'And I dare say you would, if you could speak. Wait now, I will open it, no need to tear into it like that!'

The smell, together with the picture of the cat working his way through the snout of the fish, chewing with the side of his mouth, his eyes closed, meant Rebecca felt no need of her own supper, even though darkness had fallen by the time she got back. The season was such that the days seemed to barely come into being before they went out again. It was cold, freezing even. She must keep on her bonnet and her shawl, and warm her hands by rubbing them, for when she sat down at her desk again the cold air shot in through the window frame where it rattled and made the cobwebs in the corners sway and shake.

But Rebecca did not mind it. She was even – could she say it? – happy. If happy it was to start about the business of getting revenge on her husband. Say, then, not happy. What then? The fulfilment of her plans. The writing of herself, as she sat on the chair with one leg shorter than the other three, at her spindly desk that creaked and groaned at every press as if it might at any moment collapse, into the story. A feeling of her place in the world – just for a moment, under darkened sky – that was not too far away from the feeling her draught had once lent her.

Rebecca took out the papers and set them before her. She took out an old envelope and set it next to the papers, very close. No, she could not see well enough, she would have to light one of the candles. The flame on it twisted and gave off an uneven light, but if she set it close to the papers it was enough.

She fixed her eyes on the first page. Alexander's hand was angular, vigilant, with very small gaps between the words. It was like being in a cloud of swarming bees, to look on it. And he pressed on the paper very hard, sometimes rucking it up in front of the nib.

She took a breath. The writing was so unlike her own that she doubted her ability to copy it.

Women have many traits in common with children, wrote out Rebecca, trying to press as hard as she could.

But that would not do! The *h, l* and *d,* were all wrong. And the *W,* and the *o.*

h,l,d

h,l,d

h,l,d,h,l,d. Words, letters, only marks on a page.

But marks on a page are all I have, and they are enough to imprison me, and all women, inside them.

h,l,d, There now, that was a little better. But her hand was already aching with the pressure of the nib on the paper, and the upright stems were the only letters that looked anything like at all. There were still all the rest to get right, with their loops and curves and the occasional letter, such as V, that Alexander wrote in a way that was all his own.

Women's field of understanding is very narrow, ruled by sentimentality.

No, no she had not got it. But she worked on till the candle was halfway gone, Kitty threading his way between her legs.

Women's moral sense is deficient, she wrote out.

They are irrational, jealous, inclined to vengeances of a refined cruelty.

But Alexander's S's were sharp at the corners and when she attempted to match them, they were unrecognizable. Ink blotted her hands and stained her cuff. She was getting nowhere! She flung the pen down and stood up, glad to straighten her legs and feel the air on the back of her thighs.

She had not put up the shutters, the night was windy and the trees slashed about near her window. She stared out at the blackness. This was going to be harder than she had first thought.

She let Kitty Kat's tail run through her fingers, his purring the only sound in the house, until the knocker sounded, loud enough in the darkness to make her jump, though it was not late yet, only dark.

It was Alexander! Her pulse beat in her ears. He had seen her on the street, and had followed her here.

She would not go. He could not get her, not if the door was locked.

Thumping now, hammering. And her name being called.

But it was not Alexander's voice, it was Gabe's. Only Gabe. Rebecca put her palm on her chest to slow the beating but instead her heart gave a leap, in spite of herself.

And how nice it was to see his face, to have a little company, on this lonely night.

'Are you well?' he asked her anxiously.

'If you mean, have I stayed away from the drops? I have.'

'Dearest Rebe, you are strong, I knew you would be. Only, it is so easy to fall back into old habits, and when every pharmacy sells them, even easier.'

'Sit a moment, will you? I have nothing to offer but chicken bones and a little tea.'

'I should rather tea, but chicken bones will do if I must.' He grinned. Sitting there at the table he made it look flimsy, with his hands spread out on top of it. Her heart, again, twisted in its socket. She turned to the stove and busied herself with the kettle.

'I have come, well, perhaps you would have rather I sent a note,' he began.

'Oh no, it is fine that you came. I am struggling in my work and I am glad to have a break in it.'

'Are you glad? Then I am glad too, and to see you looking so well.' He dropped his eyes and his cheeks reddened. 'Though I don't know what work you are bent on, but if it has to do with the Royal Society, that date you asked of, 'tis tomorrow.'

'Tomorrow?' Rebecca put her hand against the stove. 'Oh, that soon? Tomorrow, you say?'

'Is it too soon? It is bad news?'

Rebecca blew out her breath. ''Tis not too soon, but sooner than I had hoped, oh much sooner! I think I will get no sleep tonight. I think I will have to work the whole way through it.'

'Is this the work?' Gabe picked up the sheets. '*The Formula of Happiness*. This sounds promising.'

''Tis not! The title is a lie, and the reason my husband has been persecuting me. Turn over and see for yourself.'

'*An Attempt to Correct the Feminine Problem with Reference to Heroin*—' Gabe broke off. 'What's this?'

'Read on.'

'*For Millennia human society has been run on the equable division between the sexes, men and women in their separate yet equal spheres. But now we find to our dismay that the "Angel in the House" has come under threat, from womankind herself, in the guise of monstrous females who call themselves "reformers" but who would take on the role of men in the public sphere by expanding their brains to an unnatural and dangerous degree.*'

Gabe stopped again. 'Who wrote this?'

'My husband, the chemist.'

'Now I see why you ran away!'

'There is more, much more, that I have not told you.' The kettle was starting to steam and she took it off the stove before it shrieked. She had burned herself already on the handle, which was only a bit of twisted wire. 'I was happy to take the medicine he offered, at first,' she said. 'I wanted to disappear too. But I ought never to have married him.'

Gabe started to talk but she cut him off. 'I can't blame you for that! I was greedy and I thought that being a wife, to anybody, would be better than being a spinster.'

Gabe looked at her, and then, as if he could not bear it,

dropped his gaze back down onto the papers and started to read again.

'*None are more at risk from the ministrations of these women than their gentle sisters, and it is these females with whom we chiefly concern ourselves.*

Every day beset by the pressures of the modern world, these wives and mothers – and even, dare we say it, fallen women too! – find themselves tempted by the supposed freedoms espoused by their more manly counterparts. They are desirous to be good but are torn asunder by anxieties from all sides. And it is this anxiety that puts in jeopardy the very future of our race, and the future of the Empire!'

Rebecca came to Gabe's side and set down his mug; some tea slopped out and onto the paper and blurred several of the words. 'No matter,' she said.

'But will he not notice?' said Gabe. 'Or will you hide it from him, so he cannot make the speech?'

'I will do better than that. At least, I had a plan, a good one, but Alexander's hand, see here, is so heavy that I cannot make its likeness. P'raps if I work all night it might come right. But look here, at this,' said Rebecca: '*And this is added to the weakness that females must inevitably suffer thanks to their grandmother Eve: less capable in mind and strength than a man, narrower in perception, more volatile in emotion, beset by sentimentality.* But what is the matter, Gabe?'

'I see here my own sin,' he said, pushing his fingers over his forehead.

'Where?'

'My own sin of hubris. I, too, wanted to change the world.'

'Oh Gabe, there is no need to look so grim. I don't think that is a sin! It only matters how you go about it.'

But Gabe shook his head. He stood up. 'You will need the fire if you are to work all night. Let me make it up for you?'

Rebecca went to the fireplace and knelt next to him. A flame leapt up, she could feel the heat on her knees. Gabe took up her hands and kissed them at the fingertips and at the knuckles. 'I left you,' he said, hardly louder than the flames.

'None of that now,' said Rebecca. 'We have been through this.'

He dipped his head to her hand again. His moustache was soft where it tickled her palm. She wished he would kiss her more. Instead, he raised his face. 'Let me try.'

'Try, try what?'

'Try to copy Alexander's hand. If that is what you need to have your plan come right. I have the weight behind me, at least.'

'Oh! Yes – yes, you do have a stronger hand, you may do better. But Alexander's hand is strange, I cannot get the loops, or the S or the B, or the C.'

Rebecca went to light another candle and Gabe took up the pen, squinting in the gloom. 'He must run through a great many nibs.'

'But your attempt is much better than mine already! Look there, that *g* looks quite alike.'

'Let me try some more.'

An owl hooted, once, and then the sound was Gabe's breathing and the nib scratching away at the scrap of paper. His tongue stuck a little way out of his mouth as he worked, and again, Rebecca's heart twisted to see it – the diligent schoolboy!

After a bit he looked up at her and grinned. 'It is not bad labour this. I am good at being someone else, look.' He held the paper up for her to see.

'Why, it is almost exactly alike, and so quick to do it!'

''Tis not bad, though I say it myself. Shall I do more?'

'Yes, please – that G there is perhaps a little too rounded, and the odd way Alexander forms his Vs, that might be hardest of all. But then I think no one would know the difference!'

Gabe squinted down again. 'There now – how about this?'

'Just a little sharper – and the V – it does not join properly – there now – well done, Gabe – it is perfect! Oh, perhaps my plan has a chance after all! But it may take most of the night – are you tired?'

'Not at all. This is easier labour by far than the tannery.'

'Will you help me, then? For there is still so much to do.'

'I should be glad to, gladder than anything,' said Gabe, his cheeks flushed. 'Even if it should take up the whole night.'

CHAPTER 29

It did not take all night, but they laboured long into it, working side by side. Rebecca dictated and Gabriel wrote, pausing only to flex his hand or throw more logs onto the fire, until at last Rebecca said that for all its imperfections the work was done.

She fell into bed then, and slept, but it seemed only moments later that the window rattled loud enough to make her sit straight up out of bed -- it was hailing -- and she had overslept. Everything was ruined! She had no way of knowing the time in here. Rebecca threw off the covers and went to the window, rubbing her eyes, they had grit in them.

She looked up at the sky. The cloud was too thick to tell where the sun might be. It was low, anyway, at this time of year. But a whistle sounded out from beneath her -- the boy, with a pea-shooter, waving his cap at her.

'Thank you, yes, I am awake!' She waved at him through the glass. And now she saw that there was a factory boy on his way to work, and a girl straightening her cap and going round the back of the next-door house, to start her day's work.

She had an hour then, before Alexander would leave the house for the Society, even if he left early, as she knew he would. Rebecca went to the stove and made herself a little tea, and breathed into the steam. She picked up the cat and rubbed his whiskers. She thought about cooking an egg, but her heart was hammering too hard to eat.

Calm now, courage! She had put in motion half her plan. Now for the final part. She took off her nightgown and hurried to shrug on her chemise and her gown, shivering against the cold. She had washed her old dress herself, the one she had fled her house in, with soap meant for washing hands, and she had not lifted all the smell away from the bodice. Never mind, it was better than before, and a dress that was not quite clean would help her cause too.

Now where to put her papers? Oh, she had not thought of that! She had only the reticule, or the bag, both lent by Gabriel – too big or too small. Under her cloak – but they might be seen if she had to take it off. No, her bodice, that was the only place, wrapped around her ribcage – careful now to crush them! Smooth them down and now fumble with the hooks and now slowly, carefully, downstairs, all the time her heart banging like piano keys. 'No, Kitty, you must not follow me. 'Tis not safe for cats.' She pushed open the door and prodded the cat back inside.

She rang on the bell again and heard, behind the door, a shout: Alexander's voice. And then the shuffling steps of Mrs Bunclarke, looking befuddled as she pulled open the door.

'Who is it?' called Alexander from the dining room.

'Your wife, sir, come back home from her aunt's.'

The sound of a chair being pushed back. 'Rebecca, you say?'

Rebecca stood up on her toes, took a breath, and ran towards his voice, meaning to launch herself at him. Alexander, too, had got up to see her, so she met him sooner than she thought, in the doorway, awkwardly, where she fell onto his chest, keeping the side with the papers away from him.

He staggered back, in horror or surprise.

'Oh husband, forgive me! I have been a fool. You were right, in everything you said. It was only my own stupidity, which prevented me from seeing it. I am a woman, after all! But now I have had time to reflect, and I have come to see that you are right.'

'What's all this?'

She was glad to see his face was not furious but bewildered. His eyes were red-rimmed, as if he had not slept either. He had shaved his face bare again but behind it he was thinner, his cheeks more sallow.

'I have come to see that you are right about all of it,' she said again, reaching out her hand and touching his neck. He flinched. 'I *am* grateful, I know you hold only my best interests at heart! I ...' She let her voice falter. 'I ... can hardly believe that I could have done such a thing to you. Are you recovered? I see that you are. And to think that I hurt you! Husband, I am sorry. Only … I was afraid. But I see now that anything you had in store for me would be right.' Pray God he did not bring out another syringe and try it again, straight away.

But now Rebecca saw the use in being married to a husband so dogged.

'I knew you would see the truth of it. I am only surprised that you did not see it at once. If anything the wound you gave me convinces me further that I am on the right path.'

Rebecca nodded, keeping her eyes on the knot in the floorboard.

'I know where you have been. And who you have been with.' He spoke very reasonably, but a pulse jumped in his temple.

'Oh husband, I can explain, 'tis only—'

'You have been with your aunt, the cook told me. But why you had to leave in that manner—'

'I needed to think things over!' Her heart jumped with relief. 'And I see the error in my part of it, as I said, and I am determined to be a good wife.'

Alexander passed a hand over his eyes. 'I am glad to hear you say it at last. But I am afraid I cannot concern myself with you today. I must prepare myself.'

'Why, what happens today, husband?'

'It is a great day for me – for Mr Badcock and me. It is our lecture at the Royal Society, and I must get ready for it.'

Rebecca watched his face. But there was nothing in it to

suggest that he had missed his papers the night before. She let out a little breath. 'Ah yes, I forgot. What is it that you are talking about?'

P'raps she had gone too far, for he looked at her sharply. But seeing nothing in her face he said, for he could not help himself: 'Mr Badcock and I are giving a talk about nothing short of human happiness, or rather, female happiness! Men's happiness lies in other directions.'

'Well!' Would clasping her hands together give the right wifely vision? It would, she saw it in his smile, though, she was also glad to see, there was something strained around the corner of his lips. And even though his face was bare again, he had missed patches of hair here and there, and had cut himself on the cheek.

She let the tremor come into her voice. 'I need my medicine, though, before you go.'

'Yes yes,' he said. 'You may have to wait until this evening. I don't know if I have the syringe here.'

'But p'raps, husband dear,' she cut in quickly, 'as I do tremble so at the injection, could I revert to my draught? At least, till you have managed to get another syringe?'

'Your salts, you mean?' He let out a sigh. 'If you like. You will have to find them for yourself.' He glanced at the clock. 'I am following the time very closely, and I must meet Mr Badcock at the Society in less than an hour.'

'But, are they here? For I fear I will sicken, and then …'

Tears came easily to her eyes. If he did not tell her where they were, all would be lost.

'What have you been taking, at your aunt's? Laudanum, I suppose. Take some more of that, for today.'

'But – the laudanum is as nothing compared to your medicine, your salts. I can run to the pharmacy and return. Do you not need it for your lecture?'

He looked at her now, surprised. 'I do have a bottle here, for that purpose, yes. How did you know?'

Rebecca put her hand to her neck and pulled at her collar. 'I thought as much,' she said quickly, 'when you told me the subject of your talk. Your invention is the best thing of the age, is it not?'

He scratched at his cheek. 'Yes, yes it is.' He blinked. 'I suppose there would be no harm in you taking a little, though you will have to measure it yourself. You have seen me do it often enough. It is in the parlour, on the mantel.'

Rebecca went to the sideboard and took up a glass. She filled it with a little water and went to the next room, to the parlour. There it was, just the sight of the blue bottle made saliva run into her throat again, as if she might be sick.

Come now, calm! She took up the bottle with a trembling hand, uncorked it, and tipped out the crystals into the glass. Had she put too much? She squinted into the depths of the bottle. More than she had been used to taking. Oh, it would have to do, she could not pinch it all up and put it back!

Now, swirl the water about, and about, until it is dissolved. 'Thank you,' she called. 'I have it here. I will bring it through.'

She came into the dining room again with the glass, her fingers covering the bottom of it in case all the salts had not dissolved, and put the bottle near his plate, forcing her breath to come evenly. 'Here is the rest of it, husband, for your lecture. Would you like some more coffee?'

'Coffee, no. I must go up.'

'But husband, you cannot go out to speak without coffee! You need it to stimulate the brain.'

'Do not fuss,' he said. But he had a little piece of kipper still on his plate and he turned to that and put it on his fork.

'Let me fetch you some,' she said in a trembling voice. She took the coffee pot to the sideboard and stood with her back to him, barely breathing, wondering if Alexander's eyes were fixed on her.

If they were, he was still eating, she heard the scrape of his knife and fork across the plate.

She opened the lid of the pot pretending to look inside. 'Oh, I am being foolish! I think your day at the Society is affecting me too! There is quite enough coffee in here.' Enough dregs too, to disguise the taste of the draught. She dare not look back, not now. Keeping her elbows close in to her side, and almost fainting with fear, she swirled the salts about the glass and quickly tipped it into the coffee pot.

When she turned around again Alexander was looking down at the newspaper, but ineffectually, turning page after page. She picked up the pot, her hand quivering so hard that the top of the coffee pot rattled in its groove, and brought it to him.

'Here it is, husband,' she said, as bright as she could, pouring him as much liquid as could fit into the cup. 'It may be a little cold, and I'm not sure that Mrs Bunclarke made it rather strong today, it tasted a little bitter.'

Alexander closed up the paper and pushed it away. And then – thank God for his nerves! – without looking at it, he picked up his coffee and flung it down his throat.

He grimaced. 'You are right. It *is* bitter. You'd best speak to Mrs Bunclarke about ordering different beans.'

Rebecca waited until he had gone upstairs, and then, quickly now, she crept across the hall, holding her breath at the creak of a board – what if Alexander were to come downstairs and see her outside the door of the study? She turned the handle, holding tight onto the knob as if she could force it to go quietly, her hand slipping on the brass. Now she must unfasten her bodice, but her fingers were trembling too hard to do it!

She stopped her breath. Forced her hands still. First one hook, and then the other. Now she had enough space to pull up the papers out of her bodice, still warm, and put them back on his desk. Gabe's hand was good – it looked very like. But the papers curled a little from where they had bent around her body. She could do nothing about it. Alexander would return downstairs at any moment.

Rebecca ran back to the parlour and sat on the sofa, all her attention pointed towards the stairs. Soon enough she heard Alexander come down and go to the study. He was in there an age, more than an age!

But here he was now, in the hall, putting on his coat, the papers in that bag there.

Rebecca leapt up. 'Are you leaving? But will you let me accompany you, as far as the Mound? For I would so like to stay with you. It is my duty, I think, to provide succour, is it not?'

'Accompany you?' He was buttoning up his coat.

'Accompany *you* as far as the Mound. Look, you have done this button up wrong.' Rebecca re-did his button and stepped back to reach for her cloak. She did not *have* to go with him now, but she could not bear to stay at home without knowing if it had all gone off as she had planned.

But Alexander said: 'You stay at home. The Royal Society is no place for you.'

'Are women not allowed?'

'I doubt it. And I don't think you should listen to the lecture,' he said, taking up his Gladstone bag. 'Wish me luck!' And he smirked at her.

The smirk, she knew, signified that he would be talking about her, and Evangeline. He thought it funny! Oh, she could not stay indoors, not now! She must know whether he was to be brought down, or whether he would come back triumphant, if he had learned his speech off by heart – pray God he had not! Or whether he would suspect her and come back this time to do her real harm. Rebecca reached for her bonnet and stuffed her hair up underneath without any pins, and drew on her gloves and her cloak.

Outside it was not raining, but it was damp enough, as if the air itself contained water. The sky leached the colour from the houses, from the pavement, even from Alexander, as he strode on round the corner, working his mouth and worrying his lip.

They passed along several streets, Rebecca keeping well behind, for she knew the way to the Mound. Now he turned to cross the street, only, without looking, he plunged straight into the road, into the path of a velocipede, a great wheeled thing, the young man up on top dressed in boots and breeches.

The young man swerved violently and shouted out a curse. The velocipede swung off to the right, into the path of a brougham, the horse reared up.

'Hey, hey!' shouted the driver.

Alexander was flung back to the kerb and sat on it in a daze, his hand pressed to his forehead.

'Damn you!' shouted the young man again, leaning forward over the handlebars and swerving off to the other direction.

Rebecca stopped, her hand before her mouth. Was he hurt? Would he still go on? A woman, a servant by the look of her, took Alexander's arm. 'Are you all right, sir?'

'These damned velocipedes! They ought never to have been invented.' Even from where Rebecca stood she could hear the thickness in his voice.

'Should you like to get up?'

'Yes, get up.' He let the woman pull him to his feet. 'Thank you. I am distracted this morning.'

'Yes, you are distracted, nearly got yourself killed!' She brushed off his trouser leg.

'Oughtae look where he steps, the next time!' said the driver, pulling himself back on top of the carriage with a grunt.

'I don't think I slept enough last night,' he said, leaning on her quite heavily. 'I feel slow, slower than usual. No doubt it will clear. Thank you, madam, much obliged.'

But it did not clear, of course. Alexander's steps grew slower the nearer they drew to the Mound. Even Rebecca's steps began to falter at the sight of the grandness of the building, its pillars ranked along the front portico as if they had been transported back to Ancient Greece. Mr Badcock was waiting for Alexander at the top of the many steps, chewing on his glove. 'You are late! Let us go in,' he said, putting his watch back into his pocket. But over Alexander's shoulder his eyes met Rebecca's.

'What is she doing here?' he hissed.

'Rebecca?' Alexander half-turned around.

'Never mind, we are very near to being late, Alexander, hmm? Are you well? You look out of sorts.'

'I think I have been afflicted by something,' said Alexander.

Rebecca held her breath. Would he know the symptoms of his own medicine when he had asked so much about its effects of everyone else? Then he would turn on her, and would not go in, and everything would be lost.

'A cold or influenza, something making my head slow. It is the time of year. Have I a fever?'

Rebecca smiled. Mr Badcock put his hand to Alexander's forehead. 'There is no heat, some moisture. Nerves, I should say, quite understandable, yes? But we ought to go in.'

Now she must wait for them both to go through the main doors and try to slip in herself. If she were turned back for being a woman, she would have to wait outside, but no, as soon as she went in she saw there was another woman in the audience. But she kept her bonnet on, which was plain and with a broad rim, to hide from the men underneath.

Most of the audience were already waiting, men drawn from the medical profession, the pharmacists in black jackets and waistcoats, black bowties and cravats. Several had notebooks and pencils hovering over them sharpened to a point. But there *was* one woman, with black feathers in her hat.

'A proud day for you, is it, Mrs Palmer?' said Mrs Shrivenham, turning in her seat.

'Oh yes, very proud,' answered Rebecca, hardly able to speak. She would take the seat behind, Mrs Shrivenham's feathers would obscure Alexander's view of her.

'I saw the title of the talk and I must say I could not resist, and from your own husband too!' Mrs Shrivenham looked at her.

'Yes, yes, indeed. Oh, I think they are beginning!' Rebecca wished she had eaten breakfast, her stomach churned horribly. Mrs Bunclarke would have swept it all away by now, sitting in the kitchen with her legs stuck out towards the fire.

A thin-faced man dressed in a pair of tweed trousers stepped out in front and began an introduction. Rebecca heard nothing but the beating of her own heart, and a few, entirely expected, words: esteemed colleagues ... scientific endeavour ... important new drug. She noticed that on the table behind him lay a syringe, and behind that, a blackboard, polished to a shine.

And then Mr Badcock stepped out, dabbing at his face with a handkerchief. Alexander stumbled up the step and had to be helped.

Alexander fiddled with his papers, squinted at them, and began to speak.

Rebecca could see nothing on his face that suggested surprise, nothing to imply that he was reading Gabriel's writing, not his. Although his face wore the same blurred look that she had seen so often on Evangeline's.

Evangeline ought to be here, to see this, if it went well! And if it did not ... But Alexander had begun to speak.

'It is of utmost importance that we are gathered here today, in light of the Pharmacy Act now being drafted by Her Majesty's Government.'

Several nods from the audience and murmurs of agreement.

'We who are pharmacists oppose the regulation of medicines, especially opium. This new Bill will take our business from us and put it in the hands of physicians. Otherwise, its requirelent ... requirement ...' he passed his hand across his lips, '... that we register ourselves and record all purchases of so-called dangerous medicines questions our ability to carry out our work.'

More nods, more agreement. Someone wrote busily down on his notepad.

'But my colleague and I are here this morning not only wish to prevent this act, but to prevent ... present ...' he shook his head again, '*present* some explorations of the use of opium that have not been explored before.'

A pencil fell to the floor and rolled to the front.

Not yet, not yet. It was all the same speech that Alexander had written for a few pages more; that way it would work better when the words were not his own.

First Alexander must explain how he had made his new medicine, how high the hopes he had for it were. His head sunk lower and lower as he spoke and Mr Badcock had to dart forward and catch him by the arm, and apologize.

'Are you well, Mr Palmer?' asked the sharp-faced man. 'Ought we to postpone?'

'Yes, Alexander, we ought,' whispered Mr Badcock loud enough for everyone to hear. But Alexander shook him away. Thank God for his obduracy!

'Many, if not all, will be aware of the habitual nature of opium, and that is where the benefits can be said to fall down. But heroin is not only four times more potent than morphine, but also *decreases* the desire for morphine by an equal amount.'

A questioning hum and several more note-takers scratching away on their pads. Alexander was leaning back against the table, and, Rebecca was glad to see, had need of frequently consulting his notes.

'I learned from my many years working in my laboratory that chemistry may be defined as one substance working on another to create a different, often more powerful, substance. Heroin, for our purposes here today, may be seen as analogous to laudanum, only far more effic … efficacious.'

Alexander paused and fell silent and Mr Badcock had again to leap out from behind the table and plead with him: 'Really, Alexander, what on earth is the matter? Let us reconvene, I beg you!'

But again, Alexander shook him off, like a drunkard told to leave the public house. 'I may have been working too hard in preparation for this speech and find myself over-taxed. For which, please, excuse me.' He stared down at his notes, turned over a page, and began again.

'Philosophy, for its part, could be said to be the study of the nature and meaning of life. And this morning, if I may ... if I may ...' Alexander's eyes grew vague and his eyelids fluttered ... drooped ... drooped lower. In the room the atmosphere grew tense. A book fell on the floor, and Alexander snapped upright and started speaking again.

'If I may be so bold I will attempt to bring the two branches of knowledge, chemistry and philosophy, together. The Stoics of Ancient Greece practised self-sufficiency, so that, in the words of Epictetus, a person would remain, "sick and yet happy, in peril and yet happy, dying and yet happy, in disgrace and happy". And yet the females of our species lack the will-power to be able to enact this triumph of mind over matter. Heroin acts upon chemical substances already in the brain, and the resulting compound alters how the brain perceives the world, not the world itself – we do not lay claim to that much!'

He paused, to wait for laughter. Someone guffawed.

'We believe that heroin, in short, may be seen as a replace-ment to Stoic Virtue, for the frailer half of our species, in the light of their own more powerful brains.'

That part, in Alexander's notes, had read *less* powerful, and before it the phrase, 'more childlike'.

Rebecca held her breath – would he notice now, and call an end to it, too soon? Now – at last – she clenched her hands into fists, here it was ...

But instead of reaching for his notes again, Alexander turned sideways to the end of the front row and crooked his finger, to bid someone come – which was strange, for Mr Badcock still sat behind, and Rebecca in front, and there was no one else ... save ... Violet. Violet! Who came to the centre very stiff. Arms hanging loose at her sides, her gaze slack, her rosebud lips parted, and her hair very beautifully put up into a net of tiny violet flowers.

'Thank you, Violet; now you need not be afraid.' Alexander stood on one side of her, Mr Badcock on the other.

She did not look afraid; she gazed into the audience with a perfectly blank expression.

'We merely want you to answer a set of short questions. Will you do that for us, Violet?' said Mr Badcock.

She nodded.

'Good. Here is the first. Are you, would you say, content?'

Violet's eyes came into focus. She rubbed her nose. She nodded.

'And were you, before we started this treatment, happy or unhappy?'

Her voice came very low. 'I would say, unhappy.'

'Why would you say that you were to be found in that frame of mind?'

'I thought it was simply the way my mind was made. And I thought I was not made for marriage.'

Mr Badcock looked pleased. He pressed his palms together.

Some of the audience shifted about in their seats. 'And now you are quite content, you say?'

'Yes,' said Violet, looking out with eyes that had never seemed more blue.

Now Alexander spoke again. 'I trust you will not consider me as possessing any sentiment of vanity when I say that the equation of happiness lies within our reach. Just as Lord Owen collects the ephemera of the natural world to fill his museum in the environs of Kensington, my associate Mr Badcock and I have been collecting the feminine emotions, to harmonize them and make them bearable.'

Rebecca sat forward on her seat, her fingers pressed to her temples.

Everything now depended on this.

Alexander looked – thank God for it – down at his notes.

'For women are strong and bear much punishment.'

Nothing still.

'Women's intelligence is manifold and more broadly encompassing than a man's, whose field is narrow and only intent on their own ambition.'

Mr Badcock's mouth fell open. But Alexander had not noticed anything was awry.

'There will come a time when women shall throw off the shackles of men and not submit to being dosed and pierced by needles for the taking of medicine they need only because of their state of oppression.'

Mrs Shrivenham laughed, which Alexander, in his befuddled state, took for praise of his experiment.

'Alexander, stop!' said Mr Badcock, trying to take his arm.

'Until that time, Mr Badcock and I have been taking women, and even my own wife, against their will and turning them into depraved opium eaters' – Rebecca had decided on the use of 'depraved' for its sensationalism. The medical men set up a murmur that grew louder as Alexander went on.

'We have administered every sort of pain, which we have called *P* in our research, and given them the antidote, which we have called *H*.' This just like the original document, to keep him going on.

'And in the course of my research I have been a constant visitor to Mrs Bard's House of Flagellation where—' Here at last Alexander broke off. He turned to Mr Badcock in confusion. He turned back to the papers. He swallowed. Pushed a hand across his face. 'What is this …?'

From the floor there started up a slow clapping.

Alexander turned the page. He rubbed his forefinger back and forth across his lips. He turned another page. 'A working formula … what's this?'

Oh, it had worked better than she had dared to hope! Rebecca had never dreamed he would go on so far.

'This is not fit!' cried someone in a high voice.

'No, no, this is not the paper I meant to bring before you. It has been changed.'

'By whom? A woman?' called out Mrs Shrivenham.

Laughter. Alexander gave a twitch, one corner of his lip drawn towards his ear.

'I meant to say, a working formula that will have great implications for the human race!'

Mr Badcock's face underneath his beard had turned the colour of paper-hanging paste. He put his hand to his cheek, as if in a trance, and shook his head.

'I have it here somewhere, or I can go on, I remember it all … Heroin may be the most important medicine yah … yet discovered!'

'Get off!'

''Tis a disgrace to the Society!'

'No, no,' said Mr Badcock.

'We are scientists, man, you bring shame on us!' A ball of crumpled paper hit him on the forehead.

At last Alexander came to a stop and looked about him, bewildered. 'John?'

'No, no no no,' Mr Badcock said, shaking his head. Another ball of paper was thrown and hit his cheek.

'What has happened?' asked Alexander. 'I think this is a dream.' He pinched his arm. 'John?'

But Mr Badcock had already stumbled up the aisle, being pelted with balls of paper as he went, leaving the doors swinging behind him.

CHAPTER 30

The audience rose up in a babble and quickly went out, bending their heads together. Violet had been left standing alone on stage in her white dress, her cheek as pale and glossy as a pearl.

Rebecca took her hand, which was very lightly trembling. 'Was it something I did wrong? Mr Badcock was so insistent I get it right, and I didn't, did I?'

'It was nothing you did, Violet; it was I who ruined it all.'

'You? You were not up here. But what should I do now? Mr Badcock said I should go with him – but they have gone – do you know where?'

'No,' said Rebecca, though she thought they would have gone to Albany Street. 'Why do you not come with me?'

And so Rebecca sat with Violet in her rooms, that night and the next, trying to help her. She wrote a note to Violet's husband to say that she had been invited to stay with her for the weekend. Her habits must have become more erratic of late, for he made no objection.

The first night passed without incident, Violet snored all through it. The day after passed slowly, tolerably, with Rebecca reading aloud and starting a tapestry, and taking Violet on a walk out of town when their confinement grew too hard to bear. Towards the end of the day, however, Violet grew fretful. 'You are holding me here against my will,' she said. 'Do not try to save me!'

The second night, as Rebecca knew, was the worst. If she could help Violet through the dark hours of it, Violet would be on her way to throwing off the medicine for good. But Violet took it worse than Rebecca had. Every quarter hour, as the evening grew into night, she started up from her chair, her hair matted with sweat, her pupils wider and wider with anguish.

'You must have some drops. Where are you hiding them?'

'No drops, not here, no, Violet, not now. Wait awhile.'

'But if we wait awhile the pharmacy will close – let us go, let us go now!'

'If you have the drops you will not be free of the heroin. It will pass, this craving for it, I know, for I have felt it too.'

Violet grew angry then. 'I don't think you have, for then you would not be so cruel. Why are you keeping me prisoner? All I want is my medicine! I am not like you! Do not force me to be someone you think I ought.'

Rebecca stood at the door and they grappled, facing each other, breathing heavily. But after a while Violet fell back on her chair and sobbed. 'You are a bitch for stopping me. I only want to carry on as I was before – content – as Alexander says!'

'I am sorry, Violet, to have brought you to this! You are right, it *is* down to me that you are here, but I am trying to rectify it now, if you will let me!'

Violet seemed to calm then, and after a little while lay on the couch and slept. But later, just as Rebecca was falling into a fitful sleep of her own, she heard Violet pacing about. She heard her go to the door and rattle it, and then try the windows, but Rebecca had locked the door and hidden the key under her pillow and the rooms were three storeys up.

She did not hear Violet again until a watery sunlight quivered over the mustard-coloured walls. Violet was gaunt and drawn but her mood was sweeter.

'I have done it, haven't I? I have lived through the night! But how I long for a bath! I think that would mend me more than anything.'

Rebecca pushed herself up from her bed and pulled down her nightgown. 'I have no tub here,' she said.

'Oh dear!' Violet looked as if she were going to weep again. 'For I don't know what I will do without one.'

Rebecca sighed. 'Very well. There is a shop nearby that sells tin baths. I suppose I could buy one there and boil up some water for it.'

Violet clasped her hands before her and smiled sweetly. 'Oh, would you, would you really? What a good friend you are, Rebecca. I owe you my life!'

So Rebecca went to the shop and came back up with the bath, her back aching from awkwardly bending over the two handles. Violet would only be able to crouch in it and pour water over herself, but it ought to soothe her a little.

She was boiling the first pan on the stove when she heard the door open. Rebecca had forgotten to lock it behind her. The next instant Violet was out on the stairs; she flung one backward glance at Rebecca, her lips wet, her eyes streaming.

'Violet! Do not go – the worst is over!'

But Violet made no reply, Rebecca only heard her clattering down the stairs and out onto the street. Too late to catch her, even as she started to. As she turned to the door she saw a bit of paper, with a scrawl of writing on it, laid on the floor.

I am sorry, Rebecca, I cannot! I know I ought to want to stop, but I don't. I am not strong enough and life is better with the medicine than without it.

Thank you for trying to help me – I did not mean what I said.

V

Rebecca sank down and pressed the heels of her palm into her eyes. The pan was boiling heavily on the stove, slopping out water and making it hiss. She got up wearily and tipped the water into the bath: better not let it go to waste. She went to the stove and boiled another one, and another, until she had enough for a shallow soak.

The first moment, as she sunk her body into the warm water that was meant for Violet, cheered her. But the water soon cooled, its heat dissipating into the sides of the bath, and in another moment she was too cold to stay in.

For a week Rebecca watched number 19. Violet came but she left a short while later, setting her face against the cold and frowning. Nobody else, not even Mr Badcock.

'But you cannot go back!' said Gabe, when she told him of her plan. 'He may try to hurt you again.'

'The experiment is finished with,' she told him. 'He will not come at me with the syringe, or anything else, I think.'

'But he may want to punish you,' said Gabe. 'He can still overpower you; he is bound to be angry.'

'But where else am I to go? I cannot stay here.' She waved her arm round the little room. The glum light of the winter afternoon had made it look even worse.

'You could take another set of rooms – better ones.'

'And who should pay? I have taken enough from you already.'

And for the first three weeks back in the house it was as she'd thought: Alexander kept to his study. He did not go to the pharmacy, or to the parlour, or anywhere else. The only sign that he was in the house at all were the plates that Mrs

Bunclarke carried to and from his room, and they came out almost as full as they went in. Rebecca did not seek him out; she found after all that to see a man broken down was not something to gloat about.

Christmas came by; wreaths went up on the front doors and at dusk candles were lit on all the trees up and down Albany Street. Lionel knocked and asked for Mr Palmer, only to stand at Alexander's bedroom door until the latter opened it by not more than the width of a hat's brim and told him to go away.

'But Lionel, now is your chance to run the shop for yourself,' said Rebecca, when he came back downstairs.

Lionel rubbed his chin. 'I cannot manage it by myself,' he said. 'Even though custom has dropped away since the Act and we have lost half our custom—' He broke off.

'Oh Lionel, there is no need to be embarrassed on my account,' said Rebecca. 'I know you heard of my flight. Jenny misses you, I think. She has kept a piece of soap—'

'Aye.' Lionel nodded. 'The rosewater and glycerine. I made it up for her.' He blushed and put his knuckles to his cheek. 'Jenny told me you suffered, but bore it bravely.'

'That sounds like someone in a book! I suffered, yes. I don't know about bravely. I suffered, because I had to. But Jenny wants to come back to Edinburgh, she said so.'

'Aye, she does, but she cannot find a position from there and she won't travel without one.'

'It's a pickle, then.' Rebecca looked up the stairs, she thought she had heard a footstep, but Alexander's door was closed tight. 'But she could help at the pharmacy! Could she not?'

Lionel's eyes widened. 'Aye! The work is too much for one, and I think her so sensible she would learn quick enough!' But then he shook his head. 'But what about Mr Badcock? He might trouble her there.'

'You would be there; I don't think he could get to her at a shop. 'Tis not like being in service. And I could be there too, now that Mr Palmer is out of sorts. Yes, that is true. I could help you and Jenny. I am not experienced either … still, between the three of us we may be able to manage. I have been married to a pharmacist, I may have picked up something along the way.'

'It is a grand idea!'

'I could not pay her much. The pharmacy has gone slow, as you say, and we need to think of a way to make it go faster again. Perhaps Mr Palmer has neglected the business side of things, always being in his laboratory. It needs a woman's hand – forgive me, Lionel, but I think it does. And Jenny always did advise me, in worse times. Write and tell her, Lionel, do it today!'

CHAPTER 31

When she came, not more than ten days later, Jenny turned out to be far better suited to the pharmacy than she had been to maiding: thanks to Mhairi she had an immediate talent for order and display. The labels on the shop-rounds had got blurred, so she soaked them off and wrote out new ones in her neat looped hand. 'I knew it would come in useful, you see, this writing! Mother said it wouldnae, but look here. Is it right?'

'Aye, Jenny, just right,' said Lionel.

Then Jenny scrubbed the counter and straightened everything on the shelves. While she was doing it she noticed that some of the powders had been put into narrow-necked jars when they ought to have been put into wide-necked ones, for ease of pouring, so she swapped them over, creating a deal of mess for several days. But when all the jars were in their right places at last, and the corners had been dusted, and the windows polished with vinegar, and the tiles swept clean, the shop looked brighter, and more competent, and Lionel had more people to serve, even if they did not know why they had come in.

And if sometimes the two of them took their break out in front of the shop, under the beech tree whose roots pushed up the paving stones, and if sometimes their heads bent together as if they were laughing, or kissing, then what was the harm in that?

'And what do you think, Jenny, of the carboys?' Rebecca asked her one day, pointing to the great glass jars in the window.

'The carboys, Mrs Palmer? Yes, I see what you mean.'

'What does she mean?' said Lionel.

'You wouldnae see it, Lionel, but they are looking dusty.' Jenny ran her finger across one of them. 'See?'

'I suppose I had forgotten about them in recent months.'

'But more than that,' said Rebecca, 'they look old, and they take up a deal of space.'

'Space?' said Lionel. 'That is what they are meant to do. Else people might think we are a … I don't know … a fishmonger.'

Jenny laughed. 'They will not!'

'I know, it is a strange idea,' said Rebecca, 'to get rid of them—'

'Get rid of them? Why?' Lionel said.

'Only because we should stand out from the rest. We ought to look modern.'

'But what would we replace them with?'

'Fishes, Lionel,' said Jenny, sucking in her cheeks. 'That is the latest thing.'

'Stop!' He tugged at her apron.

'I don't know,' said Rebecca. 'Shelves, p'raps, with the latest medicines displayed along it. Though they will have to be displayed in the right way. In the cleanest and most arresting jars and pots – but you can see to that, Jenny. P'raps I shall have a look around and see what we might get.'

And so the next day Rebecca found herself peering in at all the windows of all the pharmacies in town. Some were dirty, some were clean, some were busy and some were desolate. But Mrs Shrivenham's pharmacy still seemed the most welcoming and the busiest of all. Even though Rebecca got there late in the afternoon it was still filled with people.

'I am glad to see you, my dear, glad indeed!' said Mrs Shrivenham. 'Anthony, look to the shop for a moment, will you, whilst I talk to my friend here. How is your husband?' They moved along the counter and Mrs Shrivenham dropped her voice. '*Not* well, I hope. That lecture of his was the most execrable load of tosh I have ever heard. At least, it started so. And ended, most unusually, in the defence of women.' She looked at Rebecca and the corners of her mouth twitched. 'I think someone – a woman, say – got to his notes before he read them.'

Rebecca dropped her voice. 'I was very lucky, if you can call it that, to be married to a devil, but I never thought my plan would work out so well!'

'It was the talk of the town, my dear! Chemists, apothecaries, apprentices and women – especially women – could talk of little else! I think the excitement will carry on for some time. The Society has never seen anything like it; the old boys are in uproar, there is talk of a general meeting to see how such a paper got through. And good, serve them right, that's what I say, my dear. Serve 'em right!' She gave a chuckle. 'I think you have done women a great service.'

'I am glad for that,' said Rebecca.

'You must be, dearie, you must be.' Mrs Shrivenham swept away a little powder that had fallen on the counter with her fingertips. 'But did you come here to hear the gossip? You would be welcome any time, my dear, but perhaps you had something else on your mind?'

Rebecca glanced around the shop. Anthony was grinding down something in his pestle and mortar. A woman in a velvet hat was turning over a package of herbs, finely wrapped and tied with ribbon. 'Now that Mr Palmer keeps to his room, we – I mean, my apprentice and his sweetheart, who used to maid for me – have taken the pharmacy over and are trying to make a go of it.'

'Mrs Palmer, that is good news!'

'But since we have lost the trade that comes with opium, the place is much emptier. Which is why I have come to you – for advice. I know hardly anything about the business,' said Rebecca.

'Neither did I. Although you will know more than you think. If you come back after the shop closes I will show you all these.' Mrs Shrivenham waved her arm round the glass bottles behind them labelled: *tinct assaf*, *oil eucalypt*, *oil juniper*, and a thousand more. 'Tis not nearly as hard as it looks. There is a great book, *Pharmaceutical Formulas*, as heavy as a boulder. That will tell you everything.' Anthony had come up to ask her something but Mrs Shrivenham waved him off.

'I wouldn't like to take up your time,' said Rebecca.

'I am glad to do it, Mrs Palmer. You are not imposing on me, not at all, my dear. The men like to make this business seem complicated, as if they alone can hold the keys to it. But it is not, not really, so long as you are taught in the right way.'

'But do you really think I might take charge of it on myself? Jenny and I have been seeing to the look of the place more than anything. I don't think I had thought any further.'

'Of course you can! You need not use the laboratory, if you don't like. I do very well without any laboratory above my shop.' Mrs Shrivenham tapped her nose. 'I'll tell you a secret. There's nothing so remarkable about my methods, and this is the key: buy tons where others buy hundredweights, if you have the cash that is, my dear, so you can knock off tuppence or so and still make a nice little profit. And you have the other trick already – 'tis a woman's trick: make all the articles you sell look as attractive and neat as possible. That is all there is to it, my dear, I promise you.'

Though there was no tree, no baubles, nor any other sign of the festive season at 19 Albany Street, for Christmas Day Mrs Bunclarke had cooked a turkey. As the smell of it came out of the kitchen Rebecca thought Alexander would be drawn from his room at last. The table looked almost proper, with cranberry sauce on it, and peas, and potatoes, only the tablecloth was stained due to the girl they sent out the laundry to being pregnant, and dust, as ever, was on the mantel, this time because Rebecca was too busy to see to it herself. She must hire another maid.

The table was laid for two. Mrs Bunclarke must know more than her, for she saw him more than Rebecca did now. Perhaps he had said something. Well, she would start without him anyway – the potatoes were giving off steam and the buttered carrots were hardening in the dish. And if Alexander did come, well – she must see him some time. Though when she picked up her knife and fork she found her hands were trembling.

The food was good, and she ate for a while with only the grandfather clock for company. But after a bit she got to thinking about her Christmases as a child, all those ordinary Christmases with her mother frowning over the oven, pulling crackers, toasting the Queen ... But now her mother and father were both gone ... and Eva too.

She blinked. She would not be lonely, not today. Though perhaps Christmas *was* a time to be lonely, if you were on your own.

Gabe would be having his Christmas dinner with his parents. It had been more than a month since she had seen him. Their labour, to bring down Alexander, she missed even that, sitting together in the candlelight, with the soles of her feet towards the fire. And now she had one last favour to ask of him, another loan, but this time she hoped to pay it back, and he always did love to help out the poor; she imagined his serious frown as she asked him it, and that was some consolation.

It was not until Boxing Day that Rebecca heard Alexander's door open and his tread, slower than usual, making its way down the stairs.

'Is it turkey again?' he said. 'I imagine it is. How I hate cold turkey!'

Rebecca put her knife and fork down and half stood up. P'raps Gabe had been right, Alexander would come for her, try to throttle her … But he was not making for her after all, but the sideboard. She tried to take him all in: his face was overgrown with hair, as if by shaving it down for so long now it burst from his skin with desperate vigour. His beard was tinted red, even though the hair on his head was black. His jacket had lost two buttons, the shirt was stained with every kind of brown. His trousers were grey at the seams and hung off him.

He spooned a large amount of cranberry sauce onto his plate. 'Will you let the cook go, or shall I? Though I dare say we will not find another who will work here. But her food grows worse and worse.'

'Yesterday was not too bad.' Rebecca did not mention it had been Christmas Day.

After a few bites Alexander put down his fork. 'You could have been rich, you know, if you had not destroyed it all. And I could have been famous.' His eyes glittered as he spoke. 'Someone else will happen upon my invention, in one year, or two, or twenty, and then they will be rich and famous, and remembered for the greatest invention in history.'

'I do not care for being rich,' said Rebecca. 'Not any more.'

'I ought to have concentrated on my solution, and not tried to apply it to the wider human good. That was where I fell down ...' Alexander's eyes drooped and seemed to close, but then he fixed them on her again. 'Women are devious, calculating and ruled by their emotions.'

''Twas a pity you read out the opposite then, to the Society,' said Rebecca.

'But why would you want to let emotions govern you? That is what I do not understand. I have been thinking of it over and over. Far better to be reasonable – like a man. My medicine only made you – and Evangeline – and Violet – more stable. Is not life better when lived that way?'

'Life is better when lived, not half-lived. That is what you have taught me.'

'A tautology! You were alive when you were on my medicine. A better, more suitable, way of being alive.'

Rebecca paused, her elbows on the table, and looked outside. 'You are right – sometimes it *was* better. But, then, and I do not know why – it changed, and was worse. My life was happening somewhere outside of myself. I couldn't feel anything, not good, not bad.'

'And that is what I hoped for. Yet you have sabotaged it.'

Rebecca sighed and put down her fork. 'Someone else will stumble across it, as you say.'

Alexander sighed also and laid his knife and fork together. Thinness did not suit him, the fine bones of his face were too sharp, his eye-sockets too deep.

He stared at her morosely for a moment. 'I have not lost all hope,' he said. 'Something may still be salvageable.'

'With us, do you mean?'

'No, no! With the experiment. I have something up my sleeve, so to speak.' He chuckled mirthlessly, then he scraped back his chair and shuffled from the room, holding on to the door frame for just long enough to leave a greasy mark.

CHAPTER 32

A week later Rebecca was at the pharmacy awaiting delivery of her new orders: French chalk and powdered starch to make up perspiration powder, tincture of capsicum to mix in with eau de Cologne for the relief of dandruff, and much else. It had all been bought with Gabe's money and she wanted to be sure it was all there.

But instead of French chalk, there was Alexander at the door, sweating about the eyes. Jenny shrank back behind the counter and took hold of Rebecca's arm. Lionel stood with his hand before his face. But Alexander only strode through with a nod directed at the floor and stamped on upstairs, as he always used to do.

Lionel started up the stairs behind him, but Rebecca shook her head at him. *Wait*, she mouthed.

'But what if he has come to stay?' whispered Lionel.

Rebecca shook her head again and turned her palms to the ceiling, as if to say, *What can we do?*

Their eyes were fixed on the ceiling. They could hear Alexander thumping about, a bench scraping back with a shriek, a glass beaker dropped. Eventually Alexander reappeared on the stairs, rubbing his cheek.

'Have you taken anything from up there?' he said.

'No, Mr Palmer, nothing at all,' said Lionel.

'I could have sworn, I could have sworn I had some acetic anhydride, in the big bottles there on the shelf, but perhaps I ...'

'We have not been up,' said Rebecca.

'I could synthesize it, perhaps, by heating potassium acetate with benzoyl chloride, only ...' Alexander came back downstairs as he spoke and pulled on his beard. 'Only they are hard to find too, and it will take too much time.' He stared at Rebecca unseeingly. 'I have no other option, though, I see no other way.' He was at the door now. 'Yes, yes, I will do that. Though it takes longer, it will be more satisfying.' He pulled open the door, still muttering to himself, and went across the outside of the window with his head bent down.

'What was that about?' said Jenny.

'He is gone at least,' said Rebecca.

'But what if he returns?' said Lionel.

The three of them were uneasy all day but he did not come back in. Although when Rebecca returned to Albany Street an unfamiliar figure started up out of the gloom of the parlour and came towards her.

'You are not in your room?' she said anxiously.

'I cannot bear to be in there. I must move about! I mean

to ask you something of great importance. My salts – do you have any left, hidden away, say, in your bedroom?'

'No, I threw the last of them away.'

Alexander turned away and put his face into his hands. 'And I was hoping, oh! I was sure …'

Rebecca came a little way into the room and put her hand to the back of the sofa. 'You are feeling the need of your salts.'

'I could not find the chemicals I needed … They take time to prepare, and I had no time, not enough. And now they have passed that damned act I can no longer go to a pharmacy for drops, or even a twist …' He slumped down on the arm of the sofa. 'But I will manage! I will brazen it out until tomorrow.'

'Very well, then,' said Rebecca. 'Perhaps I will see you in the morning.'

'Wait! Tell me. Does it hurt?'

'Does what hurt?'

'Tonight – what must I go through?' He still leaned on the sofa, as if he had not the strength to stand up, worrying at a loose thread.

'How long have you been taking the salts?'

Alexander faltered. 'Ever since the talk at the Society.'

'That is not too long. Not as long as I took them for. It will be easier for you. You will not sleep, though, I doubt. Perhaps you will feel as if ants crawl about under your skin. You will long for a draught more than the religious long for God.'

'I see.' Alexander sat back down again and put his hands to his forehead. 'And I am sweating. Is that usual, or does it mean I have a fever? I think I do! I think I must send for the doctor!'

'It is not a doctor you need! You must bear it. A freezing kind of sweat is one of the first signs of the sickness. There is no other way but to go on.'

Alexander shook his head again. 'And I will not be able to master it any other way? Say, through will alone? No, no I can see I will not, for the craving for a draught has begun already. Though I push it from my head a thousand times, it returns, to snap at me.' He turned his face to the back of sofa. When he looked back his face was damp.

'It helps not to be alone,' said Rebecca, with a sigh. 'Dark thoughts come when you are alone. I will sit with you a while, if you like.'

'Sit with me?'

'I have been through this before. It may be some comfort.'

When Alexander put his hand to his face it was trembling. A tear fell onto his fingers. Rebecca knew those tears – they came from the lack of salts. If heroin was a cloak that smothered all, when it was lifted, everything sprung again to unwelcome life. But she would not tell him that – let him feel his tears, let him feel that he could not stop them.

And so, once again, Rebecca kept vigil, as the night closed in on them both. She lay on the daybed with a blanket thrown over her, whilst Alexander paced, wrung his hands, pressed his arms to the glass, and sobbed.

Even so she must have fallen asleep because in the darkest part of the night he shook her awake.

'I cannot do it! I cannot take it after all!' A white speck was lodged in one corner of his lips. 'There must be another way.'

'There is no other way,' she said, rubbing one eye and pulling up her blanket. 'Alexander – this is part of the sickness. You must let it go. The quicker you lose hope of salvation the quicker you will accept your condition, and the quicker you will move on. Can you not rest?'

'Rest? No, I cannot tolerate lying down even.'

Rebecca sighed. 'I will read a little to you, if you like. It is a means to pass the time.'

So she picked up the first book that she brought from the shelf – Charlotte Riddell, *The Race for Wealth* – and read him that, as he paced the room and sighed, and wrung his hands, and drew back the curtains, gazing out into the blackness.

As it was just after Christmas the nights were very long, and this one longer than any Rebecca could remember. But somewhere in the early morning he asked her kindly enough to stop reading and leave him to his thoughts, so she went up to her bedroom and slept.

Her eyes were very dry, but there would be some drops for it at the pharmacy. P'raps it would be a slow day, and she could sit down. But as soon as she arrived Lionel pulled her to the back of the shop.

'Mr Badcock came, yesterday, as I was closing up. I met him at the door and managed to persuade him to leave. He wanted you, I think. He said he would return, in any case, today. What should I do? P'raps we ought to put up the shutters for the day.'

The thought of closing was tempting. Her temples throbbed. But she said: 'I think we cannot. If not today, he will only come back on another day and we don't want to lose business for him. P'raps we ought to have a boy ready to run for the constable, though, if we need it.'

But before she could send for any boy they heard the sound of the bell jangling on its arm, and the door flung open, and a heavy breath.

'What shall we do?' said Lionel.

'I will deal with him,' said Rebecca, coming to the front.

'What is the maid doing here?' asked Mr Badcock.

'Jenny is working here now,' said Rebecca. 'Jenny, the white powders need to be written up, in the back. Can you do it?'

Jenny stared at him. 'But he can do nothing to me now!'

'But best to go to the back.'

Jenny stood staunchly, with her arms crossed. 'Jenny!' Rebecca said again.

'He has got even more foul; I didn't think it possible,' said Jenny, but she turned away as Rebecca had asked, to the back.

'Does Alexander know that you women are running the pharmacy?'

'He takes no more interest in the place,' said Rebecca.

'Yes, since you ruined him, hmmm?'

Mr Badcock, too, was changed. He was fatter, but he had not yet visited his tailor to tell him of it. The buttons of his jacket gaped, his shirt no longer covered his belly, leaving a wedge of bare skin above his waistband. 'Don't forget, will you, that the pharmacy belongs to me.'

Rebecca paled. 'The pharmacy belongs to Alexander. You own what is made in it, I understood. What do you want here?'

'I only want what is mine.'

'The pharmacy?' She glanced outside. He had not brought a cart. Some new stock was still behind the counter, hidden. If she stood in front of it she may prevent him taking that at least. Much of Gabe's money had been used up in the buying of it.

But Mr Badcock came towards them. 'It is mine, and I will have it!'

'It is not all yours!' Rebecca said desperately. If he took all her new stock she would be ruined. She ran to stand between him and the counter but he put out his arm and shoved her aside.

Then Lionel ran to him and pulled him on the arm with both hands. 'I ought to have said this before – you are a disgusting pig-headed tramp!' But Mr Badcock only shook the boy off with a grunt and Lionel stumbled onto the floor, still cursing.

Mr Badcock passed them both now. He was making, as Alexander had, for the laboratory.

'The salts! He wants the salts!' said Rebecca. 'But there are none.'

She climbed the stairs, two at a time. 'You will not find what you are looking for, not here,' she called after him. 'Not here, not anywhere!'

Through the open door she saw that a chair had been pushed back from the table and had fallen on its back. Several candles had burned down to their wicks, the wax was spilt all over the tin candle-holders. A glass bottle with a metal tap on the top had been caved in, the glass pieces still strewn around it.

'Last time I came 'twas all lined up, just here.' Mr Badcock pointed with a fist to the shelf. 'Here. And now nothing, hmmm? Nothing!' He wheeled round to face Rebecca and came towards her, his hands out in front of him as if he would grab her by her collar. '*You* know, wee wifey! You must have sneaked some away for yourself. You can never be free of it, you know, not once you have tasted it. Evangeline taught us that.'

'It is not here, or anywhere. Alexander was looking for it yesterday.'

'Alexander? That is good, then. He may have made some more, and then we will get it to the patent office, as we planned.' Mr Badcock lifted his hat and scratched his head. Then he turned and trod down the staircase, shaking bits of dust free from under it as he went.

'I am going to follow him,' said Lionel.

'Whatever for? Let him go!'

'He is going to Mr Palmer's – to your house.'

'What will he do there? He is not in his right mind. Alexander has no more salts.'

'I think he may damage the place. We may need to call the constable after all.'

Rebecca worried at her lip. 'You are right. He must be followed, but not by you, by me. I must see that he does not throw a chair at the parlour wall, or break the china, when he finds there are no salts there either.'

'You are not going on your own.' Lionel was already pulling on his cap. 'Anything may happen.' Jenny had come out again, her cheeks flushed. 'Jenny, dearest – stay here. And if we are above an hour, call the constable.'

It was a mild day for January but they went on at such a pace that Rebecca's neck was prickling under her cloak by the time they arrived at Albany Street.

'No need to hang on the bell, I will open it,' she said at the door.

'Why are you here?' Mr Badcock said. 'This is my business. Nothing to do with *you*, either of you.'

'It is my house,' said Rebecca. 'I do not want you in it. But if you must go in, I will be there.'

'Your house? I think you will find the house belongs to your husband. And why are *you* here, boy? It was a mistake ever to take you on; Alexander saw that from the first, and I,' he laughed incredulously, '*I* was your supporter. But, never mind that now.'

'I am here to protect Mrs Palmer,' said Lionel.

Mr Badcock laughed again. 'You – skin and bone, hmmm, a protector of women? Just like the last time, yes? Last time I seem to remember you only stood and watched.'

Lionel paled.

The cook was in the hall, a plate in her hand. When she saw Mr Badcock she put it down and smiled, showing her crooked teeth. 'Mr Badcock! I wasn't expecting it to be you. How well you look.'

'Thank you, Mrs Bunclarke.' He slid his eyes over to her. 'As are you.'

Mrs Bunclarke pinked.

'Is Mr Palmer here, by any chance, hmmm?'

'He is upstairs, in his room,' said Mrs Bunclarke, lifting her chin and pushing a lock of hair behind her ear. 'He ate a great deal of breakfast.'

'That is good to know, Mrs B,' said Mr Badcock, turning for the stairs.

As she went to follow him Rebecca saw a blur go by at the side of her vision. And then a crack. Mr Badcock staggered back, his hand covering his jaw. 'What the devil—'

'Oh, sir!' cried Mrs Bunclarke. 'Why you little varmint—'

But Lionel was on his toes, his fists out in front like a boxer. 'You bastard,' he said. 'That is for Jenny. And so is this.' He hit him again.

Mr Badcock fell to his knees. 'Oh!' he cried. 'Oh! I am abused!'

Lionel was readying himself again but Rebecca stood in front of him: 'Not now, not here – Lionel!'

Mrs Bunclarke rushed over and pulled a filthy handkerchief from her sleeve. 'Here now, Mr Badcock, we shall have you right in a moment.'

'How it stings,' Mr Badcock cried. 'Oh, send for a doctor!'

Lionel was shaking. 'I am sorry, Mrs Palmer. But I—'

'I know! I understand. But not now. Not here,' Rebecca gestured around the hall. 'Aren't we here to prevent this kind of thing?'

'Blood – look there!' Mr Badcock held the handkerchief out to her; there was a spot on it. 'I am undone – he has broken my jaw! I will have you arrested, I swear it. A boy, from the gutter! I rescued him, did you know that, Mrs Bunclarke, yes?'

'I can well believe it, sir. 'Tis a crying shame to see a man such as you abused by a boy.' Mrs Bunclarke turned to squint at Lionel. 'Shall I call the constable now?'

'Yes, do!' said Mr Badcock.

'But perhaps,' Rebecca cut in, 'we ought not to trouble a policeman with a domestic incident. He will want to know the background to it, and I'm sure Lionel will have a deal to say in his defence. Besides, the jaw is not broken,' Rebecca went on. 'You can talk quite well.'

Mr Badcock sat for a moment more, nursing his cheek, then he got to his feet, leaning heavily on the cook. 'P'raps you are right. But it is luck that it's not, else I would have you in jail.'

'Take a seat still, Mr Badcock, stay a while!' said the cook.

'I cannot, Mrs Bunclarke, I cannot! For I am come here on important business, which cannot wait.'

'Mr Palmer, is it, sir? You will find him in his bedroom. I tend to him there, every day.' She turned to stare at Rebecca. 'I am the only one he can bear to see.'

When Mr Badcock got to the door, he found it closed, as usual. 'Alexander! Hey, Alexander, 'tis your old friend John. Let me in, now. Come now, let me in!' He rattled the door handle.

And now, to everyone's great surprise, the door creaked open.

'Alexander – I have come for our medicine.'

He waited for a reply.

'Alexander, I have come for the medicine. I know you have it.'

This time Alexander did reply, but so quietly that neither Rebecca nor Lionel could hear. They both crept a little way up the stairs.

'But surely you have it,' said Mr Badcock. 'Or can make it, come man!'

'I can make it, but I will not,' said Alexander.

'Will not make it? But why?'

Alexander shook his head and blinked slowly.

'Do not tell me you too have turned against our medicine! Not like those women, those foolish women? No, not you!'

Alexander blinked again, shook his head again.

'It is the greatest medicine ever invented; the cure for every ill. The value of it is impossible to gauge. We only need to patent it and we will be rich!'

'I have never cared about the money, you know that, John.'

'But it is your life's work! Never mind about the Society, that matters nothing! The thing, the medicine, the cure, will stand by itself, yes?' Mr Badcock leaned heavily on the doorframe, still nursing his cheek. 'Why, we need not even advertise it! Word will spread and we will have more people knocking on our door, and more chemists clamouring to order it by post, hmmm, than we can possibly make by ourselves!'

Alexander made no answer, only stood at the door of his room looking over his friend's shoulder.

'Why, we will have factories, no? Hundreds of them, just making up our salts, and our liquids, and I dare say we could make it in other forms too! Powder, say – but you know all this, Alexander. And yet you stand here, looking like this.' Mr Badcock came to a stop and raised his hands. 'You do not look like yourself, man, I hardly recognize you! And you tell me you have no heroin and will make none. What has happened?'

'What has happened?' Alexander said at last, bringing his hand to his beard. 'What has not happened, you had rather ask me.' He stopped again and rubbed at it with his thumb. 'My wife, in the devious way of women, worked some of the salts into my coffee, or tea, on the morning of the Society. That is why I was confused.'

'What?' exclaimed Mr Badcock.

'But that gave me the idea, John – I would experiment on myself. Women are too sly and too weak. I would be the subject of my own experiment, just as Mr Davy had been the subject of his. And so I started, using controlled amounts, just as we had been, taking notes, just as we had been. And at first it worked very well. I was observing myself, whilst feeling the effects. No emotion, no impulse, was out of place. Everything was ordered, to the last degree.'

'And there we have it, Alexander – the key!'

But Alexander closed his eyes again, for a longer time. When he spoke again, Rebecca had to climb two more stairs to hear what he said.

'But on the nineteenth day I found I must increase my dose to achieve the same effect—'

'As we know already, but that only means greater sales, Alexander, as we discussed!'

Alexander put up his hand. 'With the increase in dose I noticed a tendency to slip away into the most fantastical dreams, or non-dreams rather. Such as real-life is, only with nonsense in it.'

'Again, as we have observed, come now—'

'Disturbing memories would surface, over which I had no control.' Alexander closed his eyes again and seemed to shudder.

'Surely, though, Alexander, they could not be that bad, hmmm?' Mr Badcock brought his hands to the front of his belly as if he were praying. 'Not to put our whole project, all our work – all my fortune now, my old friend – into jeopardy? Come now.'

'Dark memories, black ones, which the medicine should have made better but only seemed to make worse.' Alexander looked to the floor and rubbed his knuckle in his eye. 'And then the greatest revelation. Only two days ago I experienced a craving.'

Mr Badcock shook his head, as if to say again: *We know this already!*

'The craving was unlike any I have ever encountered. Every part of my being was driven towards the syringe, and the medicine. Only there was none left, and unaccountably I had not thought to make more.' Alexander passed his hand over his face again. 'Most unlike me, but I can only explain it by saying I had fallen into a reverie and I believed there was another bottle of acetic anhydride in the laboratory. There was not.' He raised his eyes to meet Rebecca's. 'In consequence, I passed a ghastly night – this last one, to be exact.' He rubbed his nose and blinked, and sniffed, and looked away from them both.

'Come now,' said Mr Badcock, fainter.

'Damn this!' Alexander blinked more rapidly and three tears fell down his cheek. He wiped them away angrily but could not stop more from falling.

Mr Badcock's voice took on a wheedling tone. 'I shall be ruined, Alexander, if we do not patent this heroin, hmmm? And you too – you too! All my money is sunk into the research!'

'But do you not see? The foundation upon which we based our research is false! What seems to be governance evaporates into its opposite in the absence of the medicine. Acceptable perhaps, if it is only the women, who are more inclined to loss of control. But if it can affect men in the same way, then it is no good at all! We have already seen the effect of opium on the working man, and this is worse. A hundred times worse.'

'But we mean to market it to women, not to their husbands! Men will not feel the need—'

'So I thought, before I had tasted it. But it is so sweet, and its power so seductive, that I fear everyone will want it, even men.'

Mr Badcock wiped his lip. 'If what you say is true, nobody need know, not yet, not until we have heroin patented and sold in every pharmacy in Britain, and America. It will take months, years even, for the truth to out. And it will still cure a cough – it is the best cure for that!'

'Everything I have worked towards for all these years was based on error. I cannot go on with it. That is all.' Alexander turned away and made to close the door.

'Wait!' cried Mr Badcock, clutching at his sleeve. 'Alexander, I beg you, for a friend.'

'No, John! I said that is all.'

Mr Badcock's face changed and grew red. 'Damn you!' he shouted in a high-pitched voice. 'Go back to your whores, then. No wonder your wife betrayed you! She got the best of us, you know, and now you are letting her!'

Alexander turned. 'And you, John, to go bothering a *maid*, with all the dust from the hearth and the floor about her skin …' He laughed disbelievingly. 'I should never have thought it of a churchman.' He turned again and shut the door with a click.

'Fuck you, *friend!*' Mr Badcock yelled. 'Fuck you all. I shall make it myself! It cannot be too hard.' He pushed past Rebecca, shoved Lionel away and knocked into Mrs Bunclarke's shoulder before getting to the front door and slamming it hard enough to make the whole house shake.

CHAPTER 33

'And now he says he is leaving – to Canada, of all places!' Rebecca and Gabe were in the pharmacy, putting up the shutters. The nights, little by little, were growing shorter, and the days longer. The lamps had not yet been lit outside.

'Canada! What is there for him?'

'A new life, that is what they say about the Americas, is it not?'

'A new life? I have tried that! Good luck to him.'

'And good riddance!'

'He will take his problems with him, wherever he goes.'

'No self, but only problems. That sounds like a way to live!'

'Only feelings. Only that.' Gabe kissed her lightly. 'I am glad he is going.'

'He says he will leave as soon as he can book a passage. Imagine it, Gabe, I will be free of him at last!'

'Yes, Rebe, it is the very best news!' Gabe grinned and tapped her on the tip of her nose. And, silly as it was, it pierced her heart, something unchangeable in the human soul! Sick and yet happy, in peril and yet happy, dying and yet happy, in disgrace and happy. Did the Stoics not speak of the same?

She moved her face towards his and kissed him. She had not really kissed him since the night in the hotel in Glasgow, and it took her a moment to get used to the feel of his lips again. But at the touch of his tongue a jolt ran through her, and she began to tremble, and now they were kissing as they had used to, until he too was shaking and she could feel his heart beating under his clothes.

At last they drew away. 'Come now, we are in a shop,' Gabe said. 'A place of work.'

'That is shut up for the night—'

'And you are still married, to *him*,' said Gabe, his cheeks flushed. 'There will be a scandal if it gets out – that we are together.'

'But do you know? I care not! I have fallen so far out of the way of any respectability, I care nothing, if you visit me here, or were to stay with me, here and there, say ...' She faltered and grew shy. 'For a night or two. I care nothing for the looks cast at me on the street. I think there are looks cast at me anyway, with all the scandal I have had.'

'Oh Rebe, how I have longed to hear you say that! Say it and mean it, as I think you do.' He put his head to one side and grinned. 'Here and there, you say?'

'Here and there, or here and here, if you like ...'

'Here and here sounds better.' Gabe raised his eyebrows.

'No – I meant – not here! Albany Street is a big house to live in on my own. For I think the cook will leave when Alexander does, though I shall have to get a new one …'

'Ah, Albany Street. What a fine address.'

'I used to think so.' She let her cheek rest on his shoulder. His hair had grown longer, now that he did not have to shave it for the tannery. 'I should never have taken you for a dandy.'

'And I should never have taken you – no, scrap that. I should *always* have taken you, wherever I went.'

The light was fading now but inside Rebecca and Gabriel stayed on. The pavement was busy with people walking home from work, and when there was a knock at the door they thought it was one of them, come to ask for something.

'A customer most likely, with a migraine,' said Rebecca, going to open it.

But it was not a customer – they could see that by his air of importance that was generated by his tailcoat and his whiskers.

'Have you seen a man by the name of Badcock?' said the man at once, his voice very nasal. 'If he is in here I pray you, do not hide him. You are liable to go to court for it.'

'Mr Badcock? No, he is not here. If he were I would gladly give him to you. What has he done?'

'He is wanted for non-payment of debts. Are you sure he is not here?' The man craned his bony neck to see over Rebecca's shoulder.

'No, I swear it! He would not hide here.'

'I always catch up with people in the end,' the man said, 'no matter how they try to run. If you are a friend to him you may tell him I am on his tail. It is better to end the misery quicker than try to elude it.' He pinched his nose. 'Though many still try to flee, it always looks worse in the courts if they do. Tell him that, if you see him?'

Rebecca nodded, and smoothed her dress. 'But I will not see him – I hope.'

'He has probably tried to get away – but tell him, I say, that I am on his tail.' He smiled. 'Bailiffs will be along tomorrow, in any case, to collect the equipment. I understand there is a laboratory?'

'Yes, upstairs—'

'And anything else that belongs to Mr Badcock.'

'This down here belongs to Mrs Palmer,' cut in Gabe. 'I have the receipts.'

'Not all of it, I'll wager. I expect there'll be a few pots and pans, as I always say.' He shut his eyes and pinched his nose again. 'A few pots and pans as belongs to us! Good evening to you.'

'How much is his, Rebe?' Gabe asked, after the man had gone.

'I do not know. Not much – we have sold any stock Mr Badcock bought for the shop long ago, and there is only the equipment, which I do not need. The newest stock is bought with your money and, oh Gabe, I ought not to be happy,' she brought her fists up under her chin, 'but Mr Badcock in a debtors' prison! Nothing would please me more.'

'No, Rebe, to be happy for another's misfortune is a terrible sin.'

'I know, Gabe, you were always better than me, and you are right—'

'I jest! Do you think me such a stiff, even now? Mr Badcock is a horror, from everything you told me.' He bent and touched her forehead with his own, and took her face in his hands. 'But I *am* better than you, that part is true.'

'Why you devil—'

He kissed her. 'And if you do not mind ejecting one husband and getting another one soon after, I will gladly come to Albany Street. I cannot live with my parents for ever. And there is the small matter of never wanting to be apart from you again.'

'And I you! But, Gabe – let us never marry.'

'Not even if I stick a twig in my turban?'

'Even that!'

'But – what should we be to each other?'

'I will be your wife-in-watercolours,' said Rebecca.

'And I – what do they call me?' Gabe frowned.

'There is no term for you, I think.' She put her hand to his cheek.

'But will you have me anyway?'

'Oh yes, I will. Oh, I will!'

AUTHOR'S NOTE

The setting for the novel is 1869. However, heroin was first synthesized by an English chemist, C. R. Alder Wright, in 1874; he was trying to find an antidote to the addictive properties of morphine. But it wasn't until Bayer marketed heroin as an analgesic and a sedative for coughs in 1888 that its popularity really took off.

Whilst I have used this as an inspiration for the character of Alexander, obviously in no other way does C. R. Alder Wright compare to my anti-hero.

X